THE GODHEAD

www.thegodhead.net

The Godhead

by

Edward Barr Robinson

Bloomington, IN Milton Keynes, UK

authorHOUSE

AuthorHouse™
1663 Liberty Drive, Suite 200
Bloomington, IN 47403
www.authorhouse.com
Phone: 1-800-839-8640

AuthorHouse™ UK Ltd.
500 Avebury Boulevard
Central Milton Keynes, MK9 2BE
www.authorhouse.co.uk
Phone: 08001974150

First published by AuthorHouse 3/2/2006

ISBN: 0-7596-1016-9 (e)
ISBN: 0-7596-1017-7 (sc)
ISBN: 1-4107-9944-1 (dj)

Printed in the United States of America
Bloomington, Indiana

This book is printed on acid-free paper.

1stBooks - rev. 01/21/06

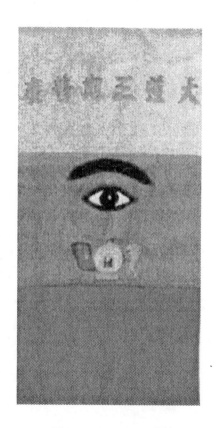

Flag of the Caodai
(followers of the Cao Dai)

This is a work of fiction. Names, characters, places, and incidents are either the product of the author's imagination or are used fictitiously, and any resemblance to actual persons, living or dead, business establishments, events or locales is entirely coincidental.

One underlying theme of *The Godhead*, not in the original plan, turned into a hunt for the Answer to Everything, which might not be as presumptuous as it sounds. Everyone seems to take a run at this search in his own way, although for this book I first needed to broach a few of the mothers of all questions. How existence came into being, maybe for openers, because that answer might logically lead to what the goals should be for those of us still floundering around inside this dimension.

This isn't absolutely pertinent to the story, by the way. It's more like background music that I felt necessary to properly frame *The Godhead*. Anyway, thanks to the revelations of quantum physics we might no longer have to go through a fictional looking glass to find, most mystical of all puzzles, the origin of existence. And strangely enough those quantum findings--that the elemental stuff of existence might well be *non*-existence, for example--agree word for word with a large tract of eastern mysticism, most of it stemming from the Tao.

Maybe we're onto something here. Maybe we all somehow exist only within our own self-created, virtual matrix of unreality. Whatever, the hoped-for result of this writing is the providing of something a reader can re-think, take off the shelf and stroke occasionally.

For instance, is it possible that just one man, Lao-Tse, in writing the *Tao Te Ching* twenty-five centuries ago, perceived the exact world that the quantum studies are just now proving? *Exactly* proving? And is it possible that someone of such perception, then, could also have perceived the goal of existence?

Stop and listen a moment. I've been working on that.

E. B. Robinson
www.thegodhead.net

To Jean, *my wife, my beautiful friend, my life companion*

ARJUNA, the Warrior:

Swift as the rivers stream to the ocean,
Rush these heroes to your fiery gullet:
Mothlike, to meet the flame of their destruction.

SRI KRISHNA, the Godhead:

The wise see knowledge and action as one:
Take either path
Tread it to the end:
There the followers of action
Meet the seekers after knowledge
In equal freedom.

> From the battlefield dialogue
> of the Bhagavad-Gita.

Chapter 1

This, then, will be your touchstone, and this will be your light...

Dao Chien Thieu, trying to remember the words, knew this would be the last incantation of his life. This was such a bewildering thought. Yet the thoughts, the words, stuck in the tight place in his throat, for he asked this grace from the searchlight of a French boat and not from the light of the Cao Dai, not from the Eye of God.

"Glorious light," Chien whispered, allowing this deception, squeezing the words past the tightness in his throat, "let your prophecy and guidance be fulfilled in me, please, on this night."

The French LSSL patrol boat, the *Arquebuse*, had been scanning Chien's freighter, *Erroa*, from the moment she secured berth in the harbor of Da Nang. Their discovery was so unexpected, so completely unexpected here. He thought the *Erroa* would easily pass through Da Nang Bay unseen, only one more freighter harbored within the veil of rains--how could she be detected in these monsoons? The rains in the early summer of 1953 were the second heaviest since the keeping of records, and yet here they were, the French with their gun ship.

Dao Chien had already dismissed his men and told them to scatter inland after hearing the first hint in the transmissions, mainly from the *Arquebuse,* that the French had identified the *Erroa* as a munitions carrier. The French boat carried three-inch cannon and ran at twenty-two knots and carried sixty troops, and the *Erroa* had no chance against a gun ship like the *Arquebuse.*

Dao Chien stepped down the ladder of *Erroa's* midships hatchway and shuffled back to the unlit aft-cargo where the more volatile munitions were secured, where the fume of bilge-diesel lingered and its taste clung to the air, and it stunk heavy in his mouth. A brown canvass shroud covered the container of plastique but he couldn't risk using the overhead lamp to find it. The French would notice that. Instead he used the emergency wall-flashlight to locate the pen detonators, still in their plain wooden carton, snugged between the containers of 81mm mortar rounds and the anti-personnel mines, packed in calcium silicate crystals and stowed atop the center container marked in English: "Caution--Granular PETN--Plastic Military Explosive."

He heard the French commandant calling from the gangway. The soldiers, noisily wharfside now, were boarding the *Erroa* off the pier ramp,

1

rattling along the iron railings, deploying down the main deck, down toward the companionways, down into the holds and lower cabins, and Chien fumbled to get the timer set but his fingers wouldn't hold steady. He put his hands under his arms and squeezed hard, then groped the indicator to the fifteen minute mark and stuck the ends of the circuit wire into the clips on the detonator, which would give him enough time to get the ship's manifest and bills of lading. If he could get by the soldiers... Little hope of that.

If he couldn't, he would stay in the navigation room, shut its armored door and let the documents be destroyed with him, because their destruction was necessary. Dao Chien Thieu knew at least this: There was no longer a choice.

French soldiers were running through most of the corridors but Dao Chien reached the steel-enclosed room next to the navigator's quarters without being seen, and had to gasp for breath as he did so, before he stepped inside. This was young men's work and he realized on this day of all days that he was certainly no longer young, and he rested his shoulder against the bulkhead wall before he saw the officer, and heard the words, obliquely, "God in heaven...Dao Chien?"

A French officer stared at him from behind the navigation table. "Dao Chien Thieu?" Major de Larocque said again, almost dropping the pistol as he re-gripped the sweaty handle. The barrel banged against the steel table. "God, the brother of the *Minister of Defense* is behind these shipments?"

"Major de Larocque..."

"Only last week we had dinner with your brother, for God's sake. Now I find you *here?*"

Chien tried to think but was too tired, too isolated to think of a believable lie. He lowered his head, reached his hands out to either side, surrendered to his world of lies. "I carry no weapons, Major de Larocque."

"God in heaven, the Minister of Defense had reports that some *American* was supplying the communists." The major began to shake his head. "Now look, we find his damned brother here." Major de Larocque thumped a stack of documents on the navigation table and stared down. He continued shaking his head.

Dao Chien felt the beginning of a cramp burning his shoulders but he kept his arms out, and the quickness of the pain told him of his frightful oldness. "An American supplying the rebels against the French occupation? Major...if my brother thought the Americans were taking sides with the Viet Minh," Dao Chien swallowed painfully, "he would join the rebels himself. But I don't really know who sends these weapons."

2

De Larocque's eyes, narrow, sitting tightly over his long nose and weak chin, made the 40-year old officer look too much like an aging ferret, thought Dao Chien. Not at all like the tall mustachioed regimental officers of the *Tiraillers Tonkinois* who once visited his family plantations in Tan Am. "Your brother is a big admirer of the Americans, monsieur..." Without moving his pistol the major began gathering the papers with his other hand. "But even they would never, never persuade him to supply the Viet Minh guerrillas against the French, if such a thing were even thinkable..."

Dao Chien closed his eyes and blocked out the words. He remembered the metal door, still open behind him, a step away, and wondered if he could take this final step.

"You are thinking, perhaps, of trying an escape, Deputy Minister," said the Major, seeing Chien look toward the door. "Please do not. Please. You would not succeed. I have no desire to hurt you."

A squad of footsteps went by outside, along the passageway. A thin voice shooing men into the cabins and sleeping quarters of the ship's crew. The door swung in as a disheveled young lieutenant stepped through and saw Dao Chien and stopped, and fingered the flap of his holster. "Everything all right here, Major?"

"Everything's all right, Lieutenant Aumont." Major de Larocque waggled a hand toward the lieutenant's holster. "I think you know Deputy Minister Dao...What about the weapons?"

"Sir, the boat is loaded." Lieutenant Aumont gave up trying to unsnap his side arm. "We can start an inventory-"

"-No. No inventory right now," said Major de Larocque. "Secure and post watches. Get those worthless Headquarters people to take inventory."

"I'll do that, sir." The lieutenant, seeing that Dao Chien presented no threat, saluted himself out, but Chien felt his chest cinch up at the sight of the young officer. At least a company of men remained on or around the *Erroa* now, and there was the patrol boat alongside...too many men. He never thought of himself as a field soldier and he did not want to die like this, with the killing of so many men, but he needed to keep the documents inside this room forever.

He reached toward the door... "Jesus--*no!*" The major yelled and raised the pistol and fired as the door clanged shut, and Chien felt the bullet thread into him, and he sagged against the wall, and he slid awkwardly down, groping the bulkhead as the major came over him, bent over him, reaching at the wound--"Christ in heaven, what in hell were you *doing*?" De Larocque lifted Chien's white shirt where a scarlet rose of blood was soaking through. "I thought you were trying to escape. Have you gone *insane*?"

3

Chien could barely hear the words. The old Vietnamese squirmed upward, propping his back to the wall, and waited, waited, for the stinging in his chest to stop. "You must give an order... Make your men leave the ship, Major."

"Leave the ship?"

Dao Chien felt the blood leaking warm through his hand. "You need to give an order, Major. Tell your men to leave the ship. Now, please." He heard the pounding at the bulkhead door and the lieutenant's muffled voice hollowing through a quarter-inch of steel: *Major! Everything all right in there?*

"I'm okay, Lieutenant." Major de Larocque tried to turn the door handle. "Wait there a minute." Looking back to Dao Chien. "What have you done here, Deputy Minister? Where is the key?"

"We've only a few minutes, Major. Please, order your men from the ship." Dao Chien felt beaten, terribly disoriented, but thank God, blessings from the Cao Dai, the pain was beginning to slip away. "I'm sorry. I'm very sorry, Major, that you have to be with me."

"What are you saying, Deputy Minister?" Major de Larocque squinted at the old man. He yanked at the door handle. *"Lieutenant! Break this door in--now!"*

"He won't be able to, Major," said Dao Chien. "There is not enough time."

De Larocque aimed his pistol at the lock as the thud of a body, or foot, crashed against the other side of the door. *Give me some help here,* they heard the lieutenant yell. On this side, the report from the major's pistol reverberated like a cannon in the steel room, the bullet spat into and away from the lock, ricocheting down past the major's knee.

Major! You all right? A tremendous bump shook the door. *It's solid, sir. Need to get tools.*

Major de Larocque gaped at the lock, only a moment. He pushed at the door again, once, and let his hands drop--"Lieutenant, get the men off this ship!"

What, sir?

"The ship's going to go up--get the hell off this ship and tell the patrol boat to pull away! Do it NOW, Lieutenant!"

The other side went silent, for a heartbeat. Then a short mumbled discussion took place before they heard the junior officer begin shouting away from the door, and steps banging up the metal stairs of the adjacent companionway, and a mixture of running and scuffling and yelling that lasted only a minute on deck before the two men in the navigation room felt the rumble of the patrol boat backing its screws.

Noise accelerating, whining to a higher pitch and then fading, fading, until everything became quiet.

Quiet. The quiet of death's approach, thought Dao Chien. The final quiet of the Cao Dai, perhaps.

Major de Larocque watched the bulkhead door before wiping his forehead with his gun hand, still loosely holding the pistol. "You could open this for me, Deputy Minister. You can't...I know you have the keys here, somewhere in this room."

"I'm sorry, Major. I do not have the keys," said Dao Chien. He prayed that the soul of Major de Larocque would understand the reason for this one last lie. "I'm so very sorry, Major," he said, "but I cannot open the door."

"Mother of Christ," whispered de Larocque.

"Nothing else I could do," apologized Dao Chien. "I couldn't let you take the papers. Forgive me, I couldn't."

"There are other documents... Someone else will just be assigned..." The major's voice wavered, then limped into silence, and he walked away, unsteadily, to the navigation table, laboring himself onto the edge of its elevated seat. "Even your brother's son has been assigned to this... to the investigation of these shipments, Dao Chien."

"I know, Major. I know." Chien tried to nod. "Such a mixture of loyalties in this land, even in my own family." He stopped while the major made a trembling sign of the cross over himself, and Dao Chien thought. What a waste of this man. If only I had another choice... "My brother says the Americans are sending his son and another Army man, by themselves, to do their own investigation of these shipments," said Dao Chien, succeeding this time at producing a weak smile. He felt his words might help the major in these last seconds. Such a frivolous token, while taking a man's life.

"My brother feels these Americans will find who is right and wrong here." The major didn't answer, and Dao Chien, struggling to sit upright, felt himself getting weak. His left side felt very cold and weak.

"Whoever could tell right and wrong in Indo-China could explain rightness everywhere, *n'est-ce pas?*" said Dao Chien. "If such a thing exists."

Chien's voice, his last words, had begun to rasp as the first discharge went off, searing into the two men and jolting the *Erroa* like ship collision a moment before the giant yellow firebloom tore the ship from gunwale to waterline, swallowing masts, booms and kingposts into its hold, destroying the pier and cranes, destroying even the dockside warehouse.

*

Tan Am

Dao My Linh lifted the hem of her white *ao dai* where it circled the top of her ankles, and settled quietly on the wooden ledge of the irrigation mound. The villagers and tenant farmers in grey calico tunics gathered around, an activity they did each week to hear the girl-priest of the Cao Dai speak, although some of them still preferred that she speak in the temples like the older, more orthodox priests did.

Her father, Dao Phuong, owned these fields. He owned the rice lands, the banana trees, the coconut palms and corn crops. He owned the breeding grounds of the cream-colored Peking duck. The family of Dao Phuong, in fact, used cows instead of buffalo for the shallower rice fields, an indisputable sign of wealth.

They, the workers of Dao Phuong, had almost completed the first picking of rice that brought in over seven tons per hectare, almost a record for their region's January-June crop. They had already filled many of the lower paddies with water for the six-month breeding of carp, so if they could not hear her in the temple then this clearing made the next most desirable gathering place, certainly better than the lower and wetter fields to the south.

The affluence of Dao Phuong had spread through the area--seven families out of ten owned *radios* here--but his presence was not the reason these people came today. The villagers had not expected to see Dao Phuong today, in fact, for everyone heard that he still wept over the death of his brother Dao Chien, who had died so terribly, they heard on their radios, in the ship explosion at Da Nang.

The earth around the irrigation mound was still wet from the recent flooding. It soiled the white blousings of My Linh's hem. It distracted Dao Phuong, for he was a fastidious man, while his daughter waited for the people to become quiet before she began in her soft clear voice: "Do you remember the philosopher I spoke of last week? Socrates?" The people looked at one another. Some grinned self-consciously.

"This week I found a passage in his dialogues that describes the joy of finding the true goal we spoke about." And she beamed her enthusiasm for this discovery, her crescent eyes widening, her pink unpainted lips smiling, releasing this dazzling whiteness over them. And they thought, *Aiyee, but she is beautiful, is she not?* A porcelain goddess, and what ideas she had! And she, only a village leader, had not yet taken the next step in the Cao Dai of becoming a student priest, and she wore an *ao dai* rather than the

6

white robes, and she spoke of this Socrates rather than the decreed saints of the Cao Dai such as Christ or Confucius or Winston Churchill.

Indeed, she was a special gift to them.

"The Tao says our world is only one of many world-illusions, so if we wish to bring meaning to an existence that is only one of these illusions, the people within it must then *create* a goal..." She took a small brown book from her satchel as the villagers tried to look thoughtful for her. She delicately opened its cover.

"What goal could be more sensible, then," she said, "than to make this world as good as we can for each other, since we are all in this one particular illusion together. Even if this requires our own personal sacrifice, which would give the highest meaning to our lives."

Enchanted by that idea, My Linh began to leaf through the pages while the villagers poked and nudged each other, but only when she could not see them. They intended no disrespect. These gestures were their way of paying attention: *See our leader?* they would indicate. *See our own village leader? See our girl-priestess here?*

"It is found in a dialogue written by Plato called 'Georgias,' where Socrates attempts to explain these things to a man called Callicles... Yes, oh..." and she began to read: "Socrates talks to Callicles and he says 'Callicles, if my soul happened to be golden, don't you think I should be overjoyed to find a stone to test the metal, the best stone possible which, when I applied it, if it proved that my soul had been well cared for, then I need no other touchstone?'"

Delighted with this beginning, she continued her reading from Plato, and the words sent chills through her father Dao Phuong, like blessings from God. She far surpassed him now, he knew. For she had approached her touchstone, this thirst to make life better for everyone, although neither he nor the gentle villagers nor anyone in the world might ever understand her.

But he would try.

The word had distracted him from the writings of Plato.

It was such a perfect word, his daughter's most favored word: touchstone. The Americans had asked him for a key word--a *secret* word--as a reference for this mission they were sending his son on, to find the reason for the ship explosion at Da Nang.

Touchstone.

Chapter 2

On the morning of July 10, 1953, at the Eighth Army headquarters in the upper Pusan Delta, Korea, the investigation of the arms merchant John Bryan began. It was triggered by the last straw, at least for the French allies, in a series of unexplainable, or maybe *too* explainable, events: the explosion of the munitions freighter in Da Nang.

"Quantum *mechanics*? What in hell... Army's putting some sergeant into college to study--what in hell's this, Captain? Quantum mechanics? Is that some kind of *physics*?"

"Being sent to Kumsong first on the Da Nang investigation, remember, Colonel. So whether he lives long enough-"

"-What's his name? Let's see his file there, would you?"

"Marion Apollo, sir. Sergeant Marion Ramirez Apollo."

"What kind of name's this, *Marion*? Isn't Apollo the name of a vacuum cleaner? Look, 201 file says he's Mexican American--a Chicano? Bullshit, we're sending some Chicano to college to spy on school kids, for Chrissake, so here he applies for...what the hell's quantum mechanics?"

"Don't know exactly, sir, but he could handle whatever...look there at his AFQT and aptitude scores."

"Screw his aptitude scores."

It was a hell of a bad time to start any kind of investigation. The peace negotiators were within days of signing the truce at Panmunjon. The Chinese, to keep Kumsong in North Korea, had thrown eighty thousand people into a twenty-mile line between the Iron Triangle and Finger Ridge, just above the 38th Parallel. G-2 had neither the manpower nor the will to begin an investigation of arms shipments to Vietnam, wherever the hell that was.

"Look here at his record, Captain. Another bastard-kid street fighter who joins up to dodge a manslaughter rap. Now we send this guy to college, right? Another goddamned *eight*ball?"

"Going to Kumsong first, Colonel. Might never live to see any college."

"Bet your ass. Why bring him from Okinawa?"

"Novinger's memo asked for a noncom familiar with the Kumsong sector-"

"-Great choice for a high-security assignment, isn't it? Look here, Okinawan CO reports he *daydreams* half the time. So now we send him to college--that make any sense?"

8

"Minority with high aptitude scores, sir. Great fit for campus surveillance."

"Well, give a shit, I suppose. Who's the other poor bastard?"

"The one they specifically requested for Kumsong. Name's Kim Chau Dao."

"Oh, God..."

General Arnold Novinger of the National Security Council had started this investigation with NEED-TO-KNOW-ONLY instructions through FECOM G-2 in Tokyo, ending at the desk of Colonel George Purdy, requesting that he send two men to make the inquiry. It was quite specific about one of them: "A lieutenant in *our* Army, sir," the captain continued, "Born in Indo-China, attended a French military academy there called Da Lat."

"I thought the Chinese already took Finger Ridge-"

"-Dao's father requested this investigation, Colonel. He's the Minister of Defense in Vietnam there? Name of Dao Phuong."

"What in hell do we know or care about *Vietnam*? We got our own goddamn war."

The French Bao Dai government, following rumors about the freighter explosion in Da Nang, had accused an American arms merchant, John Bryan, of continuing the arms shipments to the Viet Minh that were started by the OSS against the Japanese during World War II. The memo "anticipated" that the investigation could be opened and closed quickly to avoid problems for a man of Mr. Bryan's stature and possibly--more than possibly, if Purdy was reading this right--to the U.S. Government itself. Even Colonel Purdy recognized that someone high up preferred not to dig too deeply into this investigation: "There are considerations involved here," said the memo, "that certain members of the Administration would prefer not to complicate at this time." That was clear enough to Colonel George Purdy.

Future communications were not to mention Vietnam or John Bryan by name. They would use only the name suggested by Lieutenant Dao's father, Dao Phuong, the Vietnam Minister of Defense... Touchstone.

"Shall I call them in?"

"Finger Ridge, how's that for a screwed-up place to start?"

Captain Hensley nodded through the door at the men in the corridor and, as they came in, Colonel Purdy noted with peripheral satisfaction that they were about what the memo was looking for: a tall motley grunt sergeant and a lieutenant who looked more like a samurai. A Cervantian duo. The sergeant wore unpressed combat fatigues that were faded to uncamoflaging green-white while the lieutenant was razor-starched, forest-green. Exact opposites. Perfect, except, maybe, something about this sergeant... Shadow-grey eyes, for instance, too light for some 25-year old half-breed. Droopy-lidded eyes, the man looked half-asleep, or drunk, or dim-witted. His looks didn't fit with those big aptitude scores.

"Come along, step in please, Sergeant," snapped Captain Hensley, who was barely noticeable in the same room with the large, bald, heavy-jowled Colonel Purdy. A big foul-smelling spittled cigar stuck out from a series of skinpuffs composing the colonel's eyes, cheeks, nose, chin--a coalescence, with the cigar anchoring his face, that was described by the local E.M.'s as a toilet bowl's view of a fat woman defecating.

"Lieutenant Dao, sir." The lieutenant's hand split the air. Hair whitewalled to a spray on top. A face that resembled small rocks, symmetrically piled.

"Sergeant Apollo, sir." The sergeant touched the edge of his fingers to his eyebrow, which shadowed over his defined cheekbones. Full brown hair combed flat back--some kind of barrio pachuco hairstyle, the colonel supposed. Purdy's cigar slid to the middle of his face, forcing the remaining bad taste through his teeth, aiming the cigar at the sergeant's mid-gut. "File says you're going to college as 'campus surveillance'. What kind of background you have for spying on school kids? You got any college experience?"

The sergeant's eyes closed and opened again. He seemed to lean away from the question. "My father's a professor of quantum physics."

"Quantum shit, Sergeant. I read your file. You don't know who the hell your father was." The colonel squinted down the length of his cigar. "You really kill some L.A. street punk?"

The sergeant almost rolled his eyes. "Name was Chuy Gonzales, sir."

"What?"

"His name was Chuy Gonzalez," said the sergeant, sniffing. "He w's more than just an L.A. street punk."

Purdy eyed the sergeant. "Sergeant, you been drinking?"

"Stayed the night in the village, Colonel. No one said t'get here sober."

"God Almighty." Colonel Purdy took the cigar out to spit into his trash can. "This's how you been going through life, Sergeant? Drunk in the villages? Signing up to spy on a bunch of *school* kids? Can't find a better way to use these big aptitude scores?"

Sergeant Apollo tried to focus on Colonel Purdy. "Maybe I'll go look for the 'splanation of existence, or something."

"Be careful, Sergeant," Purdy growled. "Be *damn* careful. You're just lucky we're under pressure here, or by damn... You have any idea why you're here?"

"I think so, sir," Chau answered. "My father said we'd be assigned to the Touchstone investigation-"

"-The *what*? Where the hell'd you hear that?"

"He--my father--thought up the code word for the assignment, sir." Seeing the colonel's scowl, Chau retreated to a blinkless forward stare. "Said he got it from a sermon that my sister-"

"-Okay, enough, Lieutenant." Flesh moved along the lines where Colonel Purdy's jaw hid: Top Secret my ass, he thought. The gook lieutenant hears about this assignment before *I* do. "Lieutenant, I was asking this *sergeant...* You ever hear of Daniel Bryan, Lieutenant?"

"No, sir."

"All-American at Stanford?" said the colonel. "Don't you follow football?" Colonel Purdy waited, shrugged, swiveled back into the stare of Sergeant Apollo, who watched Colonel Purdy now and didn't look away as a sergeant should do and in fact should be goddamned *obliged* to do. Colonel Purdy felt he was being *appraised* by this enlisted sonofabitch. "I understand you were at Hadong with the 29th, Sergeant."

The eyes, then, tiredly moved away from Colonel Purdy. "We were overrun."

"Yes...right." The Colonel leafed through the 201 file. "An F.O. for Third Battalion, says here. Watched Third Battalion get their asses shot off, right?" Hearing no response he continued flipping the pages. "Didn't fire a shot yourself?"

"Where I was, Colonel, that would've gotten me killed. Not much more."

"Who's to say? Here you didn't even *try*? Don't you put any importance on self-esteem, Sergeant?"

"Self-esteem? Not sure what that means, Colonel."

Colonel Purdy grunted and turned a page. That answer seemed sufficiently eight-ballish. The tone of the general's memo warned him to check out the lieutenant's escort to insure that he wouldn't get "too involved" in the investigation. No danger of that from this half-drunk sergeant. "Last C.O. says here he can't find you half the time. What've you been doing? You got a happy-girl, a *joson*, on Okinawa?"

The sergeant shook his head and looked away. These were strange goddamned questions. "Spend most of my time around the north end."

"North? Hell, not even a good *whorehouse* up there." The colonel glanced at the captain for his accommodating snigger, delivered on cue.

"I go to watch th' albatross mainly, Colonel." Not an eyelash flickered as the sergeant said that, not a muscle in his face moved, although Purdy at first thought the sergeant was trying to make a joke. Not hardly. The man's face showed no sign of humor.

"Something wrong with you, boy? Something addled up there somewhere?" Colonel Purdy stabbed his own forehead with his finger. "You're supposed to help reorganize an RCT that gets its ass shot off and you go watch birds--that what you said? What the hell're you talking about, *albatross*? The '45 invasion blew away any birds up there."

"Things've a way of coming back, Colonel."

How the hell'd he get into this? Colonel Purdy ended it with a sideways swipe of his hand. "Anyway, you've got one more assignment before you go spy on *school* kids, Sergeant. You get to take the lieutenant here through the Iron Triangle near Kumsong, right below Finger Ridge." He watched for a reaction that didn't come. "Like the lieutenant says, we've been told to investigate some arms shipments to some postage-stamp country in order to satisfy some higher-ups. You're assigned to get the lieutenant to Kumsong, do this investigating, then get him the hell out again. All secret. No mention of Bryan, Indo-China, any of that crap. From this point we refer to this investigation as 'Touchstone,' like the lieutenant says. You follow?"

"I'm s'posed to go into a zone like Finger Ridge with one goddamned green lieutenant?"

"What the hell'd you say, Sergeant?"

"Sorry, Colonel."

"What am I supposed to be investigating at Kumsong, Colonel?" asked Lieutenant Dao.

Purdy tapped on his desk and watched the sergeant for a moment before turning back to Chau. "This lieutenant I mentioned--Bryan--he's a platoon leader in the 23rd Regiment there...probably only battalion-size by now, from all reports. Probably doesn't know shit about his father's arms business but since he's with the Army he's the easiest place to start. Just ask if he knows anything about his father's shipments to Indo-China, write down what he says and then get the hell out." He slid two sets of mimeographed orders toward them. "These'll tell you what to ask and get you through the lines to Kumsong. That's it, gentlemen..."

After the two had left, the colonel poked a new cigar from his five-pack and winked toward Captain Hensley. "If there's any can of worms here, it's not going to be opened by *those* two. What was that half-drunk son of a bitch saying? He was looking for the *explanation of existence*? Did I hear that right?" The colonel laughed as he lit his cigar. "Hell, then, Finger Ridge should be the exact right place to start."

Chapter 3

The Life Journey of Marion Ramirez Apollo
by K. Marisa Paviso

I crossed his path but once,
A strange sort of man he was.
Searching for truth in the strangest places,
He surely was not one of us.

But I am, said he.
And yet, he was not.

Searching? Sergeant Marion Apollo snorted as he read the weathered "bon voyage" poem from his ex-girlfriend K. Marisa Paviso, and thought about what a *cabron* he must have been in City Terrace. He slouched against the splintery corridor bench and waited for Lieutenant Dao to get out of the head. What a phony image we all tried to create, he thought. *Searching for Truth.* Lord, he didn't need to search around Korea any more, though he always had this feeling he'd end up back here. This forced enlistment for the death of Chuy Gonzalez wasn't about to end with that massacre at Hadong, was it? No, no, hell, this assignment was just another part of his lifelong damned penance for the death of Chuy. Maybe.

He had never shaken the last sight of Chuy lolling against the peeling lapped-wood sideboards of Chanson's Mercado, with Apollo's buddies the Tessa brothers screaming *Peencha-ay!* at Chuy's face. *Ese, ese!* the brothers yelled into Chuy's face, yelling for "Ram el Cuchillo"--Ram the Knife--to demonstrate his skill with the blade, and, hey, Ram was happy to show it off, thunking it deep in the phone pole next to Chuy's ears, but no one knew Chuy was overdosed. No one thought he'd die on them. Christ, Chuy was once the big chingon in City Terrace, wasn't he? A long time ago he was. The vatos were only screwing around with him.

Lieutenant Dao finished his nervous-piss and they got in the jeep and Apollo drove off with the same looseness he'd shown in Colonel Purdy's office. Rolling with the road. When the grooves in the cold-hardened dirt

13

swung to the side he'd let the wheel slip lazily with it in natural syncopation, tipping and sluing past the slat board structures of Eighth Army HQ.

Even this chauffeuring job to Kumsong reminded Sergeant Apollo of Chuy Gonzales, who used to get driven around by his vatos in Chuy's chopped red Ford, before the guy became a gutter-hype. Apollo remembered that last night when Paco Mena found Chuy on the sidewalk: *In the spoon by noon, chingon!* followed by Paco's dummy asthmatic burro laugh, followed by Paco flashing a finger underneath the street light at Chuy, next to Chanson's Mercado.

Apollo sped up after they passed the secondary outpost and skidded the jeep onto the main road.

"Is your father really a professor of...what'd you tell the colonel? Quantum mechanics?" Lieutenant Dao gave Apollo a curious peek. "And you go into that colonel's office *drunk?*" He started to giggle. "What was it you told him? You were searching for the *explanation of existence?*"

"Yeah, well, I read that existence isn't much more than--I dunno--some kind of pass've, um, accident . . . I think. Bothers hell out of me, though. Don' know why."

"What's that mean?"

"Don' know. 'S no reason to be here, I think--'s why I need to look into that quantum bus'ness, not just because my father... This stuff might be the answer to everything, if I'm readin' it right." Apollo could hear Paco Mena's response to that: *So what're you, vato, the brainy humpin' sunflower in our crappy little weed patch?*

"Your father was *Doctor* Apollo?"

"*Mi madre* said it sounded like Apollo--took the name from a movie marquee. Then stuck me with Marion because it sounded like somethin' a gringo-professor would stick me with," Apollo saw one of the lieutenant's eyebrows rise. "John Wayne's real name, y'know--Marion," said Sergeant Apollo. "My mother was a movie freak."

"So you want to take up physics too, be another Albert Einstein?"

Apollo clucked his tongue. "Tried t'read Einstein once, like trying to read goddamned Egyptian. Y'know that people see things different, depending on how fast they're going?"

"What the hell's that mean?"

"-'s why a space man would come back younger than the people he leaves behind. Each second goes zippin' into space at the speed of light, y'know, so if you go zippin' out with it you'd stay right with that second for goddamn *ever* as far as those people watching you . . . " He stopped, jerked his head to the side, losing his train of thought.

Lieutenant Dao shifted in his seat. "You don't seem to worry much about it--your father I mean."

"Being illegit'mate? Nah. She, my mother, met him when he used t'eat at her cafe, near downtown L.A. Used t'go there when he'd lecture at USC."

"You know where he's at now?"

"You said your sister was a priest," the sergeant changed the subject. "How can a girl be a priest?"

"In our religion?" The question, as intended, put the lieutenant on a new tack. "Women can be priests in our religion--the Cao Dai--though she's only a *student* priest right now. It's kind of a combination of all religions, ah, Taoism, mainly..." Stopping as Apollo sat up to look over the rock and brush around them, thinly lit now by an approaching dawn. "What're you looking for? There's no enemy around *here*, is there?"

"Looking for a road along here."

"What's wrong with *this* road?"

"Won't take long. Tell me about...what'd you call it? Taoism?"

No answer. The Lieutenant just remembered they were headed toward a battle zone, thought Apollo. The lieutenant had nervously stuck his envelope, the orders Purdy gave them, on the jeep floor behind them and put his carbine over it.

"What do they really expect us to do in Kumsong?"

"Nothing, probably," said the sergeant. "Just gets some problem o'theirs out of the way." Like Detective Halperin, he thought. Big-jawed bastard wanted *me* the hell out of the way. Did a good job, too, since here the hell I am. "What were you saying about this Cao Dai?"

"Yes, well..." Dao tried to recall what he was saying. "Like the Catholic Church--Christ the Redeemer and all--but Buddha and the ethics of Confucius are all mixed in."

"Then this Taoism-"

"-Glues it all together, sort of." Chau fidgeted his hand over the carbine behind him, through the gap between the seats. "My sister could explain it better if she were here. She's flying up to meet me on Okinawa when we get through here, actually. Maybe you can ask her yourself."

"Okinawa? You goin' to the Rock?"

"Assigned to the 29th now, same as you." Dao reached back to finger the envelope under the carbine. "But, Jesus, until then...don't these orders bother you? Just to investigate this they send us to a *combat* zone?"

"The whole damn world's a damn combat zone, Lieutenant."

They rode on in silence another half hour while a morning glow spread behind them, but they were circling toward the mountains to the west--

not the right direction for Kumsong, not as Lieutenant Dao understood it: "Shouldn't we be heading more north, toward that saddleback?"

"Pretty soon."

The answer quieted Lieutenant Dao for another few miles.

"Why're we going toward the mountains?"

"There's a place I went when I needed to think, last time I was here," said Sergeant Apollo. "Like to stop there before we head north."

Well, no hurry, Chau supposed. It would take at least a day, whichever way they went, to get to the Triangle, although they seemed to be taking a high-country route. Through clearings along the road he could see the landscape below running down to the Chaktong River where grey splotches of an army camp appeared on the hill section of the Pusan outskirts. It wasn't really light yet, although Apollo didn't use the headlamps.

They had reached the highest pass in the Ch'ongdo coastal mountains when Apollo stopped, pulled the brake and got out, while Lieutenant Dao stared about him. An unscenic, scrubby place, this: a rock mountain in front of them and a view of the rice paddies along the terraces and valley below, barely seen from this side of the road. No lights or signs of life anywhere along this stretch of road.

Dao reached back for the orders and got out to follow but the sergeant had already climbed up the first section of hill, and the smaller lieutenant had to navigate over a ladder of rocks to catch up. Rock to rock, grabbing onto the wiry shrubs speckling the mountain, he could already smell the sharp weed-stink on his hands.

Apollo stopped on an extended shelf a short way farther up the mountain and squatted, facing the coming sun where the wind, only tickling the shrubs on the road below, had started a serious blow. Apricot light from the new sun began to warm his face, reminding him of the hills above City Terrace after the warm Santa Annas had cleaned the air... "How'd you say your name, Lieutenant?"

"Chau...is my given name," answered Lieutenant Dao, wheezing from the climb. "Sounds like Joe--Dao Kim Chau... In Asia the family name comes first." He stopped himself from explaining about the Dao name and its reputation, the wealth of his father Dao Phuong and the ugly death of his uncle, Dao Chien, in the explosion at Da Nang. Apollo didn't seem to be paying attention anyway. He was watching the clouds streak to slivers of metallic reds above them, billowing to enormous bursts of color, into separate copper sunrises. "Bad place to meet anyone," said Dao Kim Chau. "Could be a short acquaintance once we reach Kumsong."

The sergeant frowned and spat. "Don't plan to die in any goddamned Kumsong, Lieutenant. Need to keep that in the front of your mind, all the time."

"Then I don't plan to die there." The lieutenant was trying to smile as he hunched against the wind. "Got too much to learn before I do any dying." Under his jacket he felt the envelope holding their orders, fumbled them out, handed a stapled sheath to the sergeant. "Might as well keep your set of these."

Apollo took them, weighed them in his hand, then stood and steadied himself, then began to tear the orders. Carefully, though, not with anger. He tore the orders carefully until he held a stack of scraps, while the lieutenant watched him. For someone like the lieutenant, the sergeant figured, this was probably like tearing pages from the Bible. Good analogy. These orders might be his--Apollo's--one last supplication for Chuy's death.

"I understand all hell's breaking loose around that place--Kumsong," said Lieutenant Dao. "Doesn't that scare you?"

"Almost everything scares me, Lieutenant." Apollo tightened his hand around the scraps and raised them over his head like a banner, and the wind caught his sleeve and flapped it along his arm, and he let the papers go. The wind streamed them to the air.

"These're for you, Chuy vato," he explained to the sky, and the airborne flutter became angry, scattering the scraps toward the cloudmass, along the sunrise.

The heavens winked. Pulses of light, dimmed by their ionospheric reach, sent a glow over the sky for a moment. An electric storm that high up...kind of strange in this region, this time of year, thought Sergeant Apollo. Like a special grace.

It happened again, this sudden penumbra, a flashed code that covered the world and then disappeared.

*

Ramirez Apollo remembered how, when not much more than a muchacho, he had looked up to Chuy, Chuy's collar always flipped up to frame his slick duck-tail, so damned dangerous-looking. If someone as cool as Chuy could turn into dog crap, Ram remembered thinking, later, then all heroes must end up as dog crap. So now the Army wanted him to go be a hero again, for--what did they call this investigation? Touchstone? Hell, first he needed to find himself a *real* touchstone, at least then he might see some kind of purpose in all this.

Apollo had stooped over Chuy that last day, looking into the hurt of Chuy's face. The injuries were down inside the man, a deep serious hurt, and Apollo remembered how the man's lips opened, and how the air hissed in his teeth. Chuy looked like a run-over animal, and Ram Apollo kept this picture of himself over Chuy, rocking over him, folding his hands on the pavement in front of him. Ram had only wanted to show off, needed to let everyone see how good "Ram the Knife" was with the blade, throwing it so close Ram thought he'd scared the poor bastard to death.

But the coroner said Chuy died from overdose, not from the scare of Ram's knife or from the kicking the Tessas gave him, but that didn't help all that much. Ram had held Chuy's pulse and the man looked into Ram's soul that day, for a moment. The thump of life had stayed for a moment in the pulse on Ram's fingers and then, like all of Ram's heroes since, Chuy Gonzales just flickered away.

Chapter 4

Gunfire murmured on the hills to the front and left of Sergeant Apollo and Lieutenant Dao. The firing skirted the southern flank of Finger Ridge, with a salvo of howitzers answering, bellowing far behind.

They had continued north from the Pusan flatlands and watched the flurry of retrenching along the shattered roads where a hodgepodge of U.N. forces dug fire bases along hilltops, where shouting men directed their trucks south to grind over now-worthless fields. Joining the heavy-booted armies, mincing the Korean farmland into grey powder.

"Where in hell are we?" Lieutenant Dao's fidgeting was getting worse. "I think the war's gone *past* this place. Where the hell's the war?"

Sergeant Apollo shrugged and pulled over to eat near a fresh crater, reeking with ash-smell, where a mortar had disintegrated an American halftrack. Apollo bit into his bricklike C-ration biscuit while checking their provisions: standard thirty pound field packs. Twenty pounds of rations, sleeping rolls and ponchos, four canteens, twenty clips of ammunition, four grenades.

"Spooky, isn't it?" said Sergeant Apollo, pointing toward the crater with his bayonet, then opening a can of hash with its blade. And when they started driving again the scene got spookier. There was miles of this abandoned debris. The jeep finally surfaced over a gutted pass where a constricted valley ran parallel to the road, where the sergeant, quietly more alert now, eased the vehicle to the side and stared down the valley: Two knolls, garlanded with barbed wire and sandbags, rose from the valley through the grey Kunai grass.

"That our base?" Chau stood and leaned over the windshield. A line of shallow chogi trenches ran across each knoll between the horseshoe outguard bunkers, slashed concentrically around a large square pile of sandbags. It was a command post, an American-style fire base.

"Probably the 23rd Regiment," said Sergeant Apollo. "What the hell're they doing here?" The sergeant rubbed the back of his neck. "We can probably make it through, I suppose."

He turned the wheel to the right and drove off the road, sliding down the side through lumps of sumac, toward the base. Not one rifle shot, not a sound came from the farther ridge. Dao waited for the flashes that should have followed them but it didn't happen. He saw the strings of spiraling concertina wire around the base and thought that if the ridge didn't fire,

19

then the people up there--good Jesus--might be *U.N.* troops. Which would make the bunkers in front of them *Chinese.*

He thought about mentioning this too late. Apollo had downshifted and gunned toward the perimeter of wire where a bulked mass of double-aproned wire was getting yanked jerkily to the side. "Get ready, Lieutenant..." The sergeant skidded the jeep into an upward slalom and Lieutenant Dao banged against the windshield as Apollo jammed the brakes and rolled out while the lieutenant, thrashing his gear, followed, jumping, crawling, huddling behind a sandbagged defilade.

"Where the hell'd *you* two get from?" yelled someone through an embrasure above them.

"Pusan," Sergeant Apollo called back. "Division G-2."

"How the hell'd you get past that Ridge?" A skinny staff sergeant, pointing an M-1 and eyeing the oriental lieutenant like a Nazi, was crouching his way from the trench.

"No one fired on us," said Sergeant Apollo.

"Why the hell *didn't* they?" Sergeant Knapp--the name on his pocket patch--was apparently none too sure about the dark sergeant either. He eased up the rifle a little as Apollo shifted along the bags to squint at the valley behind him.

"Damned if I know."

Another soldier came out behind Sergeant Knapp. A freckled kid-corporal, tripping at the entranceway and bunching himself against the bags. "You call that being right *behind* me, Weissman?" growled the sergeant, whose cheeks were barely visible beneath the shadow of his helmet.

"Damned equipment, Sarge."

"Screw your equipment. Watch while I check their papers... Sorry for the precautions, Lieutenant. Can I see them?"

"See them? Sure, certainly." Lieutenant Dao groped around inside his field jacket. "We come from Division Security. Came to see Lieutenant Daniel Bryan. You know him?" Nervously wrestling the papers out. "Just routine."

"Routine? Lord Jesus." That from Corporal Weissman.

"Something wrong?" asked Lieutenant Dao.

"Oh *hell* no." One of Sergeant Knapp's cheeks could be seen now, like beef-jerky twisted sideways. "Been here three days now yelling for those assholes to come get us, and every time we try we get the shit shot out of us, and now you drive right in on a *routine* security check?"

"What kind of security check?" Corporal Weissman had a long doggy face that hung open as he talked. His mouth barely moved.

"What the hell's that to you, Corporal?" Knapp turned back to Lieutenant Dao. "You can talk with our C.O. here, Lieutenant. Major Vickers is what we got left. Watch your head." Bowing himself back into the trench. "Least, he's the highest rank we got left. One captain left, no real majors, no colonels. Only this one damned tin major and a captain and about seven lieutenants left."

"Why didn't you get out with the rest?"

"Ask the tin major that," growled Knapp over his shoulder.

*

Trailing the group, Corporal Weissman straggled to a stop and slumped against a trench wall alongside an 81mm mortar--"Lord, it's all the hell over..." A security check on Bryan? The words lodged in his head like warts on the brain--this *had* to be about him and Bryan. Didn't Division always send these investigators first, before shoving a perversion charge up your ass?

The shit was about to fly.

*

"What *is* this, Lieutenant?" The long narrow head and neck of Major Henry Vickers snaked from Lieutenant Dao to Apollo and back while his right hand picked at a soiled, sloppy bandage that extended along his left arm from elbow to fingertips. The skin beneath the gauze glowed dull orange. "We're about to be wiped off this piece-of-shit hill and G-2 sends an *investigation* team?"

The major had directed the second question at Sergeant Knapp but Knapp didn't answer. The major shuffled away from him, around the sepulcher-like CP bunker. The air was choking in here, reeking with the fume of packed wet mulch and honeypotted dirt.

"You see what we accomplished by waiting?" said Vickers, pacing back to the silent Sergeant Knapp. "The road's open now. *These* two got through."

"That road's not open, Major," said Apollo.

The captain stopped, cocked his head around to find the source of that voice. "Sergeant Apollo, is it? Are all sergeants insubordinate now? Is that the way the Army *makes* sergeants now?"

"The Chinese let us get through, Major."

"He's probably right, Major," said Sergeant Knapp. "The Chinese're most likely still there. These two're bait-"

"-Who put you in command here, Sergeant? Can I ask who put *either* of you in charge?" The major paced again, veering past a radio transmitter

21

manned by a PFC who sniffed himself alert. "Something's caused them to pull back," said Major Vickers. "Probably not more than a skeleton crew left up there." That sounded right to him, apparently. He swung his good hand toward the PFC. "Tell the hotloop to cover Sergeant Knapp's company--if there're any radios still *working*. Sergeant Knapp, you get your people across that valley, then cover the pullback of the nearest units past the Ridge-"

"-Major, what in hell're you talking about?"

Major Vickers put a hand on his holstered .45. "Move your ass right now, Sergeant Knapp, or by God I've got the right to shoot you where you stand--you understand *that* much, don't you?"

Knapp hesitated, gave Vickers a long look, then began talking to himself, spitting to one side, kicking the doorway on his way out. "Lordalmighty stupidity..."

"You are not in command here!" Vickers yelled after him, and moved his face for emphasis in front of Lieutenant Dao. "Damned non-coms. The Chinese've bypassed us. It's a tactical maneuver on their part but you think this idiot sergeant sees that? You report to G-2 that Major Vickers has this regiment under control, right?"

"That's not why we're here, sir," said Lieutenant Dao. He had to lean back from the intense pink beak, and breath, of Major Vickers. "We just came to see Lieutenant Bryan."

"Bryan? Jack Armstrong his damn self?" Vickers had to think about that. He rubbed the unbandaged part of his arm. "His platoon's on the other side, you'd have to circle the hill... He in some kind of trouble?"

"Just a routine investigation, Major."

Vickers stared from Dao to the dark sergeant as a stocky captain slid through the door, forking wire military-issue glasses around his ears so he could stare through them at Vickers. "What the Christ am I hearing on the radio? Sergeant Knapp is taking a whole *company* out? Who came up with *that* asshole idea?" The officer had ferocious coal-black hair poking beneath his mushroom helmet, the captain's railroad track insignia slashed up the back of it.

"Stay out of this, Griggs. You just concentrate on the damn mortar company, all right?"

"Major, what the hell--you're talking about losing maybe four *platoons*!"

"I know what I'm doing, Captain Griggs. Get back to your company, *now*."

"Damn it, I won't *do* that!"

"Move your ass, Captain. You understand a godamned order?"

The captain swayed from one side to the other, then banged his helmet against the wall and swung back through the doorway.

"And you two..." Vickers turned back to Dao and Sergeant Apollo. "Until we get out you're under my command, you understand that?"

"Our orders are just to see Lieutenant Bryan, Major."

"If the Chinese *let* you, Lieutenant." Major Vickers waved his finger at the radio operator, who busied himself on the three-wire board. "Knapp's company has to show us the way."

"Where can we find Lieutenant Bryan, Major?"

"You can't right now, Lieutenant, don't you hear me? His group's circling the hill to the east. Can't get through in daylight."

Apollo swallowed. This half-ass had the companies cut off even from *each other.*

"Yes, sir," said Lieutenant Dao. "At least we can go to the point nearest his hill-"

"-Go. Go!" Vickers flapped his good arm up and away. "Go on see him right now for all I really care. What can I lose, a couple of desk-jockey *Gee-Too* men?"

Lieutenant Dao waited for Apollo to step through the entrance first, and as the sergeant did so he grinned, for the second time that the lieutenant could remember. "Welcome to the front damn lines, Lieutenant."

They stepped over a sleeping private in the trench outside.

*

Ramirez Apollo moved along the firing perimeter with a veteran's ease, leading the lieutenant to an alcove lined with double-bagged walls. He leaned his M-1 next to a rifle notch, Dao Kim Chau did likewise. The sergeant squinted past an embrasure down a lumpy sinkage of limestone humps, lousy with potential enemy redoubts. "Lord, what shitty positioning," the sergeant grumbled.

"What the hell're the chinks up to now?" Just above ground level, in the next hole, a pair of eyes emerged under a helmet, enlarging when they saw an oriental looking back. "How the hell'd *you* two get here?"

"Wondering that ourselves," said Sergeant Apollo. "How many men here?"

"About eighty or ninety along this particular line." The soldier periscoped his rifle up next to him. "Sergeant Knapp came by to gather a shitload from here for recon. Must've been three platoons moved out--hoo, Jesus! Kiss them *all* goodbye. Probably not more than a couple hundred men on the other hill either."

Dao leaned over to see the other hill, Bryan's hill, but only the slope of it was visible from this position. It ran about two hundred yards down to the dry wash in front of them. "Where's the Chinese?" He stared beyond the wash where, on the other side, enough brush and jack pine stood to hide a division of people.

"Man, all around us," said the soldier, still watching Chau's eyes. "Pushed 'em away a day ago but I don't believe for one damned second they left. Major thinks they've pulled back but that's plain horseshit. Knapp's platoon is dog meat."

Chau shrank back into an ungraceful crouch and strangled his carbine to his chest, shifting his tail bones to fit a dirt bench around the cavity... "Long way from Okinawa, isn't it?"

Apollo nodded, still watching the Chinese hill. "I been here before, Lieutenant. There's worse places we could be."

"Do me a favor, just call me Kim Chau as long as we're in this hole together?" Chau didn't look at Apollo. He began to fingernail dust out of his trigger housing. "I'd like somebody to call me by name for a change, if it wouldn't bother you."

Sergeant Apollo shrugged. "Okay by me. You call me Ram if you like."

"You seem to take everything so calm, Ram. Even when you get a shit detail like this."

"Calm's not really my first nature, Kim Chau." The sergeant thought about that. "Everybody gets their share of shit details, it's just our turn."

"Sounds like my sister's view of life." Chau felt inside his shirt and jiggled out a crinkled photograph. "Her name's My Linh. Want to see? Took this last year."

Ram wiped his hands on his fatigue jacket before taking the photograph by the edges. It was a soft picture, not well focused, fuzzy bamboo stands backgrounding this girl in white cambric muslin, arching toward the camera on tiptoe. Her shoulders back straight as eagle wings.

"Pretty young to be a religious leader," said the sergeant, without taking his eyes from the picture.

"She and I don't agree much on religion, or most other things for that matter." Chau looked from the sergeant's face to the picture. "Like me being here. Thinks my coming here to kill a lot of communists won't help solve anything."

The sergeant leaned on the muzzle of his rifle and handed the picture back, and inspected his M-1. "In East L.A., once, we were accused of killing a man..." He rubbed his sleeve on the barrel where perspiration acid had tarnished the bluing. "Never thought of it as something that might

24

solve anything." He spat on the barrel while he rubbed, and changed the subject. "Can't reach our own flank during daylight. Never heard of such shitty positioning. Worse even than the damned 29ᵗʰ."

*

Later, in the late afternoon, the skies began to drizzle into sleepy rain. Diaphanous grey shades of cloud that were interrupted, near nightfall, by the white flares and noise of a firefight beyond the valley. Sergeant Apollo and Lieutenant Dao heard the firing and knew it was Knapp's company but neither man said much about it. There wasn't much to say.

*

But during the remaining daylight hours one man got through to Bryan's hill. Corporal Weissman, anticipating that Knapp's company would divert the attention of the Chinese, made it to Hill Two.

Two Division men waited in the fire base to question Bryan. The last time that happened, Weissman had remembered, one of the HQ queens disappeared on a Section Eight, so the coming of these men meant just one thing for Lieutenant Bryan and Corporal Weissman. The delivery of that message, at least for Corporal Luke Weissman, was worth the risk of his life.

Chapter 5

A pinpoint of fire flickered up the Korean sky, hung a moment, then popped, dully at first, then dominated, floated, burst into sun-brilliance. The flare spread its light across the battlefield, so close that Lieutenant Bryan could smell the burning sulfur.

Char and twinkling wire. Bright-black ugliness. Bryan raised his head above the outguard bunker and blinked toward the Chinese and hunkered back to his crouch, folding his arms across his knees. No movement out there. No attack tonight, probably.

The new light caused a stirring among the muzzles and helmets along the main trench but Bryan watched only Luke Weissman, who remained with him, still silent, so relaxed now. A security investigation would be the end of both of them, Bryan knew, and here's Weissman so damned... Maybe we deserve what's coming, he thought. How would the barracks talk describe them? Section-Eight bait? It brought the taste of bile to his throat: Daniel Bryan, All-American screaming-fag football hero--how do you explain that to your son Sean?

Weissman, the flamingo, stayed loose, elevating his boot to the wall. Dying light from the flare sparkled off the concertina wire, twisting in front of them ninety yards away, reminding Bryan that they had no high-ground advantage here. The wire along here stretched straight out, at just about eye level, just about *asking* for an attack.

He'd prefer an attack rather than his coming humiliation, though. Fat-ass staff officers sitting around him, maybe relishing the idea of nailing Dan Bryan, the hero. Some kind of jewel in the crown of the Army's homo-hunt, but he would not ever face those two Division investigators. He peeked above the bags and saw blackness, saw only the shell of his own helmet above him. No flares, no moon. He could see the knot on his nose that was broken in '49, before face guards were invented.

"Notice anything on that right flank, Luke?"

"That what?"

"When the flare broke, you notice anything on the right?"

Weissman sniffed, sat up, wasted a look toward the invisible flank. "Whatta you mean, *notice* anything? What's there to notice?" The flamingo still spoke with the honk of an adolescent.

"I wonder if they're covering the right flank?"

"The Chinese?" Weissman was getting real alert now. "Hell yes they're over there. What the hell're you talking about?"

Bryan craned his head forward. "I don't think they're covering that side."

"For Christ's sake, Lieutenant. Course they are." Weissman squatted down, brought his knees tight to his body. "Course they're out there. What the hell're you saying?"

"I could get through the wire, Luke, probably get some help up here."

"Jesus, Bryan, we already told them on the radio."

"It's not the same. Got to have someone get back there and *tell* them. Division doesn't understand unless someone gets back and tells them direct."

"Bullshit." Weissman began a rocking motion. "No reason to get yourself killed, Bryan. What're you thinking about?"

"I'm going to test that side."

Weissman huddled and went silent. In the valley to the west some shots startled the night and then stopped. M-1's. Nervous people on Hill One.

A drizzle feathered Bryan's face. "Got to try it, Luke."

"Shouldn't have told you about those two," Weissman mumbled. He looked at the lieutenant sideways and Bryan leaned against the gun port and saw the clouds break up, unveiling a slit of moon. The rain had cleaned the sky, the stars came through crystalline. The universe opened above them... It's expected of me, thought Bryan--John Bryan's son, all-around perfect human, trapped in a mud hole at the ass-end of the world with a perversion charge hanging over me.

The stock of his carbine had gone clammy, wrapped in a membrane of dew. He held it close, thought about firing it to heat the barrel, something warm to hold on to while he tried not to think... Somewhere in the world of his father, of Bryan Enterprises, inside the fortress of Jonathan Bryan there still existed Sean, son of Dan Bryan, hero.

Sean, he who was about to go fatherless. I hope he's straight, thought Dan Bryan. I hope no one tries to make him perfect.

Rivulets of water traced down the brown-porridge trench walls, sluicing around the stones. Corpuscling little streams. His hands pressed the cartridge release and fumbled with the casing, testing the spring hold. Only two rounds. He ejected the casing and inserted another jacket, and then it was light again, flare-bright, the Chinese keeping watch on their prey. The flare re-lit the huddle of Luke Weissman, wisps of red hair straying from the helmet, his slow sad stare remaining on the mud wall while Bryan watched for the climbing fizzle of another rocket. He saw none, and folded his poncho and laid it to the side, and felt the muscle strain beginning to respond, already, the butterfly tension prepared to give him speed, like in the glory days.

Weissman was watching him, Bryan knew, but the corporal's face remained inside the shadow of his helmet. Bryan climbed over the sandbagged parapet and he knew Luke was watching, and in a breath Dan Bryan shook off that burden and ran, jumping up, over, away from the trench like a hare from its flooded warren.

Toward the multi-toothed barrier, and his legs felt like they weren't part of him. There was this senseless giddiness, a disconnecting rising in him as he plodded through the sloppy ground. The terrain seemed to become smooth as he ran. The mud and mortar holes smoothed to long green fields, sunlight opening above him, hash marks whirring underneath, the goal growing larger. He smelled again the mown grass, heard in his head the crowds yelling. He tucked his carbine in his arm and stumbled through a bomb pit and imagined the crowds standing and yelling and waving, screaming these meaningless sounds, falling together and laughing like a long sustained explosion rolling across the field. Like an attacking army, Dan Bryan ran. Men loomed up, in his mind, to the front and side of him and then flushed by, he twisted and sprinted from them. Hands grabbed at him and hit at him but he spun from them and ran.

Bryan watched his knees settle to their stride and the field open before him--the freedom he searched for. The tall white posts welcomed him and embraced him as he approached the flags.

The first bullet caught Dan Bryan as he reached the wire. It hit bone in his shoulder and spun him spread-eagled into the spiny concertina, his feet tangling beneath him. He slipped but didn't fall, the wire held him there and he sank deep into it, struggled to regain a lopsided stance and wrestle himself upward, but his arm didn't respond. It flapped angrily around the barricade and sent a wrenching pain across his chest. The bone separated. He collapsed against the wire. The barbs ripped his skin.

His hoarse scream sang along the trenches.

Other bullets exploded in ballet precision around him, a new flare opened the sky. Dan Bryan laid back and tried to fill his lungs and the warm taste of blood came to his mouth and he surrendered himself to the distant flashes that were beginning to fade, but the bullets laid only patterns around him. They did not strike, and he thought that these Chinese were indeed badly trained if they couldn't hit a man dangling a couple hundred yards away. The noise of their rifles were hollowing into mocking sounds but he felt nothing hit him.

Instead, he heard the voice of his childhood: *Don't you dare fail me!* Bryan tried to laugh but couldn't, could only cough, and that hurt terribly. *You're Dan Bryan!* came the voice. His thoughts insisted this, this nonsensical crying-out to hold onto his bubble of life, and he imagined the form around that voice, above the hill where the men gaped at their lieutenant; the dreadful white eyebrows of death, scowling like his father Jonathan, above the watching men.

The cheering crowds were transformed and hushed. Somber now, unable to help. Bryan tried to straighten his feet beneath him but felt no strength in his legs. He tried to hold his mind in place, he could at least do that. He prepared himself for the Chinese to finish this, but they did not.

The Chinese continued shooting flares that night, and in the first morning light Bryan understood. They left him alive to lure the heroes out, but no one came. Fortunately no one was that dumb, not even Weissman.

The ground mist had not yet dissipated. The Chinese still watched, he knew, but this game was just about over. If no one came to the wire last night, certainly no one would try it now. No more reason to leave him alive. And when the morning haze began to clear the Chinese started their play-shooting. Bullets stung the steel and rocks around him. One shot cut his forearm and another punctured his calf, he could hear the whistling of the ricochets. They would pick him apart now, he knew. The Chinese riflemen were in no hurry; they would use his body parts for practice, he'd seen that done before.

Bryan could distinguish the bunker that he and Weissman had shared, except two more men were in there now, all of them watching. He couldn't be sure--one looked Chinese. A row of shots filled his legs with distant pain. They had begun on his legs, and that roused him for a moment--his swift *runner's* legs. The thought of his body disintegrating for the amusement of Chinese riflemen... He would not tolerate that.

"Weissman!" He was surprised that he could still yell. "Luke! Don't let them do this!" He could see Weissman's face, his eyes widening, for Luke understood what the lieutenant was asking. "Luke, you do it! ... *Luke!*"

Then the third man, a sergeant, stood, above the other two and just above the ditch. His rifle hung in the crotch of his arm and Bryan thought, Death comes for me. In his blurring vision Bryan could at least see this: The man who stood in shadowed silence was an apparition of Death.

The Chinese bullets worked their way around Bryan's arms. "*Weissman!*" But he knew Luke would not shoot him. He's not like me, thought Bryan, and realized he wasn't thinking about Weissman. That dark sergeant is not at all like me, a hero still playing to imaginary crowds, even in death. Shallow, meaningless asshole that I've always been.

The Chinese interrupted him. They intensified their fire, tiring of this game, and Weissman turned away. The corporal could not give Lieutenant

Bryan this last request, and Bryan thought, don't feel bad. I didn't really expect you to shoot me, Luke.

The oriental next to Weissman still, only, watched, although Bryan could see the man was petrified--no hope there. Bryan rolled his eyes upward and tried to clear them but the sky would not stop spinning, and he brought his vision down to the third man, whom he could see better now. An Indian sergeant, he looked like, or some kind of Latin movie star. Portraying Death, for Dan Bryan's benefit.

The sergeant raised the stock of his rifle to his cheek and squinted at Bryan across the nub sight. At this distance it should be so very clean, thought Dan Bryan.

The jaw of the man portraying death twitched, but Bryan did not see any burst of flame, for the explosions from a Chinese machine gun also bracketed him, and traversed toward him, and raced through him.

> Death itself was not all that dramatic.
> He felt only a distancing from this field.
> He felt only a little faint.

Chapter 6

The rain came down heavily that morning, on the day Dan Bryan died. Not a pleasant rain, a Korean downpour that left the soldiers on Hill Two ankle-deep in their trenches, forcing Ram to hunch into his poncho, and wonder how the hell he'd gotten back into all this. He had already seen this unit, the mighty "Manchu Raiders" of the Second Division, begin its disintegration inside the Triangle and now here he was again, trapped with this one fractured regiment for no understandable reason, just a howitzer shot from rein-forcements.

Major Vickers had already jumped on the PRC-10 field telephone yelling for an explanation--"Two men saw one of *our* people shoot Bryan, that's what they're saying here! Now you find what happened and you do it now, Lieutenant." He called Dao because the G-2 lieutenant, when Bryan died, was apparently the nearest officer to the shooting. "You do it now or I'm coming over there myself, you got that?"

"It wasn't clear what happened, sir," Kim Chau had almost convinced himself that he might have only imagined he saw the sergeant fire at Lieutenant Bryan, or at least he wasn't really sure what he saw.

"All right, goddammit, I'm coming over."

"In daylight, sir?"

"No one's going to see me in this rain."

"Whatever you say, Major." Chau stuck the field telephone back on its cradle and squished himself down in the mud embankment. He stared at Sergeant Apollo and Corporal Weissman seated at either end of the firing alcove. With the mud covering their ponchos they looked like mummies.

"The major's coming over," said Kim Chau, spitting the grit taste from the radio's mouthpiece. "Says two men saw someone here shoot the lieutenant."

"Jesus, the sergeant only did..." Corporal Weissman pushed his feet in front of him, and didn't finish the sentence. He began digging two mounds of mud with his boots. "The major's going to want somebody's ass for this."

"Unless we didn't see what happened." Lieutenant Dao waited for something from Apollo but the sergeant just shifted himself on his bench, which was only a short lump of wood between two sandbags.

"Well, I didn't actually see anything," said Corporal Weissman. "I was turning my head when it happened."

"Think what you're saying, now," said Sergeant Apollo.

"Neither of us saw what happened, Sergeant," said Chau. "That's the truth."

"He died before we could've done anything to him anyway," said Weissman. "Wouldn't've done any good for us to shoot him."

Decided simple as that. Ram watched the corporal for a minute and then, leaning forward, held out his hand. "Name's Ramirez Apollo, Corporal. Didn't catch yours."

The corporal awkwardly shook hands. "Luke Weissman, named after Saint Luke. Had a Catholic mom and a Jewish pop." Giving Ram a weak grin with that rehearsed explanation. "Appreciate what you did, if you really did it." Weissman made this confused twisting with his mouth. "He was really asking *me* to...do that."

Ram turned away from him and began to check the chamber of a Browning .50-caliber machine gun they'd carried from an empty back bunker. He ran his thumb down the chunky cooling-jacket: Too narrow a cone of fire from here, he thought. He aimed the gun in the direction of Lieutenant Bryan, hanging before them like a flag of truce, reaching down like a baseball shortstop.

"Lord, it was strange seeing you two come in." Weissman began to straighten up. "Like a postman just delivering the darned regimental mail, or something, the way you drove in."

"Look what we delivered." Apollo tiredly rubbed his eyes, then squinted down the gunsight at Bryan. "A whole company shot to hell, and a dead lieutenant."

"I heard a lot of Knapp's men got back." Weissman saw where the gun was pointed and looked away. "We planted a mess of bouncing betties and Claymores out there awhile back. Don't know how the lieutenant didn't step on one." His voice, not very strong to begin with, was almost whispering now. "Must've been two thousand Chinese coming up a couple nights ago, blowing whistles like they only do at night now. Trying to scare us. Hell, doesn't take two thousand men blowing whistles to scare me. One Chinaman with a rifle can do that."

Using his poncho as a tent, Weissman started field-stripping his rifle. The three remained quiet until the rain began letting up. "Bryan was the only real hero around here," Weissman said from his tent. "Once I tried to discuss the issues of this war and he says the only issue we should think about here is who kills who. Hell, he even talked like John Wayne."

Neither of the other two answered. Ram rested against the scratchy burlap bags and watched the opposite hill, and thought about this unspoken conspiracy over the death of Lieutenant Bryan, with these two, and wondered if only wars produced such men. He remembered the five-thousand man Turkish Brigade at Wawon, assigned to the Second Division and left stranded by the screwed-up Eighth Army staff, so the Turks throw down their hats in the custom of the Turkish military and refuse to move farther. Every man gets killed. Everyone sticking it out to the goddamn end for no real crystal-clear reason--like we three conspirators, he thought.

"It was you that shot Lieutenant Bryan, Apollo!" Major Vickers landed in the trench behind Ram in a smack of water, slipping into mud three inches deep. He held his festering hand and waved it at Ram, and the bandages flapped around it like soiled wings, exposing the brunette skin. "This Private Peterson saw you do it! A Corporal *Barnes* saw you do it!--you point that rifle away from me." Ram had turned his rifle toward the incoming commotion and Vickers pointed his finger at it and then at Ram's face. "You move that rifle *now*, Sergeant."

"Right, Major." Ram propped the rifle between his knees.

"They said the shooter had a sergeant's stripe on the back of his helmet and *you're* the only damn sergeant along here." Vickers struggled up from the mud in the direction of Kim Chau. "Lieutenant, you're a witness. I'm bringing charges against this man."

Chau took a look at Ram, from Ram to the major to Ram again. "I didn't really see what happened, Major. So much going on--we'd just got here-"

"-What the hell're you talking about? You've been right next to this man since..." Vickers squinted at Chau, then saw Weissman, who was in the corner trying to get invisible. "What kind of shit-conspiracy's going on here? Corporal, you're not in this, whatever the hell these G-2 assholes are up to. You saw it, right?"

Weissman made his baleful chewing motion again and Ram watched with an expression that Weissman couldn't figure out. Curiosity, it looked like. "I was looking away, Captain. Turning my head when it happened."

Major Vickers wasn't buying that. "What in hell's wrong with you--*all* of you. A goddamned crime's been committed here."

"Even if someone had shot him, Major, would've been better than what he was getting out there," said Weissman. "The Chinese were cutting him up."

"That's not for you or *anyone* to decide-"

"-The Chinese'd probably already killed him, sir."

Major Vickers kept his glare on Weissman. "It's people like you, Corporal, and Sergeant Knapp and even Lieutenant Bryan out there--all *undermining* me... So you didn't see him killed, right? So if nobody here saw him killed then maybe he *wasn't* killed, right? If nobody saw him killed then maybe you should crawl out there and *see* if he was killed, Corporal."

"Pardon, sir?" Weissman's stare went to the ground between the trench and wire, ninety yards of muck, black, undulating, down to the circular crucifix of Bryan. "Jesus, Major..."

"The man's dead, Major."

"You stay the hell out of this, Lieutenant. I'm giving this corporal a direct order, or are you deaf *too*?" Vickers saw the look the lieutenant gave Sergeant Apollo, like some kind of school kid. This officer was looking to a damned *sergeant* for help.

"That doesn't make sense, Major." Ram lifted a foot from the mud and placed it on the jerry-rigged bench, which slipped the rifle over, aiming down at Vickers' feet. "That lieutenant was a dead man, soon as he decided to make that dumb-ass run."

"Sergeants don't talk to me that way, Sergeant. Stay the hell out of this." Vickers made a sloppy pirouette around the alcove until he faced Ram. "Bet your life I'll be talking with you later--*you point that away from me!*"

"You're putting a man's ass right in the line of fire, Major." Ram shifted his M-1, not much. "What the hell for?"

"Shut your mouth, Sergeant." Vickers moved his pointing finger from Ram to Weissman. "Corporal, you go see if the lieutenant's alive. *Now.*" Weissman hesitated until the major again unsnapped the holster flap on his .45. "Can't you hear me, Corporal?"

"Going, sir." Weissman lifted himself to where he could see the wire and Lieutenant Bryan.

"This doesn't make any sense, sir," said Lieutenant Dao.

"*You* make no sense, Lieutenant. You let a goddamn murder take place in this bunker."

"That's a strange word to use here, sir."

Vickers waved off Chau with his bad hand as he drew his pistol. "You just stay down, Corporal. Stay down and crawl."

"Yes, sir... Oh shit." Weissman inhaled, snaked over the sandbags. His feet kicked above the edge for a moment and then disappeared.

Ram eased his rifle away from the major. "That's the second time we've seen you pull that pistol, Major. You do that a lot?"

"Okay, Lieutenant, at least you heard this son of a bitch say *that*."

Dao didn't look like he had. "I'm not sure what he meant, sir."

Major Vickers backed away. "We're playing some kind of game, is that what we're doing here?" He felt behind him for the wall of the trench. "You think I can't get both your tails in the stockade?" He was clumsily maneuvering his body over the side as he talked, backsliding away to a crouch. "It's daylight now, you remember that. A lot of men are watching us."

The major turned and squatfooted down through the arroyo between the two hills of the 23rd Regiment. Ram made something that might pass for a wink toward the lieutenant and rested a forearm on his rifle. "The major thinks I might shoot him, Lieutenant. Think I should oblige?"

Kim Chau wasn't sure that was a joke. He kept an eye on Apollo's rifle. "Got a mission to accomplish first, remember?"

"The investigation of that lieutenant's father? Hell, our part ended the minute he stepped out of this hole."

"It's my homeland that's involved in this arms business, remember. It hasn't ended for me."

Ram shrugged and put his rifle down. "No need to shoot him. That arm'll kill him if someone doesn't take it off, real soon."

"Take his arm off?"

"The arm's gone, at least the hand part is. The dumb ass probably doesn't understand that yet."

"You a doctor too?" Kim Chau *had* noticed the veins on Vickers' arm, like little black rivers. But, well, Christ, that wasn't really their problem. "How the hell could you tell that?"

"Seen it before." Ram was studying the terrain between the bunker and Bryan's corpse. He watched where the mud moved, watched the outline of Weissman's helmet. The corporal was belly-crawling between two fat depressions in the earth. "Could I see those binoculars?"

Ram took Chau's glasses and adjusted them on Weissman, gulping air inside the second crater, about thirty yards from Bryan. Weissman was clutching mud in front and pulling himself along like an iguana, using his big spindly iguana-hands while his cheeks rubbed earth that still reeked with the stench of fallowed paddies. Reminding Ram of the mud of Kunu-ri during the retreat through Sunchon Pass, the Valley of Death where the soldiers fell in bunches from their trucks, sliding like Weissman to their muddy ditch-graves or falling back to the battle at Chipyong-ni where the Algerian units, the Moroccan mercenaries, in their childlike enjoyment of war had cranked hand sirens and bayonet-attacked the attackers. Ram's top sergeant had told him about that attack, laughing so hard he had to lean against his rifle in the telling of it. Ram chewed the mud-taste of his saliva and wiped it off his mouth with his sleeve... Now everyone's gone from here, he thought, except this major and this scraggly-ass command. We sit and wait for reinforcements that never come while a whole ocean of Chinese re-group along the Ridge.

Weissman had reached the wire now, a few yards from Bryan. A flock of starlings bickered around them while he inspected the wire, snarled around Bryan like a road map. Weissman stared up at the wire with his face still wet with that fecal stink--probably couldn't smell it anyway, Ram thought. Fear seems to shut off the sense of smell, though the stench would be welcome to Weissman right now. Shit was, maybe, most of all, life.

There was a quietness in Bryan's face that Ram hoped the corporal would see, to help keep Weissman quiet, because if Weissman got up and ran now he'd be like a moose in a shooting gallery. But they both stayed quiet, Bryan still leaning over, spreading his arms above Weissman like some grey Christ.

Corporal Weissman looked up at the eyes and shied away.

Christ's death-gaze followed him.

Weissman tugged at Bryan's ankle but the lieutenant stayed fast, so he made a small jump, sprang, just to his knees, grabbed the lieutenant's arm and tried to pull him off the wire but the lieutenant didn't move, and Ram's stomach tightened: What in hell was the man *doing* out there? Weissman went to see if Bryan was dead and he *was* dead, now what the hell was he doing? Everything but wave a goddamned flag at the Chinese.

Bryan had instead lodged tighter into the wire. The Chinese still didn't open fire. They either didn't see the corporal or didn't care. The rain had stopped in the valley and the wind picked up and the sky would be clearing soon. The Chinese would not miss another move like that, but Weissman did not back off. He reached for the hanging hand of Bryan, feeling for a pulse, and Ram could hear the wind sing through the stretched concertina as the two remained silent, the corporal and his dead lieutenant in this frozen tableau, and Weissman looked like he was crying when the first shot cracked from the Chinese hill. He tried to wedge into an old plough rut while the bullets began to smack and fluff around him, and tracers from the company of soldiers to Ram's right began streaming at the Chinese hill as Weissman jumped up and ran under the canopy of fire toward the American line.

"*Oh God! Oh God! Oh God! Oh God!*" The corporal's voice howled above the firing.

"*Run*, you son of a bitch!" someone yelled along the line.

"Oh God! Oh God!" yelled the corporal. He fell hands and knees into the trench thirty feet from Kim Chau. A PFC tried to catch him and they both fell in the mud.

"Get the hell off me," said the PFC.

"You okay?" Chau called over to him.

"What the hell were you doing out *there*?" someone else yelled.

"I was ordered out." Weissman tried to catch his breath.

"The tin major strikes again," came another voice.

Ram breathed easier. Weissman lives, he survives, he would be around to go "south," as the survivors of the Sunchon massacre used to describe it.

"You okay?" asked the PFC, who stayed in his sitting position as Weissman got up.

"Got to get back to my position..."

To get south, like Weissman, you needed to survive. Hell, Ram realized, even the massacre site at Sunchon was south of them now.

Everything was south of them now.

*

John Bryan learned of the death of his son, Lieutenant Daniel Bryan, in the late afternoon of July 27, 1953, the worst day of the old man's life. And he wept for the first time in his life, and he sent his chief officer, Harry Crosse, to find the reason why the Army had sent his son to a combat zone like Kumsong. And he swore to Harry Crosse, and to God, and to anyone who would listen that day, he would find the people who were responsible for doing this to his son.

Chapter 7

In their daylight assaults the Chinese troops no longer came with the whistles and child's bugles shrilling and tweedle-tooting. The screaming and hissing stopped with the killing of the first ten thousand Chinese by the U.N. forces, for it was too costly to announce their attacks in that way, and they no longer made those sounds when they came.

The Chinese assault began with the rustle of twelve hundred padded feet and Ram heard it first, instantly, like leaves in a wind. Lieutenant Dao didn't understand the meaning of the whisking cadence but to Ram it came like a fire bell, and it still sent a shudder through him, more than all the yelling and all the noise-making.

It began in the late afternoon of their second day with the 23rd Regiment, a strange time of day for an assault, with no warning along the American line. No artillery barrage preceded it. Ram nudged his foot against the lieutenant, who was asleep on the wood ledge. "Time to earn our pay, Kim Chau."

Chau rolled to a standing position and stared toward the valley. He fumbled with his carbine and began to breath in short nervous gulps.

"Deep breaths. Long deep breaths, Kim Chau. Don't pass out on me." Ram pulled the bolt on his M-1 and pushed a cartridge to the chamber. Quietly, quietly, he thought. Wait till you can hit something, amigo. "Hold your fire, Kim Chau. Don't shoot till I do, okay?"

Farther down the line he saw Weissman take his position with the men there. They listened to the rub of jackets and leggings, to the muted clack of buckles and wood and metal, rising to a hushed crescendo. The cold mist lifted from the ravine below the American hill, churning with movement. Ram saw the grey pantlegs and grey-brown boots of the Chinese before their bodies came out. The bayonets emerged.

Another sound, barely audible, murmured somewhere behind them. "What the hell's that?" whispered Kim Chau.

"Doesn't matter right now. Don't fire till I do, understand?" The nearest man was still the size of a flea in Ram's gunsight. He exhaled, tried to shake the butterflies, and tightened his grip.

Ram felt the lieutenant jump back from the rifle's explosion--"Holy Jesus *Christ!*" The man Ram had aimed at reeled to the ground. Chau came back to the parapet and stuck his carbine across it and pulled the trigger, copying Ram, and the M-2 instantly rose.

"Switch to *semi*-automatic." Ram grabbed and flipped the selective-fire switch on Chau's carbine as the lieutenant groped for another clip.

Not time yet to get on the machine gun, Ram thought. Not yet, not yet. He didn't want to use up that ammunition until the Chinese got closer. The assault was beginning to return disciplined fire and the Chinese were keeping a good spread in their line. The spattering of Chinese rifles joined the noise from the American hills, then bursts of mortar covered both sides in a curtain of smoke as the attackers started uphill at a jog.

Now the bracketing *crump crump* of incoming mortars churned along the American lines. The front sappers, loaded with bangalore torpedoes and recoilless guns and satchel charges, chugged and wove toward them and Ram's eyes began to water from the cordite fume, melding the uniforms into a grey diaspora of people wavering around him. He put the M-1 down and gripped the slippery wood-spade grips of the Browning machine gun, flipped the feeder. The belt fell into place, the cocking lever slid and locked the first cartridge. He tapped on Chau's helmet--"Feed this thing, Lieutenant."

He pulled. The machine shattered the air, the belt leaped like a snake from its can. Ram brought the fire down until it hammered through the nearest group of men, screaming, sounding far away, although a few sappers got to the first concertina and the *ba-room* of their charges blew out twelve-foot gaps in the wire. And they poured through. They crumpled magically. Ram swiveled his magic machine--it felt like it would shake his wrists apart--and huge pellets sucked life from the assault, they chewed through the men who danced at the edge of the perimeter while the Norkor burp guns answered with their quick *b-r-r-rup-p-pt* stutter. Potato-masher grenades from the Chinese spewed dirt over the bunkers but the grenades weren't well thrown, the attackers died too quickly.

Lieutenant Dao looked over the field as he stuffed in another belt. "They're slowing up! I think they're slowing up!"

The.50-caliber gun, the death monster, had ripped apart the charge in this sector though they still came in twos and threes. The sergeant still sought them out. A group on the left stayed afoot and Apollo sprayed into them and the attack straggled as a round hung up in the belt. Ram felt his guts flip--"*Son of a BITCH!*" He shook the rigid cocking lever but it held tight, the belt webbing jammed. He grabbed his M-1 and searched the fire zone but the rest of the assault had gone to ground. The Chinese soldiers on the flanks were sprinting back downhill and the Americans tried to bring them down but most of the Chinese made it back past the valley.

Huddled bodies remained, some squirming, drowning face-down in pools of rain, and the sound of crying remained.

Chau peeked above the parapet. "We got them *all*."

"Don't talk shit, Lieutenant." The assault troops, Ram knew, had faded down the rock ledges, into the craters and into the stunted pine along the other hill. About two regiments had charged and fired and withdrawn, he guessed. Like the knife thrust of a *vato*. I've cut them bad and now they bleed, he thought. They retreat from my goddamned maelstrom, my great goddamned maw of death.

"Lord Almighty," said Kim Chau.."I think it's over."

"Not yet, not yet." Ram's stomach was scrambled from pumped adrenalin and he sagged against the parapet while Chau, still elated, kept grinning at Ram, and seeing the sergeant return the look he stretched the grin wider, baring a crooked front tooth. They still lived, and Chau's face locked into that relief, and Ram finally smiled back. "Nothing like that feeling, is there, Kim Chau?"

"We're going to make it, aren't we?"

"One way or another."

"Can't die yet." Chau grinned again. "Haven't finished the Bryan investigation yet."

"You're an obsessed bastard, Kim Chau."

During the hiatus, during his check on the ammunition, Ram noticed a message scratched below the print on the olive-colored ammo can, and he tried to read it before the humming began again. He picked up the field glasses instead. The noise was still too far away to hear clearly but Ram didn't need to hear it any more.

He knew the sound. Tanks. In the valley he saw the Chinese forming up but the sound didn't come from there. The din of engines drifted from the valley behind the Americans, a tiny buzz prickling the air then falling away: heavy, *mean*-sounding machinery. The whine of Norkor Russian tanks or maybe the growl of American Shermans or the new American 48's--one of the sides would be getting armored help soon. Ram doubted if the battalion had stockpiled any HEAT anti-tank weapons or 3.5mm bazookas on this hill. The .50-caliber machine gun had anti-armor capability if anyone had the sense to pack armor-piercing rounds. Fat chance.

Wait, then.

The noise, still a distance away, made that unmistakable clank, a dim intermittent rattling hum that faded with the shift of wind, bringing with it the faint smell of diesel.

"Are they ours?" Chau finally stopped his smiling.

"Coming from behind us, Lieutenant. I hope that means they're ours." Ram was busy trying to pry the hung cartridge from the gun with his bayonet as the jarring thump and blast of the mortar rounds came in again, and dirt cascaded into the trench for the thirty feet visible to them, sending men crouching against the sandbagged escarpment. Dirt filled the inside of Ram's collar and scratched its way down his back. The bags along the wall jiggled under his hands with the thud of mortar. The shelling scattered away from them.

We might be in luck, Ram thought. Green mortar people on that Chinese hill, or maybe they were just too spooked by the tanks. The first break in the explosions brought him up searching the tree line but the grey army wasn't attacking, they looked confused and busy on the other side of the valley, people scurrying around trying to sort themselves out as the tank noise got louder.

He went back to the machine gun but the belt wasn't coming loose. He picked up the M-1 as clusters of men started toward the American hill again, but not in any military skirmish line. The attackers *were* confused. They came up the hill like a disorganized mob now, huge numbers, tumbling like army ants from the tree line over the crags of purple rock--a panic charge at the Americans. If they needed the higher ground this fast, Ram guessed, the tanks *had* to be American. The Chinese wanted the higher ground as the better position against tanks, probably the reason for an assault at this strange time of day, and the reason for the weak preliminary barrage.

Smoke and uniforms meshed again to a solid shifting grey body around the American line. Chau switched back to automatic fire on his carbine and swept the air before him and Ram hit the stock of it with the back of his hand: "*Switch to SEMI-automatic, God DAMN you, Lieutenant!*"

The nearest Chinese soldier came so close that the man's chest filled Ram's gunsight and there was no time to help the lieutenant. The impact of Ram's shot, at this range, jerked the Chinese soldier back. Behind him the tank 105's discharged. Yellow-white blooms of fire tore up clumps of Chinese in the valley but the tanks weren't where they could take out the attackers near Ram's position. The Chinese swarmed around what little wire the sappers hadn't blown away and Ram's cartridge magazine ejected and he grabbed another and saw Chau kneeling bloody-chested on one knee, trying to fix his carbine. *Help your damned self, Lieutenant*, he thought. *I can't help you now.*

More men got to the sandbags as Ram slid in the new clip and swung the barrel toward them. A soldier rose above the parapet and fired down on him, simultaneously with him. The man's face sprayed red as Ram, stepping sideways, stumbled and fell, but he wasn't hit. He kept his rifle up and waited for other faces to come over the rim of the bunker.

Kim Chau, his carbine working again, was back to the embrasure by the time Ram got up, but nothing was moving in front of them.

"Where the hell do they go?" Chau asked.

Ram could only raise his shoulders. *Christ in heaven,* he thought, *quit asking these asshole questions. He* looked over the field of dead, the contorted handiwork of his machine gun. In the field the golden hands of dead Chinese punctuated the air like runt corn stalks. More heroes, he thought. Miserable bloodied things. They reminded Ram of the lieutenant's smeared jacket but he was too tired to think about Kim Chau. The lieutenant was working on the jammed machine gun and he seemed to be okay, and Ram needed first, right now, to rest back, and as he did he saw again the hen-track scrawling along the back of the ammo can--an elegy of some kind. An ode to some corporal named Hill:

> *Dreamed I saw Joe Hill last night,*
> *Alive as you and me.*
> *I said, hey Joe, you're three weeks dead.*
> *I never died, said he.*
> > *To my buddy, Cpl Joe, ?/34 to 5/13/53*

Ram reached to touch the words. Like thin, scratchy Braille. He let his eyes close.

The tank sounds muted. He could hear only the dialectic mumble of Chau working over the hung round. Ram put a hand on the still-warm barrel. "Take a break, Kim Chau. I'll do it."

Chau fell back on command, spraddling against the parapet, dropping his hands. "You think they'll come back?"

"They always come back." Ram nodded toward Chau's wound. "How bad is that?"

"Tore some skin, I think. Think I have time to rest?"

"Christ, yes." And Ram thought, Christ, yes, rest, even if there *weren't* time. Death might be a fair price for some rest. The heroes out there were resting now, their bodies will be changing hues soon, while they rest: fusions of purples, blacks, greens... Ram freed the round and pulled the cocking lever back, which smacked against his hand as the next cartridge slipped down the chamber.

"You t-two okay?" A private's mottled face peeked around the corner of the slit trench. Just wide green eyes and helmet showed, no more, in case somebody here still had trigger nerves.

"We're okay."

"The Major asked me to r-recon this hill. Brought some rations. A-anybody hurt here?" The private carried a bantam duffel half-full of cartridge belts and C-rations.

"Not right here." Ram was too tired to ask how the hell he got over here, but Weissman crawled over to check him out.

"Whyn't you just call on the radio?" asked Weissman.

"Can't." The private slid by, toward the next bunker. "The damned radio is..." he kissed the last word off his fingers: "*gone*, man. Like we'll be i-if those damn tanks don't get here soon."

"You sure they're ours?"

"If they ain't," said the private, "then we get to go out like old John W-Wayne hisself."

Ram let his head rest forward on the cold barrel of the machine gun, for a moment. Other men were watching the line, any new attack would certainly wake him anyway. Hell with it either way.

Ram saw the boy as he closed his eyes, and Ram retained the picture of this Chinese boy kneeling behind an outcropping, not eighty yards away. The boy was visible from the neck up, watching Ram like a tanned Chinese Buddha-doll, like a brown chimaera on the rock. A screaming began behind the boy but that came from Ram's own mind, Ram knew. The screaming in his head had happened before, in firefights, although the warning scream this time came so insistently. Calling for him to awake--this was no illusion--and the kid grew to a distorted apparition in Ram's head, hovering over a scene not earth-connected. A terrifying door seemed to be opening behind the boy and the voice screamed for Ram to be awake. He *was* awake.

Probably not ten seconds had passed, Ram wasn't sure. Everything seemed quiet enough. He couldn't see the boy now but Ram knew the kid was on this hill, and Ram's bunker must have been--was--his target. The young Chinese could have moved nearer to Ram's bunker, maybe on this side of the wire. The slope still steamed from spent shells and cooling blood but no living thing moved out there, not that Ram could see. A.50-caliber hitting any part of the body tears tamale-sized chunks from it. If that kid was still moving out there, Ram doubted if he was hit.

The head came up behind a cedar stump and stared at Ram and vanished again, scared and uncertain, his face so close that Ram could see gaps in his teeth. Damned dumb place to hide, Ram thought, using that stump as a redoubt. The.50-caliber gun could scramble it to pulp. A dumb position for some kid to be in. Ram couldn't remember ever being that young, or dumb.

He wrapped his hands around the spade grips and swung the long barrel into alignment with the stump. The boy might slide back to the run-off behind the stump but he probably wouldn't. He was probably too scared to move now. Ram hoped so. He didn't want to kill this one.

43

His ears droned with the hush that fell on the field and the air hung moist on Ram's face. He tasted again the dry fear in his mouth, like dirty cotton, and he listened for insect sounds or bird sounds but there weren't any, and this reminded him strangely of the large silent birds of Okinawa.

The break in the silence came undramatically.

Footsteps. Running feet splashing the earth with this quick steady rhythm. Ram adjusted the gun to the boy-soldier, where he emerged without the yell of defiance that Ram expected. Only a steady, intent run. A stupid kid running, earnestly, concentrating on Ram with earnest, frightened eyes, but he didn't seem to make any headway up that hill. The boy was like a person running in a dream, and the dream hypnotized, the cobra-effect of steady movement and danger and a reluctance, on Ram's part, to end it here.

One boy, lugging this ugly black can-like grenade by its rolling-pin handle, the weight throwing him off stride as he runs.

Ram squeezed the grips, the gun rattled his forearms, the roar of it punched acrid white smoke to the air, clamoring into the silence. Through the cloud Ram saw the boy divide, his stomach shredding in the point-blank discharge. The boy's arm jerked forward in muscular contraction, hurling the grenade over them. Ram saw the dark blur of it pass overhead, heard it drop with a metallic *clunk* behind him.

Releasing the grips, spinning backward, Ram shoved the lieutenant away--"*Grenade!*"--while the lieutenant, confused, tried to stand and reach for the ammo belt. Ram ran and pushed him again just before the grenade detonated and Ram saw for an instant the flash of Chau's face as Ram catapulted over him. Ram felt the machine gun tumble in on him, slamming the air from him. A loud blare and then the clatter and the falling gun and then a silence. Shadowy vacant stillness. A vague serenity taking him into darkness.

Ram was drowning in a sea of silence, the taste of sulfur in his throat, while other men rose above the ledge. But they seemed farther removed now, telescoping to a different and faraway battlefield. They came into the hole with slow grotesquely distorted motions, their boots and calves so close and so greatly out of proportion to their faces and helmets, a long steep distance away. The man nearest Ram came down holding a bayonet crooked to the side and Ram tried to move but couldn't, and he felt then the horrifying euphoria he had heard men speak of, of total release, of knowing he was about to die and accepting it.

The incision of the black bayonet brought quick dull pain and caught him in mid-breath, and Ram coughed and rolled to his side as it slid from him. And the sound diminished. He tried to open his eyes in the blurring bottom of the trench where he could just make out the boots of other men scuffling within the hole, or lying still, jumbled into browns and greens.

The boots and the colors and the scuffling faded. He still had fear, but no longer of death. He could not distinguish this new fear, could not remember its source. He remembered, instead, in his last thought before unconsciousness, the "bon voyage" poem of K. Marisa Paviso, and wondered if, wherever he was now going, he would be shown the Truth that she wrote of.

Chapter 8

Harry Crosse stepped off the Bryan Industries helicopter like an athlete, which he was, once, as one of the first black running backs in Stanford's history. Best thing that ever happened to him, he always realized, being on the same team with Dan Bryan, buddying up with the main limb of a giant money tree. That's where Harry now was, and where Harry planned to stay.

The helicopter ride from Monterey Peninsula scared hell out of him, like always, not for the usual reasons. This time it felt too much like the flight he just took around Korea. Lord, he wanted no part of any war zone again, not for *any* kind of money.

Harry hunched himself beyond the reach of the decelerating rotors, adjusted his Magnin tie and waited for the personnel carrier that scuttled around the Bryan grounds. When it arrived he checked the seat for dust before getting in, turned the rear view mirror to check his hair and, yes, slick as Mr. Tyrone Power's, though Harry's nose was a little wider and a whole lot darker.

The driver was typical Bryanesque, a thin pale guy who didn't look once at Harry while the vehicle rolled toward the forest surrounding Bryan's compound. The rock wall bordering the trees split two landscapes like a granite zipper: On the ocean side, wildflowers tumbled through the palisades, perfuming the breeze with zygadene lilies, seaside daisies, Indian paintbrush. In contrast, the other side was a spectered woodland: gnarled Monterey Cypress twisting at the cliff's edge, Australian blue eucalyptus jumping like ghosts at the skyline, heavy with lichen and Spanish moss.

Spooky place, thought Harry Crosse as he got out at the Fort and hurried along the steepest part of the cliff. A skein of brown pelicans skimmed the ocean below, toward the marshes of Elkhorn Slough, disappearing behind the Fort's sawtoothed balustrades.

Bryan's bodyguards, Sorry Ochoa and Charles Trevors, were playing gin in the miniature Viking hallway, its stave walls and dragon-style portal jammed against the side of the building, as a guardhouse. Appropriate for those two, Harry thought. Trevors and Ochoa were themselves Viking-sized, geological outcroppings, hands that could crush dictionaries, although Harry never made the mistake of regarding them as lummoxes. Not likely. These two were professionals, not to be screwed with.

"*Gin*, ass hole." Trevors' voice had all the articulation of a falling tree.

"Crap," whined Sorry Ochoa. "What kind of crap cards you dealing me? Lemme win *one*, would you?"

"Morning, Mr. Crosse." Trevors noticed Harry and stood and grinned with that strange expression. Suppressed rage, as Harry saw it.

"Morning, Mr. Trevors." Harry took a long step toward the door as Trevors bonged the door's hanging iron lion's-head against it. The man's biceps strained the knit of his navy blue coat like the wrapping around a cotton bale.

A servant in white livery opened the door.

"I'll join you, Mr. Crosse," said Sorry Ochoa, as head bodyguard around here. Sorry had no visible neck. Harry'd heard rumors that Sorry's nickname came from his habit of apologizing to his victims before hurting them. No one knew his real first name.

Inside, along the hall, paintings of wars from the Peloponnesian to WW II were paneled around a cupola housing a Gallic catapult. Slits of skylight streaked through long thin windows, highlighting sheets of floating dust, moving with the sun across the ancillary truncheons, bludgeons, cudgels, rams and pikes that lined the wall.

Harry quick-stepped behind the simian stride of Ochoa with no great enthusiasm. He preferred the slums of the tenderloin district around Bryan's San Francisco headquarters to this bad replica of Dracula's castle. He waited for Sorry to wrestle the vestibule door open and allow him into Bryan's library, which seemed to Harry like some kind of church, built around a ceiling of brown nubbins, silver intaglios, green gargoyles.

Harry could barely see Kenneth Willy Carson half-hidden behind the bookshelves. Bryan's voice, soft as a cat's purr, came out to find him. "Do you remember what my father's last words were, Harry?" The old man was in his high leather chair, facing the window. "Did I tell you," said John Bryan, "the last words he ever said to me?"

Harry stared toward Bryan's desk, blotted inside the burnt-orange window. "I was able to get that information-"

"-Did I ever tell you what he said, Harry?"

"I think you did, once." About a hundred times once, thought Harry.

"*Satan*, he called me. Seller of death--can you imagine? My father asked the Lord to forgive him because he had spawned the *Antichrist*. He meant *me*, Harry." John Bryan turned and watched Harry beneath clipped white brows. "Can you imagine such a curse on me?"

"No, sir, I absolutely can't."

"And for that, because I took up selling arms, he threw that spewing malediction at me, like a firebrand on my soul, Harry. 'If the Angel of Death does not punish you,' my father said, 'I'll send the messenger *myself* for the shame you bring onto me.' And now he has done that, hasn't he?"

Harry looked away, toward the private chapel recessed into the paneling. From Harry's view only the yellowing, placid Christ-hand could be seen. "That has nothing to do with the death of your son, Mr. Bryan."

"He condemned me as a coward for selling arms rather than *fighting* in that war, Harry. I can't easily dismiss such a condemnation. My father was a Pentecostal preacher, remember, a wrathful man of God and a great evangelist and a Christian Soldier, as even he himself was born into the parsonage of his own father, Josh, oh, God, himself a preacher."

"He shouldn't have condemned you like that--as a coward, Mr. Bryan." Harry said that like a court page. That wouldn't do, coming from the Executive V.P. of Bryan Munitions.

"Yet I *was* in battle, you know, in the battle of Belleau Wood, full thirty-five years ago now. My father never knew that, so he had no right to condemn me like that, threatening to send his *messenger* after me, after my *seed*...to kill my son Daniel, as he has now done."

Harry shook his head and listened and said nothing. He'd heard this before and he knew that Bryan never fought in any war, anywhere, but then who was Harry to deny the old man? Harry himself stayed out of Korea because of a long-healed football injury, which, fortunately, he'd acquired by running interference for Bryan's son. His friendship with Dan and a fake injury had gotten Harry here, and he wasn't about to rain on anyone else's hero-fantasy.

"I even received a leg wound there. Even now it causes this limp, do you see?" The old man actually limped in front of Harry, as he'd done before, but now with a more pronounced dip.

"I certainly see that, sir." Harry thought about his own heavily-mortgaged house on Union Street in San Francisco, and Bryan's 120-foot yacht where Harry was allowed to stay in L.A., and Harry wasn't about to question Bryan's "leg wounds." John Bryan was the closest thing to family, in fact, that Harry had in this world.

"I originally intended to be an evangelist preacher too, a spiritual giant like my father, Harry, but the crowds they would never...they would not listen to me. I believe my father relished that failure in me but, oh, when I visited the battlegrounds of Verdun and the Meuse-Argonne and the six hundred miles of trenches across France and Belgium, when I saw these instruments of war in piles--in actual *monuments*, Harry--stacked on the roads from Arras to Laon, in this metallic pyre I saw this...destiny.

Unrestricted profit, Harry, without national boundaries, without politics. The arms trade wings like an indifferent spirit above our little world conflicts."

Harry knew better than to interrupt. The old man would now go on about the Russians using Krupp cannons on the Germans, the Bulgarians bombarding French 75's onto the French troops in Bulgaria, etc.--a *phantasm* of free enterprise, as Bryan liked to put it.

"I studied the lives of Francis Brannerman and Basil Zaharoff, Harry, the Merchants of Death who could start and *end* wars, so the blueprint was already laid out. The materials were at hand. So let the young men die--much as I, a good Christian, dislike that thought, Harry--but let their survivors mourn over the dead husks of their heroes if they must. I will harvest this fallow wealth no matter who He sends after me, no matter what *He* does to me."

Bullcrap, thought Harry. *I'm* the real runner of this company now, I'm the one who's harvesting your goddamned fallow wealth for you. But he said nothing, and waited, instead, until Bryan seemed to be through. "About Daniel, sir. You asked me to find out the circumstances-"

"-I didn't think he could be killed, Harry," said John Bryan. "The Lord should not have permitted my father's damnation to be carried out like that, considering how I have served Him and tithed and lived in accordance with His tenets."

"You took your sweet time about getting back to us, Mr. Crosse," said Kenneth Willy Carson, apparently figuring it was safe to speak now. Kenneth Willy Carson's official title was Assistant to the Chairman of Bryan Industries, whatever that meant.

Harry stared along the paneling until he found Carson, still inside the shadow of the bookcase. Only the left side of his short skinny frame could be seen, the chest lapel of his silver-colored Italian suit glinting from the window light.

"Let Harry talk now, Kenneth," said John Bryan. "He's been all the way to Korea for us, hasn't he? Let's hear him out."

Carson remained still as Bryan turned again to Harry. "Kenneth--both of us, in fact--have heard stories, Harry. We want to know if you verified them." Bryan was unbending himself to an unsteady stance, his eyes worn and blooded, reminding Harry of the black dots the editorial cartoonists always punctuated into Bryan's caricature. The old man's slippers flapped between rug and heel as he limped back to his chair. The limp, on cue, had become worse.

Harry's gaze wandered around the library, tracing the grain of cherry wood paneling, ending at the paintings: Flemish landscapes, western cowboy scenes, pre-Raphaelite realism, their varnish crackled into sickly glue-yellow.

"Tell me about the death of my son, Harry."

The mid-bone of Harry's throat bobbed as he swallowed. "I couldn't get to the battle areas, Mr. Bryan. They required me to stay mostly in Seoul, and they hadn't brought out Dan's...his body yet, but I located the officer who commanded his regiment." Harry stopped to adjust his tone. "Danny's unit was trapped behind Chinese lines for a while. He died before the reinforcements got there."

"*Before* the reinforcements?" Bryan leaned forward. "How did Daniel die, Harry? Did this officer say how he died?"

Harry had considered, before coming, just letting the rest of this story go away. That was rumor and trouble he didn't need. "Seemed to be some kind of peculiarity about his death, Mr. Bryan," said Harry, too up tight now to take his own counsel. "At least according to the major I spoke with. This Major Vickers lost his arm there."

Bryan rid himself of the last part with a flip of his white hair. "Never mind the major's arm, Harry. You said *peculiarity*. Tell me what that means."

Here we go, thought Harry, into some real deep shit. "As I understand it, Mr. Bryan, there were two men, a lieutenant and this sergeant, sent in by Army Headquarters--CID or G-2 or something--they drove through enemy lines just to talk with Dan. But before they could, Dan tried to break through the trap his regiment was in. That's when the Chinese killed him."

"We heard there was more to it," said Kenneth Willy Carson.

"Be still now, Kenneth. Let him finish."

They already know, thought Harry. Bryan had already linked up his brass-to-brass communications and Harry's report was just verification. Or maybe, more likely, some kind of *test* for Harry.

"Tell me what the major said, Harry." The eyes of Bryan were not pleasant to look into. They never were a real treat for Harry anyway, but it was worse this time.

"It isn't proven, sir, but the major--Vickers was his name--claims that one of these Intelligence men...one of these people shot your son."

Silence. The ocean's distant rush was suffocated by the silence of John Bryan. A slight rattling of wind against the burnt-orange window. The clacking of a timepiece somewhere in the room. A draft of air, causing feathery undulations across the thick drapery, lightly brushed the back of Harry's neck.

Bryan waited before speaking, and he spoke now in a kind of hollow tone, like a high priest. "Tell me the name of this man, Harry."

"Marion Ramirez Apollo. A sergeant, Mexican-American."

"Apollo, the god of light. So he has come."

"God of light?"

"The Angel of Death, Harry. My father's avenger."

"The, uh, sergeant hasn't officially been accused of this, Mr. Bryan. His Division hasn't accused him of anything yet--they're not even sure the man's still alive."

"Explain that, Harry."

"Their Division sent in two regiments and a whole tank battalion to get the survivors out. These two G-2 or CID men were pretty shot up, but they were still taken away and hospitalized with their permanent unit on Okinawa, and this Major Vickers wasn't sure whether they died there. No one would talk about it, but there wasn't any mention at Division of a court-martial."

As he listened, Bryan pushed his fingers together until his knuckles went white. "You didn't find out if these men were still alive, or why they killed my son?"

Harry tried to get more saliva into the dry part of his mouth. "The Army laid heavy security around these two--until they're either dead or awake enough to be de-briefed, Mr. Bryan. I had a tough time finding out even this much. If it weren't for this major..."

"When do you think you can get back there, Harry?" Bryan's brows softened. His eyes narrowed to cracks in the skin, but they were quieter now, it seemed to Harry, which cued a new perception on this--a pedestal, maybe, for Harry to mount himself on.

"I'd like to get back on it right away." The Black Avenger in Harry came awake. "Dan was my close friend, Mr. Bryan, and there's something about his death they don't seem to want us to know." And, bingo, Bryan nodded toward Harry, even though Harry had no conception of who "they" might be, or what "they" would not want Harry to know.

"I think it's a bunch of crap myself, Mr. Bryan." Willy Carson came to the side of Bryan's desk, bringing with him a sickly fragrance, bay rum cologne, or something. "Why would anyone want to kill Danny?"

"No, hush now, Kenneth. Harry's right, there's something more here than anyone wants to tell us, I *know* this." Bryan wasn't taking his eyes off Harry. "You go after this, Harry. Spend whatever you need, bribe those military people if necessary. Spend whatever needs to be spent, you understand?"

Harry understood a blank check. Harry could make like *Batman* against the bad guys with a blank check.

Bryan struggled to the window, his hands clapping behind his back. "We must somehow get them here."

"The G-2 people? We're not even sure they're alive."

Bryan ignored him. "We get them here, to start with. You were a psychology major in college, weren't you, Harry?"

"My graduate degree was in business." Harry would usually use an opening like that to pump up his Stanford business-school education, but not this time. Bryan wanted him to bring those two here? What did Bryan have in mind--*kill* them?

"I believe firmly in the First Commandment, you know," said Bryan, watching Harry. "I would hesitate to take a life, as you know, but there can be worse things than that in this world, can't there?"

"Mr. Bryan, I don't think..."

"*I* do. I think you will use your psychology on these people, Harry." Bryan's voice rose a little. "I think you can do that."

"Mr. Bryan, I wouldn't know anything about...using my psychology."

Bryan paid no attention. "If I assigned you to these two men you could find their weaknesses, couldn't you, if you wanted to?"

"That's beyond my scope, Mr. Bryan," said Harry, and he wanted to add *and beyond my duties.* What kind of crap were they heading toward here?

"If Mr. Crosse doesn't have the stomach for it..." Kenneth Willy Carson wanted a piece of this action but Bryan waved him off. "You find if they're alive, Harry, and if so I want you, for the moment, to stay on them, to be the bane that follows them, you understand?" As Bryan talked, his attention turned to a Remington portrait of an Indian warrior. The reddish-brown face gazed placidly back at the old man. "I have always considered you, Harry, as a black man with the inclinations of a Mediterranean."

Harry didn't know how to take that. He let it alone.

"Reminds me of myself at your age," said Bryan. "So I'm saying this to you, Harry, you do these things for me and your earthly rewards will be great, as long as you're with me."

If earthly rewards is what that means, thought Harry, I'm all for being a Mediterranean.

"A great injustice has been done to me, Harry, by my father from his grave, by God Himself, for that matter, and you must rectify it. I would take revenge upon God Himself for the death of my son." He turned sideways so he could better think about that.

Harry wanted no part of that subject. Whatever happened to Bryan's "Christian Soldier" concept of making the world God-*fearing*? he thought. Bryan had used that Christian Soldier concept as a defense in surviving the ad hoc Nye Committee arms investigations of '34-35: *The Bible has proclaimed that in the Millennium swords shall be turned into plowshares, but to accomplish this you first need the SWORDS! Only the well-armed Christian Soldier can bring this about!* And the Nye Committee, Harry remembered from his history books, actually bought that bullshit.

Self-righteous religious megalomania, Harry thought, though it didn't interfere much with Bryan's shipping of arms to the anti-Christian--or at least anti-Catholic--forces in Indo-China when General Novinger requested it. As Novinger put it, quoting Secretary of State Hull, who in turn was quoting Roosevelt: *America didn't go to war against fascism only to re-allow French imperialism.* That's all very well, Harry supposed, but he sure couldn't shake the feeling that their corporate tit might be getting caught in some real large political wringers here.

The old man could be coming unwrapped, and maybe that was to be expected, but Harry planned to take no revenge on any *God.* "Will that be all, Mr. Bryan? I'd better get started."

Bryan, distracted, calming, cocked an eyebrow at Harry. "Eh? Yes, go. You go work on this, Harry."

Harry closed the door behind him and retraced his way along the funereal hallways as Sorry Ochoa, from an adjoining alcove, fell in behind at a semi-trot, because Harry needed to disengage himself from this place, quick. He needed the action of downtown San Francisco around him. He needed a drink.

Outside, the weather had turned hot with the white sun reaching mid-day, an agreeable coastal heat. The ocean and its offshore wind kept the warmth in check but the temper of the day had turned nasty, the wind possessed a pugnacious shove, a fierceness that raged below at the fortress base.

The fortress now sat awaiting the human sacrifices that he, Harry, needed to offer up: a couple of poor-bastard grunts who'd already had the crap shot out of them. Whatever, the Mexican sergeant sounded like the easiest place to start, since the man took his basic at nearby Fort Ord. If he was still alive he'd be mustering out through Fort Ord on his way back to L.A., probably.

What a creepy assignment, Harry thought, and wondered what this man was like, an L.A. Mex who was about to become the specific target of Bryan International. Hardly an equal match.

Still, who's to say? Harry thought. From what I gather from the people who were at Kumsong, this sergeant is, or at least was, an awful tough fighter.

Chapter 9

The shuffling of feet inside the trench, the rumbling of trucks, the watching down on him by these white-shirted people. Then he dreamt of floating until he heard her voice telling him to be at peace, telling him softly, with such marvelous sincerity, that he had approached the Touchstone: *You are so near, Ramirez Apollo. You are very near the glorious light.* And he knew in his soul the truth of this. *By sacrificing yourself for Dao Kim Chau you have approached the Touchstone. You are so very near.*

The only response he could manage was his own one thought: "I'm afraid of being killed."

"Shh...shh. Don't try to move." Her dark hair cascaded around him as she leaned over, carrying with her the feathery smell of jasmine.

"The Touchstone? The Bryan thing?"

"Not your investigation. That was my father's idea. I use the word only to mean the Tao." She was still a formless shape above him. He tried to focus his eyes.

"You were full of the sleep-medicine, Ramirez Apollo, when you asked about the Tao. It is not surprising you do not remember."

"Your brother said you understood those things."

"Dao Kim Chau believes I know everything, but I understand almost nothing. I am ashamed of my small knowledge."

He thought for a moment that he might still be under the sleep-medicine, for she was fading from him again.

"Don't leave me, Ramirez Apollo. It isn't time for you." Her words came to him without context, but they had such a melodious quality, and her presence, and the wonderful smell of her, brought with it...exhilaration.

"I don't plan t'join the Tao, Kim Chau's sister. Too afraid of dying."

"Death and Reality are only illusions." Her voice betrayed her confidence in this, and she added, "Don't leave me."

He lay within this river of black hair, tickling along his arm, she watched him so very closely. "Illusions?"

"Shh."

"We aren't really *here*?"

"Shh. The Tao is like an uncut block of marble, in which any statue can be imagined." Her voice grew fainter, and it seemed more urgent, for she wanted to keep him with her. "To actually see any world-forms inside

54

the Tao, we have to be part of the form ourselves. We are prisoners within our own illusion."

Ram blew air through his dry lips, like a whistle, but no sound came. "These people you preach to," he whispered, "they understan' that?"

"These ideas are more easily understood by a Buddhist. The Buddha taught that in the Void, form does not exist."

"We're not real?"

"We are, but only inside our own illusion. We rejoice that there are other observers with us here to share this experience, because we are in just one of many possible illusions."

Rejoice? Even if this is just a dream? he wanted to ask, but he couldn't speak now. She put her fingers to his mouth to keep him from trying.

"As long as we are in this illusion together, we should make this dimension as good as we can, even to sacrifice ourselves if necessary. As you have done for my brother."

I sacrifice for no one, he thought. I'd like to see anyone *sacrifice* himself to reach your Touchstone... For a moment he could see her, and make out her face, a young girl's roundness surrounding these small red cushion-lips. Dark cloth strapped over her breasts, pushing up golden skin. Her hand had the touch of cool velvet to his cheek.

"They will be back to see you now," she said. "They think you are dying, but you will not die here."

He was too tired, now, to care.

"You are not destined to die here," she said.

Before he went into his unconsciousness, and smelled again the penetrating ether-smell, he tried to remember if she had said whether Kim Chau survived. But he didn't really want to know that, not right now.

His thoughts instead slid away.

He floated instead toward the Touchstone.

Without a beholder only potential dimensions exist, he had read these things in his books on physics. He had been told these things by Kim Chau's sister. These perceptions merged: the red illusion of Earth forming from illusory spatial dust, primordial fluid, collapsing into boiling matter, trapped in its gravitational heap. Sergeant Apollo could see the all-reaching protoplasmic mush-space, just matter-potential. Subatomic spin-outs dividing into something in space where no thing and no space really were.

Apollo floated and witnessed this phenomena: dimensionless fields forming quantum packets forming matter into blue worlds, mutating protozoa into life forms. Worlds forming in dimensions where time and space warped, to be gauged only in relation to non-existence, misnamed lightspeed. Emerging in spinning equilibrium. He had lain wounded and alone in the trench that night at Finger Ridge while the universe metamorphosed for him into its essential state. Patterns of energy, the universal hum. He needed to shake loose from that craziness.

No use. He had been unable to move in his trench. The universe swam over him and explained itself, all stimuli colliding and crystallizing. The coagulation of data--the books of physics, the words of Kim Chau's sister--blossoming into dark revelation, chemihistoricanthro-philosophy all clamoring to fit in, gorging up this terrible conclusion: There is no existence. Just mysterious whorls, gyrating illusions, illusory life-forms chasing illusory purposes.

All humanity thus, in his fever, lumped into purposeless broil. No good and bad, no right and wrong. The patriot lumped with the traitor and the murderer with the priest, the answer filled the night sky above him with ten billion clues. Star systems swirling outward, a pageant to this irrelevance, all just shadows flitting in and out of existence like quantum particles.

He had to find his way out of that nightmare.

"Is he still out?" came a voice--"Hey Weissman!" Truth cannot be hidden from, said the old weiss man, thought Ramirez Apollo.

Heads wheeled above Ram but they would not leave the white fog, yet he knew they were staring down at him. "What's your name?"

" 'pollo."

"*Damn.*" A whistle came from a corner of the room. "He know where he is?"

"You know where you are?"

"Where's Kim Chau?"

"Lieutenant Chau? He's alive, Ram." A familiar voice this time, it *was* Weissman. "Most of us made it out, in fact."

Ram forced his head to the side, beginning a small whirlpool in his brain. He saw the corporal in tropical khakis and cap, and below the base of his cap a band of white gauze circled his forehead. Weissman grinned when Ram looked up. "The lieutenant's one big band-aid right now, but he'll be all right. And lookit me." Pirouetting in front of the bed, arms out. "Not a scratch, 'cept where that shrapnel bounced off my head."

"Wha're you doing here?"

"Sick leave, Sarge. You and Lieutenant Dao were sent here to Okinawa and they said you were pretty shot up so I grabbed a MATS flight down to see you."

"S'appreciated." Ram could taste the bitter fluid that his i.v. was dripping into him.

"You're welcome. Now all you got to do is lay around and talk with pretty young girls. Looks like *that* part's being taken care of. You remember talking with Lieutenant Dao's sister?"

"Wasn't sure if she was real."

"Wasn't real?" Weissman looked into Ram's face. "Doc said you probably wouldn't remember much of it, you were so doped up. You still look doped up. You getting sleepy again?"

"Again? Hell..." Ram was too weary to keep his eyes open. He'd survived, that would do for now. His chest and legs felt like they were sinking through his cot.

"Kim Chau'll be over here soon's he hears you're awake. He's in the *officer's* ward, o'course."

Ram didn't hear much of that, but he now knew this exquisite girl had sat with him a few days, and he made a sleepy smile.

Weissman patted him on the arm. "Happy dreams, Sarge."

When he woke, she was with him again.

"I have to leave, now."

"Leave?"

"Your Army took my visa. Civilians are not to talk with either you or my brother, they said. Not yet."

"We're not that important."

"You're truly an attractive person when you sleep, Sergeant. Your jaw remains shut like a field horse, but the rest of your face softens, as if you dream great visions."

He opened his eyes and found the room less cloudy, the fibrous images knitting together. He saw the sterile room and the bed next to his and the strict T-frame looming over him, over which a mosquito net was folded. And he could see the radiance of Kim Chau's sister.

"Haven't seen your brother yet," he said.

"Corporal Weissman has gone to tell him you're awake. They will be back soon."

He wanted her to lean over him again.

"Welcome back, Sergeant Marion Ramirez Apollo," she said. The moving of her lips, the nearness of her sent a small tremor through him. "The doctor said you would not remember me, from when you were full of medication. Do you remember anything?"

"Not much."

"They let me shave your face yesterday."

"Sorry I missed that." He touched her forearm and moved his hand away again, but the warmth of her skin stayed on his fingers. He felt a stir in his groin, thank God the grenade hadn't taken *that* away from him.

"Our family owes you the life of my brother," she said. She smiled her thankfulness. He wondered if she had seen the stirring, if there really was anything going on down there. "He says you saved him from a grenade."

"Just pushed him out of my way."

"He says you have the essence of the Buddha."

Ram almost laughed, but that tightened his chest and he made a noise that sounded more like gas. "I never had an essence before."

She giggled, and he liked the sound of that, and he liked the way her eyes smiled. Her sweet jasmine odor filled his head.

"In your half-sleep you talked of being heroic—'machismo,' is that the right word? You called it *bullshit*." This sent her into a trickle of giggles which gave him an unusual pleasure, like being stroked with a palm frond. "In my country the droppings of a bull are highly prized to enrich the crops," she said, "but it didn't sound as if you mean it that way. My brother says that you give the answers of a Buddhist priest."

Ram wanted to shake his head but his skull gave a warning throb against that. "I've got no touchstone..." He couldn't think of her name.

"I am My Linh," she smiled. "We had long talks while I thought you were asleep. I thought you would not remember."

"You said nothing was real."

She hid her mouth in her hands, although her face brightened. "You were not supposed to hear me."

"Said the world doesn't exist."

"It is embarrassing that you heard such talk." She put her fingers on his shoulder between the bandaging.

Ram tried to scratch a serious itch on his chest, through the tape, which created a thick aroma of bandage-gum, but his fingers were too weak. "Tell me about your reality, My Linh." He only wanted to keep hearing her voice.

"I would rather talk of other things, now. About your home in America, if you like." Her hand moved to the location he couldn't scratch, and she worked her fingernails into the padding and dug her nails there. "Well...to understand reality, the Tao teaches that all thought must first be cleansed from the mind." She tilted her head and seemed pleased at his attention. "There is nothing we can think of that can help us understand reality, so we must think of nothing."

Ram closed his eyes and tried to picture nothing, but he saw men with bayonets coming over him instead; he saw hissing grenades exploding in the floors of trenches. *That* was reality, he thought.

"Don't talk now," she said, taking a damp cloth to his face. "These are the ideas of a young girl. You should not be burdened with them." And she hummed and felt his cheek.

"Since we are all in the dream together," she said. "We should just be happy that we are all here together, and try to make it as good as we can for each other."

Fatigue pressed the sides of his skull, but her words came through unfettered and clear, like freshly cleaned fruit. His mind closed around them... "But we are killing each other."

"Conflict might be needed for real purpose. To sacrifice to preserve the good, in the face of conflict, is the highest possible touchstone."

Then let others preserve the good for me, he thought he said--he might have said--for she looked at him in such a sad way.

"For some it is not a matter of choice." She brought her face closer and her hair brushed his chest. He wanted to put his hands against her, if he had the strength. "In our religion," she said, "certain people are thought of as superior beings, those who have taken steps toward nirvana."

"Those thoughts are way beyond me, My Linh."

"My words are only dreams," she said. "I should not even say them aloud."

They are great words, he thought, even though I don't understand them. I don't understand this Touchstone thing. In the streets no one sacrifices for anyone.

He wanted to say this, he just didn't have the strength.

Chapter 10

"A week ago old Carl here tried to pull a sheet over you." The large-headed man in the blue robe stuck a thumb toward the orderly and made a laugh like a whinny, breathing in as he did, almost choking. "Some doctor, ain't he?"

"Go screw yourself, Hegelmeier." The small man in the white coat was tugging on Ram's eyelids, staring inside, breathing a licorice smell in Ram's face.

"You a doctor?"

"Him? Shee-it, Sarge, he's just a medic." Again the bigger fellow with the shaved sidewalls grunt-laughed. "No doc's gonna pull a sheet over a live man, is he?"

"Look, Hegelmeier," the orderly poked a finger into his larger companion, "I'm not a medic. I'm an *orderly*." He turned back to Ram. "Everything looks okay, Sarge. Doc'll be right in." He walked off and Hegelmeier followed, giving Ram a wink: *The little guy gets pissed off easy, don't he?*

Behind Ram a screen door, unoiled, squealed open and popped back to its stopper, preceding the voices of Weissman and Kim Chau, jabbering like schoolboys--"No shit, I tell you he's been awake since *morning*. Just ask the doc there." Ram had a hard time looking anywhere but up, but he could see an arm waving to the side of him.

"Hey, I just said he didn't make sense last time I talked with him." Chau's voice sounded hoarse, like a Japanese prison guard in an old war movie. "I don't think he was really awake."

The first face above Ram belonged to neither of them: "Dr. Moley here, Sergeant. Glad you decided to stick around." Dr. Moley, cheeks sagging with tanned overflesh, draped himself above Ram as Weissman and Kim Chau appeared over each shoulder like perching crows. The doctor felt around Ram's chest with a stethoscope.

"How's it going, Kim Chau?" Ram tried to look sideways at the lieutenant.

"*Big* headache, Ram," Chau grinned back, touching his temple. A crown of gauze circled his head like the top half of a volleyball. "Subdural concussion or something."

"How's the vision?" asked Dr. Moley as he ballooned a blood pressure belt around Ram's arm. "Any double vision? Dizziness?"

"Don't think so."

"Heard you met my sister." Chau had to stand on tiptoe to see over Doctor Moley's shoulder, and Ram nodded, which made his head swirl. He had to close his eyes.

"I'm not sure 'met' would be the right word."

"The brass made her leave the island," said Chau. "No civilians allowed to talk with us until Colonel Purdy gets here. For our de-briefing, I guess."

"Strong like an ox--a badly wounded ox, though," said Dr. Moley, standing back up. "Your wound sheet reads like the damn battle of Gettysburg." He marked his note board and turned to leave. Weissman moved into the space he left. "I'll get back this evening," said Dr. Moley.

"Kind of gorgeous, wasn't she?" said Weissman. "The lieutenant's sister I mean."

"Glad to have you back, Ram," said Chau.

Ram tried to raise up on his pillow to see the rest of the room: the churning of overhead fans, the row of cots beneath gauzed clumps of hammocked mosquito netting. Three other cots were in the ward and in the bed next to his another patient slept, his face swaddled in bandages, his shoulders matted with bunched black hair. "We were both pretty shot up," said Chau, staring with Ram around the room. "Some *routine* investigation they sent us on, wasn't it?"

"They can stick it up their ass now."

"The investigation? Well, first listen a minute, would you? You know where Bryan's main staging point is in the Far East?--it's at the Machinato Dump, right smack here on Okinawa."

"What're you two talking about?" said Weissman. "Bryan's dead. What's there to investigate?"

"Not Lieutenant Bryan. We were investigating his father."

"His father?"

"What's wrong with you, Luke?"

"His *father*?"

"What the hell's wrong with you?" Chau cocked an eyebrow at Weissman but the corporal just gaped back at him. "Anyway," said Chau, going back to Ram, "right here on this island we're in one hell of a position--"

"Don't want to hear it." Ram needed to lower himself back; his chest wrappings were stabbing into his stomach. "We went to Korea to check out Lieutenant Bryan, and we did, and now we're done."

"It's the enemies of my country that they were supplying, damn it." Chau pointed a finger toward the scrubbed wood floor. "And Bryan's got the stuff running right through *here.* We can use those orders they gave us for the investigation--"

"Those papers wouldn't even get us on the dock, Kim Chau, let alone on any freighter."

Chau made a sucking noise with his teeth and turned, and started toward the screen door. "Right, Sergeant, you keep going your own way then, *alone.* Find yourself a *reason.* I'll do this by myself."

"Like your sister says, I need to find that touchstone first."

"Hell with your touchstone." The door squeaked open as Weissman sat down next to the bed and watched the door bang behind the lieutenant.

"Didn't think Chau ever got pissed," said Weissman. "You mean you were on the Ridge just to investigate Bryan's *father?*"

"What'd you think we were doing?"

Weissman looked down at his hands. "I thought...Christ, it's not important what I thought."

Ram watched Weissman watching his hands, and Weissman made an attempt at smiling. "Know what?" Weissman changed the subject. "Found out I can get into UCLA on the G.I. Bill, and the lieutenant says you're going there to spy on school kids, or something. I was thinking maybe I can join you there, if that's okay with you."

"Sounds fine to me, Luke."

In the next few days Ram learned how to shift his body, but not without a cymbal accompaniment in his brain, not without the breath-stopping cinch of his chest wrappings. Chau came by each morning after Hegelmeier and Carl the orderly had gone through the ward, but the lieutenant never brought up John Bryan again. "Even when my sister was really young, you know, some people saw her as some kind of new and original shaman, like the Trung sisters, the girl-priests of the ninth century." Chau knew Ram preferred to hear about My Linh, so he stayed with that. "Here on Okinawa they call their female priests 'yutas,' I think. Would you like to hear what she used to say, when she was just a kid?"

"Rather wait for her to tell me."

"Right." Chau slapped Ram on the arm. "Only My Linh can explain this stuff."

From then on Kim Chau added religion to the one other taboo subject--the Bryan investigation--until the day Colonel Purdy arrived.

*

"You just *had* to create a shitpot mess at Kumsong, right?" The stink from Colonel Purdy's cigar stuffed the air of the tiny O.D. office. "Now I got this one-armed captain in Korea yelling for your court-martial, I got a dead lieutenant to explain to the rest of the world, and I hear some rumor in Division that we sent you there to deliberately *shoot* the son of a bitch."

"It's not easy to explain, sir," said Chau.

"Really?" Purdy bent over and held his cigar to the side. "Well now I got this Major General Arnold Novinger himself, of the sonofabitch National Security Council, on my ass thanks to you gentlemen creating a big episode over what his memo *specifically* said to keep low key. So now we have to fight just to keep this investigation out of the goddamned evening news, and that is the *only* reason why I'm now on my way to save your butt from a court-martial, Sergeant."

That dialogue was more or less the beginning and end of their debriefing session. Colonel Purdy caught an MATS plane back to Korea that same day, that afternoon.

"You have any idea what a court-martial *means*, Ram? You just sat there like you could give a shit less. That's not normal, you know, not seeming to give a shit about anything."

"That word 'never' covers a lot of territory, Kim Chau."

"See? You won't even give me an argument about whether you give a shit about anything."

Ram caught a mosquito with his thumb against the opposite forearm, mashing it to a tidy red smear. "That's because I don't have any argument right now." He inspected the red speck on his forearm. "But I'm working on it, Lieutenant."

*

In the days following Purdy's visit, the patient next to Ram, Staff Sergeant Marshall L. Lementke, came to life. A patch over one eye eventually replaced the gauze there, and he started gaining weight, and in a few weeks his stringy frame started looking more like a side of beef. A *noisy* side of beef: "The world's just one big anthill of people, Lieutenant," he told Chau as soon as Ram introduced them. "Big crawling mess pushed into different groups by mountains and water and we live and fight for whatever group we happen to end up in, and we're supposed to die for it just because that's where we happen to *be?* Well, up the world's ass." When he laughed he displayed jiggling lines of fillings, his mouth opening up like a suitcase. "From now on, first I determine who the bad guys really are, then I'll rectify the shit out of *them*."

"You let me know when you find out who the bad guys are, Marsh," said Ram.

The grounds of the hospital consisted mainly of a bashed, beer-stained bench within a weedy gravel enclave, looking over the East China Sea that flattened out over Nago Bay toward a sunset that set the whole ruffled afternoon sky on fire.

"In combat, you go too long without sleep and your mind starts playing tag with your ass hole," was Lementke's typical comment at the setting of the sun, which strengthened Ram's image of Marsh Lementke as some sort of undiscovered primary conduit, transmitting impressions directly from perception to vocal chord with just a minimal swirl through the cerebrals. But what the hell, Ram figured, the man sure provided a different look at things: "Them defense pacts got us into wars like Korea because the politicians are scared white of commies--see 'em under their pillows," said Lementke. "But after we get done in Korea they're gonna tear up all that paper, watch and see."

"You're wrong there," said Chau. "Another war is coming up right across the South China Sea there. That paper will bring you people to my country some day soon." He didn't intend to refer to Vietnam as *his* country. He saw the glance Ram gave him.

"Pigballs," Lementke retorted. "Everyone's had enough of this police work."

"By the end of the Fifties we'll be in Vietnam," Chau corrected his affiliation. "The French will get pushed out, the U.S. will come in. Inevitable as the sunrise."

"And you'll be there to greet us, Kim Chau," said Ram.

"Why should I? I'm an American now."

"You'll be going back," said Ram.

"What makes you so sure what *I'll* be doing?"

Ram smiled. "Because you're one of the lucky ones, Kim Chau. You've got a calling."

*

"This's plain horse shit, Major." Captain Lyle Griggs respectfully laid the papers back on the desk of Lieutenant Colonel Dale Simpson, head of the Advocate General of the 8th Division. Simpson had called him to Division headquarters in Seoul, Korea, for a preliminary hearing on a possible court-martial for Sergeant M. R. Apollo.

"I have two *witnesses*, Captain," argued Major Vickers.

"I'm not talking about the shooting of Lieutenant Bryan, Major. I'll get to that. Right now I'm talking about this charge of cowardice and..." The captain scruffed through the papers on the long table in front of them. "*Dereliction of duty*, whatever the hell that means. You forget, Major, *I* was on that hill too."

Captain Griggs stared down at the sitting Major Vickers and the major, in turn, stared at Colonel Simpson: This harangue from a subordinate officer called for *some* kind of reprimand, didn't it? But the colonel only gazed back at the major, whose hand groped across his knee for its phantom mate. The fourth person in Colonel Simpson's office, another colonel--a full "bird" colonel--a heavy, bald, brutal-looking man, was not introduced to Vickers, but he plainly was not there to help Vickers.

"Before we got to him, I saw this Apollo fighting like a goddamn Cossack in the middle of that assault, sir." The captain turned to Colonel Simpson. "Meanwhile the major here...I heard from the CQ people that he was playing dead."

"Stay to the point, Captain," cautioned Colonel Simpson. He had a long, hollow-cheeked, stony face. A hardass ex-paratrooper.

"I lost an arm in that battle, Captain!"

"That arm *rotted* off," corrected Captain Griggs. "You cut it on a goddamned ammo can you were using as an ashtray, then didn't have the brains to disinfect the damned thing."

"Captain Griggs. Enough." Colonel Simpson patted a hand on his desk toward Griggs. "You're here only to comment on the major's request for a court-martial. Please concentrate on that." Settling back again. "Now, as far as this shooting of Lieutenant Bryan-"

"-That man was *sent* to do it, I think," said Major Vickers.

"What's this fool talking about, *sent*?" The heavy-set colonel was addressing Colonel Simpson. His eyes, however, stayed on Vickers.

"I'll take care of this, Colonel." Colonel Simpson held up his hand toward Purdy and turned back to Major Vickers. "Those two men were there to see Lieutenant Bryan by order of Colonel Purdy here, Major." He was saying this with great deliberation. There was obviously more to this meeting than he cared to discuss, mainly with Major Vickers. "I can assure you they had no intention, they had no *reason*, to harm the lieutenant."

The three officers around Vickers waited for him to answer, but the major was no longer anxious to respond. He stayed quiet.

"In our opinion it'd be a lot better for you just to drop the charges, Major," Colonel Simpson continued. "From what Captain Griggs and others told us, in fact, it'd be best for you to stay away from *any* discussion of what happened around Kumsong."

"I lost an arm there, Colonel." The major's complaint dissipated into the circle of blank faces.

"At the time, you still could have fired a rifle--" Captain Griggs began. A glance from Colonel Simpson stopped him.

"You really don't have any good witnesses," said Colonel Simpson. "We talked with the one survivor who you said would testify--a Corporal Peterson?--and he wasn't at all sure what he saw. And the man in the trench with Sergeant Apollo, Corporal Weissman, says he saw nothing at all."

"It's still my word as an officer, sir," said Vickers.

Captain Griggs turned away from that to stare out the window. It was dismally grey outside. "You realize, Major..." Colonel Simpson's prelude hung in the air above Henry Vickers. "You realize that the defense could bring in questions about your own record, could bring your own men in for character reference."

"I'm not afraid of that, sir."

"I would be, if I were you." The colonel slipped a pair of Ben Franklins over his nose and stared at the papers in front of him. "You've got quite a few weak performance reports here." He let his finger slide along one line. "Is it true you pulled your troops out the wrong way, just before Kumsong?"

The major's face paled. "My staff sergeant misread the maps. He should have... He had a lot of experience in the field, sir. He was reprimanded."

"He was *killed*, Colonel, when the major sent the sergeant's company into a Chinese ambush," said Captain Griggs. He was still staring out the window.

"I did the best I could. I lost an *arm* in that battle. What the hell *more* do you want?"

"Screw your arm," said Captain Griggs, without looking around.

"Captain Griggs, that's enough. And sit down, please," said Colonel Simpson. "Now, I don't have the authority to order you," he was talking to Vickers. "If you demand charges then we'll have to open it up, but the witnesses are disputing your testimony, remember, and in fact might bring evidence detrimental to you personally, and maybe embarrassing to us all. The last thing we want is for the damned newspapers..." His voice wavered for a moment. He cleared his throat. "In my opinion you don't have a basis for bringing charges here, Major."

"But he also threatened me with his rifle. At least *twice* he did that."

"Threatened you, Major?" Colonel Simpson began to bring his hands together in front of him and then stopped. "That's only because of his youth, Major. I probably *would* have shot you."

The statement startled even Captain Griggs. The heavy colonel, Purdy, shifted his weight on the seat from one buttock to the other, trying not to look as surprised as he was, but a statement like that... That went way beyond any legitimate dressing-down, even for this guy.

The major's cheeks had sucked into a silvery ash, making his mouth a tight wrinkled hole. "That isn't fair, Colonel." Through the hole, his voice sounded more like a whistle.

"Major, the only question we need to answer here," said Colonel Simpson, "is whether you wish to press charges... Do you want to press charges?"

Vickers looked to each of the other officers in turn, searching for support, in vain.

"No, sir," Vickers mumbled, finally. "No charges."

Chapter 11

Ciro's and Copacabana, the Stork Club, Club 21. Brass and chrome and coal-black signs lined "The Street of a Thousand Pleasures" with sad imitations of New York glitz, just beyond the city of Koya, just off the main highway through Okinawa. Onto one of its side paths the Naha bus bumped, stopped, dropped Ram and Lementke off with half a busload of people, then mashed its way back to the main road.

"A thousand pleasures!" Marshall Lementke stuck a finger toward the hand-scrawled street sign. "That's about the right number for *my* present needs."

"Where the hell is this?" Ram wasn't all that excited about going into the villages. Any kind of serious drinking, with Ram's low booze threshold, usually ended in disaster.

"It's called Village Fifteen, Sarge. A little bit of heaven right here on the Rock--but don't try to look it up. It ain't on any map."

Ram could almost *taste* the sweet-sour aroma, like sweet burning goat milk, wafting from the three-sided dwellings that were crammed together like rabbit warrens, cooking fish and sweet potatoes. Sukahatchi hags offered oral satisfaction in the alleyways for "one dollah." The half-pretty ones were actually boys, Ram had heard, but whatever they were, they weren't *that* pretty, certainly a lot uglier than their painted sisters in the bars.

"Where the hell is the Blue Goose?" Marshall peered through the saloon windows with his one good eye. "Used to be right about here."

Shrunken mama-sans in scratchy burlap shawls skittered across the paths. Potbellied cherubs ran behind, waving their arms for balance. It was early afternoon, not many Americans on the street yet. Lementke stopped before a shanty with a yellow neon sign blinking its one-word message: *Beer.* "This is it, Sarge," said Lementke. "C'mon, I'm dry as a sonofabitch camel."

"Lementke, this place is a goddamn dump." But Marshall had already rattled through the front bangles--strings of purple marbles hanging across the doorway like grape vines. As in most of the whorehouses, there was a thin no-peekie panel just inside, requiring the customers to step around it like a matador entering the ring. Two girls wearing slit-to-the-hip dresses were rousted from the back by their wizened mama-san as the two men ducked inside.

"Hey, G.I., you need girls?" squealed the mama-san.

"Who doesn't need girls, mama-san," said Lementke, sitting and then whispering toward Ram, "You got to admit how good it is to order up one of these little wonders, like you would a damn beer. 'S why I call this home, Sarge, hell, even the *smell* is home to me." Lementke inhaled a lungfull of the thick village vapors, which weren't hard to summon up. "Gonna take my pension and know-how and stay right here, 'cause we're at the gut-center here. The services're going to be all over FECOM from Korea to Siam for the next fifty years and half of them'll be stationed right here, dropping money on their way through, and China'll be *keeping* 'em here, b'god, with their finger up everybody's ass."

Three sailors came in as Marshall talked. Maybe four. Hard to tell with the daylight fading behind them. The elusive fourth man, the one no longer there, looked to Ram a lot like Kim Chau. The Kim Chau look-alike had appeared then disappeared, quick as that, slipping behind the shoji-screen at the entrance.

Two more girls came from the back room to join the sailors. Ram scraped his chair back and looked for the door but in the growing dimness the entrance became obscure, the walls and the no-peekie screen had blended together. Ram aimed himself in what he thought was the right direction until he came to the panel and, sure enough, Chau was just outside.

"Thought you were off to spy on Bryan, Lieutenant. You come to join us?"

"You kidding?"

Ram looked over his shoulder. "There's a lot worse places, Kim Chau. What're you going to... You still going to Naha?"

"Two of us would have a better chance of getting on board."

"Two of us would have no chance at all, Kim Chau. No more than you will by yourself."

People passed between them on the uneven walkway: two boy gum-sellers and a man carrying shoulder-buckets. "Just wanted to let you know I'm not pissed off at you," said Kim Chau. He held out something wrapped in brown, waxy, souvenir-stand paper. "Bought this up the street."

"What the hell's that?"

"Peace offering, kind of." The package in Chau's hand looked like a heavily wrapped Churchill cigar. "It's a custom."

"What's it for?"

"A custom. Just want to let you know I'm not really pissed off at you... for not coming with me, I mean." Chau kicked at the ground, sending a small spray of pebbles sprinkling around. "What're you going to do here? Going to get *laid*?"

Ram held his arms out to his sides, embracing the village. "Hell, Kim Chau, Lementke says everything in life is right here. Maybe I'll find your sister's Tao around here."

"Not funny, Ram. My Linh must have caught you at a real weird moment. That touchstone thing's become an obsession with you."

"Everyone's got his own obsession, Kim Chau."

Chau had begun walking back to the highway. "Maybe you do belong here," he said, over his shoulder. "The village is where all the give-a-shitters end up."

"I'm still trying to find something to give a shit *about*, Kim Chau."

The lieutenant didn't turn around. "I'll let you know how this turns out." He dodged around some servicemen who sat smoking and talking, sitting in their adopted Okinawa-squat postures.

Maybe he didn't hear me, Ram thought, as Chau blended into the flannel shadows. I'm still trying to *find* something, okay?

"It's so pretty," said the blue-dressed girl when Ram came back in and unwrapped the package. She leaned over, rubbing warm breasts along his neck.

"What is it?" asked Marshall.

"Switchblade."

"Hell, I know it's a switchblade, for Christ's sake."

Ram found the button and pressed and the steel flew out and snapped into place. The knife, compared to the plastic handles and cheap steel of the L.A. blades, was a work of art. A red serpent inlaid the ebony handle. "You could become a real killer with this."

"Doesn't take any switchblade to be a killer." Lementke held out his hand and Ram passed it over. "They make these little suckers by the dozens in these villages," said Lementke, fondling the handle before giving it back. "But that's a special beauty, looks like."

Ram balanced the knife on his forefinger and let the weight of it even out--about ten ounces of lacquered wood and nickel-plated steel. He poked Lementke on the elbow with the tip. "Chau thinks if you're from East L.A. then you must love switchblades. Hell, he's probably right, that's how we got our kicks. One of these days we'll probably even use guns on each other."

"God help the big cities when *that* happens. You know how to use one of those?"

Ram set his drink down and gave Lementke a wink. Fifteen feet to the side hung a poster depicting the kabuki theater in Tokyo, an actor's mask in the foreground, a row of pink-robed actors behind it. Ram weighed the flat of the blade in his palm before pressing his thumb across it, until the edge pinched his skin, and then threw it, thumping the blade deep in the exact center of the mask.

"God Almighty." Lementke almost broke his chair as he fell back, smacking one large hand against the other. "You're really *good* with that sonofabitch."

"Should've seen me in my prime." Ram waved for two more Kirins as spotlights lit up the multi-mirrored ceiling ball. A new Okinawan doll-person tittered her way toward the two men through the snowflakes of light.

"Fifty cent, two beer," she said, turning her midriff to rest against Ram.

"Lookit the face on that girl," said Lementke, putting down fifty cents in orange military occupation script. "A face like that could bring back *kissing. Naysan*, how much push-push?"

"Three dollah," the girl giggled. She kneeled to wipe up spilled liquor and the slit moved up her pantyless hip, her knees parting, allowing hints of available pleasures. "You wanta push-push, G.I.?" She was asking Ram.

"Well, hell..." Ram began to stand up, stepping back to catch his balance, and followed her through a back door that opened outside to a row of truncated compartments, like large crates, painted pink, neatly kept, stacked on cement blocks.

Ram felt like he was crawling into a low bunk bed. In her small room, on her crinkly reed mat, she handled him with the caress of a professional- *-rubber to go on before push-push*. She groaned mechanically, utilized the tight actions, that made quick work of his overprimed need, and his whole groin seemed to explode – "DAMN!"

She scratched his back after rinsing herself and refilling the steel basin. "You like Yoshiko a little?"

"Hell, Yoshiko, you're one of the few people I *do* like."

She slapped his shoulders gently and tickled him, the universal whore-signal. *Turn's over, G.I.*

Lementke was getting comfortable behind a lap-sitting, butt-ugly naysan as Ram made his way back to their table, no longer an easy journey. The bar was filling with people wearing uniforms, or wearing the short-timers' semi-transparent mosquito-net shirts. Ram made it to the table, sat, took Lementke's bottle of unlabeled brown liquor and poured a glass. He took a swallow and banged the glass on the table. "Lord, Marsh, how can you drink that shit?"

"I see your bride's back," said Marshall. Yoshiko was sliding between two tables next to them, bringing a handful of name bracelets: steel, bronze, Siamese silver, some lined at the edge with gold plating.

"These man's bracelets fo' you," she said. "One dollah fo' stainless steel, three dollah fo' silver, ten fo' gold. One dollah fo' have name put on. Can do right now."

"Whyn'cha buy one for Kim Chau?" said Marshall.

"Buy him a goddamn *bracelet*?"

"He bought you that knife, didn't he? That's the way it's done in the Far East, don't y'know? He gives you a knife, you give him a damn I.D. bracelet or something. Lets him know you're not pissed off either."

"You're full of shit, Marsh... Here, Yoshiko, two dollah. One of those steel ones, put Dao Kim Chau on it, okay?" He fumbled the script out as she wrote the name. Lementke refilled Ram's glass as Yoshiko made her wonderful smile again and left for the engraver. Ram slid farther into the unforgiving wood chair. The juke box hammered out some hillbilly quadrille, yowling into his nervous system, and a string from his stomach started jiggling his throat.

Lementke eventually whooped off for the commode to "unbeer," and never came back, leaving Ram with his knife and his engraved bracelet, and Ram decided it was about time to move out, and he tipped the table in his effort to stand up again. The room started a slow turn and he knew he had to get outside now, fast, but the bullpen-style door had blended into the fuzzy red-brown griffin-patterned wallpaper. He took a step to the wall and felt along the surface, leaned next to it, looked down the wall for signs of the hatchway while the thin paper-covered plywood creaked and flexed away from him. The wall sloughed forward, away from the makeshift beams and studs that were anchored only in dirt.

A chair fell near him, four legs pointing at him like a Gatling gun, like a cornered crab, and Ram felt the rage of being cornered too. He stepped back to aim himself at the wall. His arms and body crashed into the thin cratewood, crunching forward under him, with him, into a toppled clutter on the street outside, thudding flat out atop a large panel of the wall which had ripped and splintered around him, drowning the bar noise. The wood shards tore loose and scattered pinpricks along his back.

He rolled his head to one side and breathed the cool night air. Not much light in the street. The nearest lights--what appeared to be an assembly of jack-o'-lanterns--silhouetted the heads and shoulders of the curious people gathering around him. Between the crisscrossing of legs Ram saw a ghostly luminescence reflecting off the dirt road. He laid quiet on the remains of the plywood--a cold, hard mattress.

He needed rest. The curious street people split a path for the jeep that slid to a stop behind them, allowing a pair of tall, grim, white-helmeted uniforms through, and Ram couldn't help admiring how polished they kept those boots. White spats, hand-polished billy clubs, starched, tailored fatigues, looking down from Olympian heights. The MP's began pulling him up by his arms, which extended from him now like ramps to the moon.

*

"Head wound, very serious, causes him to act like this." Doctor Moley was making excuses to an MP captain *sotto voce.*
"Ran right through a damned wall, Major."
"I know, I know. We'll keep him in longer this time."
The MP captain, as short as Doctor Moley but a lot more muscular, didn't look like a military policeman from where Ram was, back on his cot. The MP captain looked more like a small gorilla.

*

"Is there any communicating with that closet world of yours? *Hey,* there." Major--Doctor--Moley stood over him. It was daylight outside. "Holy" Moley nudged him again with a note pad and Ram lifted his head to see if Lementke had made it back. He had. Snoring like a drugged bear.
"What was that craziness about last night, Sergeant?" Only a swaying effigy in a white frock circled above Ram, bending sideways over him. Ram shifted to get his mouth off the pillow. "Acted like a *cabron,* Doc... Couldn't find the sonofabitch door."
"You acted crazy, is what you did." Moley scratched his tongue with his pencil and continued writing. "What the hell's bugging you, Sergeant? You think you're going crazy?"
"Poco a poco. Chau thinks it's 'cause I don't give a shit."
"That the reason you break down a wall?"
"Scared of going through life without finding that door."
"So you felt the room was closing in on you?" Doctor Moley tried on his globular grimace. Analyzing. Doctoral omniscience sealed into these small bulbous eyes.
"Wrong analysis, Doc. Lemme alone."
The rebuff didn't bother Doctor Moley. "I get real concerned when a patient starts acting crazy, Sergeant. And you...first we had that babbling about the universe or something when you were brought in, now you act even crazier the minute we give you a little freedom."
What the hell'd you expect, Ram thought, before he fell asleep. Want to make a choir boy from a knife-man? Why do I run through walls? I don't goddam know.

Trying to get away...from what? he tried to ask himself.

The killing, he answered himself. The crummy bars with those dancing *cabrones*. The back bedrooms where I always seem to end up. I don't goddam know.

*

On the afternoon of November 12, 1953, John Bryan learned that the charges had been dropped against Sergeant Apollo and Lieutenant Dao. He called Major General Novinger of the National Security Council directly, demanding a meeting, threatening his own reprisals if the Army refused to punish the murderers of his son.

Chapter 12

Henry Vickers walked down the customs ramp of the San Francisco Airport with his left sleeve folded to the side like a flag. He felt the rush of his self-endowed martyrdom here, which was almost worth--it *was* worth--the price of an arm to Major Vickers.

"Welcome home, Major," said one of his admirers, a lady of aging bulk who had sat next to him on the plane. Over-perfumed, smiling earnestly. "Bet you're glad it's all over."

"Yes indeed. Yes I am," Henry replied, bravely.

He shook off a porter, even though the bag *was* a bit heavy. He shifted his right shoulder upward to compensate for the lack of a counterbalancing forearm. He struggled from the building toward the taxis, where the Bryan people said they would meet him.

"Major Vickers?" A man at the taxi pick-up watched down on Henry over cliffs of nose and jaw and, having spoken Vickers' name, smiled, exposing rows of teeth that flashed above Vickers like sheet lightning.

"Mister Trevors?"

"First name's Charles, Major. Call me that. Over there's Sorry Ochoa." Trevors indicated a chunk of brown in an identical, badly rumpled grey jacket. It looked like someone had tried suiting up a water buffalo. Sorry Ochoa waved and pointed to their limousine. "Don't let Sorry scare you," said Trevors. "That's his normal face." He removed the bag from Henry and took the major by his good elbow with a grip that numbed the bone.

"Quit looking at people like that, Sorry," said Trevors. "Makes people think you don't like 'em."

"Sorry," said Sorry Ochoa, withno trace of sorrow.

*

Ochoa and Trevors took their places on either side of the window in the library section of Bryan's den. The two had dropped conversation as soon as Vickers was in the limousine, and they didn't look in his direction during the ride. They certainly did watch him now, though.

The major shifted in the center of the room until he faced the window, toward the desk of the white-haired man. The man, John Bryan, stayed still.

"Do you know, Major, where my son got his great speed? His great *football* abilities?" Henry could discern only this leonine whiteness in the chair's silhouette, the back of which blocked half the orange window light. "Got it from his mother Dorothy. Before the tuberculosis caught her she was very... She could run faster than me, but anyone could do that, I suppose. But now *both* of them are gone, aren't they?"

Major Vickers didn't know whether the man expected an answer. Bryan's chalky hands folded together on the desk. "Tell me about my son, Major," said John Bryan. "I need to know about the death of my son."

Vickers blinked. "There was...he was very heroic, sir." Vickers held his tongue for a painful moment between his teeth. "He died very heroically."

"Of *course* he did! But that's not why you're here. I want to know *why* he died, Major."

"Why? He was trying to run for help, sir, and he was caught by machine gun fire-"

"-Why was *he* running, Major? Couldn't you have some *private* running?" Bryan talked with a throaty rumble now. He watched the wordless movement of the major's lips: "I'd like an answer, please."

"He did it on his own, sir." For a few seconds Major Vickers thought he was going to shout the words--this was *unfair.* He had expected a much warmer reception from Lieutenant Bryan's famous father.

Bryan made a low, humming tone, like a circling cat, while the bodyguards on either side stayed silent, entombing Vickers in this hissing stillness. Then, "You implied to my emissary there was something suspicious about his death. What did you mean, Major? *Suspicious.*"

"It wasn't exactly that, sir. I felt it my duty to report on the circumstances--" Vickers groped for words. "A new man came in that day, sir. A Sergeant Apollo. Came to find Lieutenant Bryan."

Bryan leaned forward. "About this Sergeant Apollo, you reported that *he* killed my son?"

Vickers needed to lick his lips. "He was seen aiming a rifle at your son, Mr. Bryan."

A chill came through the room. The pale man before Henry took odd shapes, like something underwater, undulations without real movement, and Vickers knew his mind was playing tricks. Bryan was in fact motionless.

"Sergeant Apollo," said John Bryan. "Marion Ramirez Apollo?"

"Yes."

"A Mexican." Bryan said the word distastefully, and Vickers thought of the brute Ochoa behind him. "Why would this Mexican sergeant kill my son?"

"He came specifically looking for your son." Vickers chose his words carefully here. This situation could still turn out in his favor, but he must handle this conversation very carefully.

"He came *looking* for Daniel?"

"Yes, sir."

The room whispered again. Henry saw a fluttering in the draperies, moving like hands through a shroud.

"Why would the Army send someone to look for my son?"

"A lieutenant came with him, sir, a Lieutenant Dao, but I don't know why they were sent," said Major Vickers, and Bryan waited for him to continue. "...Those two were sent by G-2, sir, but he was caught on the wire on our perimeter. But it wasn't necessary to shoot him--for *any* reason."

The face of John Bryan dipped between steeples of touching fingertips, the glint of spectacles peeping between his passing hands. "Are you suggesting, sir," Bryan stopped to think about what he was asking. "Are you suggesting that my son's death was a *mercy* killing?"

"Oh, no, sir. No way to know--I mean, he could have survived. I don't know how this Apollo could take it upon himself to..."

"There's a larger meaning to this," said Bryan. "You don't need to understand it." He removed his green-tinted glasses but Henry could still see only deep shadows beneath the trimmed white eyebrows. "I want to know what this man is," said Bryan. "This Sergeant Apollo."

Vickers needed to steady his chin before answering. "This much I know, this sergeant's a violent man, comes from a poor background, some kind of ghetto. Maybe he just resented your son. A rich man's son, I mean."

"A violent man, is he?" Bryan swiveled away from Henry. "We could teach him violence." Henry felt the words spreading back at him from the cherry wood panels. "In my son I created my concept of what a perfect man should be, Major, and then this Mexican sergeant dares...What proof do you have? Did anyone else see him kill my son?"

"The oriental lieutenant must have seen it, sir, but when I tried to bring charges, this oriental lieutenant would not testify."

"Then these two are in this together."

"Yes sir, I think so." Vickers wished he had better answers for someone like John Bryan. His report sounded more like tattle-telling. "I absolutely don't know why-"

"-I do, Major. I know full well the being that sent them, and why they came after my seed, but I have my own preparations for them." He brought his chair back around, nodding in agreement with himself, re-acknowledging Major Vickers. "However, that is not your business, is it? He will now come after me. I'm the reason he's been sent here, after all."

Bryan raised his hand, Ochoa went over to open the door for Henry. "I'll be prepared when he comes, Major. You see the proof outside I've been constructing? I'm preparing my *own* message for him to carry back... Anyway, you go now, Major. We will talk further about this later."

Henry's audience ended on that weird note. The bodyguards took him back to the steel front doors where a black man in a charcoal suit met him. The same emissary, Vickers recalled, who tracked him down in Korea. "Mister Bryan would like you to stay in the Bay area for the time being, Major." The man spoke in a low private-school cadence. "I think you'll find it rewarding."

"Yes, certainly." Vickers' voice, in contrast, sounded like the squawk of a macaw. "Thanks for the offer, Mister Crosse."

"Don't thank me," said the black man. "I'm just making a request, Major."

"Well, thanks anyway, Mr. Crosse." Vickers slid past Harry, scraping against the steel door. As the bodyguards drove him out Vickers did notice the earth-moving equipment--backhoes, tractor-plows, cranes, steamrollers--surrounding an immense tract of freshly turned dirt. That would be the construction that Bryan mentioned, Vickers thought. What'd he say about it?--Bryan was constructing some kind of *proof?*

Whatever it all meant, thought Major Vickers, Bryan did intend to reward him, at least according to Mr. Crosse.

*

Claire Bryan heard the cane stumping past her front walk long before John Bryan came to the door, but she didn't leave her bed. Her son's nanny, Ingrid, answered the rap on the pane.

Bryan had lifted his cane again as Ingrid pulled back the curtain, and dropped it again. "Mrs. Bryan, you awake? *Mr.* Bryan's outside."

"It's okay, Ingrid." Claire slowly got up, out of her room, past the door into the kitchen. "He say what he wants?"

"I didn't ask him, missus."

"Let him wait." Claire took her morning glass of orange juice, added vodka and went to the door while tying her robe with one hand. She opened the door just enough to look through the crack at her father-in-law.

"I take it you have heard of the death of my son." Bryan was making one of his attempts at sarcasm.

"Mr. Crosse brought over the telegram they sent--after you opened it, or don't you remember."

"I have a lifetime of remembrances, madam, but none I would share with you." Bryan inclined himself onto the cane. "You and I have very little--only one thing, actually-- to talk about."

"We have nothing at all to talk about, Mr. Bryan. What're you doing here?"

"We have something of importance to discuss, madam. If you would walk over to my library now, we can settle this."

"Settle what?" She noticed he was leaning oddly to one side. "What the hell're you talking about?"

Bryan tried to step back but the favored leg almost buckled. "You look slovenly, as usual, madam. How your child must suffer."

"Dan thought I look sexy this way, Mr. Bryan." Claire emphasized this lie by lifting her drink. "Don't you think I'm sexy, Mr. Bryan?"

"How *dare* you!"

"What can I do for you, Mr. Bryan? Any sexy little thing you need from me?"

"Courtesan! You can leave this compound, that's what you can *do*. Go back among those file clerks where we found you. My son had no personal money to leave you, you fully realize that?"

"Sean and I can get along without your money."

"That is precisely why I'm here, to insist--*demand*--you do what is right for my grandson."

"He's your grandson now?"

"There is the Christian bloodline of my son in him, madam, which needs nurturing. You cannot raise my grandson in your condition--a prostitute, a heroin addict."

"I don't have to listen to that shit--" She caught herself. She would not let him get her angry. "I haven't taken drugs since I met Dan, I think you know that."

"I have reports all the way to your childhood, including interviews with your Emil St. Amand in Paris--you remember *him*, don't you?" He obviously enjoyed that, letting her see how much he knew. "You were a heroin addict then, you will always be a heroin addict. I will not allow a prostitute and a heroin addict to raise my grandson."

"Go screw yourself, Mr. Bryan." She said this as calmly as she could and, God, that felt good. Bryan hated profanity even from men. From a woman it was like Christ giving him the finger.

Bryan's eyes widened, his face blotched to a nice redness. "The courts will never allow a prostitute and a heroin addict to have custody of my grandson!"

"You got it wrong, Mr. Bryan. Prostitutes charge money." She gave him a smile and, worst of all obscenities, winked. "No one pays me a dime."

"If you had any feelings for my son, for *anyone*, you would be in mourning now."

"You have no idea what my arrangement was with your son, do you?"

"I know he married a harlot. Promiscuity is just cause for assuming guardianship--"

"-Stick it up your ass, Mr. Bryan." She closed the door.

"I have prepared all my life for this!" she heard him say. "You remember this day! This is only the beginning!"

Claire sat in the entryway chair and tried to decipher what Bryan was saying. Hot air, probably. Probably. She shivered. Bryan could never take Sean from her, but how in hell did he know about her in Paris? Or about Emil St. Amand?

"Granpa mad?" Sean had woken up and climbed into her lap.

"Granpa's sick," she said. "Granpa's a sick person, Sean." She scruffed his hair and thought about the real irony in Bryan's accusation. Claire's "promiscuity" was the exact reason Dan Bryan made his weird proposal: the ultimate open marriage, the nymph and the fag, just to keep up Dan's football-hero image while they both chased other men. Lord Almighty.

But when Dan Bryan first came to work for his father, she remembered, into the office came *God*. A waist the size of a napkin ring unfolding to a quarry of deltoids, laterals, pectorals. Teeth like Carrara marble--too good to be true, she thought, which turned out to be exactly right. The image wasn't true at all.

"You want me to take Sean, ma'am?"

Claire looked from Ingrid to her son, who had fallen asleep in her arms. She handed the boy up to his nanny. "Make me another vodka and juice, would you?"

The big round-shouldered nanny looked sideways at Claire. "You might've had enough for this morning, Missus Bryan."

"Bring me another anyway, would you?"

John Bryan only needed to check the shipping department of his own headquarters, Claire knew, if he wanted to get any dirt on her. She'd probably slept with at least half the men there. Among the other clerks in that trap she drew attention like a butterfly in a cattle car.

She could vividly recall when she and Dan, to provide John Bryan with a grandson, had consummated the marriage. Just once. An absurd memory, Dan climbing over her with teeth-gritting concentration, like she was slipping an ember down his crotch. But, still, that marriage was the perfect arrangement for both of them, while Dan Bryan remained on earth.

Except for the night-demons that visited him, decrying the All-American fraud, waking him in the night, leaving him sweating, fearing the fate he thought he deserved. That was the reason he arranged his *heroic* exit from life, she knew. Banners waving, trumpets blaring above the flames of war and all that. Danny would probably like to think of the problems of his life ending in such a glorious way.

But the problems wouldn't end that way. Christ, there was no way he could end them so easily, just by getting killed.

Chapter 13

The telegram went to their processing unit in Japan. To Camp Drake, not Fort Buckner.

"The man must have one hell of a recon on us." Ram handed the yellow page back to Kim Chau. "How'd he find us here?"

"That's no problem for a person like John Bryan." Chau was obviously happy to get the message, though it didn't provide much information: *Jonathan Bryan requests a meeting with Sergeant Marion Apollo and First Lieutenant Kim Chau Dao upon their arrival in San Francisco Stop Please respond Stop Harry Crosse Executive Vice President Stop.* Giving a return address and telephone number in San Francisco.

"Why would we want to meet the guy's family? That'd be a dumb idea, Kim Chau."

"Think about it a minute, Ram. We're being invited right to the *source.*"

"We're not on that damned investigation any more. How many times... We're about the last people who'd want to meet the guy's father."

"Ram, every man in the battalion probably got one of these telegrams." Chau was going through this nervous see-saw exercise, sitting and standing next to the card table in the regimental recreation hall. "Bryan's not interested in us, why the hell *would* he be?"

"Because I might've killed his son? Think that might be a reason?"

"You're a real riot, aren't you? How could he know about that? He just wants to meet people who were there when his son was killed."

"There's no reason to see him." Ram had received a letter from Weissman saying that everything was turning out swell at UCLA: room, registration, books, girls. He didn't need to screw that up chasing this Bryan investigation.

"You didn't go with me to the docks and look what happened," said Chau. "You end up in the drunk ward, right? That's your subconscious, you know, it's a way of telling you you're wrong."

"How the hell'd you put *that* piece of logic together?" Ram laughed. "Christ, Kim Chau, you never let up."

For the two days they had left in Japan they decided to take the rattly Odakyu train to Kyoto. Chau felt it was *imperative* for Ram to see something called the Temple of the Thousand-Armed Kannon, adding what he thought would surely sell Ram: "Went there when we were kids. That's where My Linh got her ideas about her *touchstone* theory, at least that's what she once told me."

That, thought Ram, was horse crap. But then, hell, what else was there to do?

They went to see the temple, where statues of the Kannon's twenty-eight followers stood behind the main icon like colorful Christian seraphim, fusing human and animal, parading all forms of human emotion: *All Carved in the Thirteenth Century by The Master Tankei, while in his Eighties,* the tourist sign explained in English. And here the icons still sat, forever gathering dust in this lusterless, dusty, barn-like building. "Reminds you a little of the Catholic Church, doesn't it?" asked Chau.

"The Catholic altar's built around a dying man," said Ram. "Isn't anyone dying in here."

But all other parts of life did parade themselves here: anger and love, envy, greed, justice, loyalty, compassion. "Can you see what he's saying, Ram?"

"Who?"

"Who? Dammit, the master Tankei. You see what he's saying in those sculptures?"

"The touchstone's in there somewhere?"

"He's saying each emotion contains its own form of beast. Each person chooses which beast will be inside him. It's impossible to live without choosing one of these paths."

"You saying I need a path?"

"Tankei shows that no man can live without a path."

Ram grinned again, although Chau didn't see it within the big darkened shed. "Dao Kim Chau," said Ram, "you ever going to get off my ass?" But he did study the myriad of carved gods, the thousand and thousand mutely gesturing hands, limbs, the life of a thousand branches. He patted the nubby wood railing that surrounded this pantheon of gods. "Anyway...this Tankei, what makes you think he's offering anyone a choice?"

Chau didn't answer, and Ram watched the Thousand-Armed Kannon. A choice to do what? He thought. Chase the Army investigation? Help some little cowshit country find out who the bad guys are? I don't think even the Army really wants to know that.

The Thousand-Armed Kannon gazed down as it had for seven hundred years, in this room, according to the tourist hand-out. The hands of the Thousand-Armed Kannon reached forever in its thousand directions, holding their scepters and seals, maces, balls, hatchets and cymbals and scythes.

Maybe this once, Ram thought, I will *choose* to see if there's something more to all this than...what? Street-survival? That's the only "true path" as far as I know, everything else is dream-shit. But, hell, I'll probably end up seeing Bryan with Kim Chau, just to get that thrill of risking my ass again. Like in Korea, or in the streets of East L.A.--what the hell is wrong with me?

Maybe Doctor Moley was right, he thought. Maybe I *am* going nuts, poco a poco.

*

The Pan Am terminal resonated with the loudspeaker's female contralto: "*Sergeant Marion Apollo...Please respond...on the...white... courtesy...telephone.*"

"They must already be here," said Kim Chau. He and Ram waited for their duffel-unloading from the Pan Am Clipper Ship, the last stop on their three-week passage: two weeks on a troop ship from Yokohama to Seattle, one week staging through Fort Lewis. They paid for a commercial flight themselves for their last leg to San Francisco.

"Your party's at the Pan American ticket counter," said the loudspeaker voice, softer now inside the white phone. Ram checked the antiseptic pale-blue counters where a flock of ladies had assembled around a stern-looking woman holding up a small American flag. The only other person there was a lean, tall, small-breasted girl--too long and narrow in the legs and hips, Ram thought.

She began waving a beach-bag purse toward them. "Sergeant Apollo?" Moving past the scrutiny of the ladies' tour with a slow longlegged stride, she was half-naked: strap sandals and textured cotton play-sheath, unbuttoned and open, showing a cone of brown bareness from the waist up. "I'm Claire Bryan. Can we go for some coffee? I need a *tub* of coffee right now."

She had turned toward the airport cafeteria before finishing the last sentence.

"Name's Ram. Never cared for the name Marion," Ram said when they joined up in the coffee line. "You related to John Bryan?"

"I am--was--his son's wife," she looked up at him through sleepy, dark-lidded eyes. "*Mrs.* Dan Bryan, Lieutenant Bryan's wife." There was no accusation in her voice. She had a scent that assailed the brain, a carnal fragrance that mixed surprisingly well with residual vapors of bourbon. She leaned past Ram to look at Kim Chau: "And you're Lieutenant Dao?"

"Dao Kim Chau. Yes ma'am."

"Your orders put Dao as your *last* name."

"In the orient the family name comes first-"

"-I've been hearing a lot about you two," she interrupted as Ram paid the cashier. "Need coffee before we talk--do you mind? Nursing a goddamned *gangbuster* hangover. I probably need another drink."

"We were told someone named Crosse would meet us," said Ram.

"I persuaded Harry to let me come instead." She gave him a curious look. "Why'd you agree to meet him?"

"We're searching for purpose," said Ram.

"Where're we going?" asked Chau.

"Eighty, ninety miles from here, about." Her eyes stayed on Ram a moment before turning back to the lieutenant. "To Bryan's little fiefdom near Carmel." She found a booth and sat. The two men laid their duffels alongside the booth and sat.

"How'd you find out about our orders, Mrs. Bryan?"

"Call me Claire. As I said, I've heard--Christ, I *know*--a whole bunch about both of you. My good father-in-law's done a real study on you two, gets passed on to me through Mr. Crosse. I'm very persuasive with Mr. Crosse, like I said."

"I can see why." Kim Chau glanced at Ram. "Why us?"

She took a package of cigarettes from her purse and tapped one out. "He thinks you, Sergeant, killed my husband. In fact he thinks you were sent by his long-dead *father* to kill him." Her hand shivered over the flame that Ram held up for her. "That's why I talked Harry into letting me come, I thought someone should let you know." She sucked deeply through the filter. The smell of menthol filled the booth.

"He thinks his dead father sent us?" Ram couldn't tell if she was joking.

"Bryan's mind doesn't work real well any more." She fidgeted with the cigarette. "You and I and the lieutenant here, we're all his enemies, in case you don't know. You say you don't like the name Marion?"

"Call me Ram."

"Well, Ram, in case you're wondering, I can't help you, but I did want to talk with you." She leaned in as she said this, her pink blouse folding out, the soft edges of two very persuasive young breasts blossoming within the folds.

"What's he plan to do at this meeting?" Kim Chau leaned closer too, but he knocked over a flower-holder and brought his arms back.

"Jesus, who knows. But if I were in the place you're in, I'd think twice before going there." She looked at Ram. "You didn't really kill Daniel, did you?"

"I'm not sure."

"The Chinese were picking him apart, Mrs. Bryan." Kim Chau stopped himself. That would be the last thing a widow would want to hear, he thought, but her eyes showed nothing, moving placidly around the table from the artificial yellow daffodils to the steel napkin holders. "He was screaming for someone to shoot him, Mrs. Bryan," Chau decided to continue. "I'm sorry, but someone almost had to help him."

"Didn't think anyone could kill Danny in anger," she said. "Poor Daniel." She touched Ram's arm like the brush of a catspaw as she said that. "If his father starts up with his Christian act, about how he can't harm anyone because it's against God's *will*, don't believe that crap. He's too screwed up to know how dangerous he is." She let her hand play on the muscle of Ram's forearm.

A Pan American Stratocruiser, on the runway near their window, whined high and angry on the line, then gusted into its long forward lurch. Ram waited for the comparative hush that followed: "Mrs. Bryan--Claire--why'd you come here?"

She drew on the cigarette, arched her chin to the side, spread a thin smoke stream against the window. "Dan and I had a long--how do I say this?--we had a different relationship, Sergeant. He was homosexual, but you probably already knew that."

"Sounds like a different relationship, all right," said Chau.

"Dan was my savior, Lieutenant Dao," she said. "Got me off dope, made me feel...we lived together under kind of an open agreement, for appearances."

"Okay, but why tell us?"

"You and I are both the enemies of Mr. Bryan now, Sergeant, and I'd like the company of some co-enemies. I'd like us to know each other, if that's okay. It's lonesome out here by myself."

"It might be time to talk this over, Ram." Chau was losing enthusiasm for meeting Bryan, real fast. "This looks like *way* more trouble..."

"I thought you wanted to meet the man, Kim Chau."

"Come on-"

"-Chance to go right to the source, you said."

"Christ, Ram, now that there's real risk in it you *want* to go, don't you? I saw that back in Korea. You kind of *like* this stuff."

Ram gave Chau a sideways grin and turned back to Claire. "What's the man got against you?"

She shrugged. "I thought that was apparent. I'm the tramp that married his son."

*

She drove them to Bryan's compound in a '50 Aston-Martin, a candy-apple wire-wheeled DB2 coupe, with Chau crammed with the duffels into the narrow back bench. "The only thing Dan owned personally," Claire explained on the way. "I wouldn't even have *this* if it weren't already in Dan's name."

They drove for almost two hours before she swung into a driveway flanked by rock walls, barred at the front by a thickly-woven wrought iron gate. Claire pushed the code buttons at the gate and it cranked open, and she accelerated across a long bank of land, pulling up before they reached the front portico. "I'll leave you two here. Going to get myself a drink."

"You *live* here?"

"In a separate building." Her mouth made a weak smile. "Just don't have the guts to leave all this." She stopped Ram's hand as he reached back for his duffel. "Leave it. I'll be chauffeuring you back when you get through here." She didn't take her eyes off Ram. "But I could think of a whole lot of better ways to spend an afternoon."

"I hope you mean what I think you mean," said Ram.

Chapter 14

Sorry Ochoa was the first to get up from his cards. Charles Trevors stayed down and stared at his. "Mr. Apollo?"

"*Sergeant* Apollo, amigo," said Ram. He wondered if this Samoan-sized doorman was Chicano. "Como esta', my friend."

"I'm just dandy, amigo." Ochoa nearly, not quite, smiled back, gesturing at the two men with his open hand. "Been waiting for you." The words came in precipitous grunts, like stepped-on frogs. He pulled a door handle the size of a night stick and the doors swung open and Trevors, flipping his cards away, fell in behind.

Inside, down the hall, Ochoa and Trevors moved to the side and ushered the two guests into a room that had an ancient, fusty smell.

"Sergeant Apollo? Lieutenant Dao? I'm Harry Crosse." A black man dressed like a banker approached them while Trevors and Ochoa took positions near the door. "And this is Kenneth Willy Carson, assistant to Mr. Bryan," said Harry Crosse. The room wasn't as dim as the hallways but Ram still had to look hard to find Carson. The smaller man, Carson, didn't move from the bookshelves. He nodded.

At the end of the room a desk large enough for table tennis was pushed against an overstuffed chair, housing itself around a white-haired man. "And this is Mr. Bryan," said Harry Crosse, circling behind them. "Mr. Bryan..."

"I see him, Harry," said John Bryan. "I know who he is." Bryan's eyes strained through the space between him and Ramirez Apollo. "That harlot who brought you here warned you of this meeting, didn't she?" He frowned toward Harry. "And still you come. Only someone like you would continue coming after me, after the warning I know she gave you." As the man spoke Trevors moved nearer, folding his forearms in front of him. They looked like stacked fireplace logs. "And now you've accomplished what you came here for, haven't you?" said Bryan. "You took my son... You think I'm incapable of doing anything about that?"

Ram's response was a curious, inspecting look at the old man.

"You won't defend yourself?"

"Don't need to defend myself, viejo."

"You deny killing my son?"

"Don't really know," said Ram. "I might have."

Bryan's mouth had begun to form his accusation before Ram spoke, but now it trembled into a tight line.

"Your son was dying in an awful way, sir," said Kim Chau. "There was nothing anyone could do for him."

"No, that's enough from you." Bryan cleared that reasoning from the room. "I don't accept that from people like you." He coughed, caught his breath. "The two of you are lying. My father is the one who sent you, I *know* that." Wetting his lips with his tongue. "You did that without justification, there is no...I am not guilty of those charges. I am no coward, as I fully intend--will certainly--prove to you, very soon."

Ram watched the man a few moments and then rose, and turned to look at Charles Trevors. "You were right, Kim Chau. We shouldn't have come. The man's a nut case."

The black man, Harry Crosse, made a quiet move back.

"I recommend you stay where you are, Mr. Apollo," said Willy Carson, "till Mr. Bryan says you can go." He stepped away from the shelves and put a hand in his pocket.

"Got a blade in there, chingon?" Ram nodded toward the pocket, which wasn't large enough to hold any other kind of weapon. "You know how to use one?"

"No, Kenneth, stay there," said John Bryan. "There is something I need to prove to this man first."

Ram turned from Carson back to Trevors, who was now grinning back at him: "Want to try me out, pachuco?"

"No, Trevors," said Bryan. "He would only keep coming back. It's clear what needs to be done first."

Kim Chau could feel his skin crawl--what the hell was going on here? Ram seemed to go along with this creepy shit, so what the hell was Ram doing? Trying to *hex* the old bastard?

The rest of the room stayed quiet, waiting to see if Bryan was through. He wasn't. "The person you killed was my only child, Sergeant Apollo, I want you to understand that. I deliver the swords of war to people like you so that you--men like you--can kill each other all you want, but that was never meant for my son. And yet you, a half-breed, accepted the mission to take his life. Don't you see the terrible inequity, the *wrongness* of that?"

Ram rubbed the side of his nose. "You may not follow this real well, Mr. Bryan, but all this money and power doesn't mean shit to me."

Bryan's eyes widened. He sucked in his breath. "I buy and sell your kind for *taco* chips, Sergeant. I would advise you to be careful here, be very careful here, and stop this mission you're on."

Ochoa shuffled alongside Trevors and Bryan. The small man, Carson, stayed somewhere behind, but Ram saw the effect that the fourth man, the black man, had here. This Harry Crosse was their safety net, probably, if Ram was reading this right. Only for the moment.

"I did not want, ever, to harm anyone." Bryan tried to continue. His mouth worked hard to keep from twitching. "It is against all Christian law, against all...but you have violated-"

"-Mr. Bryan," said Ram quietly, "you're a messed up old man, and you already know that, don't you?"

"Holy Christ," Harry whispered.

"That the hell does it, ass hole." Carson drew a turquoise-handled knife and pulled the blade open.

"No, Kenneth, stay put. Don't you see what he's trying to do?" said Bryan. "For the love of God put that away, and do not *profane*--it is this... Satan, who brings this out in you."

Ram didn't move. He watched as the old man tried to return the stare but the effort demanded too much. Bryan squinted instead at the top of his desk.

They waited but Bryan said no more. They waited, and Ram turned away from him. "Your sister was right, Kim Chau," he said. "For some people the world is one big illusion."

Chau hesitated a step forward. Seeing no resistance from Trevors he continued toward the door while Ram kept his eyes on the bodyguards.

"You are the killer of my son, Sergeant Apollo," said Bryan. His gaze worked its way around the room, at his carved ceiling, his cherry wood paneling, his ancient black armor and giant walnut clock. "Your mocking indifference to me will be repaid."

Ram reached for the oversized door handle but didn't follow the lieutenant, and Chau's heart skipped--they needed to be *out* of here. "It's not your son's killing that's behind all this, Mr. Bryan," Ram was saying. "That isn't what's screwing you up."

"I hesitate to destroy you, Sergeant. It is against God's laws."

"That isn't what's stopping you, Mr. Bryan." Ram turned and Chau followed him, but they could hear Bryan's voice as they walked through the hallway. "We're not through, you and I, Sergeant Apollo," said John Bryan.

"For Christ's sake," Chau whispered. "What the hell were you *doing* back there? You get some kind of kick out of shaking this guy's cage?"

"He was going to be our enemy anyway, Kim Chau. Just wanted to clarify his reasons for him."

"You think we could take on those two goons? You think you're that street-tough?"

"In the street we only act tough, Kim Chau. Those two were genuine tough. We'd have gotten our asses kicked."

"Jesus, Ram, you don't make any sense."

*

Claire had just enough time to go to her place for a glass of Smirnoff over ice and a change of clothes. She brought the car back to her private spot on the cliff side of the fortress, where the on-shore breeze always gave her this scary feeling. Airy nakedness. Like the windblown bosomy ship's witches she'd seen in town, pried off the prows of whalers...a sexual, airy feeling.

When Ram and Chau came back she made a toast, waving her leather-bound flask at them. "Good show. I thought you two might have to be *carried* out of there."

"Wasn't all that bad." Ram was watching the dress blowing against her body, and she turned to give him a good front view. "I think we came to an understanding with the old fellow," he said.

"Certainly you did." She looked away and fingers of hair brushed along her face. "Let's go to the city and find you a nice hotel room, Sergeant Apollo. Some place you and I can come to our *own* understanding."

*

On the way back, Kim Chau kept a glum silence in the cramped back seat. This Bryan business was *serious*, however casually Ram chose to treat it. The man's threat was real, this was no drill. It made him think about his own family in Saigon, but he shook that idea off--Bryan's threat could carry no risk to them. How would John Bryan know anything about the Dao family?

*

The jangling outburst wouldn't stop. The shriek of the telephone ricocheted across the room and stripped Ram from his sleep and went right down his spine, and with his wrist he sent it racketing downward, and he lay on his side a moment. He wondered if anyone was still on the other end of that thing.

"What was all *that* about?" Claire--both of them, Ram seemed to recall--had gone to bed drunk. No serious love making had gone on, not that he remembered, not after finishing her flask of bourbon plus some other stuff. Just a little sniffing and fromping around until his low booze-capacity dropped him. She reached for a glass on the night stand and he propped himself up to take a closer look and she moved the sheet aside with her foot to show long cream-white legs, tapering to her thatched auburn vee like a brunette rose, atop two thin stems. From the floor a small voice continued talking to him.

"Hold that position." He reached for the receiver.

"Sergeant Apollo." Wrong answer, he remembered. From here on just a damned hello would do.

"Welcome to the land of the free, Sarge." The twang was unmistakable.

"Weissman? How'd you find me?" Ram couldn't recall for a moment exactly where here was. A beat-up hotel in North Beach, as far as he could remember.

"Chau called me this morning," said Weissman. "Said not to phone you too early." Giggle. "Said you'd probably be indisposed for awhile."

"Just woke up." Ram checked to make sure Claire was still in that pose. She was. "Weissman, you in town?"

"In San Francisco? Hell no, just called to say you're all set up here at the university. Picked up a registration packet for you. You're all set soon as you muster through Fort Ord. Even got us a place to stay."

Claire flattened out next to him and rotated a knee in the air, stretching back. She was creating this musty-sweaty fragrance that was clogging Ram's brain. "Luke, I'll call you back."

"Chau said he'll meet you in the coffee shop in the lobby 'round noon," Weissman persisted. "Wanted me to pass that on."

"Got it. Thanks."

Claire sipped from the glass and folded the sheet away as he rolled over and smoothed his hand along her. "Feeling a little friskier this morning, Sergeant?" said Claire, turning on her side to give him a better look. "Like what you see?"

"Be hard not to."

"That's only the surface, Sergeant," she said. She felt for him, and he was sufficiently enlarged, and she climbed over him. "Gotta go deep to find real joy, isn't that what they taught you in the orient?" He had to grit his teeth to keep from exploding too fast, that felt so good.

Afterward she twittered and relit a half-used cigarette and finished her glass of sweet rosé. And watched him lay back into the mattress. "Most people would dampen their shorts with a man like John Bryan after them," she said. "But how does Sergeant Apollo respond, folks? He responds by screwing Bryan's dead son's wife. How's that for cajones?"

Ram thought about that, and it did seem funny. This old man growling around a quarry who was too busy screwing his dead son's wife to care, that was damned funny.

*

Chau met them in a windowless enameled room labeled "Delicatessen": bottled pickles, boiled eggs, pre-wrapped sandwiches. Burrowing into a section of the Andrews Hotel lobby where signs announcing breakfast specials blocked the windows. The counter waitress stood tail-to-tail with the fry cook.

"Where do you two go now?"

"We muster at Fort Ord," said Chau. "Then I might go back to Saigon for awhile."

"Saigon?" Claire raised an eyebrow. "Aren't you an American now?"

"I might be needed there, for awhile."

"Chau has family in Vietnam," said Ram. "French are getting their asses kicked there. All hell's breaking loose, I guess."

"And dear old John Bryan will keep stirring the pot there too, selling guns to both sides, making piles of money--" The stare from Kim Chau made her stop. "Did I say something?"

"You know about Bryan's shipments?"

"I worked as a file clerk in his company." Claire, puzzled, looked back at Ram. "That's where I met Dan."

"And that stuff was *known* around the company?" Chau persisted. "About him supplying both sides in Indo-China, I mean."

"Leave it alone, Kim Chau," said Ram.

Claire sat back, a little. "Known? Not really, just rumors. But I was *married* to Dan Bryan, remember."

"For Christ's sake, Kim Chau-"

"-Could you get them now?--those documents, I mean," asked Chau.

Claire nodded. "I'd know how to get to them, if that's what you're asking. But I sure as hell don't plan to. What're you talking about?"

"We need to prove that Bryan supplied the guerrillas in Indo-China."

"Like hell we do."

"You weren't listening, partner." Claire held up a hand. "Right now I'm just the old guy's enemy, I don't plan to become his *target*. Besides, those papers probably have fake end-users on them, what would they prove?"

Chau leaned toward Ram. "You heard what Bryan said. He's coming after us anyway. Might as well fight back, shouldn't we? We have a choice?"

"There's always a choice, Kim Chau. Remember the old master?"

"Doesn't apply here, dammit."

"S'cuse me," Claire interrupted. "Weren't you listening? If you're thinking of starting a war with John Bryan, leave me out, hey?"

That distracted Chau, for a moment, allowing Ram to change the subject. "Speaking of fighting--" He searched through his jacket and brought out a cigar-shaped package, still wrapped in its waxy brown souvenir-stall paper. "Need you to keep this for me, Kim Chau, would you? Give it back when--if--I ever get to Vietnam. Illegal to own one of these in L.A."

"Come to Vietnam? You're thinking of... I don't have to give you back my steel bracelet, do I?"

Ram smiled. "That only cost two dollah, lieutenant. Besides, it's got your name on it."

"You kidding about coming to Vietnam?"

"Who knows? Might need more instruction from your sister some day."

"Instruction my ass." Chau peeled a corner of the wrapping, revealing the red dragon on the handle. "Lementke said you handle this thing like one of those carnival knife throwers."

"It's a fine knife, Kim Chau, but I don't plan to use one of these again."

"You say those are illegal in Los Angeles?" asked Claire.

Chau grinned. "Since when does 'illegal' bother you, Ram?"

"It's a symbolic thing, Kim Chau. Gives me a reason to come visit you."

Chau laughed. "So you can come get it back in Saigon? Hell, that'd be great." Chau tucked the knife in his pocket. "Just hope you won't be coming there as a soldier, when you do."

"Not very damned likely."

Chapter 15

The entry of Major General Novinger seemed casual enough. He came in quietly, gave Purdy an incurious glance, stared around the sickly green G-2 offices like a house guest. "We need to talk, Colonel Purdy, about that...assignment, the one you handled last July. You remember?" General Novinger sounded tired.

"Of course, sir." Purdy felt his usually tolerable fatness squeeze his windpipe, tuning his voice to a wisp. "The Bryan investigation?" Something had gone terribly wrong, he knew that. There was this terrible, salty taste in his mouth.

"Yes, the Bryan...of course, as I thought I said in my memo, we'd like to refer to that investigation as the Touchstone file, drop all reference to Bryan." He sniffed the stale cigar smell in the room. "I thought I went over that."

"Yes, sir, you did." Oh, God, thought Colonel Purdy.

Novinger allowed the silence to settle around the colonel. "About those two men you assigned..." He fingered a scruffy leather envelope he'd brought with him. "This Sergeant Apollo and Lieutenant, uh...Dao, is it?"

"Yes, sir--they were assigned to-"

"-Yes, I know what they were assigned to." Novinger cleared his throat. "Colonel Purdy, didn't you interpret my memo to mean that we should go lightly on this investigation? Hit and run, so to speak, to avoid any kind of a, ah, political rhubarb, concerning this matter?"

"That's all we did, sir--less than that, as a matter of fact. Lieutenant Bryan died before he could even be questioned."

"Then it should have just dropped there?"

"It *did* drop there, sir. Both those men were wounded, they were sent to Okinawa. They're not even *in* Korea now."

"I know they're not in Korea, Colonel." Novinger shook his head at the floor. "They're on Okinawa checking freighters for munitions shipments, that's where they are. And they're in the U.S. meeting with John Bryan himself, *that's* where they are, Colonel."

Colonel Purdy's cheeks sucked in. "That's not possible, sir. Where did this-"

"-Comes from the people at Bryan Munitions, Colonel. Bryan apparently went through the Defense Department to have us put some shit on these two. And Bryan's people don't even *know* about the investigation, I don't think."

95

General Novinger reached inside the leather envelope, pushed some papers along the front of Colonel Purdy's desk and put a finger over one of them. "These," he said, "are the orders you drew for those two. They were taken from Lieutenant Dao aboard a freighter called the Santa Ynez. He tried to use these to inspect a Bryan shipment."

"Lord Almighty."

"Lord Almighty," agreed General Novinger in this iron voice. His eyes looked like slits in a pillbox. "We also know that both men went to see the man personally last week. You have an explanation?"

Colonel Purdy was starting to feel light-headed--what in the world was happening here? "I can't...explain that, sir. They were *disabled*."

"You were asked to stay directly in charge of that investigation, Colonel, and to make the assignment?"

"Yes, sir."

"You read my memo?"

"Yes, sir."

The general moved the papers until he came to a manila folder, a 201 file. He flattened it out, looked over the charts inside.

"This sergeant you assigned, Colonel, this Apollo, you picked him out?"

"My aide did, yes sir."

"And you approved it before you called this man in?"

"I think so, sir." Colonel Purdy wanted to go pull his own files but wasn't sure his legs would hold him up.

"Did you catch my meaning that we don't want to pursue this Touchstone thing too energetically? That meant--I hope I made myself clear--we'd prefer not to send men who could grasp the meaning--"

"This sergeant, his record indicated he was kind of an *eight*ball, sir."

The general didn't change his sad expression. He slid the folder toward Colonel Purdy. "I'd like you to look at these, Colonel. Tell me what you see."

Apollo's AGCT and aptitude-battery test scores lay before Colonel Purdy. The numbers blurred in the sweating humidity but he could still see them, all three-digits, all with a "1" in front.

"Well, sir, these are Sergeant Apollo's test results, it looks like. They seem to be...they seem higher than average."

"They're higher than your own scores, Colonel. They're higher than *my* goddamned scores, matter of fact."

"Yes, sir, with these numbers, that might be possible."

"Take my word for it," said General Novinger. "And did my memo not imply we'd prefer a man who wouldn't be able to see too deeply into this?"

"Well--ah--Sergeant Apollo wouldn't really be considered a-"

"-And you send a man there--I have a hard time getting this--with the mental rating of a goddamned *code-breaker*!" General Novinger couldn't contain the shout. This was the head of 8th Army G-2 here. What hope was there for FECOM with staff like this?

The flesh around Colonel Purdy's mouth made a multi-directional twitch. The bald part of his head wetted over. "He was very impassive, sir. He showed total disregard-"

"-He can *impassively* figure out what's going on here, Colonel. Apparently he is *impassively* pursuing this assignment on his own."

"That would be impossible, sir--if you could see the man."

"I don't need to see the man, Colonel. I've been *hearing* about him. I've been receiving these reports back on him. Oh, *hell*..." Novinger pulled the files back and closed them, very deliberately. "Anyway, I'm going to explain the situation we have now, Colonel, and then discuss your reassignment to Stateside G-2. You're going to be in charge of campus surveillance. You'll oversee the activities of our people on the southwest campuses, which will include Sergeant Apollo, understand? We don't want to bring anyone else into this."

"Yes, sir."

General Novinger pursed his lips and contemplated what to air out here, not that he felt Purdy deserved explanation. He needed to verbalize this more for his own line of thought: "There are things, government policies, which may or may not be apparent to you, Colonel, but during the Second World War some arms dealers like Bryan supplied the Viet Minh to help fight the Japanese, first through OSS and then later through the NSC, through me personally, for a while--even after the war."

"Against the *French?*"

The general didn't answer. He turned to stare out the window. "The President and Secretary of State can only *imply* what they would like to have done. It's up to people like me to interpret from there, to protect their deniability in such actions." General Novinger was trying to straighten out his own logic here. "During the last part of World War II the French concentrated on re-establishing a puppet government there rather than fighting the war, and the OSS forces were caught in the middle of this French cabal. 'French greed is responsible for Americans *dying* there.' Like President Roosevelt said...do you fully understand this, Colonel?"

"Oh, yes sir."

"Have you ever heard of Ngo Dinh Diem, Colonel?"

"No, sir."

"He's next in command to the emperor Bao Dai. Diem is our *real* ally here. When he and Ho Chi Minh divide the country my--our--long range plan...our own war with Ho Chi Minh will probably begin, although Ho Chi Minh has offered to open up a rapprochement program with us. But we can't allow him to control... Why are you standing?"

Colonel Purdy didn't realize he'd stood up. He sat down again. The scale of the events, the problems those two could stir up were beginning to scare him.

"You see the problem that would unravel, Colonel, if those two proved that we, through Bryan, supplied the Viet Minh. Our European allies would come down on our ass--France, mainly. Worst of all we'd have one hell of a time selling people on fighting an enemy that we've been *supplying,* for Christ's sake. It would open a lesion of problems. The war might never get on track."

"Good Lord."

"Yes, exactly, Colonel. Good Lord." The general's strained control was beginning to dissolve. "And into this, despite my note describing the people we want involved here, you send a sergeant with the analytical abilities of a nuclear physicist? Since we had to make that inquiry, *all we needed was a driver for Lieutenant Dao, Colonel!* Any goddamned dogface private would have done nicely, he only needed to know the *area.* And this Apollo--of all goddamn things--appears to be a social renegade, to boot."

"But he *won't,* sir--"

"Won't what? Don't give me that crap about how impassive he is. The *potential* is there. And if he's so impassive, why the hell's he calling on Bryan?"

"I just can't answer that, sir."

"Well, from now on you'll be able to answer it. That sergeant's your responsibility now, him and about seventy other college moles in the southwest sector. I will expect no further problems from either Sergeant Apollo *or* that gook lieutenant, you understand me, Colonel?"

"Yes, sir... We could always just discharge him, sir."

"Release him from our jurisdiction? Colonel, that's about the last goddamned thing we'd want to do."

*

The grey-shingled shack in Beverly Glen Canyon contained these Lilliputian rooms: a small paint-chipped kitchen, small paint-chipped beds in each of the two bedrooms, a few badly painted-over yellow cupboards-- all just about right for the barebone needs of Ram and Weissman. Its main attraction was the rear porch-balcony, cantilevered above a gully which cascaded down to a craggy mash of brown chaparral. A stepping-off place, right next to a hill that was roadless, steeply unbuildable, rising alongside the balcony's railing.

"Awfully good find, Luke. Damned near at the top of the mountain here." Ram was checking through the house, walking ahead of Weissman. "Always wanted to live on top of a mountain."

"Also a darned good place to hustle young co-eds," said Weissman, following him outside.

Ram patted the railing. "Eighty-five dollah a month? Lord, Luke, you found us a home."

*

Captain Carl Mandelhouse wore a light blue suit and a gold shirt and a pale grey fedora to the meeting at UCLA. The hat sat a skosh small on his head, needing a tug at the brim to get it square. Hats might be common around his headquarters in the San Francisco Presidio, Ram thought, but they were plain out of place in L.A.--a kooky lapse in cover. Made him conspicuous as a chimpanzee.

"Feels good to wear a business suit," the captain said to Ram as they met outside the beige sandstone archways of Royce Hall, facing the quad, surrounded by lounging students. "I'm Captain Mandelhouse, by the way. Recognized you from your Army 201 file."

Ram had to smile at the gnarled gentleman in the baby-blue suit who identified his undercover students in public. Mandelhouse took the smile as a friendly sign. "Didn't want to wear a uniform here," said he. "Defeats our purpose, eh?"

"Right. Nice outfit, Captain." Ram recognized and liked what he saw in the man. A combat infantryman, probably field-commissioned, out of his element here. "Didn't expect to hear from the Army this soon." They shook hands. The hand of the captain, who stood about five foot six, was rough as a tank tread. "Haven't even registered yet," said Ram.

"Well, something's changing. They're going to replace me in a couple of months. Sending a full damn colonel for this sector."

"Let me guess..."

"Right. Name's Purdy. Used to be your CO or something, wasn't he?"

"Or something."

"G-2's sending him all the way from FECOM. Any idea why?"

"It's classified stuff."

"Well, in the meantime I still have to keep records on all the campus assholes," said Mandelhouse. "You heard of this Young Socialist movement?

Been asked to ask everyone in my sector about them." He apparently didn't take the investigation of campus radicals any more seriously than Ram was planning to. "Think it's a lot of horseshit myself. School kids are good at making noise but they're not serious threats. Armies of trained men are serious threats, *professional* spies are serious threats. College kids are no serious damned threats."

"This's the first time I've been near a college," said Ram. "I've got no idea what college kids are like."

"Me neither, but when you have the chance, check out these here Young Socialists," said Captain Mandelhouse. "Do your first report on them."

"Sounds easy enough."

"Anyway, we might both get pulled out tomorrow if the U.S. gets into this Indo-China shit--which reminds me, I'm supposed to ask you about a lieutenant who was with you in Korea. Dao? They're wondering if he's still on our side. G-2's heard his family fell out with the government there, if I understood right."

"What're they saying, he's joined the communists?"

"Who knows? G-2's tracking the players there and this Dao family's one of them, apparently."

Which meant My Linh was under investigation too, probably, and somewhere in the back of Ram's mind a bad scenario was forming up. "Why not let me ask them? You think G-2 would send me there?"

"Send? Hell, I doubt they'd send you *anywhere*, Sergeant"

"Wouldn't hurt to ask."

"Yes it would, and that isn't what they meant by 'gathering information,' Sergeant. They just want you to call him or something. Drop him a goddamned note."

"I'm expected to get that kind of intelligence over a *telephone?*"

Ram saw the captain wasn't keen about sending any request like that up the line, but, still, it got Mandelhouse to scratch his head. "Well, though, you heard about this Rapprochement program? Ho Chi Minh *wants* us to go talk with his people in the field, from what I heard, so, hell, I'll pass it on. Who knows?"

"I'd bet my ass John Bryan had something to do with hassling the Daos."

"Now listen carefully, Sergeant, 'cause this's the only thing I'm gonna say on that. I've been told this Bryan's the one subject I'm not to discuss with you for *any* reason." Mandelhouse waited for an answer to his unasked question, got nothing, and went on. "You step on toes as big as his...the Army can't protect your ass forever, y'know. They could Section-Eight your ass out of here any time, leave you to the mercies of the son of a bitch."

More links between Bryan and the Army brass, Ram thought. Every-goddamn-where, like trying to fight your way out of a gill net... "Whatever you say, Captain."

"You got that straight, Sergeant. Whatever *I* say," said Mandelhouse. "In the meantime they need a work-up on your Chinaman friend. With the Frogs gone, people like him might be important, you never know. The armistice'll divide up the land and the Army wants to make sure our part of it is secure."

"Our part of it?"

"Screw that. You know what I mean."

Ram stretched and looked over the grass slope next to the steps of Royce Hall. "I know what you mean." He could see across the street to the white and red-shirted football players scrimmaging. Red Sanders' team, number one in the nation this year, he'd heard.

"War is your destiny, Apollo, don't you know that? And maybe that's just as well 'cause that's all we really know, people like you and me." Mandelhouse obviously liked talking war to other military men, to young ex-warriors like Ram. "So you'd best hurry through this schoolyard shit and get back to your natural element, Sergeant. We're gonna have more wars to fight soon."

"I've got more important things to do right now."

"Like what?"

Ram waved toward the campus in general. "The pursuit of knowledge, Captain. What the hell you think I'm here for?"

"You learn a lot more on a battlefield," said Captain Mandelhouse, turning to leave. He began squaring his shoulders as he marched across the UCLA quad.

War is our destiny? According to Captain Mandelhouse, maybe, thought Ram. But first, sure as hell, comes this pursuit of knowledge. Then we'll see.

Chapter 16

Ram received the invitation to meet the Dean of Students before his first day of class.

"Mr. Apollo? Take a seat, please, Marion--or is it Ramirez?" asked the Dean of Students, Byron Anderson. The Dean remained standing. "You must be curious about all this, getting called to the Dean's office. Nothing to worry about here." Dean Anderson smoothed back the white puff of hair on his forehead and waited for an answer, which didn't come.

"Anyway, the reason I asked you here...I've received some strange information, wrapped in a lot of academic pettifoggery of course, more on the order of suggestions--too strong a word--*insinuations*, coming from some real formidable places within this university."

"Define 'formidable' would you, Dean?"

Anderson ignored that. "I felt we should meet." He tamped a nest of tobacco shreds into a large-bowled burl pipe, lit it, filling the room with a sweet leafy incense. "I thought a meeting might be a good idea."

"Your information come by way of a black man?"

"Why, yes. Yes." Anderson took a long draw on the pipe. "Showed me all kinds of reasons why we should kick you out of here." He straightened his blue blazer to align precisely with the grey slacks, and tugged out his shirt cuffs. "Gave me a whole file to show why you shouldn't be allowed here. Says you're really here as a member of Army Intelligence, as one reason."

"Campus surveillance isn't anything new, I hear."

"Right. That's the galling part, of course. The FBI usually has a couple of people enrolled here too, but they at least keep us posted on what they're up to." Anderson worked his voice down to a lower pitch, trying for some kind of an effect. "The puzzle is why one of the regents has made such a fuss in your case. Do you understand any of this?"

"You might not want to understand it, Dean."

Anderson looked like he would agree. Crossing a regent was bad business, probably, Ram supposed. This guy wants nothing to do with problems involving any *regent*. "So what do you plan to do about those suggestions?"

Dean Anderson jutted his chin and pulled on his cuffs again. "What do they *expect* me to do. As long as your grades hold up... Have you molested any co-eds? Cheated on any tests? *Those* kinds of things we can kick you out for."

"Haven't had a chance to yet. How far back does that file go?"

"Says you went into the service to avoid a manslaughter charge," said Dean Anderson. He began reading the memos, apparently for the first time. "Tore up a bar near your base, became a candidate for a psychological discharge, and while in Korea--my God--you were accused of killing an *officer*?" Anderson cradled the memo in his hands now like a dead child. "What do they mean here, Mr. Apollo? You killed an American officer?"

"I'm not sure. He was the son of John Bryan."

"God in heaven, why would you want to kill the son of John Bryan?"

"I didn't *want* to kill anyone, Dean."

The Dean obviously didn't want to hear any more. He looked a little pale. "If you were really guilty the Army would have punished you, wouldn't they? Certainly not send you here, so I assume this report has been somewhat bowdlerized."

"Whatever that means, Dean."

"It means I plan to stay neutral, Mr. Apollo, although I was curious enough...you being the illicit offspring of a professor and all-"

"-Where'd you hear that?"

"You're surprised? Mr. Crosse talked as if it were common knowledge."

Ram tried to think of where Harry Crosse could have learned about that. Not from Ram's 201 file, nothing in there about a professor, which left either a couple of G-2 officers in Korea, or Kim Chau, or...Christ, his mother. Crosse had probably contacted his mother. "Then he's probably trying to track down that professor too."

"Probably, and he'll probably succeed, with all the resources open to people like Mr. Bryan." The Dean tamped down the remaining ashes in his pipe with his finger, pulling it back from the residual heat. "Mr. Crosse says your father was married to someone else when you were conceived."

"You two had one hell of a talk."

"Fascinating man, Mr. Crosse. Stanford master's degree in business, you know, and him a... He seemed to fix on your psychological problem, as he phrased it--your 'potential for violence,' as this file seems to verify. What did the Army doctors say about that?"

"They said I need a purpose."

"Tried that once. Wasn't worth the effort."

"Maybe you didn't look hard enough, Dean."

*

Estella Ramirez lifted her spoon from the pot of meñudo, tapped the juice off and wiped her hands, already clean, on her pink camellia-print apron. "Marion, you always look so serious. So serious or so wild, never in the middle."

"The middle never worked much for me, madre." Ram sagged farther into the sagging couch of his mother's apartment in City Terrace, in the center of East L.A., and traced with his foot the weave of the worn Arapaho rug. "I've been hearing things about my father."

His mother eased into the wicker chair next to the sofa, but her thin body no longer drew the squeals from the chair's interlaced reed. When she was younger and heavier she would make the chair screech like a sack of crickets.

Her gaze also went to the tired Indian rug. "I know nothing more than I've said, Marion." She put her hand on the sofa's arm, near her son. "A professor of the physics. He ate dinners at the cantina where I worked, near the University of Southern California, but he didn't teach there I don't think. He was a *guest lecturer*, he said, and we were together...that way, only one time. Then I had to go away."

"Because of me." He rested his head back, smelling the oldness of the couch.

"Your father did not intend to dishonor me, but he was married. I had to go away."

"He never offered to help."

"I would not have accepted his money, or his name, although his name was very much like Apollo, I know, but I do not remember it." Saying this, Estella Ramirez looked away as she always did, and Ram wondered, as he always did, if she'd really forgotten his father's name. She was still afraid that her son would go looking for the professor of physics.

"I took your name from the movie theater on Whittier Boulevard," she said.

"I know that, madre." The strange feeling about being named after a movie theater, thankfully, had ended long ago. "What was he like?"

"Very tall. Taller than you, even, and nervous like a young muchacho. He could speak on any subject you could ask but I still felt sorry for him. He worried about *everything*..." His mother stared away from him when she talked of these things. They rarely discussed his father. Her eyes had already begun to mist up. "A man came here to ask about him, did you know that? A negro man. Is he a friend of yours?"

"He's no friend, madre."

"He wanted to find your father but I told him I didn't know. I told him I did not know what college he teaches at now, or if he still teaches, I do not know. And the man wanted to know what kind of people your father came from, which I thought was a funny thing to ask. Your father said his family came from Scotland, you remember."

"I remember." Ram never thought much about his Scottish blood. Scottish blood in the barrio would look ridiculous. Scotsmen were all as pale as geese.

"That's why you are lighter skinned than me, of course, and why you have some of this brown in your hair." He felt her fingers scratch the back of his head.

When his mother went back to the kitchen, to her ironing, Ram wandered through the small apartment. The same Formica table with its three chairs arranged within the shallow dining alcove, the same print of the Grand Canyon in its sturdy acrylic oranges and blacks, hanging crookedly above the sofa. Through the window the afternoon sun highlighted bright tips and patches of light along the top of the parapets and signs of the auto shops. Scattered pages of newspapers rustled along the street outside, bunching against the cracked cement of the stairways that traced up the hill to the higher, wavering streets of City Terrace.

The day's dust gathered in thin grey layers across the outside sill. The street corners along City Terrace Drive, where Ram's old gang, the Dukes, usually gathered to brag over their night plans, brooded empty and quiet. "You ever try to find him?"

"Your father? No, I never did."

The pungent smell of chili crowded away his questions. The peppered vapors brought moisture to his face, and good memories, the gut-filling Mexican feasts his mother used to bring home, the leftovers from banquets at the Tu Casa Restaurant.

"I didn't return here until you were a year old," his mother reminded him. "I told everyone how I married a Mr. Apollo, and left him, and I think everyone believed me."

"Everyone believed you, madre."

"It was an evil thing, perhaps, but I've never been sorry. It brought me this good son, didn't it? Who is now a *university* student?" His mother mentioned the "evil thing" so rarely. He responded to that, as usual, with silence.

His mother had first explained to him on his twelfth birthday how the "evil thing" brought him to the world. "My stomach is crying for some of that chili, madre."

"Hush, now, it's almost done."

The room tremored with the eastward rumble of a freight from the downtown Southern Pacific yards. The track next to Marianna Avenue, two blocks away, massaged the land for half a mile beneath its long, heavy load.

*

A young fellow, Middle-eastern, deadly serious, labored over the strings of a carved-up boxlike nightmarish-looking thing, a squashed balalaika, it looked like to Ram. Embellished in yellows, golds and reds. Ram sat on the floor of a carpetless apartment and listened to the garbled tune, which sounded like a metal garbage can rolling downhill.

But, anyway, he was here to spy on these people, not to love their music. He dipped another paper cup of sweet punch from its cheap glass bowl: vodka, tequila, fruit juice, 7-Up. There was a slow-flashing red light above the door. People sucked on twists of marijuana.

Army Intelligence will wet themselves when they get my report on these beatnik university pinkos, Ram had decided. Kiss some Army ass and they send me to Asia so I can spy on my old Army buddy too. Like hell.

He was wondering if those orders would ever really get cut when a redhead in sequined tights and unspeakable nasty hip movements coiled down next to the sitar person, and bit the sitar person's knee, and curled up beside him. Ram squatted as near as he could to that lady, wanted to figure her out, but the oversweet punch was starting to put a velvet headlock on him.

He could just make out a new player now, skinny mulatto in the center of the room, rising on his toes, arms swanning out to announce his spiritual rebirth. The thin overlay of mumbling was vacuumed into silence by that gesture. The sequined redhead ungracefully rolled into a relaxed sprawl closer to Ram, like a feast spreading before him. Like a sampler box of candy.

"In my talk tonight," said the mulatto in a soft woman's voice, "I will show communal integration as the answer to social chaos." He swayed his arms around to portray communal integration, and the gesture reminded Ram of Captain Ahab, strapped to the whale, signaling his men to follow... For what purpose, Captain? Ram had to ask, to himself. What purpose?

To perish chasing the whale, he answered himself. No other real purpose. *Sacrifice*, ass hole. Let's all you young heroes head to Vietnam.

He got up to crowd into the matchbox-size kitchen where a few bangled bohemians huddled: *You're new to these meetings?* Ram pushed himself past the asker, who had posted himself between Ram and the punch. Another voice: *You're the Mexican student, aren't you?* "Si," he did answer. *Then you know what the man's talking about, being a minority and all.* Voices all over him now: "Si, 'scuse me, señor." *See here, Colin? A man who REALLY knows about discrimination*, persisted that first voice: "Discrimination is the shits, señor."

Ram's leaking cup kept him near the sink. *What d'you think of mandatory ROTC?* someone asked. *FORCING us into the military machine!* The asker had a really bad body odor. Made Ram's eyes sting.

He mentally worked on his next report: *Attended cell meeting at twenty-one hundred hours...* No, maybe the word "cell" was laying it on too thick. *This red-headed comrade tried to subvert me with sexual advances. Too potted by twenty-three hundred hours to recall how it all came out.*

He searched around for the sequined girl, to keep the report honest.

Chapter 17

Colonel Purdy met Ram in Santa Monica, in the lobby of the Miramar Hotel a few miles from campus. Purdy sported a dark brown bemedaled uniform which, in the beach community, was maybe less conspicuous than a Tarzan suit, but not by much.

"What happened to Captain Mandelhouse?"

Colonel Purdy made a feint of throwing his hands in the air. "Nothing really fazes you, does it? I come six thousand miles from the goddamned Rock--what's it been, a *year* now?--and your goddamned comment is... What was that again? 'What happened to Captain Mandelhouse?'"

"Sorry, sir. Good to see you again."

"Don't get cute, you know that's not what I meant. Are you at all curious about how I ended up here, Sergeant?"

"Mandelhouse said you'd be here six months ago."

"I've been here just long enough to read some of those bullshit reports you sent in. Fact is, this meeting's taking place only because we got an answer to that request your Captain Mandelhouse submitted. Somebody decided it was a *dandy* idea."

"About going to Vietnam?"

"Just can't figure these people out. They calculate somehow that you need, to the day, exactly one damned week in Indo-China to gather everything what you can from that family of Chinese, the, uh..."

"The Daos, Colonel. When do I leave?"

"*When?* How the hell would I know?--maybe years, the way these people work. But apparently they want feedback on whether your buddy's turning red. They think people like you might find out, though I sure as hell personally doubt it."

"I'll do what I can, Colonel."

"You'll do shit, as usual, Sergeant, so don't give me that kind of talk. Mandelhouse didn't get one report that isn't pure bullshit, and for these people you better be a lot more goddamned factual than you've been on these bullshit campus reports."

"Trying my best, Colonel."

"And between now and then you better 'try' to get your ass to more of those Young Socialist meetings, or at least into some more beatnik parties or something. Give us real activities, not your screwed-up fake bullshit reports, or I'll be goddamned if I let you go *anywhere*."

*

A few weeks later the media was full of news about Einstein's death. Einstein, said the newspapers, was the genius who never realized his main goal, to find an elemental law that united all laws.

The man had searched for the essence of life, Ram read. The man was searching for an *explanation of existence*. Not even Einstein could find the explanation of existence, apparently, and Ram wondered if his father the professor of physics was also searching for this basic-essence thing.

Maybe his father would have the answer, if Ram could ever find him.

*

Kenneth Willy Carson had begun to look forward to his meetings with Sang Van Ky. They were both the same height and Carson liked that, to deal with people he didn't have to look up at. Just as important, next to the frail Van Ky, Carson looked almost bulky. Carson also liked that rare feeling of physical bigness.

Sang Van Ky held the title of Minister of Political Reorganization, something like that, but the man's power came as chief ass-kisser to Diem's brother Ngo Dinh Nhu. Sang was probably as tricky as Dinh Nhu too, from what Carson heard. The President's brother wasn't appointing any Boy Scouts here. Nhu's chief advisor blinked a lot, smiled a lot, bowed a lot, but still gave Carson the feeling he was getting measured for a box, a strange twist of perspective. *Carson* was the one who usually gave that impression, at least in the mind of Willy Carson.

"Why the family of Dao, Mr. Carson?" Ky could hardly speak through his face-filling smile. "Why are you so interested in these people?"

Willy, still bone-weary from his flight from San Francisco to Bangkok to Saigon, didn't feel like fielding any of Ky's subtle bullcrap. "Does that really matter, Mr. Sang? Considering Mr. Bryan's history of helping you-"

"-Just curious, Mr. Carson. Just curious. We don't really care about the Dao family one way or the other."

"Then why not just do what Mr. Bryan asked? We started this with your stooges almost a damned year ago." Willy waved off the tray of cigarettes that Sang offered. "Once you take care of the Dao situation, Mr. Bryan wants you to know that you, personally, will be remembered for this."

"I would look forward to meeting Mr. Bryan."

*

That went off easier than expected, Willy Carson thought during his cab ride back to Tan Son Nhut Airport. Took one god-awful long time to get to the right man, but all's well now, he figured.

Willy wondered how Harry was doing on his end with Apollo.

Not this good, he'd bet.

*

In the campus hangout called Dude's a string of low-wattage lamps gave the interior a spatial yellow fustiness. Beer, wine, sandwiches along the back wall. Redwood benches and carved-up tables, a stale-smelling place. A juke box played Ellington's "Mood Indigo" in one corner.

Harry Crosse picked Dude's for his second meeting with Ram because he liked this college atmosphere. And he wanted to meet Bryan's prey in a neutral place, one-on-one, just out of curiosity.

When Apollo came in, Harry realized that the man was taller, maybe a lot taller, than Harry's conception of the size of the average Latino. That figured, from what he knew about Ram's father. Harry made a mental note to put Ram's father next on his list, although there was no hurry for that phase of his program.

Apollo was wearing levis and a red lumberman's shirt, large and loose over his wide-shouldered frame. "What can I do for you, Mr. Crosse?"

Harry tried to smile. "Just felt like some conversation, Sergeant. You ever feel like just making conversation?"

"No."

"Figures. Anyway, Mr. Bryan sometimes sends me on these things, these *chores*, you might call them..."

"Mr. Bryan *always* sends you on these chores, Mr. Crosse."

"Not to this particular meeting."

"What's on your mind?"

"Well, let's see if I can explain this right." The sergeant was indeed a cold soul, thought Harry. Here's John Bryan gearing up some kind of rock crusher to grind this pebble, relatively speaking, and the man can't wait to get to it. "Bryan gave me express orders to mess up your life, which I will do, sooner or later. He pays me very well for it, and I *do* like the money-"

"-Why all the honesty?"

"Why *not* all the honesty? You plan to sue me?"

"You do like the money, except?"

"Except when I joined him, I never... I didn't figure on this kind of crap, frankly." Harry still tried to talk with these throaty eastern vowels, his own business-school inflection. "Don't misunderstand me, I do plan to carry out my orders, eventually." He stopped to think about his proposition. "I thought we might work out some kind of arrangement, in the meantime."

"Arrangement."

"Try to keep everyone happy while postponing your fate, my friend, for as long as we can."

"You want to go through the motions of screwing me around, as a show for your boss."

"Something like that." Now that Harry was verbalizing the idea, he realized it *did* sound a little stupid. "Hear me out on this, would you?"

Ram leaned toward him. "Listen carefully, amigo. You want to play games with your boss, and it keeps him out of my hair awhile? Okay by me. I don't give a crap whether he thinks you're working me over, but I don't want to be bothered with any *plan*."

"There's always another alternative, you know. I could just carry out my orders."

"That would complicate *both* our lives, amigo."

The man is truly loco, thought Harry. "Maybe you don't understand how rough a man like Bryan can get, if it suits him."

Ram had closed the subject. His gaze stayed on Harry Crosse a moment, then moved to another corner of the room. "You see the table over there, the empty one--not even a napkin holder on it?"

Harry turned and looked. Now what?

"A famous television comedian comes in and sits there almost every day," said Ram. "Big white-haired guy, I forget his name. Son's dying of a lung disease at the university hospital and he comes in every day, after visiting him. Just sits there and drinks beer."

"What's your point?"

Ram took a long measure of the room's atmosphere. "You say Bryan plans to make it rough? Hell, people like Bryan don't know rough."

"Very touching." But the connection was lost on Harry. "Whatever, Bryan's going to a lot of effort in preparing whatever he *does* have planned. All that construction, for instance--"

"He's preparing that for me?"

"He's preparing his 'proof' there for you."

"The man's nutty, Harry."

Harry half-nodded. "Probably true, but till he gets put away and all those per-diems stop rolling in, those bodyguards and I are staying real tight with him, bet your ass on that." He handed Ram his local business card. "This's my address whenever I'm down here, in case you want to talk about this. I stay on the company yacht, the 'Dominator,' at the L.A. Marina."

Harry tried to think of how to end this in an appropriately threatening vein. "If we work together we can put off your punishment, Sergeant, at least for a while."

"You consider yourself a dangerous man, then, Mr. Crosse?"

"Not as dangerous as you probably are, Sergeant Apollo, but Bryan hires people who are much more dangerous than me."

"You planning on scaring me to death? That the reason for this meeting?"

"With those guys, death would be the easy part."

Harry remained in Dude's after Ram left, and he saw the famous comedian come in as Ram had described, taking his place at the table in the corner. Harry was still thinking about his plan, it still felt like a workable idea until that famous comedian came in.

The tall, graying, red-haired man put the shadow of reality over Harry's plan, and Harry thought, Did I really think I'd fool John Bryan with some half-assed arrangement with Apollo? And does Bryan really think he can put the fear of God into this stone faced bastard?

The famous comedian poured beer into his schooner like sacramental wine, folded his forearms on the table and put his head into them.

For a real opponent I need someone who worries about staying healthy, who offers *resistance*. Matching up against this sergeant is like jousting with a waterfall.

Harry had to leave. The famous comedian, whenever he lifted his head, seemed to look right at him.

Chapter 18

The late fall winds pattered down the canyonways of the Santa Monica mountains, the last of the Santa Annas passing through. They warmed and dried the runty green shack in Beverly Glen Canyon. They pushed agreeably on the boarded walls, whispered leaves to their earth bedding.

Ram hadn't heard from John Bryan or Harry Crosse for almost a year. It had been a period of renewal for him because here at the university, he thought, there was always the chance to...do what? Find My Linh's Touchstone? He had to smile at that idea. Once long ago he had played with the thought of firming up a set of ideals, but those were ground up nicely in the crucibles of East L.A., and Korea.

That idea had faded away.

He was studying on the porch-platform overlooking the miniature wooded canyon. He needed to hold down the pages until, toward dusk, the bluster of air settled back, became cooler. He drank instant coffee with cheap harsh-tasting brandy in it and he felt sleepy, but sleep wasn't such a bad effect of booze, he figured. It sure beat running through whorehouse walls.

He was fascinated by the woods of Beverly Glen Canyon. They had the feel of the Japanese shrine gardens, and he began sipping the brandy without the coffee, to lock in their contentment they brought.

Economics II and Philosophy I, Keynesian demand curves, Cartesian geometric planes. Descartes: The only thing that can't be doubted is that you exist. Doubt your existence and you must then exist as the doubter... Ram poured more brandy, and thought, *Cuidado amigo*, you know how badly you handle firewater. Though it does expand my appreciation of this view, does it not?

Most certainly does. The trees, towering green demons, danced above him. He swiveled side to side to take in the diorama of his canyon and didn't allow the new addition to disrupt that until the second or third pass-by, when the oddness of someone watching him began to sink in. He planted himself, allowed his eyes to settle on the figure.

The dusk blended the shadows about the man, but Ram could still see him clearly enough. The flax-like material of his coat, the blue striped tie. The man's hands hung knuckles-forward, his wrists showed beneath the ends of his sleeves. A tall man, lean, scrubbed, white, middle-aged, face dappled in hollows and ridges.

Ram folded his hands across his belt, for he couldn't think of anything else to do. He couldn't think of anything to say. He tried to contemplate the man who, in turn, was contemplating him.

"I expected you someday," were the only dumbass words he could come up with. "Maybe not exactly like this..." Ram tried to keep his thoughts together. "The black man found you, didn't he?"

"A black messenger, yes. He told me about you." The man pointed a long and craggy finger at the house. "I knocked at your door in front."

"Couldn't hear it. Wind's too noisy back here." Ram was confused by the hint of anger he felt at his first sight of this man. Made no sense, he'd always thought this was the one person on earth he needed to meet.

"You've been refreshing yourself," said the visitor. "Do you drink much?"

"I don't do *anything* much. Mainly I don't drink much. I don't handle liquor real well."

"I understand your grades are quite high, even with the drinking."

"Well, hell..." Ram started to get up, popping the tight place in his spine, but instead changed his sitting position. "I don't drink *that* much. But you're right, I do pretty good in school."

"I would expect you to." The man put his hands in his pockets and stepped back, making a gesture with his whole body, withdrawing. Hard to tell what he was doing in this light.

"Your black messenger claimed to be in the employ of John Bryan the industrialist, but they don't sound like friends of yours." The wind was only a gentle westerly zephyr but the man seemed to lean into it to hold his footing. "But at least they told me about you," he said. "I should be thankful to them."

"You really a professor of quantum physics? I've been wanting to talk with you for awhile now."

"I'm still only an associate professor. Experimental condensed matter physics. My conclusions are too eccentric, I suppose, for anyone to recommend me for tenure. What are you reading?"

"This damned Descartes."

"Everything analyzed to the one simplest component."

"That agree with quantum?"

"Yes."

"Individual existence is the only thing that can be proven--that agree with quantum?"

"Yes. Without an individual observer, everything else only potentially exists."

"I drink, therefore I am," mumbled Ram.

"*Cogito, ergo sum*," said the professor, dryly, apparently needing to change the subject. "The black messenger said Bryan employs him to keep in touch with you. What does he want from you?"

"My mind, sir. He wants me to admit my sins." This was not the conversation Ram imagined having in their first meeting. It was not the conversation he wanted to have, but his mind was clouding up on him.

"Is he succeeding?"

"Don't know. Someday, if the black man doesn't succeed, Bryan will send bigger, more convincing people to discuss it with me."

"And you're not afraid of them?"

"I try to avoid feelings."

The professor shuffled and looked at his feet and clasped his hands in front of him. "Perhaps that's hereditary, in a way, though you've become a soldier, I understand. Just the opposite of myself." The tall homely man didn't know what to do with his hands, he tried them in his pockets. He stared up at the eucalyptus trees. "Your grandfather was a warrior too, a member of the Black Watch--have you heard of them? A McAlpin of the Clan Cameron, a real pride to our family."

"Not to *my* family, señor."

"No, not to your family, of course."

"McAlpin?" The name sorted through Ram's mind. "My name's Apollo."

"Yes, an interesting homology in names. Your mother showed admirable creativity-"

"-Came off the marquee of a movie theater."

"Admirable creativity, nonetheless." His father was slipping into the obscure dusk, the man was dissolving to a dark silhouette. Only the hint of a thick brow ridge, the hint of a rather long, thin nose.

"Who cares what we call ourselves," said Ram.

The silhouette remained still. "You have a point, of course," Ram heard him say. "Indifference can be a wonderful shield. I wish I had such a shield."

"I always thought you were the *king* of indifference, sir..." Ram stopped himself. His words probably hurt the man; he didn't want to do that.

"I failed both your mother and you, as I have failed in most things," said the man. "I am not a person of strong will."

"Sorry, I didn't mean that."

"I just felt you'd want to know your ancestry."

"Screw the Scotch ancestry, professor. I don't need to hear about my white ancestry. That's never been part of me."

"*Scottish* ancestry," Professor McAlpin took a step back. "I teach at LaCroix College. When you are more sober, perhaps, I hope to explain myself to you. I'd like to have a good sober conversation with you."

Ram considered a few responses to that, decided to give none of them. Dr. McAlpin liked to punish himself, it sounded like, and Ram had no desire to make this meeting too rough on him. He poured brandy into a second cup. "There's a lot of things I need to learn from you, professor. How d'you like your brandy?"

Dr. McAlpin was no longer there. He had retraced his steps through the thicket. Large-fingered leaves tumbled where he stood. Ram heard only the quiet groan of the taller evergreens now, and they sang of temples and wars and vendettas, and the natural mystery and of strangers on hills who called down to him, and Chinese boys who disintegrated as they ran to him.

They sang of faceless men with bayonets.

The quiet hiss of the evergreens hinted that behind these events there lay purpose, and its answer had come much closer now.

**.

February 15, 1956

Ram:

I was kind of surprised to get that note from you. It was kind of short, of course – to be expected from the Silent Sergeant, I guess – but sure better than never hearing anything from you.

Sorry for the delay with this response. The Bao Dai government let me go to Geneva for a while during the partitioning talks and then called me back here. Still have my position in the Undersecretary's office but this new president, Diem, took away any real authority from our family. Feels like we're under house arrest. Father says he expected it.

Your line about finally getting to Vietnam is a ray of hope. You going to make it? We really need to tell someone what's going on here but it sure as hell can't come from me. (I'm asking an Army pilot friend to mail this from Manila, in fact.)

This new President already started purges against the Buddhist sects and the Caodai (followers of the Cao Dai deity, like me). Already a lot of the Caodai and Hoa Hao sects needed to join forces with the Binh Xuyen--the Binh Xuyen are just a band of criminals, for God's sake. Anyway, the combined forces have taken over portions of the country where the ARVN soldiers just won't go. They're pretty much in control of the An Loc and Loc

Ninh sectors, near the Cambodian border. It's damn near a full-out war again.

Now out of nowhere a couple of Bao Dai ministers are hinting that my father, for one, is working with the communists. No proof at all! That's typical.

Regarding that Geneva meeting, the Bao Dai government came out amazingly well. The south came out with more land than they <u>had control of!</u> Figure that one out. Anyway, the agreement calls for nationwide elections to reunify the country before July. Chances of Diem keeping that promise are real unlikely.

How's the spy business going? (Bad wording!) Better yet, how's the "military scholarship" going? You didn't mention school in the little note you sent.

My sister My Linh has asked about you (a lot!). You made quite an impression on her. (Darned if I know why.) She's really looking forward to seeing you if this Army thing works out. I'd like to see you or <u>someone</u> get her out of here, if you could. This country is heading for disaster.

I know you don't want to hear it but recently we located an old Viet Minh supply tunnel full of M-2 carbines. A huge cache of weapons. They didn't ink out the supplier's name on the crates and guess whose mark was there. Right. Bryan Munitions. Doesn't give us complete proof, though, without some kind of shipping orders to match them up with. But the communists must keep some kind of paperwork, somewhere, and I plan to find it.

You'd love Saigon, if you can get here. The countryside is beautiful and Saigon has lots of hot night spots. (The saloon walls are easier to knock down, too. Some of them are made of paper.)

Hope to see you soon.

Your friend,
Dao Kim Chau

P.S.: What's that last line in your note?—"I met my father, and he really is a professor of physics." My God, is that all you're going to tell me? What the hell's his name? Does he really teach that quantum stuff?

* *

The campus of LaCroix College was a small version of UCLA. Unassuming parks, botanical gardens, glass and brownstone buildings

117

radiating from the quad to the parking lots, sullied over by the dome of bronze haze along the east end of the San Gabriel Valley.

"It's like a flower bed in a prison, isn't it?" said Ian McAlpin, attempting a smile at his son. "They plan to extend the facilities here. Big city influence coming in, lots of concrete." The smile wouldn't hold. "*Mutatis mutande,*" he mumbled to himself. "We're becoming a city."

"Cities aren't all that bad," Ram answered. "Sure as hell not this one, if you call this a city."

"I suppose not." McAlpin felt a surge of his lifelong angst. He couldn't imagine any seed of *his* surviving in mid-city Los Angeles. "The inner city seems like such a precarious existence."

"Precarious?"

They had met an hour earlier at the front of the Physics Building, where Ram listened quietly to the thinly masked apologia of Ian McAlpin. It was Sunday afternoon, the campus was almost deserted. "More concrete, more change," sighed Professor McAlpin, holding to his topic. He didn't want this talk to get personal. "You said you were studying physics?"

"Not a whole lot, not yet."

"No, of course not." Dr. McAlpin gave Ram a sliding glance as they walked. "You wouldn't be getting into theoretical physics, not into quantum mechanics, not for awhile yet."

"I tried to read it once. Wasn't very successful."

"You need the basics first. It's an awfully mysterious subject." McAlpin tried to affect a fatherly smile again. It didn't work. "Not even comprehensible in terms of western logic. The basic material of existence doesn't follow physical laws. It drives everyone crazy." The spreading mat of beige-box tract houses kept distracting Doctor McAlpin: Such intrusion, he thought. Spillage from the Los Angeles megapolis... "The basic particles, at random, come from and go back into *nowhere*. In fact they don't even *come* from nowhere, since they're non-existent to begin with. Does that make any sense?"

"Not much."

"It gets worse. At quantum level all laws of physics--the *real* world-- just plain fall apart. Things seem to be real, made up of particles and such, unless no one is looking at them. Then they go back to being *fields*, sort of. They go back to being a kind of nothing." Doctor McAlpin recognized this as a variation on the same chant he'd been singing for the last twenty-five years, and wondered if these words had meaning for anyone else. "A world falls into place only for those within its own dimension."

Anyway, Doctor McAlpin was enjoying this conversation with his new-found son.

"For its observers," said Ram.

"That's the exactly appropriate word," said Dr. McAlpin. They walked through a botanical study of vividly green fern, broadleaf maple, darkening cedar boughs. The air in here had the ionic freshness of a river cavern.

"Would you say that the world...is just one of a whole lot of forms in this quanta? Like statues in a block of marble?"

"Well, yes." Doctor McAlpin couldn't think for a moment. These concepts took him *years* to develop in the minds of his students. "Infinite worlds are in there, all at the same time, but each observer can see only the world that *he's* in. How did you think of the block of marble?"

"That's how a Vietnamese girl explained it to me."

"A Vietnamese *girl?*"

"A student priest of a Vietnamese religion." Ram studied his father with more attention now than the professor really wanted. "The marble idea's part of her belief."

"Except now it's been scientifically *proven*, although I think of it more like a foam. Each universe sort of shakes through this foam until one combination fits the world-path for each observer inside it."

"Shakes through infinite combinations?" Ram scratched the side of his face. "Seems like that would take awhile."

"Time is an illusion too. My colleagues here consider some of these ideas as obsessive--I carry their logic too far, maybe--which is one reason I'm...why I'm not very accepted here, I suppose." McAlpin paused long enough to get rid of that idea. "Where did this Vietnamese girl come up with the block of marble concept? She read the theory somewhere?"

"She probably never heard of quanta, professor."

"Remarkable," said the professor. "A natural mind flowering amid the paddies of Cochin-China, coming to the same conclusions the physics *immortals* came to in Brussels, the 'Copenhagen Interpretation'..." McAlpin was too flustered to remember the date of the Copenhagen Interpretation. "Quantum agrees completely with the Tao now, isn't that amazing? Each living thing is the creator of its own universe. A lot of quantum physicists are taking up Buddhist meditation in fact since western science has gone as far as it can in trying to understand this through any normal..." He caught himself and smiled again, weakly. "Sorry if I over-talk. I do that sometimes. Part of my basic anxiety."

Ram didn't answer.

"Quantum even proves there's a God now," said Dr. McAlpin. "Because if the forms of quanta are infinite, then anything that can be imagined within it, even a God-dimension, is not only possible, it is completely indisputable. For that same reason there *must* be life after death--do you see that?"

"That's a little steep-"

"-But *everything* is explained, even the Big Bang." Doctor McAlpin needed to quicken his step now to keep up with Ram. "An observer who's part of any formation would require a history to fall into place within the foam, extending itself all the way back to the Big Bang. My word, we *create* the Big Bang ourselves, the ultimate solipsism, just by being here. The absolute anthropic... Does this sound crazy?"

For the first time since they met, Ram smiled back at his father. "That's why I'm here, professor."

"Well, it's true. Something coming from nothing never made sense, and now we know something never *did* come from nothing. We're not really here at all. The imaginers are even imagining *themselves* into existence--isn't that amazing?"

"Sounds like what this girl was saying."

The comment broke McAlpin's concentration. He slowed down, pushed at the grass with his shoe. "Well, not many others...Around here I'm considered a strange man with strange ideas, although I'd wither and die outside this campus. But I don't seem to fit all that well *inside* either, do I?" Doctor McAlpin fell into step with Ram again, stopping himself from putting a hand on Ram's shoulder. "The religion of this girl prophet, what does it *do* with her block of marble idea? Since we're all in this illusion together, what do we do now?"

"I don't... Something about appreciating the other observers stuck in here with us, I think."

"Celebrate having fellow observers with us in our *particular* illusion--a moral value from the quantum theory. Imagine that."

"I don't think she meant any scientific-"

"-From the rice paddies of Indo-China--incredible."

Ram let it pass. My Linh was a college graduate from the landlord class. She sure as hell didn't fit the harvest-girl image his father was dreaming up.

"She's much like you, I'd say," said his father. "From the paddies and the barrios..." The thought trailed away. "Your circumstances were entirely my fault, of course. I never told my wife about you, but it didn't matter after all. She left me anyway, a long time ago." He directed his stare at his feet while he walked. His heels shuffled. "How is your mother?"

"She manages a restaurant. She's okay."

"I met her when she was a waitress."

"I know." They reached the stairs leading to the quad and its surrounding gardens, and walked alongside the stern red brick of the Physics Building. "Apollo, a euphemism for McAlpin. Highly appropriate for you but certainly not for me, although in Scotland McAlpin was a *grand* name, according to my own father. He was a war hero--did I mention that?" Doctor McAlpin was trying to control his rush of words. "I tried to call your mother once," he said, "after she told me she was expecting."

"We made it okay, professor."

"Even against men like Bryan? I still don't understand why he's after you?"

"He thinks I killed his son."

"I don't believe that." Doctor McAlpin thought he felt a chill pass through the grove of pine as Ram mentioned the killing, and he reminded himself that his son, like Ram's grandfather, had been in war. They lived in a world violent and foreign to someone like Ian McAlpin. "But if your girl prophet says we should appreciate each other, what does she say about these dangerous people? Should you do violence against them?"

"It's more like...something to do with sacrifice."

"Sacrifice?"

"She called it the Touchstone." Ram wished he'd paid more attention to My Linh's words, he could barely remember them now. "Everyone needs to help make this...whatever this is, this dimension, a good place to be in. Fight the bad guys if necessary. Even sacrifice yourself if necessary."

"And that's our dharma. I could agree with that, though most of us are not courageous enough to sacrifice ourselves."

"Most of us are not *dumb* enough to sacrifice ourselves, professor. Sure as hell not me."

*

Sure as hell not me, he thought, later, although everything these people said did kind of fall into place: religion and science both ganging up inside his head. Sacrifice for the common good as an end in itself? Maybe, he thought, but first show me someone who does that in real life, then I'll look into it.

Chapter 19

Man's highest joy is in victory: to conquer one's enemies, to deprive them of their possessions, to ride their horses, to embrace their wives and daughters.

-Genghis Khan

Jonathan Bryan was not a well man, Harry reminded himself of this for the hundredth time as he read, maybe for the hundredth time, the credo on the wall of Bryan's yacht. Bryan had given the plaque to Harry in better times. In fact Bryan once told Harry, in better times, that he, Bryan, could well be the incarnation of the great Genghis. Harry was not sure that was just the old man's attempt at a joke.

Harry'd hung that credo up as if it were a joke, though, but lately... first there came Bryan's near-total seclusion in the fortress, then this imagined paralysis in his legs and then his damn-near adoption of Willy Carson as some kind of son-figure, a surrogate--a *replacement*, for God's sake--for his son Dan. And now this obsession about Ramirez Apollo and whatever the hell that strange construction around the fortress was all about. Bryan had huddled with his own private contractors over that construction for about three years now without even a wink to anyone about what he was doing, except maybe to the contractors. Maybe not even to them.

Bryan used to keep himself fairly composed, at least it seemed so to Harry, but now every meeting with the man was getting a little more weird: "What's going wrong with me, Harry? What is...I know this man was actually *not* sent here by my... He is certainly not the Angel of Death, I *know* that, Harry, most of the time. But then my brain seems to go backwards--do you understand me?" Bryan did seem to recognize the problem, at least in his more lucid moments: "I do appreciate the way you've been running the company, I want you to know that, Harry, because lately I feel like...I'm not really part of all this."

"You don't need to be a part, Mr. Bryan. You hire others to be a part." Harry was standing before Bryan in the salon of the *Dominator*, watching Bryan try to connect the threads of his mind.

"Do you think I'm losing my mind, Harry?"

"No, sir. You seem just fine to me." Harry waited for John Bryan to finish. This rambling speech had been going on, sporadically, since the old man's arrival at Cloverfield Airport.

"This Apollo, for instance. He goes on in his college as if... He pays no mind at all to our threats." Bryan's mood was switching again, getting petulant. "For instance this--what do you *mean* they won't expel him from that university?" He made a small choleric whack with his cane against the teak cabinet, tinkling the glasses inside. The attending steward, blacker than Harry, removed the salad plate from Bryan's table and hurried it off to the galley.

"I told them about his background, sir, but I can't provide proof, any real reason-"

"-No more of your excuses, Harry. I gave you and Kenneth your assignments and only *he* has shown results." The old man gave Carson an acknowledging nod before sawing into his breast of chicken--skinned, unsalted, no sauce. Like watching a man chew rope. "Would you like to know what Kenneth is doing to that Chinaman's family?"

"I don't need to know, Mr. Bryan."

Bryan shook his fork toward Harry. "Kenneth puts my God-given power to its best use, Harry. Meanwhile, despite all the money I've given that university, you can't get this one favor in return?"

"As long as he stays in that school, Mr. Bryan, we know where he is," said Harry. He waited to see if Bryan would buy that.

Bryan was considering it. "Perhaps so. We do need to keep track of him, I suppose. Know right where he is, so when the time comes we can make him see my proof."

Harry knew better than to ask what that last statement meant, but the subject of the university reminded him: "I've found Apollo's father. Turns out he's a professor at LaCroix College."

"His father?"

"And his mother."

"Then we go after *them*," came Willy Carson's voice. Carson stayed in the corner, like always, like a nesting cobra.

"We'd never consider going after anyone's mother, Kenneth," said Bryan. "You know better than that."

"Just a thought." Carson's eyes went to Harry. "If you want, though, I could take a crack at the Mexican. No offense, Mr. Crosse, but the school might've thought you were just one of Mr. Bryan's servants, or something."

"How would you like your butt kicked, little man."

123

"Harry!" Bryan held a protective arm in front of Willy Carson. "What in heaven is *wrong* with you? Kenneth's suggestions were...he is only trying to help us with this, Harry."

Carson hooked a thumb in his waistband.

"Sorry." Harry had ruled out kicking Willy Carson's butt anyway. Carson usually carried that big turquoise knife with him, Harry knew. Somewhere in his waistband, apparently.

"You must choose your words more carefully, Harry." Bryan patted Willy's spider-monkey arm and held up Harry's most recent three-page memorandum. "These memos on your plans for Apollo, for instance, Harry, they are rabbit spit. We are pestering the murderer of my son with pellet guns. We should be using *cannons* on this man."

"I'll use more cannons, Mr. Bryan." And Harry thought, it was ever thus, trapped in my own candy-ass corner again, sending memos about how much shit I've been putting on a prey that probably forgot he was being chased. "I'll check out what I can do at his father's college."

"Don't divert yourself from that sergeant, hear? You work on him. You scare him. You turn his mind into pudding until I'm ready to see him."

"Into pudding, yes sir." Harry decided that he couldn't stay in this cabin any longer. He started toward the door.

"You worry me, Harry," said Bryan, after him. "You worry me a great deal, don't you want to know why?"

Harry did not want to know why.

Something's throwing me off stride, thought Harry Crosse, as he came topside. For Christ's sake I've got no desire to commit financial suicide, not after putting this much distance between me and them South Central alleys, but this is turning into a hatchet assignment and I just don't want to listen to what I've *got to do*, not right now.

Curiously, Harry appreciated Ramirez Apollo. Glimmers of defiance within the world-cesspool, a follower of some unwritten law. Harry could identify with someone who kept that cool, ignoring Bryan's threats like they were just so much dog shit.

That was cool. That was insane, but cool.

*

Weissman spent the morning painting this sign which read "Wee Hoose," made for the space above the door of their battered grey cabin. He embellished the lavender letters with serifs along each edge and was admiring the job when he heard, felt, the purr of Claire Bryan's car in the driveway. "Your lady friend's here," he said through the door, and went inside, and listened to the click of heels on the flagstone stairway. The sound itself was almost a sexual experience, Luke thought, even with *my* confused sexuality. I like *all* genders, I guess.

A small wobbly distraction was following her. A tow-headed child, cantering behind her, galloping up the slope like a colt.

"Does Ramirez Apollo live here?"

"Most of the time, Mrs. Bryan. Go on in." Luke went to his bedroom before Ram came to the door.

The brush of her lips on Ram's mouth had a taste of bourbon. "Come on up, Sean." She turned to wave her son closer. "All the way up here, now." Sean came, stood, let her straighten his corduroy trousers, while Ram held the door open for them. "Luke gave me your phone message."

"Needed to talk with someone, Ram. Everything's going so Jesus-Christ wrong." She stopped to read the little sign next to Ram, and he smelled the ginger-sweetness of her perfume. "Reminds me of a little sign my family once had on our house," she said. "In our front patio--I ever tell you how rich my family used to be?"

"C'mon in."

"Do you know what it's like to be rich, Ram?" She leaned back to let Sean past her. "If your parents don't go bankrupt and die on you, anything above that is rich... You never met my son, did you? This is Mister Apollo, Sean."

The boy kept his head down, shook hands, hurled himself toward the front room couch.

"You have anything to drink in here?" Claire looked toward the kitchen. "I need a stiff glass of anything."

"Stiff is the specialty of the house."

"I've had to kiss the world's ass lately. Need a real stiff drink to get rid of the taste." She stared at a light rectangle on the wall where a picture used to hang, white on white, portrait-size. "The son of a bitch is still trying to take Sean from me."

"Threats are Bryan's way of life, Claire." Ram glanced at the boy as he brought her a brandy. It was the only liquor left in the cupboard. "He'd need a hell of reason to get custody."

"His lawyers claim I'm a drug addict, among a mess of other things." Claire's voice was rasping now, beginning to break up. "Even got an affidavit from a pusher I used to...Lord Jesus, it's a real horrible report."

"It's pure crap, Claire." Ram tried putting a hand on her arm. "You and the boy will survive, trust me. I know about survival."

"Nobody really *kicks* the stuff, actually." Claire held the glass tight while the boy tried to pull her fingers away. "Bryan knows it. He's expert at finding what kind of stuff you're on, and everyone's on *something*, according to him. Sooner or later he finds out what you're on."

"He gets his kicks out of playing God." Ram watched her son's pawing against her face for a moment, then leaned toward Weissman's door. "Luke, could you do me a favor?"

"What kind?" Luke's muffled voice.

"Walk Claire's boy to the Four Oaks for a soda or something, would you? I need to talk with Claire."

"I need to study."

"It's important, Luke. A few minutes."

"What am I?" said Luke, opening the door a crack. "I look like a nanny?"

"It's important, just a few minutes."

Luke came out, a piece of him at a time, and stared down at the stocky blonde kid. The boy returned the look with impossible honesty and Luke vacillated, mugged his annoyance, held out his hand. "You feel like a malted milk, boy? Just down the block?" Sean looked toward his mother.

"It's okay, Sean. Malted milk sounds awfully good right now."

Claire watched them until they had walked past the corner. "Wouldn't it be nice just to get up and go out for a malted milk? That sounds so nice." She sipped on the brandy instead. "In comparison to *my* life, anyway. All because of this Willy Carson. Little rat-bastard got an affidavit from a dealer I used in San Francisco."

"That's history, for Christ's sake."

"Bryan claims I'm still on it, and I'm *not*, but he thinks he can prove anything he wants to prove."

"You're not still living up there?"

"No, hell no. I've moved to L.A. now--which reminds me, Mrs. Bingham's going to keep Sean for awhile, while I... I'll give you her number, in case--though Bryan knows where she lives too. Christ, how can anyone fight people like him?"

"It's not impossible, Claire." He took her hands, which had a surprisingly firm grip. "I've been thinking, in San Francisco you mentioned something about those files, that special department...hey, you listening?"

"You know what the affidavit says? Says I even made it with this pusher once, to get fixed. He had...perfumed hair."

"I'd just as soon not hear this."

She shuddered, and wiped her face. "The files? What's there to tell? Bryan Industries is an arms dealer. All kinds of sneaky crap goes on in those files."

"You know where they keep the ones on Indo-China?"

"That's a special department."

"There's a chance they might be of help." Ram tried to think where he was going with this.

"How in the world could *I* get them?"

"Your name's still Bryan, isn't it? Doesn't that get you into Bryan Industries?"

"You think *blackmail* would stop John Bryan?" She raised the glass, tinkled the ice in the remaining brandy, and finished it. "You don't really know who we're dealing with, do you?"

"We're dealing with just one sick old bastard, Claire. You think you could get back in there?"

"Unless he gave instructions to keep me out, but he'd have no reason to think... I could fly up there tomorrow, if there's any chance-"

"-Stop and think about it a minute, first. You might be getting into some real spooky territory here."

"How much worse can it get?" She started to lift the glass again, saw it was empty now, and held its coldness against her cheek. "That pusher, he brought some friends with him once. Wanted to show me off, wanted to pass me around."

"I said I'd rather not hear it, Claire."

"I might even have enjoyed it, who the hell knows? God, I don't even remember." Claire was staring at the white square on the wall. "I'm so very...so damned depraved."

"Screw it." The subject was beginning to sting. He got up and went to the kitchen.

"Maybe it's only what I deserve," he heard her say.

He poured the last of the brandy for himself. He needed to wash away that picture, the smirking pimps unzipping...the slut Claire Bryan humping pushers and gang-bangers for a fix. He could picture the hairy melee, the raised organs, the smirking pimps rolling into Claire's open legs, bringing on this moronic useless anger in him.

"I'm sorry," she said from the other room. "I'm sorry. We won't talk about it." He took another breath and went back in.

As he sat, she rested her head against him. "I needed to make that confession to someone, Ram, you understand? You probably understand everything." She nestled her cheek into his neck. "I'll repay you, if you want." And he wondered if he could take advantage of her even now, this satin creature.

Probably. Probably. The same genital ache would always win out in him too.

Just another one of the smirking pimps.

Chapter 20

The president of LaCroix College, Conrad Beane--Reverend Conrad Beane--was a man Bryan Industries could do business with. Harry Crosse was sure of this.

In recent years the LaCroix cash flow had hemorrhaged badly until Beane found a new way of raising money, in the blossoming art of television preaching. It worked beyond expectations. It hauled LaCroix College from the jaws of bankruptcy, for which efforts the president had made a few unsubtle suggestions that the college name should be changed, maybe to *Conrad Beane* College. Fat chance, thought Harry, but at least he knew where Conrad Beane's hot button was.

"Mr. Beane will see you now," said his receptionist.

"Mr. Crosse, I believe," said Mr. Beane, adjusting steel glasses along an old skinny nose bridge, focusing his eyes on Harry's blackness--the receptionist apparently hadn't warned the president about his visitor's blackness. "You're an associate of John Bryan?"

"Correct, sir," said Harry. "Mr. Bryan, a man of strong religious faith himself, as you know, is a great admirer of your work here."

Conrad Beane perked up. "Well, praise indeed. Do come in." The president ushered Harry to a room much less imposing than Harry had expected. No burl inlays in the desk, no panels, no moldings. The one blonde desk centered the room, facing two chairs of burgundy vinyl, stamped to look like leather.

"Please, sit," said President Beane. Harry sat, and brusquely, deliberately, began tapping on the stiff leather of his briefcase. "An envoy from Mr. John Bryan," said Beane, "does pique our curiosity, as you can imagine."

Yes, thought Harry, I've got the right man. "As I said, your work here has been of great interest to Mr. Bryan."

"Yes, a man of strong religious convictions, I understand. A great benefactor."

"And a great philanthropist, Mr. Beane. Philanthropy, in fact, would be the key word for my visit here." Harry pretended a search through his papers to allow the president time to chew on that word, then took his self-written memo off the top. "Mr. Bryan would like to show his thanks to you, for the education of young Christian leaders."

128

"Indeed?" President Beane stopped just short of rubbing his hands together. "We would certainly enjoy having the Bryan Foundation as part of our family. You were thinking of a grant?"

"More than a grant, President Beane," said Harry. He paused to bask for a moment in the tension he was creating here. "He's been thinking of establishing a chair for one and a half million dollars. Half a million now, half a million more each year for the next two years."

Conrad Beane straightened up, splitting his cheeks in a perfect, great-toothed smile. "Mr. Bryan is known for his generosity. What a fine gesture, Mr. Crosse."

"We felt this might be appreciated," said Harry Crosse, and he thought, This works out nicely. Bryan gets his spiritual kicks by dumping money on Bible-thumpers anyway. "And we want to make sure that you personally, Doctor Beane, receive credit for securing this donation."

"Well, that isn't really..." Conrad Beane couldn't hide his astonishment, this would make him a *hero* in the eyes of *Conrad Beane* College. "I've never sought recognition for my work here, Lord knows-"

"-But we do have one problem to work out, which has been a cause of concern to Mr. Bryan. He's like that, you know, ha, ha. He does have his quirks."

President Beane laughed with him, without grasping the humor. "I suppose he does, Mr. Crosse. But...what are we discussing here?"

"It's somewhat delicate. A delicate subject." Harry leaned forward and waited for Beane to follow suit, which he did. "You understand, as I say, the deep convictions of a man like Mr. Bryan. Such matters as proper conduct among the people he donates to is of major importance."

"Certainly none of our staff could be accused--"

Harry waved his hands in front of him. "No no, President Beane, we checked you and your staff, we find no problem with any of you, none whatever." Harry looked over his shoulder, to add a little drama here. "But we do find a problem among one of your faculty, Dr. Beane."

"Faculty?"

"It concerns a Professor McAlpin--in your Physics Department?"

"McAlpin? Dr. McAlpin is not a full professor, up for tenure now as a matter of fact, but he's in his early fifties, you know-"

"-Been here twenty-three years and never received tenure?"

"You would need to know the man. I rarely speak with him myself--I run more with the *belles-lettres* people myself--but the provost of our physics staff says he takes a rather, ah, bizarre approach to the subject. An almost mystical approach, but no one ever questioned his *morality*."

"Were you aware, Mr. President, that during Professor McAlpin's marriage, while a member of your faculty, he carried on clandestine meetings with a Mexican waitress in Los Angeles, and fathered a boy with her, then deserted *both* of them?"

President Beane registered the appropriate response, a raising of brows, but he was obviously confused. Why would the peccadilloes of one professor effect a donation to the whole college? Harry could see the president was missing the point.

"That comes as a great shock indeed," said President Beane. "But surely the larking of just one member of our faculty-"

"-This member is important to Mr. Bryan, President Beane. So much so, in fact, that he'd probably need to reconsider his offer if such a man were allowed to remain here."

"Isn't that rather harsh?" Conrad Beane was beginning to understand, thought Harry. At last. "This must have happened a long time ago. McAlpin's wife left him maybe ten years ago."

Harry leaned back, made a tching sound between his teeth. "Immorality doesn't diminish with the passing of years, President Beane. And I've read your rules. You can let faculty go for moral turpitude *or* academic incompetence. Now, according to your own words, his academic methods are bizarre, aren't they?"

"But this is coercion of a sort, don't you think, Mr. Crosse? How would this look?"

"It would look as if you applied your Christian ethics to the faculty, President Beane, as you rightfully should."

"Well, it probably *is* the right thing to do."

"I'm sure the Directorate would heed the recommen-dation of their president, President Beane."

*

The headquarters building of Bryan Industries hadn't changed. Claire last saw it the day she left to marry Dan, but the stolid old creature, a cream-colored monument inside San Francisco's industrial/skid-row district, the Tenderloin, had weathered okay. Only a small sandstone marquee marked the front entrance, located two blocks south of Market Street. For Bryan's type of business, the less visible the better.

"Morning, Mrs. Bryan." The guard at the front desk stood up as she came in. "Been a while."

"Yes it has." A garlic smell filled the lobby. The man pushed aside a three-inch high salami sandwich. "I've missed being here, Mr..."

"Curly's good enough, Mrs. Bryan." As Ram had guessed, it probably would have seemed foolish to ask for a pass from John Bryan's daughter-in-law, and Curly didn't, but she still didn't breathe until the steel elevator doors had closed behind her.

That was the easy part.

The doors hissed apart on the second floor. Four rows of desks, peopled with blank unfamiliar faces, fenced with blue glass-walled offices. Shipping clerks squatting in fixed positions, unmoved in six years.

"Claire? That really you?" A brunette lady waved at her and Claire nearly stumbled, turning, but the dumpy lady doing the waving--Naomi was her name, Claire remembered--wouldn't be put off with the finger-flicking Claire tried to get by her with.

"Claire! Don't you remember me?"

"*Sure* I remember, Naomi." Claire smiled over her shoulder. "Nice to see you again."

Naomi brightened. "Imagine, you're *Mrs.* Bryan now--my old coffee chum." Naomi, her voice shrilling up to let the office know who her buddy here was, chased Claire toward the back offices. "What in the world're you doing here, Claire? Heard you and your father-in-law weren't getting along." As she caught up, Naomi tucked her white blouse into her blue-black plaid skirt. "Least that's the scuttlebutt around *here*, though not many of the old group's left. Though Charley *Henson's* still here. 'Member him?" She snickered.

Christ, Claire thought, did anything get by this office? She'd bedded with Henson twice, maybe, he among others--among quite a few others. "How is Charley?"

"*Senior* V.P. now, all the way to the fourth floor, can you believe it? Now we got this jackass Clarence Sowers managing this floor. A real jerk. So what brings you here? I heard you weren't getting along-"

"-You heard wrong, Naomi. In fact he sent me to bring some files back for him."

"You *see?* Rumors still run amuck around here. I should tell Charley you're here."

"Not necessary, Naomi. Thanks."

"No problem, honest! I see him all the time. He'd want to know, I'm sure." Naomi hustled away toward the elevator.

Damn!

Claire walked faster toward the desk guarding the Classified Files room, which was monitored by a timid-looking secretary attempting a smile at her through a double line of silver braces. "You really Mrs. Bryan?" asked the girl. Naomi's greeting had carried to the back of the room. Good.

131

"My father-in-law sent me to pick up some files." Claire tried to sound businesslike.

The girl's owlish smile faded. "Well, but only Mr. Sowers or someone above him is allowed access..."

"Mr. Bryan isn't above Mr. Sowers?"

"Oh, never that, Mrs. Bryan! Just that we have these real strict instructions-"

"-And Mr. Bryan can't supersede your instructions?" Claire waited a moment and held her breath.

"I'll need to check with Mr. Sowers, Mrs. Bryan. He'll be back from coffee in a minute."

"Mr. Bryan doesn't like to be kept a minute, Miss. I'll take the keys and check with Mr. Sowers on my way out, okay?" For a moment Claire thought the girl was going to cry. Instead, she put her key into the lock of the drawer. Inside the drawer another set of keys, to the "Classified" files, were still in the leather case that Claire herself once used.

"I'll let Mr. Sowers know you're here, soon's he returns," the girl said.

"I'll let Mr. Bryan know how much help you've been."

Inside the Classified room Claire tried to remember where the Far East files stood. Up against one of the corners somewhere, away from the barred windows--in the almond-colored section? She fingered through the keys until she found one coded almond, tried it in the top lock, and dropped all of them jangling to the floor.

"Something wrong, Mrs. Bryan?" The girl, still in the doorway, peeked past the black stacks of North European files.

"No. I found the ones Mr. Bryan wanted."

"I see Mr. Sowers coming back. I'll get him to help you." Her face slipped away.

Lordalmighty, thought Claire. She jammed the key back in, wrenched open the file, ran her hand across the top...Indonesia, Philippines, Thailand. Right area. She pulled open the middle drawer: "Indo-China/Vietnam". Three files, thick sheaves of paper, each preceded by a Roman numeral--I, II and III--after the title. She probably couldn't get out of here with *all* of these. Bullshitting these people would stretch just so far. She took the one marked "III".

"Do you have a pass to be in here, Mrs. Bryan?" Sowers' voice sounded like he was talking through tinfoil.

"Mr. Bryan said I wouldn't need one. You *are* Mr. Sowers, aren't you?"

Clarence Sowers, a smallish man, made himself smaller by hunching his shoulders in. Rimless bifocals, white shirt, plain brown tie. "Yes, ma'am, but we can't have anyone here without a pass." A crease worked past his cheek down the side of his face. "Paula shouldn't have given you the keys, Mrs. Bryan. This needs to be reported, of course."

"Your attitude might be reported, Mr. Sowers, if I can't deliver these files." That seemed to back him down a little, so Claire pushed it. "Would you prefer I call Mr. Bryan?"

"Well, I know that nothing leaves this room without authorization. I should call upstairs first. I understand Mr. Crosse is in the building."

That was the last thing she wanted to hear. "Mr. Crosse would be most interested in your reluctance to help me." She had watched the building all morning, never saw Harry enter. Sowers here must be bluffing, but it still sent a chill through her.

"She's in there, I think," came Naomi's voice.

"Claire?" Charley Henson stuck his head around the corner. "That you, Claire?" His big smile widened and followed Naomi in. "Been a while, young lady. Sorry about what happened to Dan-"

"-Charley had to come see you, Claire!" Naomi bubbled with intrigue now. Getting the widow Bryan together with her ex-office-lover! Too much! "Didn't I tell you?"

"Mr. Henson..." began Mr. Sowers.

"I know the rules, Clarence, but they don't apply to *Mrs.* Bryan, do they?"

"I have to protest that, sir. Rumor is she's not even on speaking terms-"

"-Hey, Mr. Sowers--Clarence--what are you saying here?"

As he talked, Claire could see what attracted her to Charley Henson: fairly handsome large face, big cinnamon eyebrows, thinning hair combed straight back to accentuate the face. Meanwhile Sowers was affecting a wounded pose. "Only doing my job, Mr. Henson. Mr. Bryan--or at least Mr. Crosse upstairs--would want to know if Mrs. Bryan-"

"-Mr. Bryan *does* know, Clarence. He sent her here, didn't he? Don't you believe Mrs. Bryan?" Henson's voice softened, sounding more like a threat. He placed himself next to the door, and Sowers took the cue.

"I think Mr. Crosse might have something to say about this," said Clarence Sowers, and left the room, hurrying toward the elevator.

Henson watched Clarence disappear. "Sneaky little guy, isn't he?... Naomi, why don't you get a large envelope for Mr. Bryan's file. You need an envelope, Claire?"

"That'd be great." Claire couldn't seem to breath. *Look calm, remain calm.* "Thanks for the help, Charley."

"Hell, why would you need a file unless the old man asked for it?" While saying this he watched Naomi go searching for an envelope, then closed the door. "What a nice surprise to see you, Claire. How long's it been? Five years?"... Ah, yes, now she understood. Old horny Charley didn't give a crap about the files. He was just hoping, apparently, to cop a quick feel off his old girlfriend. She could handle that easily enough, small enough price to pay.

"Six years, Charley." She wanted to keep him on that track. She also needed to get the hell out of here. "We should get together again."

"Could be right now, if you have a few minutes." He patted her shoulder. "Naomi knows better than to come back in."

Claire laughed. "Charley, you always were an oversexed fiend, but I can't right now. Let's arrange something, okay?"

He put his hands on the small of her back, slid them down and eased her in. "You've got a few minutes, don't you?" The hardness against Claire's body *did* feel good. Even his sweat smelled good.

"Charley, I'd like that," she finally slipped to one side. "Let's make some plans, okay? But right now I've got to get this file to Bryan. Don't want to get him mad."

"Right, I guess." Charley adjusted his crotch and took a breath. "Man, though, it'd almost be worth it."

"No, dammit, we'll make some plans later, okay? Business first." Her heart bumped against her ribs. A minute more and Harry'd be down here, if he *was* upstairs. "Couple of hours at most, Charley. Let me call you."

"Be looking forward to it--" He stood on his toes to speak over a row of files, but Claire had already made her way through the door.

Claire took the envelope from Naomi and thought about following the red Exit sign down the stairs, but that would be too obvious. Like sending up flares right now, the whole office seemed to be watching. She stared up at the floor indicator: elevator coming down. Harry, probably. No choice but to stand and wait.

Empty. The hissing doors wrapped her safely inside again, at least until the ground floor. From there it was about forty feet to the street, if her legs would hold up.

"Nice to see you again, Curly." Claire waved as she hurried by the guard, who was walking toward a ringing telephone. He waved back as he put it to his ear.

"Oh, Missus Bryan!" He held up the phone toward her.

Claire had crossed the street before the door swung shut.

A great buoyancy came over her then. She hurried to Market Street and waved down a taxi to the airport. Claire had promised herself a three-day binge in Los Angeles if she ever pulled this off, and she *had* pulled it off. For once she'd done something she set out to do, an *adventure*!

Her legs were feeling like helium balloons as she walked through the airport. Right now, she thought, I need that drink more than life itself. First thing back in L.A. I'm getting a bottle and celebrate myself into a coma. Things are going to work out okay.

Chapter 21

For as long as he could remember, Associate Professor Ian McAlpin had toyed with the thought of taking his life. That was to be expected, he supposed, considering all his withered academic goals, his endless clumsy romantic fantasies.

He had a mental trick he'd use during these depression periods. He would imagine conversations with all the people he most respected in his life--all of them, coincidentally, now passed away. Sometimes these mental conversations would be with his old professors; sometimes, less often, they would be with his father; sometimes with a girl named Catherine whom he'd known once, idolized once, from a distance, one more of the youthful miseries he never outgrew.

After LaCroix College released him he needed those consoling fantasy-talks with Catherine more than he needed the harsher presence of his father, although for the task he had given himself today, he would need mostly--he would have to call on--the courage of his father.

He tried to picture what his father would say about this, Maxwell McAlpin's own awkward form of consolation: *Y'will feel death, then, Ian*, he could imagine his father saying. *Though not the same as death in battle, y'know. Nothing s'glorious as that.* He would make some nonsensical comment like that. His father would always work the oft-recalled battle at Auberg Ridge into his talks.

I am not like my son, nor am I like you, thought Ian McAlpin. Your courage passed through me like a conduit to my brown son.

But he needed to hear again his father's story of Auberg Ridge, of bravery and death, for he needed the courage they might bring to him: *Was a' Auberg Ridge tha' we o' the First Black Watch gathered t'attack the main Bosch line, y'ken that, for the Munsters and the Northants and the Second London were cut t'bits an' the Twenty Furst Brigade they wouldna attack again, so said their General Gough.* And Ian McAlpin thought, Men of action are the only real participants in life. *An' the only jocks left was the First Black Watch, then, an' the only ones tha' wen' over the top that noon. An' when our own pipers died we could still hear the jocks playing half a mile away, in Flaubert.*

We the seekers after knowledge, for the sake of knowledge, are nonessential, thought Ian McAlpin. But he couldn't keep Catherine from contesting that: *Heed your son, Ian.* Your son Ram, Ramirez the seeker--don't you see in him *Rama*, the Godhead, defender of moral order in

136

the universe? Don't you hear it in his name--the incarnation of Vishnu? Remember the Hindu tale of the Bhagavad-Gita: the followers of action shall meet the seekers after knowledge--

What silliness is that? thought Ian McAlpin. My son is not a seeker. He is without real goals, he has only this capacity for violence.

The words he gave his father were so much more relevant here: *I'll hear n'more of yer brown son. If you're bound to do this thing, donna whimper on so aboot it.*

And the tug of the bullet, when Ian McAlpin brought this about, brought no pain. Like being bumped in the head with a softly-thrown beach ball. And then he could see only the enveloping whiteness of a hospital room. The tug of the bullet and the white hospital room blended together in the fuzzy blinking of his eyes.

There were other people nearby, white silhouettes, but he defined only Catherine among them, remaining still until the others were done with him. And when the room became dark and the others left, he dreamt she came to him, and smoothed the clean linen to his face, and kissed him forever asleep.

*

The suicide of Dr. McAlpin drew a strange cloud around Harry Crosse. This was outside his experience, he'd never considered anything on this scale, and he grew quiet in his confusion. The other members of Bryan's little band began to notice the change.

The five of them--he and Bryan, Carson and the two bodyguards--had flown to Los Angeles to inspect their appliance warehouse in the industrial section, and because of the late hour Bryan told Trevors to drive them to D'Agostino's for dinner.

Carson picked up on the reason for Harry's silence first. "This wouldn't have anything to do with that professor whacking himself, would it?" He made no attempt to hide his glee. "What's happened to that tough business tycoon we've grown so fond of, Harry?"

"Now, Kenneth, Harry feels some kind of contrition about this man's death. He should be commended for that." Bryan aimed that useless reprimand at Carson before turning to Harry. "You did right, Harry. He killed himself, yes, that was perhaps unfortunate." Bryan realized that his assistant had stopped eating just to watch him speak, such an odd way to act. He picked up his fork and began poking at his skinless dry chicken breast. "The release from that college was a just retribution against his family, Harry," said John Bryan. "Justice has been done."

137

"Why this long face, Harry?" said Willy Carson. "You'd think you whacked him yourself."

"If I ever decide to zap anyone, Willy, you'll be the first to know."

"Harry! Don't *ever* threaten Kenneth like that!" Bryan nervously stabbed and sniffed at the garlicky pasta side dish.

"Sorry." Harry wondered how Bryan could protect this twerp. Bryan fairly *mothered* over the little bastard.

Sorry Ochoa and Charles Trevors, sitting at their separate table with Bryan's folded-up wheelchair, turned to check out the raised voices. Bryan's hands shook as he placed them on the table. "Anyway, we have more important matters... We need to address ourselves to this theft from headquarters, do we not? What are we to do with this woman? We need to take measures to keep her from doing us further mischief, do you understand what I'm saying, Kenneth? We need to implement our next plan."

"Next plan?" Harry felt a small cramp start up in his stomach.

"You are not to be concerned with this, Harry. Kenneth and I have worked out a plan-"

"-Mr. Bryan, I won't be part of any violence."

"And you will not be, Harry. We have no violence planned for that woman."

"Just the opposite, boy," said Carson. "We intend to keep her happy the rest of her life."

Harry looked from Carson to Bryan. "You talking about dope here? No way in the world she's going back to that."

"Harry," Bryan stroked Harry on the arm, "Kenneth has his ways. Haven't you noticed that yet?"

*

Colonel Purdy's first reaction was true to form: "Your father *what? Died?* What the hell're you talking about, Sergeant? You don't even know your father." But he let it drop--why the hell would the sergeant lie about *that?* He modified his tone, slightly. "Whatever, you're still scheduled to go on this Southeast Asian goose-chase in just two days. You ready for that?"

"I'll be on the flight, Colonel."

Everything was coming together too fast. When Weissman received the call from the doctors, he'd driven Ram to the hospital and while they waited, while the surgeons struggled over the hole in Dr. McAlpin's brain, Colonel Purdy had called.

And Ram had still heard nothing from Claire; she'd left her phone off the hook. He'd phoned Mrs. Bingham to see if Claire came back yet and the lady didn't know. The boy Sean was still with Mrs. Bingham. "She went to San Francisco for something and then came back, and then just started drinking, at least it sounded so, from the way she sounded," said Mrs. Bingham. "Gonna drink herself into a coma, she said. Seems her only way of handling *any* problem nowadays."

"Yes, ma'am, I hope that's all there is to it."

The damned documents, Ram thought. His fault for making that idiotic suggestion. It probably scared piss out of her, but Claire's problems would have to be put on hold for the week he'd be in Asia.

While he waited in the hospital lobby he began to feel the renewed isolation. His new source of knowledge, his father, had surfaced and promised a possible way to the Touchstone, and then he takes himself out. Leaving Ram rootless again, with only his father's cryptic, fathomless theories.

*

Willy Carson heard no response when he tapped on the apartment door. He slipped his latch-release plate between the jams, flipping the inset tongue. The door clicked and swung open, and Carson congratulated himself for not losing his touch. He put the plate into his leather pouch and slid inside, closing the door with a light *snap*.

Claire's L.A. apartment was a dreary place, Willy noticed. Nothing like the luxury she'd had at the Bryan compound. This was a working-girl's place, a functional cave, with the couch-kitchen room leading to one bedroom in back. The chairs rested on spindly metal legs and the beige hooked-weave sofa fuzzed up along the arms. Through the bedroom door he saw clothes across a chair, and a woman's hand. The door blocked the rest of her but he could see an empty bottle of Smirnoff laying sideways on the night stand. The drab chenille curtains were closed, changing the outside daylight to gold, like an old sepia photograph.

Drunk on her ass, Willy guessed. Like always. He pushed the door farther in.

Claire's mouth was open, just a touch. Such an invitation, such full, fine lips. Willy shivered, thinking it was about time he got to try this girl out. He could almost taste the sweetness of this. He stood fascinated by the smooth lines of pale-blue bed sheet, loosely drawn, draped over all that glory.

"Who the hell...oh shit, little Willy whatsis..." Claire tried to raise herself and slumped back again, but her voice had startled him, since she looked damned near comatose when he came in. He stood still as she turned her head away.

He waited.

"Wha're you doing in my room, l'il creep?" She was still awake.

Raw splendor among all this garbage, thought Carson. All breasts and legs spreading inside those rumpled sheets. "Now, Claire, no way to talk to Uncle Kenny."

"Outta my bedroom, creep. God..." She took a weary gasp of air and attempted to roll her eyes toward him.

Kenny opened the pouch and took out a package wrapped in white tissue, bound in a knot of rubber bands. He popped the bands and let the syringe, tubing and spoon fall onto the bed, but held the white package above her head. "See here, Mrs. Bryan? Uncle Ken's going to make everything nice. About time someone did something nice for you, isn't it?"

"Goddamn creepis." Claire moved her head across her pillow. "Know what Danny use to call you? Creepis Maximus." She chuckled at that.

"Now, Claire, no way to talk to Uncle Ken when he's only here to bring some happiness." He warmed the spoon with his lighter and drew the forming liquid to the syringe. Her eyes focused on the needle with an unreadable fascination. "You sonova bitch," she mumbled.

"I thought you'd like this." He held her hand on the bed, tied off the tube and knelt over her. "We're going to do all your favorite things this afternoon, Claire." Keeping her chest down with his knee. "I'm not here to hurt you, you know. Got no intention of hurting you. Just stay still, now"

Her head turned away as the needle went in. Her eyes closed, not quite wincing, and the dead woman's heavy-lidded stare came to her, an exhalation of remaining hope. Peace, Willy supposed, but surely in its ugliest form. He stood back to admire his work as Claire moaned once, then lay still, breasts moving in a slow narcotic rhythm.

She is a piece of work, thought Willy Carson. Not used up like one would expect. He touched her nipples, firm as baby fingers. He drew back the sheet and studied the rest of her, the lean thighs and sudden fur, the smooth, flat stomach. And he thought, I must have the morals of a vulture, but I sure as hell ain't letting this go to waste, having Mrs. Daniel Bryan under me. I must be such a vulture, I admit that.

He pulled the sheet down and unzipped himself, and she sighed and shifted to her side. He rolled her hips back with his hand, and felt around her entrance while her legs shifted lazily to allow that touch. He smoothed the tuft of hair aside.

"They all spoke the truth," he said. "You're wonderfully constructed, lip to lip." He shifted himself to a kneel between her knees, and he bit her mouth as he lay over her, pretending she wanted badly to have him do this, after all those years of dreaming about this.

Dusk sounds picked up along the street below. Cars honked, workers returned home. The still-new phenomenon of television paled a few of the shades of the opposite apartment houses.

Willy and Claire consummated their mock fornication in a mutual swoon, he swimming into this delicious warm cloud, and Claire vaguely conscious, disgusting herself, because even this, for the moment...sadly, gladly, surren-dering to the powder.

*

I've always been afraid too, Weissman thought, after he'd returned to the Wee Hoose. It was his first day of school since Professor McAlpin's death.

Ram's pop and I shared that unspoken *shibboleth*, that fear, he thought. Except Ram's father had enough nerve to do something about it. And Luke understood Dr. McAlpin's fear, of life itself, although the professor showed less fear of leaving it than Luke Weissman. Who *wasn't* less afraid of leaving it than Luke Weissman? he thought. Luke knew that he himself, while on this earth, would just barely exist, jackoff that he was, ending up shuffling papers for some insurance company or some bank, or some department store, until his mind turned into oatmeal.

When Ram received the call to go to Southeast Asia, Luke had this other premonition rattling his brain. He couldn't shake the feeling of seeing Ram for the last time, Vietnam was such an ominous sounding word. He phoned his latest love, a girl he'd met at Dude's named Gee Gee, to come take his mind off these weird notions of clairvoyance... It usually didn't take much to get his mind on a different track, Luke realized.

Ram came out of his room heading for the bathroom just as Luke was hanging up the phone. "You feel okay?" Ram asked. He threw his olive-drab duffel on the sofa on his way past Luke.

"Don't I look okay?"

"Look white as a sheet."

"I was thinking about your father."

"Can't talk about that right now, Luke," said Ram from the bathroom, over the sound of cascading water. Ram flushed the toilet and went back to his room to dress, the sound of the gushing toilet ending the conversation, taking all of Luke's intuition down with it. Where they belonged, Luke supposed.

Just the bathroom sounds were enough, in fact, to send Luke's mind steaming off in another direction: Unlike Ram, who had pissed right *next* to him, practically, Luke couldn't even piss in the school urinals if anyone was in the area. The stalls there, jammed like yellow safe-deposit boxes, looked like they were designed by Russians... See? he thought, you've got absolutely no control over where your mind wanders off to.

"Be careful over there, would you?"

"Right, Luke. Back in about a week."

That leave-taking held kooky overtones for Luke. From where Luke sat, Ram seemed to plunge into air beyond the doorway, but the crunch of his steps on the pebble walkway interfered with Luke's illusion of a man stepping into space.

*

Harry Crosse hurried along the mustard-yellow aluminum stairway and into the hangar at Cloverfield Airport, where Bryan Enterprises kept its Aero Commander. He headed toward the oily-smelling dispatcher's office, although he knew if they had gotten Claire this far, it was already too late, but too late for what? What did he think he would do, *fight* for her?--not hardly a good idea. But still, when Ochoa told him about Claire, here comes Harry running like Big Sam off to save Scarlett from the shantytown dwellers, although he wasn't any Big Sam, he knew, and Claire was certainly no Scarlett O'Hara.

He saw her sitting beside the window-walls of the dispatcher's desk. Charles Trevors, arms folded as usual, kept an eye on Harry as he entered, while Willy Carson grinned at Harry from his usual corner. Trevors and Carson, never exactly buddies, stood a distance away from each other.

"Come to kiss the lady goodbye, Mr. Crosse?" Carson made a little hopping movement on the balls of his feet, a miniature devil-dance. "Claire and me're going on vacation, so say what you got to say, would you? Plane'll be going in a few minutes."

Harry stepped around Trevors and stopped as Claire looked up and smiled, and stared away again.

"You okay, Claire?"

"I'm okay."

He led her to another bench just out of earshot of the other two.

"What'd they do?"

"They? The pricks hooked me up again." She talked with this slightly sing-song lilt. "We're going back to Paris to see my old friend Emile St. Amand. Going to stay happy there, for awhile."

"Paris?"

"To Chicago, to catch one of those big new jets to Paris, to see my old friend Emile St. Amand--my old dealer in Paris, least he *used* to be, a long time ago." She gazed sleepily at Harry. "Don't get the wrong idea about Emile St. Amand, Harry. He's a good friend, he really is."

"I'll bet he is. You don't really want to go there?"

She sighed. "I'm tired of fighting, Harry. I wasn't intended to live any normal life."

"Let me talk to Trevors a minute."

"What're you going to do, Harry? Fight him?" She smiled at that idea. "Better I go with them for a while, Harry. I need to rest. Bryan wants to put some space between me and Sean and...hell, Sean'll be okay here, and I just can't fight these people any more."

"Not even for your son?"

She stared upward, past Harry. "You never been on smack, have you, Harry? Long as I can keep one continuous damn skin-popping... Everyone here's better off without me, even Sean."

"You don't believe that."

Her gaze drifted around the drab space of grey steel hangar. "Would you do something for me, Harry? Under my refrigerator there's a file..."

"I know about your stealing the papers."

"I need them sent to Emile St. Amand."

"To your *pusher?*" Harry glanced over at the other two men, to make sure they didn't hear that. "Claire, why in hell would I--"

"'Cause I'm in trouble, Sean and I are, and you'll find a way to do it right... I need some help, Harry."

"Let me talk with Trevors a minute."

She didn't look at him as he walked over to Trevors.

"Mr. Trevors, could we talk a moment?"

"Sure, Mr. Crosse."

Harry tried to think of a good approach, but none came. "Taking Mrs. Bryan like this, don't you think we're starting to play this game kind of... a little rough?"

The roar that came from Charles Trevors took Harry's own wind away. It sounded mostly like a laugh, Harry couldn't be sure. "Mr. Crosse, what the hell're you talking about?"

So much for the altruistic approach, thought Harry. He'd forgotten for a moment who he was dealing with.

"What'd he say?" Willy Carson called over.

"He made a joke," answered Trevors.

Harry took a more confidential tone with Trevors. "You know, don't you, the old man is right on the edge of going nuts?"

"Mr. Crosse, we've known that a long time now."

"And you still do everything he tells you?"

Trevors looked down at him. "Long as we keep getting paid, Mr. Crosse, we *all* do just as he tells us, don't we?"

Chapter 22

Ram's first sight of Tan Son Nhut filtered its way through a trickling humidity. The airport jiggled in the refracted heat from the runway tarmac, concrete loading zones and metal Quonset hangars. The terminal itself was two stories, a neon-lit shed that gaped open-sided toward its parking area: third world prosaic, lackluster as a barrio schoolyard.

The air clung inside the airport, jammed with short sleeved white-shirted Vietnamese businessmen, exiting landowners, refugees still trailing in from the north. A group of turbaned Indian men moved through the crowd escorting women wrapped in silk caftans or red and yellow *sampots*. From the second level a deep gong greeted incoming travelers.

Ram purchased an orange soda from one of the machines but the liquid was warm and sugary and tasted like sweetened rust--he tossed it into a trash bin. Through the side door he saw a row of old Fairchild C-119 "Packet" cargo planes, their twin fuselages resembling swollen P-38's, except these had no Air Force identification--had *no* identification--on them.

A young man at the entrance saw Ram, wove through the cross flow in Ram's direction and then stopped, keeping his distance.

"You are Mr. Apollo?" Voice high and weak, choking inside the tight black vest.

"You from Secretary Dao?"

"I am Tran Van Loc," the boy announced. "I am sent by Dao Kim Chau, Secretary of Social and Political Research Services, and Assistant Deputy Province Chief." He emphasized the first syllable of each word to insure Ram understood that his superior, Dao Kim Chau, held no trivial position here.

"Hell of a title." Ram bent to pick up his bag but Tran had already grabbed it and took off toward a black Citroen B-2 landaulet which sported a South Vietnamese flag on each fender. He had it backed to the curb by the time Ram got to the pickup zone.

The carts and bicycles and *cyclo-pousses* on the avenue had to jostle aside to avoid young Van Loc's government car, plowing through Tu Do Street past the residences of Gia Dinh toward a huge white building, stanchioned with Doric columns, topped by a cupola of glass and wrought iron. "Gia Long Palais," said the boy, pointing. "President Diem live there."

On the rim of the Gia Dinh district the twin spires of Notre Dame stabbed the sky. At Quach Thi Trang Square, in front of the Central Saigon

Market and the pillared facade of Hotel de Ville, the prostitutes made faces at them as the black government car went by.

They stopped at the side of a smaller structure, a mini-forest circling its parking area. "Deputy Province Chief reside here," said Tran Van Loc. They went through a set of glass doors where a Vietnamese guard slopped his French 9mm submachine gun into a loose port-arms. The girl inside, at the desk, barely looked up. She pressed a telephone button, producing a scuffle from the next room as a foot, Kim Chau's, shoved open the inner door.

"God, it's happened. I still can't believe this." Chau held a telephone that had just enough cord to reach the door. He spoke some Vietnamese into the phone, hung up, reached for Ram's hand. "You finally decided to come save Vietnam?"

"Does it need saving?" Ram grinned. "You're looking good, Kim Chau. Like a damn politician." Chau was wearing a white shirt and maroon tie and a wide-lapelled, navy-blue suit.

"Hell, I *am* a politician, at least for now." Chau's smile softened as he pumped Ram's hand again. "Didn't my runner read my whole title to you? I *told* him to. Sorry I wasn't at the airport, I'll explain later. Let me show you around."

Chau led him past a row of little offices until they came to the exit near the parking lot. Chau went through it and signaled for Ram to follow--"This's where we sneak out." He hurried toward a seasoned Austin sedan parked near the black Citroen in the mini-forest. "Don't want to use a chauffeur from here," he said. "Most of the chauffeurs are spies."

"Even Tran Loc? Why the secrecy?"

"Just want to keep Security off my ass awhile. I'll give you the poop while we drive."

They went a different route out of the city, down bumpy streets where meat hung strung on soiled hemp strings, within clouds of flies, out-stinking the drying fish. Children crossed pebbled intersections on scabby skinned feet, while primitive old men pissed into the fuming gutters.

Kim Chau, with larger worries, ignored the scene. "Everyone here spies for someone, with all these big outside powers pulling on our little country, like being in a rowboat at the meeting place of two giant rivers. Helpless, you know, and us with so damned many problems to begin with. Catholics fighting Buddhists, bureaucrats fighting intellectuals, generals against students." He tried to laugh. "Even Madame Nhu against the prostitutes. Boy, if it were just us against the commies, wouldn't *that* simplify things."

"And of course, Dao Kim Chau still trying to butt heads with whatsisname--"

"Right! *Both* of us against that son of a bitch Bryan, I hope." He looked at Ram for confirmation and found none. "Anyway, that's not the reason you're here."

"Nope."

"They sent you to spy on me, right?"

"Got me a free trip to Saigon."

Kim Chau laughed. "You make a real crappy spy, Ram."

"I'll take whatever you've got, anyway. Commie activity, religious movements, how much poontang the Premier gets on the side--"

"The Premier's married, but he does have *mu tsai* on the side. The French here call their mistresses *congaie*, to keep your report straight."

"I can fill a few pages with that."

The roadside was changing. Buildings where mountains of iron-red bricks were stacked marked the end of the industrial section. They passed chugging, minuscule, charcoal-burning busses popping grainy black puffs from their side exhausts. Farther on, the exposed red loam of the outlying plantations was ploughed for the planting of maize. "Right along the coast it's so sandy you can't grow anything but sweet potatoes," said Chau.

Outside the city, flame trees rose across the land with bouquets of red-orange. A warm, fresh, smokeless breeze came up from the South China Sea. The world appeared to brighten around here, and Ram knew, as for himself, the nearness of My Linh had a lot to do with that. She was the main reason, maybe the only real reason, for this journey. He had begun to understand that.

Chau turned onto a cobbled driveway which cut through half a mile of new coconut palms, past rice fields busy with straining water buffalo, workers in mollusk-shaped hats. Near a circle of three-roofed white houses the road elevated, cresting beneath a group of tall areca-nut palms.

"My God."

"Nice, huh? My father's one of the few oriental millionaires in Vietnam who isn't Chinese--at least he *was* a millionaire. Diem's frozen most of our assets now."

"This is a damned *palacia*, Kim Chau. You grew up here?"

Chau turned off the motor and held up his hand. "Listen a minute."

Long Canary Pine needles murmured in the stir of air. Wood chimes tinkled from separate verandas. A waterfall splashed into a lotus pool surrounded by crimson hibiscus, where a pair of gardeners pottered. "Isn't that something?" said Kim Chau. "Peace, Ram. This's the one place in this land that you'll find it." He got out and started up a walkway of stones, and as Ram pulled his bag from the car he saw, at the end of the pathway, beneath a white lattice arbor, My Linh.

"Out of the jungles and paddies my father created a damned Garden of Eden," Chau continued. He didn't see his sister as he waved toward the Canary pines. "See there? We even planted our own forest."

My Linh had been watching them, but when Ram saw her she looked down, crossing her hands low in front like tiny shields. Ram didn't realize he'd stopped to stare at her until Chau came back to tug his sleeve. "You have to enter a Vietnamese house at an angle, Ram. A direct path invites evil spirits to sneak in with you."

"It's nice to see you again, Ramirez Apollo," said My Linh. She came to put her hand in his, like a wisp of cloud, and she led him to the house, where they walked in stocking feet over bamboo matting to a room of red lacquer ware, brass pots, whalebone scrimshaw figurines. And they sat around a low ebony table, talked politely of political things, of the old emperor Bao Dai and the threats from Ngo Dinh Diem toward their father: "But you must be careful about such talk, Kim Chau," My Linh cautioned her brother.

"My Linh, if we can't trust Ramirez Apollo, then there is no man who can be trusted." Then he became embarrassed, for he realized she knew this, and that wasn't why she cautioned him.

"Your sister's right, Kim Chau. Dammit-"

"-There was a teacher, Bo Cut, who organized the resistance to the communists in western Cochin-China," Chau interrupted. "He was an ally of Diem's, but then Diem executed him only because Diem said he had a *feeling* about the man," Chau patted Ram on the arm as he said that. "I am aware of the dangers of crossing Ngo Dinh Diem, Ram."

"How does he plan to keep control? Didn't that Geneva Conference call for--what was it?--reunification?" Ram had read the dossier about Indo-China that Purdy gave him, but the part about the Diem family was, at best, spotty.

"Madame Nhu'll figure out how to avoid that," said Chau. "She's the real brains of that gang." Seeing Ram frown, he added, "She's Diem's sister-in-law, the Dragon Lady. Anyway, they'll soon have the Americans here to back them up."

"I don't see any American soldiers around here."

"There will be, Ram. There will be."

Chau's father arrived at his residence at six-thirty in the evening, a punctuality that went unbroken for six days a week for fifteen years, beginning after his wife's death. A ruffled, tweedy old man, saddled with painful honesty, noted for his punctuality in the Bao Dai government to the day President Diem dismissed him.

He walked briskly to the house for his introduction.

"This is the man I spoke of, father. Sergeant Marion Ramirez Apollo, a liaison person for the United States Army," said Chau proudly, in English. "He'll be of great help to us."

"Well, wait now, Kim Chau-"

"-It's true, Ram. A truthful report on what's happening here would be a great service to this country."

Ram let the embellishment go. "I've heard a lot about you, Mr. Dao."

Dao Phuong's eyes, watching Ram, had a pleasant sadness. "So," said Dao Phuong, "you wish to know truth, Sergeant Apollo?"

"I don't really know what I'm supposed to learn here, Mr. Dao."

"So." This appeared to be statement enough. Dao Phuong put on slippers and went to the main room, bowed to his daughter and sat on a floor cushion, and didn't speak again until after the servants brought tea. "We all have truth within us, Sergeant. But in this day, it needs to be compromised to the society in which we live. It is easy to lose track of truth."

Kim Chau looked toward his friend.

"I can see where your daughter gets her wisdom, Mr. Dao," said Ram, obligingly. The words came out, he thought, sounding like horse crap, but from the family reaction they must have been the right ones. Dao Phuong clapped his appreciation.

"Even *my* thoughts come from my daughter, I think," said Dao Phuong. "She is our student-priest of the Cao Dai. We learn from her."

My Linh blushed. "It is not so, father."

"Your Army wishes to know the truth of our country," said the father. "Well, one must not speak against President Diem, even in the privacy of our home. People disappear here just as they do in South America, or Africa."

"To satisfy the Americans, first Diem calls you a communist," said Chau. "Then the Saigon police--they're called the 'white mice'--they come get you. I think my father's on that list now."

"Bryan have a hand in that?"

Chau nodded. "Remember the snaky-looking guy in Bryan's office? Carson?"

"But didn't Bryan supply the Viet Minh, Diem's enemies? How does Diem square that up?"

Kim Chau shrugged. "Business is business, Ram. Frankly, compared to these guys, Ho Chi Minh's starting to look... Does Intelligence know the Viets made contact with me?"

"Probably why they sent me."

"Said they'd make me deputy chief for the Saigon and Tay Ninh Inter-Zone, though in the field I'd be a battalion *commissar*--carries a lot of authority, except in combat. In combat I'd still take orders from the professional guerrillas."

"I'm not sure I want to hear about your talks with the Viet Minh, Kim Chau."

"But you know what else such an appointment would mean?" Chau persisted. "I'd have complete access to documents that could help us nail Bryan."

"Let it go, Kim Chau."

"In the countryside, the northern leader is referred to as *Boc Ho*, meaning Uncle Ho," said My Linh, helping Ram change the subject. "But some of his field officers are the most terrible men-"

"-But if those people could be removed, somehow," Chau couldn't be shaken loose, "Ho Chi Minh might be better than what we've got now, Ram. Even though communism's just a dictatorship too. A stupid inefficient one, but what choice do we have?"

An uncomfortable silence followed, broken finally by Ram. "Is that why you're thinking about joining them, Kim Chau? To help get rid of some of their bad ones?"

My Linh didn't want to hear the answer. "Kim says that on Okinawa you often went to the north of the island, Ramirez, to see the *albatross* birds?"

"Most people say there aren't any such birds up there, My Linh. Maybe I just imagine them."

For dinner My Linh would not let their cook serve goat. The meat, to taste its best, required the animal to be beaten until it sweats before its throat is cut. A terrible way, My Linh felt, to prepare for a pleasant evening, and, anyway, as a rule the Caodai usually did not eat meat. "Ah, but Ram, you should taste goat when it is prepared right," whispered Kim Chau.

Conversation during the meal, happily, avoided the subject of Ngo Dinh Diem. The Daos talked instead about controlling the mosquitoes in the lotus ponds, or the estimated yield for the corn and banana crops, or, what seemed to be of greatest pride, the care of their elaborate gardens:

"Would you like to see the rest of our gardens, Ramirez?"

My Linh's question surprised her father. Annamese girls did not *ask* men...but without waiting for an answer My Linh held her hand out to Ram and rose, and led him through the doors to the pine forest. Through a glade of bayberry and rosewood, scented with the honey-smells of jasmine and hyacinth.

A gorgeous place, but Ram didn't feel like musing through any forest. He couldn't get his mind off their discussion in the main room. "It'd be better if Chau didn't tell me about those contacts with the Viet Minh, My Linh." That didn't sound right. "He shouldn't tell *anyone* about the Viet Minh offer. It's already dangerous enough for him here."

"He thinks you and he will someday fight together against people like Diem and Bryan," said My Linh. "He has adopted the careless soul of the warrior. He thinks you share this with him, that you are a comrade soul." She was clasping her hands to her breast now. "Do you think there is such a thing as a soul, Ramirez?"

"I don't think about it at all, My Linh. And you should think more about your own survival right now."

"But if there is a soul, should survival be that important?"

Ram shook his head. "I don't think that much about such things, My Linh"

They walked across a bridge above a dry brook, filled with white boulders. "My father had his own ideas along those lines, though," he said. That strange word, "father," distracted him for a moment. "His ideas agreed with yours."

"I'd like very much to hear his thoughts," said My Linh.

"Who knows what his thoughts were. He was a physicist." Ram wondered why he'd brought that up. That wasn't what they should be talking about here. "He thinks--he thought--that a thing called quantum has proven there's a soul, and life after death. Even proves the existence of God." He stopped to look at the califlorous trees that nurtured, within their limbs, their tousled satellite plants. Dr. McAlpin's life within life. "This quantum shows how existence came to be, according to him. Proves it's all an illusion."

"He sounds like such a strong and independent man, to decide such things."

Ram remembered the tall middle-aged man who had run from life, and shook his head, no. "He wasn't a man of strong will."

"But don't you see, your father's science and the teachings of our eastern religions now say exactly the same thing."

"I don't want to talk about that right now, My Linh." He wasn't comfortable with this. Conversations like this always went sideways on him. "Doesn't have anything to do with your problems here."

They walked along a green berm bordering the driveway and she held his fingers with a touch that warmed his whole arm. "You must understand so much, if you can understand the things your father said."

"My Linh, I don't think I understood him at all."

"With such knowledge, people like you would bring down the Ngo Diems of this world." She said this as he lifted her from the berm.

"How the hell would I do that?"

Her legs rubbed against him when he lowered her. "You are like blind Samson," she said, "waiting for someone to place your hands on the pillars, to bring the temples down."

"And make one of those sacrifices to your Touchstone?" He smiled. "I'd need to see someone do that first, before I become a believer."

She skipped away then, lightly, having delivered her message to him.

"You expect way more than I have to offer, My Linh."

She hid a snicker. "We will see, Ramirez Apollo."

That night the Dao family gave Ram his own guest pavilion, a wing off the main structure consisting of a bedroom and a canopied outside porch, shoji-screened within its own coarse-grained sand garden. On his table the Chinese servants left custard-apples, a round bumpy fruit that did taste like custard inside, and his mattress was laid on the floor without frame or springs, as firm as pinewood.

Chapter 23

"Today we listen to My Linh read to the followers of the Cao Dai," said Kim Chau the next morning. "And we go with her to proselyte the Montagnards--the mountain people we flatlanders call *moi*. Means 'savage' in Annamese. Want to join us?"

Ram laughed. "Instead of doing *what*, Kim Chau?" He'd gotten up when it became too warm to sleep. He'd already chewed the gummy rice cakes and the purplish aromatic banana-shaped plantain the servants had set out, and drank their bitter green tea.

"We got a call that Diem wants to see my father, so he won't be going with us," said Chau. "But they insist on sending an interpreter along with us. Along with *you*, more likely."

"Interpreter?"

"Spy. They're tightening the watch on us now that you're here." Chau made a sucking noise between his teeth. "Got to stick this out, you know. Father Dao would never survive in the mountains."

Ram looked in the direction of the rooms of Dao Phuong.

"He's already gone," said Chau. "Father left for Saigon as soon as we got the call... Well, what've we got *here?*"

White-robed, glorified in mantled whiteness, My Linh came in and slipped to her cushion near the tea table, and smiled toward Ram. "I slept late." She began picking through the breakfast fruit. "Sleeping too much is considered a terrible sin here."

"You probably didn't sleep at *all* last night, you're so fixed up." Chau bent nearer to check her robe. "You look like the Queen of Winter Festival."

"Such a nice thing to say, brother Kim." She cupped a hand over her smile as she fluttered out a paper, partly rolled up, finely hand-printed. "I made this for you, Ramirez. The revelation I will read today, if you would like to see the translation."

"Sure. Thanks, My Linh." He started to smooth it out but she put her hand over the paper.

"I need you to read it when I do, Ramirez. At the temple."

They drove to Saigon in a canvass-topped red Land Rover. "Kind of worn but at least it's red," said Chau. "Diem says *all* of us Caodai--everyone who follows the Cao Dai deity, that is--are probably red."

"That's not awfully funny, Kim Chau."

"It's awfully true, though." Chau wiped his face as he drove. The convertible top, torn in spots, sucked the warm air over them. "One of our sects tried a coup in September of '54 but the *U.S.* secretly stopped it. Then Diem raided the Holy See at Tay Ninh last year to retaliate, using his mobile guillotine--Christ, it was bloody. Seven thousand Caodai troops were driven into the maquis and the Plain of Reeds to join the Viets, thanks to Diem."

*

The Cau Kho temple on Nguyen Cu Trinh Street towered over them. "You must go through the door on the right, Ramirez," said My Linh. "Men and women enter from opposite sides. Kim Chau will show you."

"They allow outsiders here?" Ram had to step back and crane his neck to see the top of the temple spires.

"Cao Dai embraces all religions, Ramirez." My Linh smiled. "Everyone is allowed in here."

Inside the temple a forest of multi-colored pillars, wound with carved blue serpents, supported the vaulted ceilings. There were hundreds of people inside, their slick wet faces lined up in even rows as they squatted along the tiled floor. "The turnout isn't usually this big," whispered Chau. They took off their shoes and slid into the men's half of the room. "I think word got out that My Linh is reading today."

Ram saw her come in with other white-robed women near the left altar, while on the right the male priests, wearing black berets, assembled themselves by robe color--light blue, gold, lavender--facing a five-tiered altar. Five joss sticks smoldered under the mandala that enclosed the Divine Eye and its offerings of tea, glasses of white wine and flowers. Above it the Christian crucifix and three carved idols spread their zombied composures over the room.

"Those others are Buddha, Confucius and Lao Tze," whispered Kim Chau. "Pretty inclusive religion, isn't it?"

Men priests attended the Divine Eye, lit more joss sticks. Ram could almost feel the fragrance on his skin. The priests began chanting rambly-noted sutras, bonged on a dappled copper disc, then became quiet as My Linh stood up.

"Is this a sermon?" Ram asked.

"No, no. Today she's reading a message from the Cao Dai. It's in your translation there, I think."

The translation, yes. Ram felt through his jacket, found and unfolded the sheet of paper:

CAO DAI

(The Very-High who comes to Annam to speak the Truth)
    To the peoples of the West I have given
    The peace of soul and comfort of life;
    But alas they continue willfully
    To deny the prophecy of Christ the Redemptor.
    The evil pursue fugitive virtue,
    With the sharpened knife, roam the bloodied earth.
    The voice of God that Moses heard,
    Over the Orient I am having it repeated,
    To fight, in time, underhanded heresy,
    Leading you toward the road of sin.
    The trumpet sounds, ready yourselves,
    Be prepared for this task, to <u>sacrifice</u>,
    For Universal Peace. This is my will.

Along the bottom margin, in longhand, My Linh added: *Ram, this message was received from the Cao Dai by Cao Quynh Cu, the medium, in 1930. Within it I think is the Touchstone.*

After the services they waited as instructed for the Saigon security officer. "Looks like they're sending a bureaucrat instead of one of the white mice." Chau nodded toward a thinly mustachioed young man in the crowd. "I think I know the little bastard."

"Dao Kim Chau, my good friend!" The man yelled and waved, and angled his way toward them.

"Name's Hanh Tuan," said Chau, before the man came into earshot. "Just a junior official. Shh... Morning, Hanh Tuan." Chau held his hand up. "Please meet our house guest, Ramirez Apollo. You know my sister Dao My Linh?"

"Huong Dao, I've heard of you," said Hanh Tuan, who looked too young to be a spy. He was shorter than My Linh.

"No need to call me Huong, monsieur," she said. "I'm not a woman priest yet."

"Yes, certainly. And Sergeant Apollo, call me Hon-Ton please. All the English call me that." He slicked his hair back with both hands and wiped them along the side of his tan safari-vest. "I understand we go convert the Montagnards today?"

"To *help* the Montagnards today, Hanh Tuan," My Linh corrected. "Near the border. You're familiar with the Rhade?"

"The tribe above the Delta? Well certainly, of course."

Chau drove. Hon Ton took the front seat. They began, after an hour, the ascent into the mountain region, where, along the road, scatterings of peasants stood calf-deep in pools of rice shoots, bending alongside their buffalo. Then mango trees and rubber plantations replaced the farms, then were replaced by runt trees and bamboo, then eventually by the tangled vines of the rain forest.

"Let's not stay too long," said Hon-Ton. "Don't want to catch the *jungle tax* do we?--our word for malaria, Sergeant." He shuddered. "God save us from the jungle tax."

"You believe in God, then, Hanh Tuan?" asked My Ling.

"But certainly. I am a Catholic, Huong Dao...Dao My Linh. But our priests are all men, you know." A hint of derision. "And they are all celibate, you know."

"Most of our priests are celibate, Hahn Tuan."

"Do you plan to remain celibate too, Dao My Linh?" asked Hon-Ton. He intended this as a joke but saw the look Ram gave him. Saigon had warned him to avoid provoking either the American or Kim Chau. From what Hon-Ton had gathered, both were considered quite dangerous. But Hon-Ton had a reputation for teasing young girls.

"I do not intend to remain celibate, Hanh Tuan." My Linh's face crimsoned when she saw Ram watching her. "Chastity is an invention of... Most societies put too much importance on such a natural function." She decided not to say anything further on that.

A shelf of land appeared, then dipped, but Chau turned off before reaching the descent. The path they now took, hardpack dirt, twisted north up the mountain like a vapor, then broke from the whorls of dark teak toward a plateau of green savanna woodlands. Within the trees Ram could see the Rhade village: about twenty elevated longhouses on elevated stilts with sides of bamboo and leave latticework, peopled with loinclothed tribesmen who, when they saw My Linh, hand-signaled the word back to the village.

The woods rustled into life. Old women smoking pipes hustled to the stick fence that circled the village. Naked kids clambered down the longhouse ladders while less elderly women, bamboo discs in their ears, hurried to the platforms of their huts. They spit the red betel-nut juice and waved and grinned black-toothed grins at the passing Cao Dai priestess.

A crowd gathered closer to the Rover as it shuddered to a stop and My Linh stepped out, rising in her white robes like a goddess above the small Montagnard women. "We might as well visit with the chief," said Chau.

"The villagers will take up My Linh for at least an hour. Soon there'll be a hundred of them here."

"Doesn't the chief go too?"

"No. He thinks everybody should listen only to him, the old turd." As they climbed the ladder to the bamboo floor of his longhouse, the chief, less than five feet high, made two long, exaggerated steps toward them, chattering at them. The sing-song, guttural yammer of the flat-nosed *Ban hoi te* blended into the screeching of gibbons in the surrounding forest. "He says the Montagnards hold good feelings for the Americans," said Chau, which was news to Ram. The chief's speech looked and sounded more like a scolding. "He's surprised by your brown skin," said Kim Chau. "He thought Americans were either white or black."

The chief, himself browner than either Ram or the lowland Annamese, displayed his finely filed teeth, and Ram smiled back, patting the skin of his own cheek: *Es verdad, Chief--you and me, amigo*, and the *Ban hoi te* laughed, pointing a skinny finger at Ram's gesture. He poured grey liquid into four wooden cups and handed the first to his brown-skinned guest.

"The juice of cassava root," said Hon-Ton. "A jungle aphrodisiac, I believe." Snickering.

"The Montagnards live here and in Cambodia and in Laos," said Chau, sipping, picking something suspicious from his cup. "But they don't feel they belong to any country. They live in the 'Land of the Big Leaves,' as they call it. Might seem kind of crappy to us, but the Rhade think they're in the exact middle of the universe here."

Ram sipped the sweet milk of the cassava root, which tasted a little too mushy, maybe, but not all that bad. "Then whose side are these people on?"

"No one's, Ram," answered Kim Chau. "They are Rhade."

*

Their ride back was more tumultuous, nearly freefalling down the coiled path from the Rhade village. Hon-Ton, who didn't have Chau's command of the wheel, drove, at his own insistence: "Like a darned bucking horse, isn't it?" And within two hours they had slid safely into and through the land of bamboo and elephant grass. Hon-Ton got off as soon as they entered Saigon. It seemed like an abrupt exit, Ram thought, for someone who was supposed to be their spy. But, as Hon-Ton explained in his own curious humor, the sun would be setting soon and the government didn't pay him to work after dark.

The reason for Hon-Ton's bail-out became clear when they arrived at the gates of the Dao plantation: "White mice" police cars blocked the entrance, and a group of them stood in the street inside a maze of blue-grey ribbon that webbed itself between saw-horse barricades.

"Oh, Christ." Chau yanked the car to the side, away from another white-uniformed policeman walking toward them.

"What's going on, Kim Chau?"

"It's an arrest, Ram. It's got to be--this is how they do it. *That's* the damned reason Saigon sent Hahn Tuan with us, to make sure we wouldn't get back before the looting was over."

My Linh put a hand on her brother's shoulder from the back seat. "Who are they after? Why are they doing this *now?*"

"Maybe they're panicking, My Linh. Since father used to be the government's Minister of Defense..." Chau turned to answer the policeman's question and the man moved his head sideways, signaling them to go through. "Maybe they're afraid of what he might be telling Ram. They're probably after father Dao--Christ, why didn't I think of that?"

"Be careful what you say to them, brother Kim."

When they came to the compound the white mice there were jamming pieces of art and furniture into the back seats of the police cars. Chau pulled the emergency brake and jumped from the car before it bumped to a stop and Ram began to follow, until he saw My Linh curling up in a corner of the back seat. She was going pale, tearing up. He reached over and took her hand. "Wait here, My Linh. Let me see what's happening first."

"Are they going to take my father?"

"Wait here, okay?" He held her fingers until she began to get some color back.

Inside, carpets and drapes were piled in the middle of each room. In the entry hall teak tables and chairs were stacked, surrounding the frail Dao Phuong, hunched and bewildered, barely raising his eyes when Ram came in. He stared through Ram for a moment.

"Sergeant Apollo..."

"Are you all right, Dao Phuong?"

"I am being arrested."

Chau was in the dining area arguing with an officer dressed in the uniform of a Saigon lieutenant: white jacket, gold-woven epaulets, white gloves. Chau made an angry wave at the officer and stalked toward Ram and Dao Phuong--"It's what I was afraid of, Ram. This Carson son of a bitch told them you're meeting with my father to disrupt the goddamned government, or something."

"I couldn't disrupt a *church* meeting here, Kim Chau. They know that."

"He told them we're still on that investigation ordered by Bao Dai, his old enemy--the former emperor."

"The President calls me a 'fellow traveler,'" said Dao Phuong, tiredly. "A term, I think, he borrowed from the Americans."

The gold-braided lieutenant glared at Ram from under his gold-cockaded hat as he came over to continue his harangue at the Daos, and, through all this, Ram wondered at the composure of Kim Chau's father. Father Dao remained still, complacent as a piece of furniture.

"The people that sent me here know this is..." Ram stopped himself from saying *bullshit*, not to the father Dao. "They know this isn't true, Dao Phuong."

Dao Phuong responded with only a slight raising of hands. Kim Chau answered for him: "This lieutenant is saying your Army has ordered you out of the country, Ram."

"Bullshit."

"You have to...you need to go, Sergeant." Dao Phuong's voice faltered when he saw My Linh come to the doorway, and he lowered his eyes as she came to sit next to him. Her presence seemed to bring to the scene, for a moment, a fragile peace.

"We won't let them harm you, father Dao," she said, a daughter's whisper, and her eyes searched Ram's face. "We won't let them do this, Ramirez?"

"My Linh...if they throw me out I'll come back. I'll go report this if I can, but I'll be back." He knew those words were meaningless.

The gold-braided lieutenant and two of his subalterns, interrupting their looting, motioned toward Dao Phuong.

The father Dao rose to go with them.

-

The Chinese servants returned when the police left. They straightened the rooms, beginning with the bedrooms, although Kim Chau explained to them that his family would no longer have money to keep them on. The servants prepared their meal anyway, but it was not eaten, and before My Linh went to her room she stopped to put her hand on the side of Ram's face.

And she came to him that night, he somehow knew she would, and she spoke to him in whispers. "I do not want our time to end without being with you, Ramirez," she said. "I want to walk with you again."

She had slipped to the side of his mat, this slimly veiled, beautiful specter, this golden being, as he hoped she would, but My Linh needed a companion now, not a tussle with an Army sergeant. He put his hand on her, only her arm, and tried to comfort that thought away.

"It's all right, Ramirez." He felt her voice next to him. "I want to be with you."

"My Linh..."

She put her fingers to his lips. "The function of our bodies is not immoral, Ramirez. It is not even that important. It is so difficult for people in both our worlds to understand that."

"We have so many problems here, My Linh. It wouldn't be...hell, I can't accomplish anything by going back. You know that, don't you?"

"Tell your people about my father's arrest, Ramirez." She rubbed his wrist and hand with a light, circular touch. "We can do nothing more here. We can lay beside each other and be at peace, this night." She rose from the bed and held his kimono robe for him. "Would you walk with me in the garden again?"

He moved himself to a sitting position, in his shorts, put on the kimono and followed her, and when they reached the forest he wanted to speak but she put her fingers again to his mouth. "Our thoughts should be free of other things first." Guiding his hand to her, leading him down.

The duff of pine needles fluffed into a thick cushiony underlayer, pillowing as he sat, and she kissed his hand, and she lay back with him on the matted grass. And he raised himself over her and felt her warmth rise to receive him.

They lay quiet on the bed of pine afterward. Their bodies stayed close, touched, the warmth continued to pass between them "We are free, now, to listen to each other," he heard her say, and he felt the marshmallow give of her breast, and her wet maidenhair, and she cradled into him. He allowed himself a relaxation that bordered the edge of sleep.

"We can be at peace now," he heard her say, and he let his head lay back and opened his eyes and saw the blunted horn of the moon through the trees.

"We could never be at peace here, My Linh."

"Peace is wherever the Touchstone is, Ramirez. When you return, we will find it together." She rose from the ground as she said this and he started to follow, but she went into her forest alone.

"We would need to defeat people like the Diems first," he said, into the shadows. "I can't even save your *father* from them, let alone defeat them."

A whiteness appeared and dissolved in the forest. "You will come back to save father Dao, and the rest of us, and then stay with us."

Her own concept of life again, so simple. Ram got up and scuffed through a mound of decaying leaves along the path. "I want to be with you again," he said.

"I know. Soon. We are almost through."

"With what?"

"We are almost through, Ramirez." Light from the three-quarter moon fell across her as she moved. "Do you remember what the chief of the Rhade said to my brother, Ramirez? About their position in the world?"

"They are a primitive people, My Linh. They don't take sides. Did you take me up there to hear that?"

"Yes."

"But the Rhade are *moi*, My Linh. Even your people call them savages."

"The Rhade think the rest of the world centers about them, Ram. They resist outside evil, without regard for which side it is on."

Ram put his hands into the pockets of his robe, and turned away. He didn't want to talk of these things now.

Chapter 24

Ram and My Linh kept to themselves the next morning, until they were on the road to Tan Son Nhut Airport. Kim Chau drove. The three quietly watched, as they entered Saigon, the increase in beeping cars and jingling cycles, and Ram tasted again the burnt waste air of the industrial outskirts.

"I'll get back here, My Linh." Ram broke the silence first, though he disliked the shallow sound of those words. "I'll be back here in a week."

"The Army might not let you, Ramirez."

"I know. This whole damned-"

"-If you try, your people will stop you."

"They won't know about it, My Linh." He felt along the rough wool pocket of his jacket. "My passport's still valid here, I'll get back. Meet you a week from today, okay? I'll try to get someone to listen to me in the States, then I'll get back here."

"If you think it's possible," said Chau, "we can't meet at the airport, or at our house." He thought his way through other alternatives. "We'd be safest in the crowds downtown, I think. In the Givral restaurant across from the Continental Palace Hotel--you know where that is? You'd be coming in before noon from Bangkok."

"Bangkok?"

"You won't be coming on any MATS flight this time." Chau made a circle with his hand. "Commercial flights come in through Paris and Bangkok. Long way around."

Ram shrugged. "Whatever it takes. If you're at the Givral Restaurant in exactly one week from now, I'll meet you there."

*

When Ram arrived at LAX he phoned Colonel Purdy's office and then reported, as ordered, to the Lorimar Hotel, where Purdy met him in the lobby. The colonel carried a small black notebook which he gripped like a pistol. "To answer the question you probably won't ask, Sergeant, I'm out here to clear up *another* one of your messes. Guess what I'm talking about."

Ram decided not to do that. Instead, he stared around at the old plum-colored lobby, at the old people pinging on a bell at the desk, and the old velvet vermillion drapes. A soup smell of vegetable-beef drifted in from an undoubtedly old kitchen. "I've got a bigger problem right now, Colonel."

"Cut the crap. You've *got* no bigger problem right now." Purdy raised his cap, mopped his bald head. "First you go on a routine inquiry and end up *shooting* the son of a bitch--that was *me* that saved your ass from the stockade, you know. Then you can't stop chasing this miserable Bryan investigation-"

"-I don't chase the Bryan investigation, Colonel-"

"-can't stop chasing this miserable Bryan investigation to where I get my butt chewed off and pulled from FECOM command and sent here just to nursemaid one goddamned sergeant, and now here comes Bryan raising hell all the way to the Department of *Defense*, and people are asking why I assign a man who's one step from the psycho ward, and you can't be shaken loose from Bryan even here in *California*. And now we send you for some minor recon in Indo-China and you get accused of aiding the goddamned *insurrection*."

Colonel Purdy, puffing noisily, stopped to breathe. "Now, you tell me what the hell this is about."

"The Dao family needs our help."

"Who needs *what?* What the hell're you talking about?"

"The family of Lieutenant Dao needs our help, Colonel."

Colonel Purdy's eyes searched the plum-vermillion lobby before falling back on Ram. "Is there someone watching us here? We being shadowed or something? Because I sure can't see any other reason for such an asinine-meaningless statement. Who the hell's talking about the *Dao* family?"

"The government there is screwing them up-"

"-Or are you talking in some kind of code? You think I've been spotted here as an Intelligence officer?"

Ram watched Purdy a moment... "We could help stop that insurrection there, Colonel, if we help people like the Daos."

Purdy jabbed the notebook toward him. "I personally think you're full of crap, Sergeant, but I have orders to take down whatever crap you give me." He did a heel-around toward a pair of French armchairs in the farthest corner of the lobby, sat, applied his pen like a scalpel to the notebook. "Now," said the colonel, as Ram took the other seat, "I need all the input you have on this Vietnam situation."

"I can put that in a report, Colonel. We need to talk about the Dao family."

"I'll decide what we need to talk about, Sergeant," said Purdy. "And right now we'll talk about the situation in Vietnam." He put a check next to one of his scribbled lines. "Apparently the situation in that little piss-ant country has reached a real urgency among our top people. They aren't at all interested in the plight of your one Chinese family."

Ram drummed a finger against his chair. "I thought you sent a lot of other G-2 into Vietnam?"

"We sent a lot of idiots, Sergeant, because of this 'Rapprochement' shit. None of them have the direct contact you've got." Purdy made a check beside his next point, it having been made, and moved the pen down a line. "Tell me about the political climate you found in South Vietnam."

"For Christ's sake, Colonel..."

"Better yet, how is the political climate in South Vietnam different from what you saw in Korea?"

"It's the same war, our dictators against theirs. The winners get to shoot the losers."

"Don't get snippy with me, Sergeant." Making a large blue check beside that line in his book. "Now this Kim Chau Dao is back in South Vietnam, and he plans to join the communists there-"

"-Plans to what?"

"He has joined the communists there, Sergeant. Haven't you been listening?"

"Diem calls anyone who disagrees with him a communist."

Colonel Purdy wrote this down. "So much for your opinion. Distorted by your relationship with that Chinese family, no doubt, but it is they, *not* President Diem, who are the enemy, Sergeant." Colonel Purdy laid his pen on the notebook, cleared his throat to a lecture-pitch. "Please remember, Sergeant, you're still in this Army, you re-upped for this 'campus surveillance' shit. You don't mind spying on school kids but now say you're worried about this communist family? Well, spare me the plight of the Dao family, would you? You're not bothered about any morality problems here, not in my book."

The colonel resumed writing, recording this speech, probably, for the applause of his superiors. "Your friend Dao's been offered the undersecretariat of something called the Western Nam Bo Interprovince Committee," he said, without looking up. "Gives him a lot of power in one of the bloodiest groups of the Viet Minh. He can call a meeting of all battalion commanders but he can't really *run* the meetings--an odd twist in their organizational makeup."

Where the hell to go next? Ram thought. The newspapers? Not hardly. A sergeant's non-news about a country most of them never heard of, not unless some kind of brouhaha came out of it... Like Bryan's arms deals? Hell, what would he show them for proof?

"I assume you've left your communications open with this Dao family?" said Colonel Purdy, through now with his scribblings. "Unfortunately you might still be needed as an information-gatherer."

"I was thrown out of the country, Colonel."

"Right. And you'll *stay* out, until we say otherwise. And when we do say otherwise, that government will let you back in. Trust me." Purdy accentuated the end of his composition with a large circular period. "We will, for the time being, keep your family of gooks--or what's left of them by now--on ice, at least until they *officially* join the communists."

"You mean when we force them to join the communists, Colonel."

Colonel Purdy blew some air between his lips, and sucked himself in. "Sergeant...you wander through life like some confused college sophomore, you know. But now you listen good, because Bryan and the governments of the world operate on a different level than you and me, and you better conform to that world with the rest of us ordinary mortals because everyone, even you, has to pay the piper some day."

Ram wanted to point out, then, that apparently Bryan *was* the piper, and decided against it. "You know the man's still on my ass, Colonel. If he keeps coming, how am I supposed to handle it?"

"Handle it? *Avoid* him, damn it. What the hell'd he say at your meeting with him?"

Ram shrugged it off. "I'll take care of it myself."

"No you won't. You will *avoid* him. What the hell'd he say?

"He thinks I'm the Angel of Death."

Colonel Purdy raised his hands, giving up. "Okay, right, you've been pushed into his spotlight and you--macho-man that you think you are--give him the finger while you're in it, right? So go ahead after Bryan and kill each other, just don't get me *or* the Army involved in it, understand?"

"Thanks for the pep talk, Colonel."

"Pep-talking isn't my job."

*

To get money for the flight back, Ram stopped at the campus Administration Building for a student loan application, then drove back to Beverly Glen Canyon. Weissman wasn't around, thank God. He didn't want any conversation right now. He lay on his bed next to the window and thought about Bryan, and the family of Dao. And about Harry Crosse...

Harry Crosse. Ram could get to Bryan through Harry, maybe--where did Harry say he stayed down here, on a *yacht*? Harry'd given him the location of it, the address was still in one of his shirts.

The street light outside turned on, buzzing, rippling a hole in the night.

But then, Ram thought, why would Harry arrange another meeting for me?

Buzz went the light. Ram had asked Weissman why no one ever fixed the damn thing. Street lights don't buzz, Weissman answered. Self-contained, inner-directed, damned...buzzing. Its call went unanswered in the canyon of little houses.

*

Harry Crosse rolled the tiny steel balls around the pits of his cardboard battlefield until one of them steadied itself above "Foxhole 10". With a tip of his hand Harry plipped the ball in, then slid the other one away from holes 3 and 4--"friendly" troops. He saw in the glass the reflection of his eye, overlaying the disc-battlefield like the dark eye of God, distracting him from his remaining ball, rolling to a friendly bunker-hole, killing "8" of his own troops there.

He swore quietly at himself. It had taken twenty minutes to put all those ball-missiles into enemy bunkers, except for this one last sonuvabitch. He'd done that despite the roll, the slow roll, of Bryan's yacht, exaggerated somewhat by a passing dredger.

He put the piece aside when he saw Ram. Charles Trevors, who had come with Harry to the yacht, met Apollo at the rigging house at the bottom of the ramp.

"It's okay, Trevors," Harry yelled to the bodyguard, over the railing. He drew back from the ripe smell of seagull leavings. "Check him out first, would you?" Trevors patted Ram down and stepped aside, and Harry leaned on the railing as Ram reached him. "Never get enough of us, right, Sergeant? You must be starting to like us."

"You and I aren't through yet." Ram had to bend his head to the side to avoid looking at the sun, which was directly behind Harry. "You were the one that got my father fired... You know he killed himself?"

The question, spoken so quietly, straightened Harry up. "No one here thought he'd do that."

"Does that make you any less of an ass hole, Harry?"

"You come here to take revenge, Sergeant?"

"I came to see Bryan."

"That's kind of a coincidence, because I think the man's about ready to see *you*. But he's in his fortress today--like all days, lately."

Ram held up his hand to block the sun but it stayed behind Harry, liquefying Harry's features to a blob inside the light. Ram could see only a grey presence in there. "I need to talk with Bryan about the Vietnamese family."

"The Daos?" said the presence. "What would a meeting with Bryan have to do with them?"

"They're getting screwed over for something I did, thanks to your chickenshit nut-case boss."

Harry's snort broke from within the glare of light. He made a slapping sound on the railing. "Hell, man, that's his whole point. You cause the death of his, he causes the death of yours. It's poetic, he thinks."

"He's a nut case. But you...Don't you give a crap where this is going?"

Harry's voice did tone down. "Well, now, Ramirez Apollo, I go with the gold, but at least I admit it. Just how much do *you* care about all your chums, amigo? How come you don't come here asking about Claire?"

"Claire?"

"Haven't you been keeping score? She's gone, Sergeant. My weasely little co-worker's taken her to doper's heaven."

"What the hell're you saying? He *killed* her?"

"Christ, he sent her back to her girlhood playground, to life among them Parisian bohemians." Harry, still resting on the railing, slumped down closer toward Ram. "If it makes you feel better, all this doesn't sit that well with me either, but the world's just not a genuinely fair place, is it?"

"Bryan thinks he can get his grandson by *doping* her?"

"Thinks? Thinks? Shit, boy, it's already done. You've heard of an unfit mother? Well, that lady's no longer fit by *any* measure, and you can thank yourself for pushing the old bastard over that edge. First you shoot his son and then you screw his dead son's wife." Harry Crosse spread his hands out, covering the sky like palm fronds. "Mr. Bryan's completing the work you started, my friend."

"Where is she, Harry?"

"I know where she is, Sergeant, but I've got no reason to tell you." Harry lowered his head, watching Ram from the top of his eyes. "You were the one who sent her to steal those papers, weren't you?"

"Who gives a shit any more." Ram squinted into the sun, then turned to adjust his eyes on the white stern of Bryan's yacht. "You liked her too, didn't you?"

Ram could make out Harry's teeth now, grinning inside the penumbra of a blurred silhouette. "You working on *my* ass now, Apollo?" Harry lifted a pinkish drink and clinked the ice. "I do like her, and I'm sorry about her kid. But she's so full of China White by now, hell, she probably doesn't remember if she even has a kid."

167

With the toe of his shoe Ram pushed against the docking cleat. "Harry, I want you to tell me where she is, then get me a meeting with John Bryan."

"You giving me orders now?"

Ram shifted his weight, turned to watch the breakwater.

"You saying you give a good crap about Claire?" said Harry. "I thought you were getting thick with that Vietnamese chick." Ram was assuming some simplistic affinity with him, which apparently irritated Harry. "Don't plan on any help from this quarter, friend. Right now Carson's with Claire, and that man is not at *all* as nice as me."

"You get me that meeting with Bryan, Harry. I'll try to help Claire." Ram put his hands in his pockets and started to walk away.

"Beneath that weasel exterior old Carson is more like these two bodyguards, Sergeant," said Harry. "*Real* killers, if you understand me. You hear me?"

Ram had already passed by Charles Trevors on the ramp.

Chapter 25

The landlady tugged her blue robe into a tidier alignment. "Naw, that girl's left last week. Good riddance. One of those dope addicts, y'know--should have seen the paraphernalia she left here. Good thing the grandaddy's taken that boy away."

"The grandaddy came here?"

"He didn't, but his personal lawyer came asking questions. Had me sign papers to that effect."

"Where'd she go?"

"Don't have the slightest, but good riddance. Why not ask the grandaddy? Bet he'd know."

"I bet he would. Thanks."

Ram pushed through the dusty etched-glass entrance door, down the agate stairs and away from the smell of this decaying elegance, with a shudder of relief. The place reminded him too much of his own neighborhood. These were working-class gringos and not Latinos, but the place still looked like the bad part of City Terrace.

*

"You getting a student loan, Ram?" Weissman's honk came from the front room, where he found Ram's approved loan application. "How'd you get one of those?"

"Not right now, Luke."

"S'cuse me, Sarge." Ram heard him open the refrigerator. "Didn't know you were *meditating.*"

The hammer of the telephone interrupted this.

"I talked with the man," came Harry's voice. "He *wants* you up there, matter of fact. Says he can now prove he fought in the 'Great War.' In the battle of Belleau Wood, if I heard him right."

"That's what all the construction was about?"

"Guess so."

"The man's a fruitcake, Harry."

"Probably, but till he's too nutty to write a check, me and the gorillas'll stay with him, betcher life. He flew our boy Trevors back up there today, matter of fact. Plane'll be back for us tomorrow if you really want to do this."

"I do."

"Doubt if he'll have you done away with up there, if that's entered your mind. Not at *this* meeting, anyway. Too many people know you're going there, including me."

"Thanks for the reassurance."

"I still wouldn't bet my *huevos* on it, though. Fruitcakes aren't real predictable, you know"

"That's not the biggest of my problems right now."

*

Bryan's private airstrip was less than half a mile from the fortress. He insisted that the pilot bring Harry and Ram into his own strip instead of the Monterey Peninsula Airport so they could fly the remaining distance in his olive-colored helicopter. Canting in around the trees just for effect, Harry felt. For Bryan's big *premier.*

Harry ducked through the door as soon as the copter runners hit the grass. He hurried past the cropped green landing-patch, past the thumping blades, then spruced himself back up. Vest, coat, tie.

Ram stretched his legs before following Harry out.

"From here it's just a walk through the woods there," said Harry, talking above the wash of noise. "But I don't think he plans to actually meet with you."

"Then what the hell am I doing here?"

"He wants to show you what he's built out there." Harry pointed toward a flagstone path that led into the trees. "You know the way, compadre. I've been told to wait here."

Ram gave a shake of his head and started along the path, toward the newly planted oak and birch, where fragments of John Bryan's work began to form. It appeared to be a battlefield, a simulated battlefield just inside the woods. Glimpses of mannequin soldiers within casings of thick clear glass. Sandbagged bunkers and artillery pieces side by side with the sea, separating the two landscapes--the battleground and the seaside grasses--like a fold in the earth. Even the smell of battle was in the air: cordite, burnt wood, rotted meat.

Within the trees a loudspeaker squealed, squelched, then allowed the purr of Bryan's voice: "You have requested a meeting, Sergeant Apollo." Ram stopped to look along the tree line where the voice came from.

"Good," said Bryan's voice. "But first I need you to look upon my construction. See the relics of the battle that I *did* take part in, Sergeant--the *Bois de Belleau.* See the reproduction of my experience there."

Ram stepped to the outskirts of the tree line. "This is your proof? What the hell is this?"

No answer.

"Have you started hiding from me now, Mr. Bryan?"

A clicking sound came from the speakers, another squeal. "Still as insolent--" His voice wavered, broke off, began again. "What you are looking at, Sergeant, is the resurrection of my experiences at Belleau Wood. I've created this proof for my father, and for you."

"Because I'm the Angel of Death?"

A long pause followed, before Bryan answered, "Yes."

"This is supposed to convince me you're not a coward?"

"This is the re-creation of my war experience."

Ram studied the scene, still mostly hidden from where he stood. But a feel of this battlefield did bring back the familiar tension, the butterflies. "I've come to make a deal, Mr. Bryan. The father of my friend, Dao Phuong, is being tried in the country of South Vietnam, and you're the one who did that."

A longer silence, then the clicking noise, then Bryan's voice: "The condemnation of Mr. Phuong was not really part of my intent there."

"If you stop it, I will be convinced you aren't a coward. Only cowards condemn women and old men."

"I cannot help you. Their punishment is out of my hands."

"Then what the hell *was* your plan for the Dao family?"

"Lifelong purgatory, Sergeant Apollo." Bryan was trying for some God-like tone here. His voice rolled through the birch and the war scene. "The same punishment I plan for you, Sergeant, as surely as I decide the fate of these mannequins. So now you are witness, now you can carry this back, when I send you to him."

Ram couldn't see, from where he walked, all the parts of the Belleau Wood scene. Just bits and pieces of weaponry: a cannon muzzle or a fixed bayonet sticking through the underbrush, a turret nestling behind clumps of trees. Continuing beyond his view was a diorama of scenes, hints of larger exhibits.

He went into the forest as Bryan's voice came back. "See the needlessness of your mission here, Sergeant."

The crazy theater expanded. A stand of trees enveloping pillboxes and slit trenches, manned by full-sized wood soldiers. A row of Howitzers in the rear, howling skyward, craning their welded trunks. Blackened fire lines, underground bunkers, a graveyard sprouting Army-regulation crosses. Sandbagged breastworks sheltered troops surrounded by tree stumps, carefully splintered, burnt to affect embattled ramparts.

Within glass boxes some of the soldiers stood in attack stances, wearing field uniforms of tin hats, tight khaki blouses, patch pockets, choking collars, breeches. Clay-pipe leggings fitted to the calf. Most of them carried '03 Springfields with sixteen-inch bayonets: American marines.

German grenadiers appeared on the other side. Grey-green field uniforms, top boots, pork-pie hats. Bandoleers of nickeled steel bullets and stacks of potato-masher grenades lay by the dugout of a crew that manned a maxim machine gun. Others aimed their Mausers at the marines through a matrix of barbed wire.

"This is fake, Mr. Bryan," said Ram. "This is fake shit. How would this prove you're not a coward?" In the silence he stepped farther into the trees and saw, caged in their glass protections, doughboys with Big Red One patches on their sleeves, standing guard beside Vickers machine guns, or asleep in their topcoats. British Mills grenades lined the top of their parapet.

"You are not to use profanity on these grounds," said John Bryan, adding a curious question: "Why are you doing this to me?"

"Why don't you come and stop me, or do you pick fights only with women and old men like the Daos, like a *coward* would?" Ram wanted to work on this coward angle, since it seemed so important to Bryan.

Stillness answered him. It lay above the battlefield like the after-ring of an explosion.

Ram walked on. A squad of French soldiers, bearded and stooped in horizon-blue coats, cradled their heavy Lebel rifles in both arms. They were standing around a French 75 artillery piece.

"You think by provoking me that I will release your Chinese friends, Sergeant Apollo? That is stupid logic, Sergeant Apollo."

"Then let's settle it here, Bryan. There's no need to punish the family of Dao. We can settle it right here."

A breeze from the Pacific rustled the woods, a sun ray glinted off things metallic inside the gun hole of a bunker, on the German side.

"In due time, Sergeant," said John Bryan.

"If you don't get Dao Phuong released, I can bring the government down on you. I know where your missing documents are."

"You are *bluffing!*" boomed the loudspeakers. "The one who stole those documents is in a place far beyond you now!"

"I'll find her, and she'll give them to me."

"You are *bluffing*." There came a choking sound, then a tapping as the microphone was covered up, then: "She does not have them with her, we *know* that."

"Then who else can get them? Your boy Carson's with her now, isn't he?--and he still hasn't got them. Well *I'm* going to get them, even if it means taking out your boy-"

"Don't you *dare* threaten Kenneth! Don't you *ever* dare threaten Kenneth's life! You have already taken my one son!"

Ram had struck a nerve worth pursuing here. "I can't guarantee that, Mr. Bryan. I may have to take him out."

"Trevors! Ochoa! Go now!"

Ram watched the two bodyguards enter the trees from the fortress side. They split around a Mark IV tank and joined again in front of it.

"Then we settle it here, Mr. Bryan."

"Not *here*, Sergeant. Not now. Not within these hallowed grounds." Bryan had brought his voice to a whisper. "You will not anger me into a confrontation here."

"Then I forever brand you as a coward, Mr. Bryan."

In response, a static hiss came through the speakers. A thin ticking noise, a clicking.

The hissing stopped.

"Time to go, amigo," called Sorry Ochoa. He and Trevors were still some distance away.

"Time to go, ass hole," said Charles Trevors, who didn't need to call out for his voice to carry. His arms swayed alongside him like elephant trunks.

Ram didn't move. "I'm reporting to your father, Mr. Bryan, that you're still a coward." He said this into the forest and wondered if the outside mikes were still on.

"Can the shit, Chico," grumbled Trevors. "Back to the helicopter now--" The sound of John Bryan's voice interrupted him.

"You do not fool me, Ramirez Apollo!" Bryan was no longer the omniscient being he tried to invent. His voice had risen almost to a shout: "I have convinced you, I *know* that! I have taken away your sanction to touch me *or* Mr. Carson!"

Ochoa, true to his name, looked sorrowful as he put a hand on Ram's arm with the grip of a professional wrestler. "We have orders not to hurt you just yet, chingon, but you gotta go."

"Just for now, ass hole," Trevors added, sticking a finger like a night stick into Ram's shoulder.

Ram turned toward Trevors but Ochoa stepped between them. "You wouldn't have a chance, friend. Mr. Bryan's in control here, don't you know that?"

"Does he sound like someone in control, amigo? Why take orders from a *lunnático* like that?"

"*Ese*, vato, I don' wanna hurt you, but I will if the man tells me to," said Sorry Ochoa. He began to lead Ram back to the helicopter pad. "What the hell's the matter with you anyway? You been squeezing the *cajones* of the jackal, man. You may be tough where you come from but tough doesn't cut it here, *believe* it. I know. Not even I'm tough in this league."

"There's no league here. This is a nut house."

"Well, you wait. We been told you was the leader of some L.A. street gang or something but that's a pile o' shit here. Mr. Bryan's the tough guy up here. He's got all the grease up here, hombre."

Ochoa and Trevors stopped at the edge of the grove where Harry walked down to meet them. "Feels like a prisoner exchange." Harry intended it as humor. Neither of the bodyguards looked amused.

"Sweet Jesus, you must have pushed the old man's button," said Harry, as he and Ram continued alone toward the helicopter. "Heard that last speech from up here. Surprised he didn't just turn those boys loose on you."

"You don't understand the game, Harry."

"You better hope to shit that *you* do, partner," said Harry.

Before they got too near the helicopter Harry slipped a paper into Ram's jacket. "This's Claire's address in Paris," he said, out the side of his mouth, more or less. "Whatever this freak game's about, maybe this'll help even it up. If you're headed back to your Chinese girl friend--and I think you are--you'll have to go by way of Paris anyway."

"Never been to Paris. How're the whorehouses there?"

"Bon voyage, mother."

*

John Bryan sat silent in his grand den-library, and prayed for the return of Kenneth Willy Carson. He shouldn't have let Kenneth go to Paris to accompany that woman, he thought. They'd already hired someone in Paris to supply her, and he needed Carson *here*. He pushed his intercom button... "Mrs. Cummings, get me General Novinger on the line, then come in. I need a telegram to Mr. Carson."

Kenneth is the nearest thing I have for family now, except for my grandson, he thought. But sometimes Kenneth fails to understand, I don't want her dead, not *that* way, and I know Kenneth does what he thinks is best for me and certainly no one blames him, but at the base of it I am reluctant to slay my enemies unless it might someday become so--so absolutely necessary... It is against God's law. Doesn't anyone *understand* that?

He is only a street pachuco, Bryan knew Carson would say to that.

You do not understand what we are dealing with, thought Bryan. He killed a *Bryan*. He is capable of killing you too, and doesn't anyone realize

174

that I am a man of God? Thou shalt not kill and so on, but I am so trapped, am so afraid. I have no control over what I do to these people any more and I just...don't know why.

He shushed that away with a petulant slap in the air, while the buzz of his telephone interrupted. "Yes, General Novinger, I'm calling again about your Sergeant. *Just* here, in fact, and he's become extremely problematic for us--*all* of us, General. He could be getting information that would harm your designs for that country--I know he's only a...but such documentation would give his words authenticity, don't you see? The *documentation*, General. Shipping orders, uh, uh, bills of lading--of course he can't prove their destination, I know this, but--"

The general had hung up.

Military people are always so afraid someone is listening, he thought.

Mrs. Cummings knocked, entered, and circumspectly went to her chair.

"A telegram to Mr. Carson in Paris, Mrs. Cummings. It needs to go right now." He searched his desk for notes that weren't there. "To Mr. Carson, in Paris..." he repeated, searching.

Mrs. Cummings nodded and settled farther into her chair. She did not, would never, look directly at him.

"Send this off, Mrs. Cummings: 'Think Sergeant Ramirez Apollo on way to Mrs. Daniel Bryan. Insure--*insure*-- that no documents exist there. Do not, repeat, do not try to stop him. He can do no harm without documents. He is no real threat to us at this time. Leave handling of Sergeant Apollo to this office. Repeat, do not try to interfere with him.'"

This seemed like the right approach, certainly, thought John Bryan. No reason to put Kenneth in any kind of jeopardy, was there? Sooner or later that woman could make contact with the sergeant anyway, or with someone like him, for all the good that would do her now.

Chapter 26

The Air France Super Constellation, reducing throttle to its four turbo-compound engines, droned over Paris, circling toward Orly Field. The groan and bump of the lowering wheels was unusually loud, it stirred a few heads in the cabin, but not Ram's. Not after the rattly MATS troop carriers he'd flown on.

The connection through Paris would work out okay. The overnight layover gave him a chance, maybe, to find Claire and still catch the morning flight through Bangkok to Saigon, with one more ticket that would get him to Okinawa if he had to get out of Vietnam in a hurry. Fort Buckner, Okinawa, might be the only safe place around here that he could get to fast. He could figure out what to do from there.

Ram was looking over the seat literature describing the Boeing 707 as the Super Constellation screeched onto the tarmac. There was this 130-ton machine coming soon that would fly at *twice* the speed of the Constellation... He put it down to re-read the note Harry gave him: *Hotel Greco*, in the low section of Montmartre, "in the southeast corner of the Ninth Arrondissement," wrote Harry, "where them bohemians all hang out."

At the cab stand Ram handed the address to a driver who, reading it, made a faint wave with his eyebrows, then drove to a hill of four-story apartments, neo-Gothics, armored along the front with iron grillwork and shuttered garrets.

Inside the Greco the wine-dark lobby crouched under a dozen flickering tulip lamps. The manager--a Mssr. Tourlotte, according to the sign on his door--popped from his office as soon as Ram gave Claire's name to the withered night clerk: "You are from the offices of Mssr. Bryan, I assume?" Tourlotte wanted to shake Ram's hand. Ram obliged. The manager had the grip of a sponge.

"Right."

"She gives us no trouble, Monsieur, ah, Apollo--such a strong name," said Tourlotte, checking the register. "She gives no trouble at all." Tourlotte, middle-sized, brows thick as asphalt, flinched a smile at Ram. "Even her friends here are polite indeed."

"You have a key to her room?"

Tourlotte dawdled a moment.

"Bryan sent me, remember?" Ram could go along with Tourlotte's assumption.

The manager felt inside a slot in the message grid. "*Ca va sans due, monsieur.* You have room 323, down the hall from Madame Bryan," said the manager, bringing out the keys. "She is in room 302--shall I show the way?"

"I'll find it." Ram took both keys and started up the stairs; there didn't appear to be an elevator. He heard the manager pick up the telephone behind him.

A tight machine-stitched Persian weave, orange and green, tiered over the stairway. Bulky ornate moldings cloaked the ceiling corners--a hooker's workplace, Ram guessed. Struggling under this decaying crap for its long-gone dignity.

Carson was waiting on the third flight. "Say, now, *Monsoor* Apollo," said the grinning Willy. "Sir Lancelot coming to save a damsel in distress?" He leaned against the wall of the landing, started cleaning a fingernail with his turquoise-handled knife.

"Nice looking blade, cabron. You got any plans for that?"

"Just keeping the cuticles trim, tough guy. Bryan asked me not to use it."

"Then you better obey Mr. Bryan." Ram walked past, looking at door numbers, and Carson began to follow. "Just don't crowd me, amigo. Don't want to spank you here among your friends." Claire's room was near the end of the hallway where a window glistened from a light drizzle, seeping through, wetting the carpet, producing a shabby animal-musk odor, while claws of peeling yellow paint and curling wallpaper decorated the wounded hallway of this wounded building.

The back of a business card, slid into a metal frame on the door to room 302, indicated "C. Bryan" in pencil. Each door had a similar card along the corridor of doors, running like parallel ladders to the opposite end, and through Claire's door he heard French music on a radio. And other sounds: bed springs, a cough, a light splashing noise.

He knocked, waited, heard people talking inside: *Was Monsieur Carson coming back?* a voice asked. *Hope not,* another answered. He knocked again, the voices went silent. Only the radio now. He tried the key and the door, after a rusty *clatch*, swung open.

Seedy graying furniture lined up uniformly inside, beneath a round dime-store ceiling light. Faded aqua prints of sailing ships receded inside their stick-frames on the wall. A man puffing a cigarillo was flopped on the sofa, head and feet rising to the arms on either side.

"Can I help you, monsieur?" The man folded a magazine on his stomach and stubbed out the acrid-smelling cigarillo.

"I don't believe this. If it isn't old Ramirez Apollo." Claire came to the bedroom door wearing a short pink slip, leaned sleepily against it and tried to focus on him. "How the hell're you, Ram? How the hell'd you find me?" She motioned languidly toward the man on the couch. "You meet my friend Jean-Pierre?"

"You've got no friends here, Claire. Get some clothes on. Let's go somewhere and talk."

Carson surfaced at the hallway door. "You go on down to the Maison Cockteau again, Claire." He winked at Ram. "We let her go there all she wants, Chicano. She gets fixed there or she comes back here, long as she stays where the sweetness is. Right, Claire?" He looked at the man on the sofa. "She had her sweetness lately?"

"Oui, monsieur." Jean-Pierre sat up and brushed back his wiry grey hair, and began to put on his shoes. "She go in not ten minutes ago."

Carson spread his hands toward Ram. "So help yourself, boy. She's smooth as silk now, though in a couple hours she'll be *crying* to get back here." He leaned intimately toward Ram. "Until then, of course, you go have fun with her, if you want--"

The knuckled back of Ram's fist cut Carson off, mashing his cheek to his teeth and snapping his head sideways, spinning him backward across the floor. He rolled over and started to reach into his pocket until Ram stepped on his arm.

"Leave the blade there, *cabron*, or I'll take it from you and use it. *Comprende?*"

"Why not just kill him, Ram." Claire came over and leaned against Ram and kicked at Carson with her foot. "Puny little son-bitch."

"Get dressed, Claire," Ram aimed her toward the bedroom door and eyed the other man, Jean-Pierre, who hadn't moved. "You have any problem with this, Jean-Pierre?"

The Frenchman clasped his hands together. "I only supply the heroin, monsieur."

"Fine. Now get him and you out of here."

"Oui, monsieur." He bent to the side of Carson, who was holding his jaw in both hands.

"You're a stupid son of a bitch, you know that?" Carson said, between his fingers. "If those papers were around here Bryan would've told me, and *I'd* have gotten her to tell me where they were, *believe* me."

"Didn't I tell you to get him out, Jean-Pierre?" Ram stared around at the Frenchman, who pulled Carson to his feet and began shouldering him toward the door.

Carson tried to shake himself loose. "I even tried searching up her ass, just for fun--didn't I, Claire? No documents there either, capish? No Sir Lanceloting around here, *cabron*, because Claire doesn't *want* to leave.

Right, Claire?" Jean-Pierre tugged at his sleeve and Carson didn't resist now. The Frenchman half-carried him through the doorway.

"So you want him to kill me, Claire?" Carson called past Ram toward the bedroom. "We'll see about that when you get back, won't we?"

Ram shut the door on them. *So I'm a puny little son of a bitch, am I, Claire?* he heard Carson say.

Ram looked into the bedroom as Claire sleepily serpentined herself into a tight one-piece lavender dress. "Puny doesn't always mean harmless, Claire. Better keep some distance between you and that little bastard."

"I'm not sure I care any more, Ram." Her words came slow and uneven, head to one side, hair falling across her shoulder. "Anyway, he's leaving this week... Let's go to the Maison Cockteau."

"What's the Maison Cockteau?"

"Didn't I mention it? That's where I had Harry send those documents. To Emile St Amand-"

"-Harry *Crosse*?"

"Help comes from weird places sometimes, doesn't it?"

In the chill drizzle drifting through the arrondissement of Montmartre they walked together down confined streets, where trash cans stood full on the curbs, where the night people huddled behind clenched hands, lighting sweet-smelling tobacco.

"It's never occurred to Carson to check *Emile* for those papers." Claire sniggered at this, and tightened her hold, pinching onto his arm for support. "Anyway, Emile would never tell on me."

They turned right on the Rue Germain Pilon, right again on the Boulevard de Clichy. They passed a purple tattooing shop, a line of porno stores, some bar-brasseries, a row of sidewalk cafes onto the Place Blanche. And Claire told him of Carson's raping her, of the way she was brought here: "I can't break loose from this again, Ram. Just take the damn papers and forget this, because all those nice, those fine instincts...even motherhood dies here."

"Here? Where the hell is *here*?" He went quiet for a moment. He'd almost called it an *illusion*. Lord, My Linh and his father had really brainwashed him. "Anyway, it's too dangerous for you here."

"I doubt if Carson would kill me, if that's what you're thinking. Killing goes too much against Bryan's Bible-waving, I think."

"Carson could go out of control."

"Against the commandments of Bryan, his father-figure? Not likely. But if I'm wrong, he'd be doing me a favor."

They approached a group of floodlit sand-blasted signs offering a saloon, *tobac, liquer* and shoes. *Vins de Propriete. Fromager.* A closed cafe with steel gates across its entrance was appendaged to the still-open Maison Cockteau. They went under the burgundy canopy into a room of tables with wine-stained oilcloth, up to a mezzanine filled with marijuana-sweet air, where large pillows in the shape of bodyless armchairs lay around petite marble tables, peopled with bizarre citizens: a chalk-skinned boy in a white silk bolero shirt, an old guy with a Julius Caesar haircut, a fat woman squozen into a burlap-weave middy. In one corner a phonograph playing loto and flute spun beneath a waiting stack of records.

A man with the large oval face of a moose, one eye half-closed, grinned his large moose-grin at Claire as she and Ram sat on the pillows next to him. "Yes-s-s, Cinderella arrives with her prince. So nice to see you, mademoiselle." He leaned forward in feigned supplication with a beefy shifting of hips.

"This is Emile St. Amand, Ram," said Claire. "Emile's the one with the papers, he's kind of my *avocat* here."

"*Alors!* Is this the prince you wait for?" Emile St. Amand beamed and extended his hand. "Our Cinderella needs a prince so badly. What is your pleasure? You need cocaine?"

"Christ no...thanks."

"Ah, well, we have the good alternative." Emile groped beneath his marble table and produced a brass saucer of hand-twisted joints. "Le Columbian on the left, Chinois Rouge on the right. *A votre sante.*"

Ram took one from the left. "Take all you desire," said Emile with a sweep of hands. "Mademoiselle Bryan's father-in-law, he pays for her *l'additions* here."

"Long as it's for dope," Claire added, lighting her own. She saw the way Ram looked at Emile when he mentioned Bryan. "We can trust Emile, Ram. He never talks about the papers."

"Claire and I, we are old friends," explained Emile. "Since over ten years now, although we don't see her for such a long time. But should that stop me from accepting Mssr. Bryan's money? Is that a *gaucherie*, monsieur? Is that not ethical?"

"I'm losing track of ethical." Ram inhaled from the twist of marijuana, which produced a sweet heavy vapor, a booster detectably blended into it. "You have the papers here?"

"Oui, *certainement*, but not here." Emile shifted himself again. "I received them just last week from a Mister Crosse."

"I'll pick them up tomorrow, on my way out," Ram said. "Write down where I can find you, okay?"

"And you write where I can find *you*." Emile slumped forward so Ram could heed his words. "The friends of Mssr. Bryan that come here, they are precarious people, don't you think? I should have someone to call if the princess gets into crisis."

"The princess is in crisis right now, Emile."

"*Tres possible.*" Emile fumbled a large finger inside his shirt, withdrew a pencil stub, scratched on a paper scrap and handed it to Ram. "You will write your address here, Emile will keep it. I will tell you if something becomes of the princess, *n'est-ce pas?* You will trust Emile." Ram wrote down his university address, and the military address of Fort Buckner, Okinawa.

"How goes it, Flower of the Night?" The falsetto voice of the white-skinned boy spoke to Claire as she rose again.

"I'm floating, Sebastian. Feeling just grand."

"Haaa! The lady's doing some hard white," said the man who looked like Caesar. He reached up, they touched hands as she passed, and she continued around the room, touching each head, humming wisps of tunes that blended into a tuneless mash with the twanging of the loto-flute music.

"Everything's okay now," she said to Ram as she passed. His lungs felt weightless with the energized marijuana. "Come float with me, Ram."

He inspected the crumbling ash-end of his smoke. *Had* to be a booster in there. "Got to keep my head straight, Claire."

"No, no," said the boy in white. "Go with the cannabis and powder, prince. Soda is the golden road."

"The young *débauche* is right, perhaps," added Emile. "After we explore everything else, do we reject this way of life? *Au contraire*, this is where all the seekers end their seeking."

"Non-fuggin'-participation," mumbled Ram.

"*Bien entendue.* Passivism, my friend," said Emile. "Until death plucks you up, enjoy the fruits of hemp and poppy."

The ultimate passivism, buried in snow and weed: another life-form to think about. Ram sucked deeply from the twig.

"Swing, baby. Come to mama." The old lady sang to Claire. "Pr-r-retty swings my *chanteuse*. Do us a fandango."

"She got the feeling," said Snow White. "Andante, adagio--slo-o-o-ow."

Ram let his head turn to a full-on view of Claire, so he could figure that out: *What feeling?* Claire smiled sleepily and swayed before him.

"What feeling?" he asked. "What do you feel?" The boosters were screwing with his head--another ray in this life-spectrum: these damned Parisian bohemians.

"The *feeling*," said Sebastian, whose accent now sounded like whining. "Go with the orange smoke, young man."

The record stuck and someone zipped the needle across it, into its arm-cradle. Claire hesitated, then stopped and sat down next to Ram. *"I'll sing instead."*

"What in hell goes on here," said Ram. The attempt to keep his head clear failed. In a roomful of dopers, here was Claire accepting this dopers' philosophical crap.

"The prince wants to know what goes on, *en passant.*"

"He is confused."

"Lost!" That from someone on the far wall.

"Lost and gone forever, oh-my-darling, Ramirez," sang Claire. Her voice trailed into a sweet overflow of words as others picked up the sleepy rhythm. "Oh my darling, oh my darling, Ramirez," they sang, in rumpled chorus.

Ram did feel relaxed, though.

"You are lost and gone forever..." the choir moaned on.

And he thought: Anyway, she's safe here, I suppose. She's found her place and I have not, so can she be so awfully wrong?

What, then--is this the Touchstone?

Lord no. Not this.

"...lost and gone forever, oh my darling, Ramirez."

Sure the hell not this.

*

Ram stayed with Claire that night, although, curiously, he didn't want to at first. An aberration of the Army-street code penetrated the grainy veneer of *puta primera.* Guilt sensations, thoughts about My Linh. Thoughts about Claire, already too damned abused by men. But the pleasure of Claire's invitation got to him, still too strong. She received her last fix from Emile before they left the Maison Cockteau and she wanted now her only other pleasure. "I need to make love to you now--would you mind? Ramee-e-e? Let me tell you what I intend doing with you..." His resolve couldn't muster the strength to resist that, certainly not from a beautiful animal like Claire.

Neither Jean-Pierre nor Carson were heard from again that night, but Ram knew Willy would be back. Claire had insulted him. People like Carson didn't let insults go unpunished. Ram recognized the breed.

And Ram didn't sleep that night, for Claire had now joined the wounded people around him, and he felt so helpless, so damned helpless. "I'll get you out of this," he said, quietly, when he thought she'd fallen asleep.

"Sure you will, Ramee-e."

"Trust me, Claire. I'll get you out of this, just give me time."

"I'll wait for you, Ramee-e."

Chapter 27

The next morning, before going to the airport, Ram had the taxi take him to St. Amand's apartment to pick up the Bryan documents. During the ride to Orly Field he went through them, a three-inch pile of pages fanning out in front of him--bills of lading, end-user certificates, letters of credit--the tissue of international commerce, signed, stamped, scribbled over.

He read them between meals and during the stopover in Teheran, where the plane re-fueled before flying on to Bangkok. Nothing in the documents mentioned a shipment of arms directly to Indo-China. Some listed light industrial and farm equipment to firms in Da Nang, some traced the movement of small arms--rocket grenades, anti-tank weapons, rifles, mortars--to the Philippines, Thailand and Australia. All in the file labeled "Vietnam, III."

During the last hop from Bangkok to Saigon he turned his thoughts to the more immediate problem: At the airport, what would the white mice do if he *were* stopped? But the question turned out to be academic, the Tan Son Nhut passport section gave his Army papers only cursory attention, even though he was wearing civvies--jeans and a denim shirt. No inspection, no check against any restricted lists.

He took one of the Saigon red-white-blue taxis along Cong Ly Street to the Continental Palace Hotel, an old, bank-like building circled by a necklace of spiny bike racks. He shouldered his backpack, which mainly contained his uniform, and crossed the beeping traffic of Le Loi Street, and as he approached the window-wall of the Givral Restaurant he saw Kim Chau inside, getting up and motioning Ram toward the door while Chau began to make his way in the same direction, through the late-morning coffee people.

When they met at the front of the Givral Ram saw the visible change in Kim Chau's face. There was a sad, blank expression about him, in his eyes... "It's scheduled already, Ram. They scheduled it for *tomorrow*, for God's sake. Diem already signed the execution warrant."

"Good Christ, for your father?"

"Took him out to Con Son Prison first, for interrogation. The military tribunal put him in one of Diem's so-called 'tiger cages' there." Chau held down a tremble that ran along his mouth. "He's back here now in the National Police Headquarters."

"God, Kim Chau, is there anything...can you visit him?"

"Meeting My Linh there in half an hour. I wanted to keep her out of Saigon until then."

Ram stared around the Givral, a gathering place, it looked like, for journalists and junior politicians and the surviving French aristocracy. "This isn't a good place for us either, Kim Chau. Why not go there now?"

"They allow visitors in about half an hour." Chau led the way back to his table, and after they sat he absently nudged the thick manila envelope Ram had carried in with him. "Those for me?"

"Claire got them from Bryan's files. Shipping documents...whatever, it's not important right now."

"Yes it is, Ram." A waitress offered them coffee and Chau nodded absently. "I can find the receipts that match up with them."

"What the hell would it matter now?"

"You've already forgotten?" Chau fixed on the pouring of the thick black coffee. "I accepted the black arm band of the Liberation Front now. My Linh and I join them in the mountains above Tay Ninh tomorrow, after...God, Ram, after they kill my father."

Ram tried to put a hand around his cup, which was scalding. It had an dreadful smell to it, like hot detergent. "I'd like to go along to the prison."

"That might not be real smart."

"What *is* real smart, Kim Chau?" Ram stood, picking up the documents. "I've still got those G-2 orders with me. That'll get me past the guards."

"If you say so. I'm not thinking awfully good right now."

They walked to a black jitney truck, one of those Ram had seen on the Dao plantation. "They told me to leave a truck at the prison if I want to take the casket tomorrow," said Chau. "Can you imagine them *asking* if I'd want to take him?" They went southwest along the dusty Tran Hung Dao Street, to the alley entrance of police headquarters a block above the Doi Canal, where Chau pointed to a walled area next to the largest building. "Inside there...the execution yard."

At the entrance two guards took them to a barred room where a short captain with a solid round chest--a chest like a Montagnard, Ram thought--did a body-massage search on them and, watching Ram, spoke in English. Then the officer sat down behind an old scratched-up pine desk: "I Captain Tran, take charge of prisoners here. Papers, please."

Ram gave him his Vietnam orders. The captain began writing the information before Chau distracted him with a newly-issued government I.D. card.

"You are member of prisoner family?" the captain asked Chau, staying with English, eyeing the card.

"He's my father."

"Hmph." The officer finished his registration and gave their papers back. "Where you stay, monsieur?" he asked Ram.

"Continental Palace Hotel."

"Not to leave hotel until we check papers," said the captain. "Until then, you visit prisoner. Wait." The captain left the room. The two guards stayed.

"They usually don't take all that information from Americans," said Chau. "This might've been a mistake, Ram."

"Won't be my first, Kim Chau. Hang tight."

The captain came back and opened the door for them. "Get prisoner's body tomorrow, you unnerstand? By ten in morning."

The guards led them to a corridor filled with the stink of human waste. In an undercurrent of coughing, people were sprawled against the walls of the grey concrete hallway. "The prisoners who don't have money get chained out here," said Chau. "Father Dao gets two bowls of rice a day, in his own cell. We bribed these bastards a hundred U.S. dollars a day for that."

They stopped before a series of doors, blocked together like toilet stalls, where the front guard spoke to Chau.

"He says we have ten minutes with father Dao," said Chau.

Inside was a noxious concrete room, six by nine feet, dimly luminescent. It looked like a cement sarcophagus, indirectly lit through a ceiling vent, graced only with a bench and a waste hole.

Two figures crouched on the dark floor. "Ram?"

"My Linh." He reached down to her, folding her hand into his. "I didn't accomplish anything back there... Couldn't get help from anyone."

"They wouldn't listen to you?"

"There is no 'they' out there, My Linh. The world is run by ghosts."

"You did what you could, Sergeant," said Dao Phuong, weakly, slumping against the wall. He watched the door. "The people in the hall have turned very white, from the electric shock they were given. Did you see them?"

Kim Chau stooped down next to his father. "Come up, father Dao. It's too cold there." Ram kneeled to help Chau get Dao Phuong onto the bench. The old man seemed almost weightless.

"I am ashamed that you see me like this, Sergeant," said Dao Phuong. He reached out to take Ram's hand, but his eyes rolled past Ram. His fingers drained from Ram's hand like a string of beads. "I am ashamed to go to my Cao Dai this way."

Even in this dimness Ram didn't want to look at Dao Phuong. This was worse than he imagined. "I couldn't...nothing makes any sense, Dao Phuong. No one would listen."

"You must protect my family from this, Sergeant," said the father Dao. "You and my son and my daughter, you will at least fight them. My daughter tells me this, that you have approached the Touchstone."

"Of your Cao Dai, Dao Phuong? No, I wouldn't know where to start."

"We don't know who to fight, Father Dao," said Kim Chau. "We don't belong here any more than we belong with the communists."

"But there are three of you now. That is a beginning, is it not?" Dao Phuong's faith remained intact. He gave Ram a brittle smile. "And you are still a writer of reports?"

"They're only filed away if I criticize this government, Dao Phuong."

"You'll find a way, Sergeant Apollo," said the father Dao. "Your enemies do not frighten you, and that is your strength." His body shivered as he spoke, and My Linh tightened her hold around the shoulders of her father. "When you find your true belief, you will not be afraid to do what you must, Sergeant Apollo. That is your strength, although you do not know that yet."

*

Chau left the truck at the jail and drove them back to the Dao farmlands in the dark blue Renault My Linh had brought, but they couldn't talk during the ride. The last vision of the Father Dao, praying on his bench, made talk impossible, for Dao Phuong had become distracted when the guards came to take his family from him. He had quietly called upon his Cao Dai then. He had shrunk and wept within his oversized prison uniform.

The police captain repeated that they could not come back until tomorrow morning, after the execution.

*

"I must be by myself tonight. I'm sorry, I can't discuss anything right now." Chau went to the back rooms where the servants used to live, and didn't come out again that evening, and My Linh didn't speak until she lay again with Ram on the matted bedding.

"The captain of police, he said to remain at the hotel."

"The captain of police can go to hell, My Linh."

She placed her face against his. "Tomorrow you must leave again, Ramirez. My brother and I go with the mountain people, it is all arranged." She whispered this so softly that he felt only the brush of her voice against him.

She drew a satin sheet over them.

*

Ram and My Linh got up early, just after dawn, before the forest shadow gave way to morning sun. They found her brother on a bench overlooking the gardens.

"It is six o'clock, My Linh," said Kim Chau.

"I know."

"Our Father Dao has been taken from us," said Chau.

"I know." His sister knelt beside him. From the yards behind the barn, the crow of a rooster could be heard.

"Kim Chau..." Ram stumbled over words he could not find.

"They will be coming for you, Ram," said Chau. "By now the white mice know you're not supposed to be here, probably." He looked from Ram to his sister. "You've told him of the Viet Minh situation, My Linh?"

"Situation?" Ram couldn't focus on what Kim Chau had said. His mind still couldn't shake off that picture of the shriveled Father Dao.

Chau was staring at his friend. "In the mountains, Ram, the Viet Minh won't allow a woman who has no man."

"She can't go?"

"They assign her to a man." Chau let the meaning of that sink in. "Single girls have to be with a man, or they cannot go."

"She'll be with her *brother* there."

"It's not the same, not according to them."

"Damn it, then you'll stay with me, My Linh."

"They've taken our passports," she said. "There isn't time, Ramirez."

"Ram..." Chau stood in front of My Linh so his friend could look only at him. "We have to take father to the Cao Dai ceremonial grounds first, in Tay Ninh. We need to take care of my father first, okay?"

"Kim Chau, what the hell're you saying here?"

"We have to go now," said Chau, quietly. "This afternoon we're to meet with the Viet Cong. We'll talk about it on the way."

*

Chau drove Ram and My Linh as far as the Doi Canal. "I'll walk from here, Ram. It's better if they don't see you. Take my sister to the Holy See at Tay Ninh, about ninety kilometers, she'll show you the way."

"I should go with you."

"Don't go near the prison now, Ram." Chau was rubbing the top of the car as he closed the door. "I screwed up by taking you there yesterday. I'm not thinking well, I'm sorry, but they won't bother *me* until my father's... I'm not that high up on their killing list yet."

187

There was an evenness in Kim Chau's voice that bothered Ram, something strange going on in his head, beyond the grief. "If they're looking for me, Kim Chau, they'll follow you."

"If they do, I'll take care of that, okay?"

Ram wanted to ask what in hell that meant, but My Linh put her hand on his arm as her brother walked away. "His mind is full of sadness, Ramirez. He cannot think about the police right now."

"What *is* going on in his mind, My Linh?"

She brought his hand to her cheek. "In the Holy See, there's an orphanage on one side of the mortuary," she said. "We won't be seen there if the police follow him."

In minutes they entered Le Van Duyet Street, veering to the northwest toward Tay Ninh, and soon the land merged into greens and yellows, pastoral stillness.

"Your brother, what did he mean, *assign* you?"

"Ramirez, what is done with me physically is of no importance. You are, you will always be, my spiritual companion. Do you understand that?"

"No, My Linh, I don't understand that at all." He rolled the window down so he could take a breath. "Should have stayed with your brother. He sounded...strange."

"I know."

Four kilometers east of the provincial capital of Tay Ninh she directed him into the holy city of Thanh Dia, where guards wore the uniform of the Caodai militia: black clothing with white boots, white belts, white holsters. With white Anzac-type bush hats, brims pinned up on the right.

"You don't need to stop at the gate," said My Linh. "Anyone can enter here." They drove past a seated bronze statue of Buddha. "Over near the temple is the Papal Residence, and on that corner is the mortuary." She said this without looking at the building that would destroy the remains of her father. She pointed instead to a cluster of masonry-block buildings. "That is the orphanage."

Ram pulled into the dirt lot next to it, and inside the orphanage a tall window at one end looked toward the mortuary next door. Metal jalosies, protruding outward, provided a screen for them. "If the police follow my brother, we can watch them from here," said My Linh.

How long? Ram wondered. Chau should be right behind them, unless the police required a lot of paperwork for the removal of Dao Phuong's body. But in Saigon, probably, executions didn't involve much paperwork. "Those black and white uniforms at the gate, they were Caodai? I thought the Caodai army joined the guerrillas."

"Not all of them. In our religion each person makes his own decisions-
-" She stopped when she saw him squint through the window, then step
away from it as Chau's truck pulled up to the mortuary outside. They
watched Chau get out, go inside and come back again, bringing two golden-
robed monks with him. They were rolling a casket-bearer.

"Guess we were wrong," Ram said. "The police didn't follow."

My Linh did not take her eyes from the casket. "They are here, Ram."
As she said that he saw the metallic-silver Citroen emerge from the road
next to what she had pointed out as the high school buildings. They stopped
directly across the street, two men in white short-sleeved shirts, and they
rested back in their seats, and lit cigarettes.

"If that's the police, they don't try very hard to hide themselves."

"They are not very clever at this," said My Linh. She sat on one of the
stairs and bunched her arms together. "I'm very afraid, Ramirez. I'm afraid
of what my brother is doing."

"What could he do here? This's your holy city, isn't it?"

My Linh watched the men in the silver Citroen. "My brother's mind is
full of sorrow, and anger. He is not thinking well."

He followed her stare to the silver car.

"He will avenge his father with these men," said My Linh.

Ram felt the skin tighten along the back of his neck. She was right,
that was the tone he'd heard in Kim Chau's voice. "With *these* two? That
wouldn't be vengeance."

"He is not thinking well, Ram."

Kim Chau *wanted* the police to follow, Ram knew that now, but if Chau
attacks two policemen here... The doors to the mortuary opened and Kim
Chau came out again, almost casually, carrying a brown shopping bag.
Something thin and metallic inside.

"Holy shit." Ram knew what it was by the shape of the bag. He turned
to run for the entrance just as the clatter of the 9mm submachine gun
emptied into the car window, withering the two men in a burst of glass,
spewing red litter through the other side. Doors along the hallway began
to bang open and a scream ricocheted through the building as Ram ran
through it and outside to the Renault, started it and swung around to pick
up My Linh. He wrestled the back door open as he drove toward Chau. *"In
the goddamned car!"* Ram braked between Chau and the shattered police
car—*"Get in here, Kim Chau!"*

"It's okay now, Ram--" Chau fell into the back seat and the car skidded
backward, circling around the mortuary as the two monks hurried out and
stood, stunned, staring at the police car.

"Slow down for the guard station, Ram." Chau's voice sounded oddly relaxed, in the back. "They might not have heard the shooting... Might not give a damn anyway."

"Why *this*, Kim Chau? What the hell were you *thinking?*"

"There was no choice, Ram."

As they neared the gate Ram tried to ease up on the gas pedal. The Caodai guards, who apparently had not heard the gunfire, or had for some reason dismissed it, watched them pass, and Ram began to turn left onto the highway.

"No, go straight across, along that farm road," said Chau. "Takes us through the agri-center to the foot of the Nui Ba Den mountains."

It looked to Ram, in the mirror, like Chau was trying to smile. Chau had this sad, painful kind of smile in the mirror.

"We bypass Tay Ninh that way," said Kim Chau.

Chapter 28

Ram turned the car onto a path through tracts of sugar cane, through an expanse of paddies and barns that bordered V.N. Highway 13, bowling onto the larger road, rebounding off an irrigation lip along its edge.

"We'll be climbing soon," said Chau, tiredly, resting his head against the window. "We'll be in the mountains soon, Ram. I think we'll be okay there."

My Linh reached back to hold the clenched hand of her brother. "What of Ramirez, brother Kim? This thing you have done, you didn't think of Ramirez?"

"He wasn't part of the shooting, My Linh. The priests will tell them..." Chau closed his eyes. "They wouldn't touch an American unless he did the shooting himself, and there were witnesses--" He shuddered. "God..."

"Don't worry about it right now." Ram, strangely, was feeling the exhilaration again. This running through walls again, taking up arms against the world's ghost-rulers. Terrible as it was, when he saw Chau reach into that bag, there was also this deep tingle, this hidden burst of freedom. "I'll get back to the plane okay."

"Back okay?" Chau let his head roll wearily to the side. "The world is getting too damned mixed up, Ram."

"It probably gets worse."

The carts and autos on the road were thinning out. The Plateaux Montagnards rose above the clouds, the synclines at their base broke from the Nui Ba Den, pushing upward, lifting plateaus of forest like great green torches. When they reached the base of the mountains Chau pointed Ram to a road between them where the pavement mutated to pock-marked asphalt, then to dirt. "We're very close here," said Chau. "They'll be waiting where this trail ends, if I understood their instructions."

The path greened over, the drape of forest rose around them, the brush screeching the undercarriage and slapping the axle. Ram drove until the road dissipated, finally, into a scruffed meadowland of elephant grass, where the jungle foliage circled them like dark animals.

"Where the hell... This is the end of the damned world, Kim Chau." Ram could see nothing but a solid wall of trees and undergrowth. "I can't leave you here."

"Only the world that we know ends here, Ramirez." My Linh was trying to sound confident. "The mountain soldiers survive here."

"It isn't this bad, farther in," said Chau. "Not where we're going..." Kim Chau's voice trailed as a group of men came out of the trees, and he struggled from the car to meet them. The two in front greeted him with raised arms, bowing, talking to Chau as they came nearer. Carrying AK-47's, wearing the black pajamas and web equipment of the regular Viet Minh. The three in back were shorter, darker, heavier-chested men--Montagnards, in their own sort of uniform: fatigue pants cut at the knees, knives strapped to the chest. But the two Viet Minh stopped when they saw Ram. They unslung their rifles. One of them began to jabber at Chau while the other, a scarred veteran, tall as Kim Chau, went to inspect Ram's face.

He didn't like what he saw. "No come--*Americain*."

Kim Chau went woodenly through an explanation and the guerrilla nodded, grunted, shuffled back to his companion.

"I explained you weren't coming with us, Ram. They won't bother you."

"They *already* bother me, Kim Chau. Why the committee?"

"They're greeting me as the new deputy secretary. And as their battalion commissar." Chau paused, tried to gather his thoughts. "Three of them're only Montagnards, they'll porter for any goddamned side..."

"Ramirez has to leave now, brother Kim." My Linh touched her brother's sleeve. She knew his mind was still on the killings at Tay Ninh, but they couldn't afford even these few minutes. "There is so little time now, Kim Chau."

"Yes, we still have wars to fight, don't we, Ram?" Chau held his hand out to Ram. "Get yourself to Ton San Nhut, okay? I'm sorry I got you into this. I'm not thinking right." They shook, and Chau bowed to his sister. "We'll wait on the path, My Linh. I'll have one of the bearers bring you along." He hadn't taken his eyes off Ram as he spoke. "I had to do that. Christ knows why, Ram, but I had no choice."

"I know, Kim Chau." Ram waited while his friend instructed the nearest bearer and signaled the others. "Keep your head down in there, would you?" Chau waved back in response. The troop fell single file behind the taller Viet Minh. The remaining bearer sat on his carton and eyed the American, and My Linh watched her brother until he'd gone into the forest.

"The trees look so dark from here," she said.

"I'm not going back to the States, My Linh." He felt like he'd choke on those words. "I'm going on to Okinawa, I won't be that far away." But he knew he might as well be going to another planet. She put her face into his shirt, held on to him, tightened her arms around him. And when she released him her porter scrambled to his feet and picked up the last carton, and followed her into the trees.

Ram stood quiet until he could no longer see her, then went back to the Renault and drove a slow circle around the meadow to look through the trees that she entered. The soldiers and the last of the Daos had all disappeared. He swung the car across the middle of the clearing, back onto the trail, and when his eyes adjusted to the deeper shade he pushed the accelerator until the forest blurred around him, until the forest became a swirling emerald tunnel.

*

The police would be looking for the Renault, Ram knew, so he ditched it on the outskirts of Saigon and paid his way onto a rattly Lambretta auto-carrier. He slid in between six other people in its four-by-five passenger space, but it didn't work. The police had stationed one of their powder-blue cars at Cong Ly and Vo Tanh streets, the junction before the airport, with instructions to look for a lone white *Nuroi-my*. For one lone American.

"Sahgent Apollo!" The nearest of the two policemen yelled when he looked inside the Lambretta. He yelled again to his partner who took off running for the car radio--"You put up hands, Apollo!" The man rooted himself in firing posture, his pistol arm toward the dangerous *Americain*--this police-killer!--staying in that position until a squad of white mice arrived to back him up.

The police didn't relax until they had Ram safely handcuffed in the back of their van, then they started a prattle among themselves about this capture, pointing to their captive, giggling, spitting toward him during the ride to Chi Hoa prison.

The guards at Chi Hoa put him on a cane chair, tied his wrists together, then tied his wrists to his knees.

"You like Chi Hoa Prison, Sergeant? You make sure come back?" Captain Tran made this joke and continued a chortling noise to himself, a tiny quacking sound, while he circled Ram's chair. His white jacket, small and tight around him, displayed--popped--the brass buttons and gold epaulets along his chest. His heavy jowls framed his face like a fish head on a gold-white platter.

"Maybe then we shoot you, like Monsieur Dao? You go find what hell like, maybe." He made a slapping noise behind Ram. The captain's rose-cologne smelled like bubble bath.

"I already know what hell's like."

Captain Tran's chest jiggled in a silent laugh. "We don't need reason, you unnerstand. You in Saigon. You look charges for Dao Phuong then.

193

We shoot. No charges, see?" His voice lowered. "So why you kill two my men? No harm you. *Harmless* men."

"There are no harmless men."

Ram didn't see the steel-rubber club until it hit. The hardened surface caught him across the face, whipping his jaw, lacing a sudden chipped pain across the bone of his cheek.

"You think we afraid to kill American? Hell no. Bad thing, why these men need to die?"

"Why did they...need to die?" Ram could only mumble through his swelling jaw. "No one ever *needs* to die."

Captain Tran grunted. "Help escape Dao Kim Chau, maybe."

"There's no escape from you ghost people, Captain Tran--" The second blow came just behind Ram's ear. He didn't feel this one as solidly, the club didn't land squarely, or Ram, possibly, could no longer feel the pain.

"You can go Con Son prison, Sergeant. To famous tiger cages, okay?" Ram heard Captain Tran say this before the lumpy floorboards rolled past his face. "Con Son build by Frenchies, they call it *Paulo Condore*, heh. Bad place, Sahgeant." Captain Tran stood over him. "Chi Hoa like hotel compare to Con Son."

The threats didn't mean much, not now. Ram could taste his own tepid blood, he could feel himself slip into a grey, whirling mist.

*

"Get the hell over there, Colonel!" General Novinger almost bellowed through the receiver. "Weren't you supposed to be *watching* him, for Christ's sake?"

"The man's a lunatic, General--there's no controlling him."

"Well you better get your shit together and *do* it, Colonel. We have a man in a Saigon prison who knows enough to do us some real damage there, so you go remove him, Colonel, one way or another, you remove him."

"Sir, wouldn't it be better just to let him sit in there?"

"Leave him in there? An American in a Vietnam prison? The papers make *celebrities* out of people in situations like that. No, put him back into that idiotic rapprochement program with the North Vietnamese if necessary, but get him the hell out of the prison. Get him out and lose him somewhere, now, Colonel."

"Yes, sir."

So once again they leave it to me, thought Colonel Purdy. What do they want me to do, *kill* the son of a bitch? That'll be the day. Send Apollo back to his gook buddies? Shit, with Ho Chi Minh's blessing, apparently, if Purdy understood this rapprochement thing. Maybe the ARVN will follow Apollo, to help them find the Viets, maybe, then maybe get the bastard shot in the middle of the firefight.

Right, thought Colonel Purdy. After everything that sergeant's already survived, the man's damn near unkillable. Tougher people than the ARVN have tried to put that sonofabitch away.

*

Ram tried to stretch along the cell floor, his feet and head bumped the opposite walls. He tried to move himself to a diagonal position and that worked better, but his knees cracked as he straightened himself. Then he felt this light, warm spray on his hands. He opened his eyes and saw the grillwork of bamboo across the top of his concrete hole.

A soldier was urinating above him and the water splashed through the bamboo bars, sprinkling over him, and Ram covered his head with his arms. And he thought, he dreamt, of better places, and thought of his father's words... If there are *infinite* possible worlds, what the hell was he doing in *this* one, lying in a hole getting pissed on by some punk midget Vietnamese dogface?

He could hear the words his father had used, which had stuck in his head like a stake: Your world-line is already fixed, his father said-- *everyone's world-line has already, always, been fixed.* Because time runs both backwards and forwards, or something.

What good are those theories here? What the hell does all that mean?
The soldier zipped himself up and moved away.

Ram woke again at dark, drenched. Rain had pounded the uncovered tiger cages and fumes from the bottom slime filled his lungs, causing an acid pungency, like ammonia salt. And the pain inside him, in his groin, spread through his ribs and arms. He could raise his head just enough to look into a tin plate hung on twine, inches from his face, containing a marble-sized clump of rice. Most of it was washed away, the remaining clump lay in the tin like a drowned mouse and it came apart in his fingers, but he scooped up what he could, and ate what he could: stale water, tainted mush.

Then the weariness came again and he folded himself back into sleep. And when the sun rose he'd forgotten where he was, he saw only this strange striped sunlight above him.

"You come now," a voice called from the top of the cage. A guard lifted the brownish bamboo grating and threw a rope ladder down to him.

"We go back Saigon," said the young white-mouse officer after Ram struggled to the surface. "Charges no more. You wait Saigon fo' you chief." From the top, Ram saw only shallow dirt holes around his concrete cell; the people inside the other, smaller holes were doubled up to fit in, their bodies atrophied from the restricted movement. He couldn't see if they were still alive--only dirty rags covering these withered brown sticks--until one of them groaned beneath a thick white powder that was being shoveled through his grating.

He saw the stacked-up sacks of lime, and looked away.

Con Son turned out to be an island about forty miles from the mainland, three hours by boat from the Delta, and the grim young officer accompanied him the whole way but said nothing more, and when they reached the Continental Palace Hotel the officer left Ram in a room there with his canvass bag. No passport inside now. No papers. But at least the bag contained washed clothes. Ram could shower and throw away the shredded things he was wearing, because the blood, perspiration and drying piss of the Vietnamese soldier had pasted the cloth--even the stench of the cloth--to his skin.

And he needed sleep, he needed so damned badly to sleep.

*

Colonel Purdy woke him by pushing a bowl of rice and meat against his shoulder. "Eat first. Then we're gonna talk. Heard you haven't had real food in a week." Purdy had to pull the bowl back as Ram rolled to a sitting position and squinted at the colonel. There was a pounding in Ram's skull, but at least it was less painful than when he went to sleep, and he *was* starving. He smelled the sharp beefy mush and took the plate and ate it with his fingers, like a Montagnard, slowly, hoping it would stay down.

"This's starting to sound like a busted record, Sergeant, but do you realize how badly you screwed things up again?" Purdy's dressing-down seemed to lose steam after he'd taken a look at Apollo's face. Diem's people had obviously beaten the crap out of the man, then starved him, and any speech from some fat Army colonel, Purdy figured, wouldn't mean one hell of a lot right now. "What the hell were you thinking, coming back here?"

"Dao's family, Colonel." Ram was too tired to explain. He wiped his fingers weakly against the pitted edge of the bowl. "I was needed here."

"Needed my ass. You're just lucky no one saw you with Dao near that damned monastery when those police got blown away. You realize what I had to go through to get you out? You're a pain in the ass, Sergeant."

196

"Sorry."

"Sorry doesn't cut it. I'm the one who started you on this shit--at least that's what the brass are trying to pin on me. Now I've got to nursemaid you around two goddamned continents, and still you chase this Bryan thing-"

"-That isn't why I'm here-"

"-Why I'm here, *sir.* And, yes I know, they shot Lieutenant Dao's father. And what the hell'd *you* plan to do about it? As of now all this shit's going to stop, you understand, Sergeant?"

"Not much more I can do here."

"Wrong again. You're staying here on G-2 business. We're sending you back with your buddy, into the hills."

It took a moment for that to sink in. "The Viet Cong would never agree to that."

"It'll be only for a short while, just to get you out of the way for awhile. But, yes, you will go, and yes, they will agree to let you in," said Colonel Purdy. "We're using this rapprochement program as an excuse."

Ram didn't want to know any more, he didn't want to say anything that might screw up a chance to get back to My Linh. "Sounds like a fine idea," he mumbled. "I'll reconnoiter hell out of them."

"Can the shit. You don't give a rat's ass about any reconnaissance. You make a lousy contact, frankly."

"When am I supposed to go?"

"Don't ask me yet, not for awhile. You just sit here till we get a handle on what this rapprochement business is about. *I'll* make the arrangements this time, Sergeant."

"Right, sir."

"Afterward, I see you scheduled a flight out to Okinawa. Good. When you get back that's exactly where we want you--Fort Buckner will be fine for the time being. Catch a MATS flight from Bien Hoa if you want, but when you get there, *stay* there, damn it, till we de-brief you."

"Whatever you say, Colonel."

"We know your buddy joined a guerilla battalion operating in the Plateaux Montagnard region. We'll establish contact with the leaders somehow and arrange a rendezvous place. That should show Ho Chi Minh some good faith."

"Right, sir. Good faith."

Colonel Purdy left then, because he couldn't stand to listen to himself any longer. *Good faith?* Trumping up an interest in this rapprochement crap just to ditch this sergeant in the jungle.

Where do I draw the line? Colonel Purdy asked himself.

He'd seemed to be asking himself that a lot, lately.

Chapter 29

In August, in the jungle humidity, heat transformed the leaves into wet tangles, green razors that arced stinging red welts along the arms and face. Even the remnant veterans of the 42nd Light Force Battalion ground to a slow stumble here. Toughened field soldiers became loose-kneed and ticklish and groin-weak here with the constant tug and push and heat of the jungle.

Chau equated this march to a wade upstream, chin-deep in the middle of some warm--*hot*--canal, trapped in the leech-ridden mangrove waters, rattan reeds, grotesque kapok trees. Most of the time, as he hacked through the creepers and *liana* vines, he would be choking on the stink of swamp gas and malarial compost.

For what? Chau couldn't fathom the reason for this march. No one but the battalion leader, Major Vo Trung, knew the purpose of this mission. This lack of direction was the main problem with the NLF policy of *dai doi doc lap*, Chau realized. The creation of independent guerrilla battalions, slipping out of control like runaway cannons, all part of the genesis of the new "Viet Congan," still trying to get their shit together within the tangled structure of the new NLF, the National Liberation Front.

"There's word that we're making an agit-prop mission to a village above the Coastal Plains," Captain Pham told Chau during the morning break. Captain Pham, who usually commanded this unit, was fuming over Major Trung's silence. "I don't like the feel of this mission, Commissar Dao."

Chau agreed. "We are outfitted like a combat company. No agitation cadre. No propaganda officers-"

"-Every man carries a Kalashnikov or a Browning Automatic. This is no propaganda mission."

"The head sergeant seems to know Major Trung," said Chau. "Can you ask him?"

"Good idea, Commissar. Good idea."

Kim Chau's one consolation during this trek was his ability to keep up with the veteran troops, the tough southern *bo dois*, some of whom even wore, still wore, the doughboy-style fiberboard helmets of the early Viet Minh. This surprising stamina ballooned his pride and endurance, although the weight of his military issue *was* becoming a problem.

Even his truck-tire sandals were starting to feel heavy. Even his sun helmet, made only of green canvas stretched over a bamboo frame, felt heavy, but at least the web equipment of the Viet Minh weighed a lot less than American gear. He carried only a mosquito net and a few square yards of light nylon to be used as raincoat or sleeping roof, plus a tube of rolled cotton, the "elephant's intestine," filled with rice, a little salt, a little monosodium glutamate and some dried fish, to which diet they added barbecued jungle moths, when they could, after plucking the wings.

The battalion didn't require My Linh to go on these maneuvers. Something to be grateful for, thought Kim Chau, although in camp they were facing the problem they knew would be coming: Major Trung demanded that she "choose" herself one of the unattached field soldiers, and Chau could make only his one lame protest: Why the hell couldn't she remain with him? He was her *brother.*

That wasn't the same thing, according to Trung. A woman without a man creates too much trouble among the guerrillas, that was the rule in most of the mountain units. And My Linh could never return to Saigon now, not while Ngo Diem was in control.

Not after the killings at Tay Ninh, Chau reminded himself.

Vo Trung had probably planned this field maneuver to get rice, not conscripts, Chau thought. The Viet cadre had recently swept the Piedmont area to the south and brought back a hundred men from the Hoa Hao and the Caodai dissidents. Although he knew a plan was now in place for a major offense against the rubber plantations in the fall. The new "Fatherland Front" had already begun.

"This is not a moral mission, Lieutenant Dao," said Captain Pham, sitting again with Chau during their four o'clock rice. "The head sergeant says we're going to the village of Binh-An, near where Major Trung grew up." Captain Pham was cleaning his eye glasses as he talked, while Chau peeled the thick, red-brown rind from a wild mangosteen. Chau noticed that Pham addressed him as "Lieutenant," a more comradely designation than "Commissar."

"Trung has expressed to me, many times, his hatred for the people of Binh-An," said Captain Pham.

Chau bit into the heavy peach-flesh of the mangosteen and spat it out. "God, this is bitter."

Captain Pham stared into his commissar's face. "He takes us on a mission of vengeance, Lieutenant."

"I understand your worry. I'll try again." Chau got up and went to the rear platoon, where Major Trung usually stayed.

"We hear that we are returning to the village of your people, Major Trung."

"*My* people, Commissar?" Major Trung watched Chau through eerily hollowed, skull-like eye sockets. "My people are highland, Lieutenant. The tea-growers. We entered Binh-An only to buy the profiteer's goods, while they treated us like Montagnards, these fat cheeks wearing laundered clothing, these *high* Vietnamese."

"We are here to teach class revolution, Major, not class hatred."

"Is there a difference, Commissar?"

"The Liberation Front does not condone vengeance," Chau answered. His own words stopped him from taking that any further. They reminded him of the killings at Tay Ninh.

Trung waved his arm in dismissal of Chau's words. "You are also from the class of the full-cheeks, a member of the Caodai elite. You would never understand class difference." He walked away from Chau and called to Captain Pham: "Get the men up. We're almost there."

Chau took his place in the middle of the column, and again, in the thick forest air, his lungs began to ache. He soon forgot about the strictures of the National Liberation Front.

In an hour they broke from the jungle to a land of terraced farms, sloping down to the valley of the Song Be River where the rains had just passed, where nearby oxen submerged themselves in newly-created wallows. Puffs of clouds patrolled the sky above the valley, the air smelled of monsoon rain.

The huts of Binh-An appeared within half a kilometer of the forest as the layers of crops around the village began to step downward, disappearing into the veils of rain inside the mountain passes. A sparkling moment, Chau thought, until he saw the fear. The villagers peeked above their windows at him, then slid from view. The few still outside ran the last few steps to their doorways. An old couple worried toward some children and herded them to the shacks circling the village, where the undergrowth was cleared for thirty meters--a common practice for outlying villages, Chau remembered: In these hills the kraits, the deadly *cham quap*, looked like dry twigs, and became invisible unless the brush was cleared.

Trung went to a thatch hut facing the village market where most of the stall-keepers had already, hastily, closed their corrugated shutters. On the porch an old man appeared wearing the white mandarin hat of a village council chairman, and held up a bough of polished pine toward Vo Trung.

"Welcome to this village, comrade Major Trung." His blank stare did not share that hospitality. "Can we assist you?"

"You received our notice, Council Chief. You know why we are here."

"We received no notice, sir. Can we help you?"

Trung brushed him aside and ducked through the hanging grass at the doorway and came immediately out again. "You have no pride, old man." He shoved the council chief sprawling off the porch and spat on the side of the hut. "We fought your battle against the French while your village got fat selling food to them. Now we will need to fight again, against the fascist Ngo Diem, and you refuse us rice."

The council chief struggled to his knees. "There is no war against President Diem now," he protested. "The north and the south are at peace."

"Diem broke his agreement to reunify our land. War is coming and you *know* this!" yelled Vo Trung, more for the benefit of the hidden villagers. "The village of Binh-An again refuses to help us. Again we need to fight your battles." Vo Trung's shaved temples, which seemed almost concave to Kim Chau, now became alive with knots of muscle. "We intend to make an example of you."

Chau moved to the side of the old man and put a hand under the elbow of the chief, to help him up, but the man swayed instead to an awkward sideways squat.

"Stay away from him," said Vo Trung.

"He is the council chief," said Kim Chau. "We accomplish nothing by hurting him."

"Punishment by example is a *great* accomplishment, Commissar," said Major Trung. "This man and all his village need to be shown the fate of collaborators." He motioned to two of his men who, apparently pre-instructed, raised their bayonets. "Do it now."

"Do what? What are you talking about?" Chau stepped in front of the council chief, who had recoiled into a shriveled white ball. "We have no sanction from the Central Committee-"

"-Spoken like a true commissar, Lieutenant," Vo Trung snapped, "but you are not a true soldier, are you? *This* is how we defeated the enemy in the French war." He pointed again at the council chief. "Do it *now*, I said."

"*No*, damn it!... *Jesus!*" Chau grabbed the hand of the old man as the bayonets slid into the white bundle. The council chief made a muffled squeal and doubled up, leaving Kim Chau staring down at him. Chau didn't let go of the chief's hand.

"You have no right to do this!" screamed a woman from behind the ring of huts. Other people, mostly older villagers, peered between the buildings at the old man and sucked in their breath, and Kim Chau thought: The major is not of your culture--don't antagonize him. I *know* this man now.

Chau had to release the man's hand as the two soldiers pulled him away. They dragged him through a cold fire pit that darkened the side of his white robe in the charred wood. They flopped his body into the village center and the black-and-white corpse lay there like a twisted harlequin.

Two more village men were brought to the square.

"You remember me?" demanded Vo Trung. They shook their heads, no. They didn't look at him. They leaned against each other and the taller one bent over so that the two stood shoulder to shoulder. The shorter man's shock of black hair stuck into the other's face.

"I am Vo Trung of the mountain people," said Trung. "I remember *you*. As children we passed on the road, and you passed me laughing, mocking that I worked the useless mountain land, while I had to beg in your streets."

"We do not remember you, sir," said the taller one. He still would not look up at Vo Trung.

"And we fought a revolution against the French, and now we are going to fight the fascist Diem, and still you laugh and grow fat and will not join us."

"We do not remember passing you on the road, sir. We have never laughed at you," said the shorter one, his hair flaring like black hay. "We are sorry if we offended you."

"Your refusal to help your *country* offends me," said Trung.

"Our young men are needed in the fields," said the smaller one. "We asked them. They do not want to fight." The villager now squinted back at Vo Trung, bringing ladders of skin down the man's face, a defiant latticework that drew Vo Trung's eyes like a raised tong.

"Ask? We are not asking you to serve!" shouted Vo Trung. "We are *ordering* you to serve!"

"Why should we help you?" asked the smaller man. "What difference does it make which tyrant controls us?"

Trung hit the man on the chest and sent him falling back across the small corpse of the council chief, and the villager crabbed away on his hands as Trung followed, kicking at him--"Parasite! Your words bring about your fate."

"Major Trung!" Chau yelled. "I intend to report this to the Central Committee!"

"And I intend to have you removed from my command!" Vo Trung shouted back, turning to his soldiers. "Carry out your orders."

The villager hissed as a bayonet punctured his side. He tried to pull it out. "*You* are the fascists," he whispered, but the soldiers did not stop. Red bayonet slits walked up his side like rooster tracks, and Kim Chau thought, What a soldier a man like that would have made. What a waste, to kill a man like this.

The taller villager was weeping now.

"You shall report this personally to the people of this region," Trung said to him. "The bullock-dung of Binh-An may pass the word that the new *Viet Cong* are here."

And Kim Chau did not interrupt him, not now, for that would do no good. And he thought, God damn the Viet Cong, and damn Ngo Dinh Diem for making us join people like Vo Trung.

Major Trung spent the next hour trying to gather the people of Binh-An, but they did not gather well. The villagers of Binh-An hid well, they disappeared well, they saw what happened to those who did not disappear. So Major Trung delivered his planned diatribe, his own version of the NLF Enlightenment, to the remaining old people. Those who were no longer good at disappearing.

"We expect five carts of rice and thirty men within a month. The choice is yours. Today we have given you just the smallest *taste* of our whip."

As the men of Company Fourteen filed out, a small girl ran past the bamboo just outside Binh-An and stuttered to a halt in front of the dead villager, and she extended a coin-sized palm toward him, and seemed dismayed that her magic no longer worked on him.

The guerrillas stayed in rank while a group of jets droned over the mountains beyond the Song Be River, like mosquitoes along the horizon. Their swept-back wings and stub noses indicated F-86 Sabres, not the long-fuselaged Starfires, and Chau could imagine the Zuni rocket pods beneath their wings, and he dreaded the thought of doing battle against those specks. They could turn a battalion like this into a hundred yards of burning men in seconds, but not this time. Not yet. The silver specks moved away.

And after the planes left, Chau looked back to see the rest of the village come out while the girl still tugged at the fingers of the dead villager. Assembling into what Chau pictured as the archetypal Asian fresco at the beginning of each war. Dead men, children, gathering villagers, women keening over the fresh mutilation, framed within a luminescent spiral of heat.

"They do not bother us, you see?" Trung had fallen back alongside his commissar, which produced a quickened pace from Kim Chau. He had no wish to talk with Major Trung.

"I am speaking of the American planes over there." The major's voice seemed more conciliatory now. "They cannot fire on us unless we shoot at them first--that is their present orders." Vo Trung made a crooked grin toward his lieutenant. "We were able to use those orders against the imperialists in the last war. We will do so again, very soon." Trung had apparently thought over the effect of a report from Kim Chau on the killings at Binh-An, and was half-kissing his commissar's ass now.

"How would you know what the *American* strategy is?" Chau growled.

"We have tried it before. You will see. This week there is another village we want punished, so we will fire at the planes from it, and then the planes will destroy the village."

"They can't be used that easily. They are not without intelligence."

"You will see," said Vo Trung. "The Americans are the same as the French. They make clumsy war against peasants."

Chau almost asked if Trung thought the major's murders at Binh-An *weren't* clumsy, but he stopped himself. He focused instead on the black calico shirts in front, carrying Kalashnikovs and 16-pound BAR's, bobbing back into the jungle like a string of black pearls.

Wars like this produced the Apollos and the Dao Chaus, he thought. The wild seeds of both sides forced by formless war into independent thought. Seeds that cannot be allowed to exist in wars that have no moral basis.

Chau's feet began to suck and slurp through a shallow between patches of mangrove, and he saw that it must have been a small rice field, once. An odor of decaying waste permeated it.

The odor clung to his legs when he emerged.

Chapter 30

My Linh kept her eyes on the fingers of her folded hands. A shiver, spider-quick, ran up her back as Loc Do, a captain in the 42nd Light Force Battalion, nodded his way through her dividing curtains. She did not look up.

No lamp burned inside her room but she didn't need to see Loc Do's face. She had noticed him before and he was not unattractive, although she had never thought about taking him into her room like this. But she knew what was expected of her, she had resolved herself to this meeting.

"You are welcome here, Loc Do."

"I found the matching papers, almost all of them," he said.

My Linh stared up at him. "Papers?" She moved to the side of her cot, her only furniture, so that he could sit if he wished.

"Your brother, the commissar, asked if I could find the matching receipts...during my visit to Da Nang?" Her stare was confusing him. "Those papers the American gave him?"

"Yes, Kim Chau's documents. That will please him, Captain." She'd forgotten about the papers. "Thank you for finding them." Loc Do had gone to Da Nang to match the documents that Ram had brought, she remembered now. The presence of Captain Loc had disordered her thoughts.

Captain Loc spoke of it first. "Your brother said that I might be agreeable to you, Dao My Linh. As your...consort, and protector." The words obviously caused him embarrassment and this made My Linh a little more comfortable; she risked a closer look at his face. He was high Vietnamese, smooth-skinned and tall, and he combed his hair to the side like the French officers. Even now he smelled of their brisk colognes, apparently for her benefit.

An acceptable companion, if it were not for the memory of Ram... She would not think of Ram now. "Major Trung ordered--asked--me to choose. My brother said that you would make an honorable companion."

"Then I am forever thankful to your brother." This event had apparently staggered Loc Do. Even the boldest among the mountain soldiers, she was told by Kim Chau, never dared approach her.

"And I will be forever honorable to you, Dao My Linh," he said, sitting, putting his hands cautiously around hers. He withdrew one hand when it touched her knee. "I am afraid of offending you," he said. "I am clumsy with girls."

"The decision has been made, Captain." Postponing Captain Loc would serve no purpose, she knew. "I will not think of you as clumsy." My Linh felt his hesitation. He again put a hand toward her, touched the sleeve of her uniform, and her cheeks reddened with new warm blood.

"I will try to please you, Dao My Linh," he said, placing his palm for a moment against her neck. He made this humming, nervous noise, a low agreeable sound that came from his throat, and My Linh drew away, and stood so that she could take off her black uniform, and Loc Do caught his breath with the sight of her. Her breasts without their strap remained up, and full. She slid beneath her bed covering, reaching from it to fold her lower garment to the floor, and the sight of the garment further disoriented Captain Loc. He had stood up when she did, and he remained standing, and apparently didn't know if he should sit again.

But he did sit, finally, to touch her cover. Seeing no resistance he lifted it to see the faint surge of skin, the fluttering spread of coin-sized hazel, the sudden tuft in that sacred region. He smoothed his hand lightly over her, the fineness of cat's fur on his fingers, but that would be a clumsy place to start. He moved his hand, instead, across her breast.

My Linh turned her head and closed her eyes. Loc Do displayed no clumsiness, she thought, and she felt a merging of sensations as he touched her. He knew where to touch, he did so now, she felt an arousal to that touch. Her body moved to that slow touch and My Linh told herself again that they gave her no choice. And she tried not to think of Ram until she realized that she *needed* to think of him.

She clung to Loc Do as she would Ramirez Apollo. She accepted him. She put the side of her face to his shoulder.

*

His answer would be silence, his answer was silence, and Ram asked, Have you, then, found the Touchstone? Is that what it means to die?

Perhaps silence was the best answer he would receive, the all-knowing Buddhist answer. I call on my father for help, he thought, but my father sends himself into the all-knowing silence. To understand everything is to become silent, then, like all colors combine to colorless white.

While Ram remained in Saigon he didn't want to go into the streets, he'd seen all the streets of Asia. He remained in his room and waited for word from Colonel Purdy, and thought of My Linh, and his father: Tell me what I should think of My Linh, who must lie down with another soldier? And what I should do about Bryan, or the coming war?

My Linh said there was a Christ and a Hitler in everyone, but above good and evil is the Father and the silent Tao, for the universal bond rises above human weakness.

*

"My God, we're bombing people in the Central Highlands," Colonel Purdy said this more to himself than to Ram. "Doesn't *anyone* communicate with us at Division?" The colonel frowned out the hotel window at the noisy esplanade below, his familiar grumble now, oddly, resigned. "Damned CIA think they *own* this piece-of-shit country now."

"We're bombing guerrilla units?"

"That would make too much sense. Somebody shot at some F86's from a town near the coast--with *rifles*, as if that would do any good--so we bomb the goddamn place off the earth. How do we explain that if the papers find out? There's not even supposed to *be* a war here, not yet."

"That little dictator of ours, Diem, will take care of that." But Ram felt better. At least they weren't bombing My Linh.

"I didn't come to talk politics with you," grumbled Colonel Purdy. He explored the inside of a leather courier's envelope he'd brought with him. "Got a safe-passage letter here from the Presidium of the NLF, right out of Hanoi, which we're giving to contact people in this rapprochement program. You're one of the few people who'll be going to an interior unit. Seems your buddy's unit is breaking camp so they don't give a crap if you see it."

"I thought this program was to check out their politics?"

"Hell with their politics, and don't question me again." Purdy drew a clump of papers from the envelope, sorted out a letter and map, handed both to Ram. "This shows the route you'll follow to the rendezvous point. You're flying north to a place called Gia Nghia. Don't know where they'll take you from there."

"Doesn't matter." Ram stuck the map in his jacket. "How soon do I leave?"

"This afternoon. My driver'll take you to the airport."

*

Compared to Saigon, Gia Nghia was a teeming smudge of population, located on an austere tract of earth. Smaller, dirtier, noisier. Mainly grass huts and tin hooches. Ram's contact was to meet him at the central market where Ram's ARVN jeep driver, plainly nervous in this territory, dropped Ram off and sped away.

"I am captain boat, sir. Go Song Dong now. Not far." An old fellow, his smile interrupted by a string of missing teeth, stepped from the market when the army car took off. He was nodding vigorously. "Name Jamie."

"Jamie?"

"French gimme name--Jam My Huu--*Jamie*. Fight for French soldiers. No good. No win. With Viet now."

"Stay with the winners, right? Where are they?"

Jamie looked shocked. "Sleep *boat* tonight. See Viet tomorrow." He darted back into the central market, picking through stalls of melons, boiled eggs, cigarettes, fish, rice, hanging bags of soccer balls, umbrellas, undershirts. "You give money," he shouted back to Ram. "Need food."

Ram gave him one of the twenty-piaster notes that Purdy had supplied. Jamie picked up two cellophane sacks of cream-white spheres, stuck together like balls of paste. He added two withered fish and had the shopkeeper wrap them in newspaper.

"*Xoi* and *banh-bo*," said Jamie, holding up the cellophane sacks. "You like. Coconut cake. Rice cake. *Delicieux*."

Jamie drove west from Gia Nghia toward the Cambodian border, passing through rocky hills and farmland, through hamlets too small to have names, down to the bend where the Da Dung River becomes the Song Dong Nai. It was dark by the time Jamie stopped alongside a sagging quay, concealed in swamp willow, where a long shallow-draft boat listed beneath a canopy of woven thatch. A tiny shrine within a cage capped the top of its hut.

"This my *Thuyen*--basket boat," Jamie said, attaching an outboard motor to the stern. "Sleep now, maybe eat." Pointing to the tiny cage on top of the boat. "Confucius shrine for worship water ghosts, keep you safe here. Be Viet Minh tomorrow." He yanked the starter cord and the motor clamored into action. He pulled away as Ram stepped aboard.

When it got too dark to navigate, Jamie placed a paraffin lamp on the bow which, with the full moon, apparently gave him enough light to steer by, and enough light to be seen by the river steamers. When the steamers passed, the Thuyen bobbed in their wash like a paper cup.

Jamie placed the sack of cakes and the fish beside Ram, but the fish smelled like dead dog. Ram let it slip overboard. The boiled rice and coconut balls were at least cooked. He finished the gooey mess and then slept, and didn't wake until early morning when the bow thudded against a makeshift pier among a bank of brown rushes.

Chau had already come aboard. "Lord, I never expected to see you again..." He extended his hand and attempted a smile as Ram pulled himself to his feet. "Welcome back to Vietnam, my good friend," said Chau.

"Never really left." Ram couldn't figure out Chau's expression. "You don't look real happy about this."

"No, I'm glad to see you, you know that, but Jesus it's a crappy time to be here. Our unit's planning a raid tomorrow--our first *real* raid--on something called a 'Civil Guard' village, whatever the hell that means. I don't know what's in their minds, sending you into the middle of this."

That didn't sound right. What the hell was Chau worried about here, Ram's *safety?* "I don't plan to go on any raids with you, if that's what's worrying you."

"No, that's not... I just didn't bring real good news with me, Ram."

Ram's stomach felt suddenly hollow. "About My Linh?"

"She's not hurt, nothing like that." Chau made a clicking sound between his teeth. "We didn't expect to see you again, didn't think things would work out this way."

"What the hell're you talking about, Kim Chau?"

"A captain of our regiment has... She had to choose someone, like I told you." Chau stared away from him toward the shore. "When she heard you were coming back, Jesus..." He hitched the strap of his carbine farther up on his shoulder. "The man she's with is called Loc Do, a good man. A company leader."

Ram studied Chau for a moment, then stepped from the boat to the pier, where he could take a deep breath. The air on shore had the pungency of dying moss. "Sure am glad she's with a good man, Kim Chau. That makes my goddamned day."

Chau managed a smile. "The two of us will be going by motorcycle for awhile, up the Bao Loc Pass, then through the farmland by oxcart so we don't draw attention. These old French cycles clatter like tanks." He pointed to a couple of rusting belt-driven Favor motorcycles, parked just inside the groves. "They run better than they look, though."

The road was hard-surfaced, iron-oxide red, compressed, baked solid. Ram could see that more than just country-road traffic went through here. Big vehicles had pounded down this road, although not one person appeared during their ride.

"Everyone's been told to stay off here a few days," Chau explained when they took a break. "You heard of the Ho Chi Minh Trail?"

"A little."

"You'll hear more, someday, but they want you to forget you saw this one."

"Forgetting is one of my strong points."

"U.S. Intelligence knows about it, but the NLF didn't want you to see what kind of traffic we have along here. They move most of the stuff by night now anyway, but that's a good sign--not letting you see the traffic. Means they don't plan to shoot you."

"That's comforting to know."

At the beginning of the farm country three men waited with a cart hitched to a brown bullock. "That's a Thai ox," said Chau, trying to keep Ram's mind off My Linh. "Looks like a Brahma bull, doesn't it? Good road animal, but balky as shit in the fields."

Two of the men who met them began topping off the motorcycle tanks while Ram and Chau settled in the cart among some empty burlap sacks. The uneven flooring, studded with wrinkled patches of metal plate, jabbed into Ram's hip. "Won't have to ride this very far," said Chau, as the third man--more exactly, a boy--went to the front. His whip slapped against the ox.

"Damned well organized around here."

"I wish the Americans understood *how* organized the Liberation Front is. Maybe that's what they sent you to find out."

"Who knows what they sent me to find out, Kim Chau."

As they got nearer the camp, Ram began thinking more about My Linh, and Chau seemed to understand that, and Chau let the cart creak along until he could no longer hold his peace: "Remember the papers you brought? We found a whole mess of corresponding documents to them--Captain Loc did." Chau stumbled over the last part. He didn't intend to bring up Loc Do's name. "Found them in a warehouse we use in Da Nang."

Ram was watching Kim Chau, but Chau wasn't sure Ram was listening. "Bills of lading listing water pumps and engine parts and porcelain," said Chau, "and on each list the ship's captain writes the freight they represent. Rifles, rocket launchers, mortars, same serial numbers on both the fake *and* the real goods: flame throwers listed as 'crop sprayers,' for instance. So we've got matching documents at both ends. Bryan would have one hell of a time explaining the shit we can put together on him now."

"But this Liberation Front...wouldn't they hang you for doing this?"

"You kidding? They *want* me to use those papers." Ram really had been listening to all this, Chau thought. "Bryan had to stop shipping a few years ago, so now the Front could give a crap less whether the world knows about his shipments to them."

"Just no loyalty any more, is there."

"And thanks to Claire Bryan we've got both ends of the shipping documents, front and back, and now we've got an official Army investigator--Sergeant Marion Ramirez Apollo his damned self--to turn it over to the authorities."

Ram held his hand up. "Better slow down about that. That'd get me a few years in the stockade, that's about all the hell it would accomplish."

"If it accomplishes anything, Ram, it would be worth it. I need you to take these before I go on this 'Civil Guard' raid anyway, just in case."

"Stop including me in on all that, would you?"

Chau sulked over Ram's response for a few moments. "You're probably right. That stuff My Linh teaches about improving this *experience* we're in..."

"Go to hell, Kim Chau."

Chapter 31

The guerrilla camp, Viet Camp Twelve, began at the edge of an abandoned makeshift soccer field, camouflaging itself within a burnt-out grove of rubber trees. Olive colored fronds and yellow bamboo thatch covered the above-ground lean-tos. A net of attap leaves weaved over a Molatova personnel carrier which, with its trailering howitzer, acted as center post for the tent of branches above a three-vehicle motor pool. In mid-camp, men cleaned their weapons while mountain peasants loaded carts with bulk goods wrapped in canvass. The ratchet of rifles, bolting and unlocking, prickled the air.

"It only *looks* disorganized," said Chau, "because we're breaking camp right after we probe this Civil Guard place. We should be back from there and out of here by tomorrow."

"It isn't an assault, then."

"Man, I hope not. Just a *probe*, as the major put it, whatever that means. Says he wants to see what a Civil Guard village is, before we leave."

"If they chase you back, this would be a crumby place to set up any defense."

Chau, checking over the area, nodded. "Got a little careless during the truce, I guess, but that's why we're moving southwest tomorrow. The dissidents pretty much control that part of the country."

The young driver held his bullock while Ram and Chau stood clear, then the boy led the snorting animal away as Major Trung, grinning, emerged from the main tent. "And this American friend, Commissar Dao? *So.*" Major Trung's face tightened as he approached.

"This is our battalion commander, Ram," said Chau, quietly. "He wants you to stay in the underground bunkers till we get back--you mind?"

"No problem." Ram wanted to ask about My Linh but Chau's edginess warned him off.

"*No problem*, see?" Trung repeated in English to Chau. "Sahgeant unnerstan."

"You shouldn't have any trouble while I'm gone," said Chau, but he didn't sound all that confident. "I've got friends among the Caodai soldiers who're staying behind. Captain Loc Do's going with us, though."

"Leave orders *no* people talk with American till we back. Only Major Trung can speak with you." Trung's smile broke down to a flat stare, aimed at Ram. "People be punish if talk with American before we come back, you unnerstand? Then me, you speak, tell why fight South Vietnam. You tell President Eisenhower, okay?"

"Okay," said Ram. The major's warning was clear enough. Anyone who talked with him, without Trung there, would be punished. That included My Linh.

"C'mon with me," said Chau. As they left Trung, Chau answered the question before it was asked: "The men we met after Tay Ninh, they told Trung about you and My Linh, of course. He'd love to catch her--sister of his *commissar*--being unfaithful to one of his officers, mainly if it involved an American."

"I hear what you're saying, Kim Chau."

Chau glanced at him. "He's trying to set you up, I think. Taking Loc Do just to leave you and My Linh alone."

"I said I understand, Kim Chau."

Chau tapped on Ram's arm anyway. "Be awfully careful after we leave, would you? Trung'll probably have someone watching you."

They came to a mound of sandbags formed around a bunker near the tree line. They walked down a tunnel-ramp beneath the trees, passing a munitions vault, and Ram had to touch his way along the crumbly dirt wall until his eyes adjusted to the lamp-dimness.

"Medical ward's just around the corner," said Chau.

"That where all the stink is coming from?"

"It's a mixture of balsam and *nua ao*, a root they burn and liquefy to give to the ailing." Chau smiled at that. "Giving us *nua ao* is the punishment for anyone getting sick, I think."

Kerosene lanterns threw achromatic colors against the dirt walls, creating hues of grey-brown that looked like fried liver. The underpass widened to squeeze a row of cots between two supporting buttresses. A nurse in camouflage fatigues, carrying a clump of food--corn and mashed bananas on palm leaves--squeezed by them.

"Trung looks like one sneaky bastard. Is he your C.O.?"

"Kind of. In a lot of ways I have more authority when we're not in the field, but..." Chau couldn't keep his mind on the question. They were coming to another opening and he concentrated on just getting through it--"My Linh?" he asked the room in general. "Is my sister in here?"

People were packing papers beneath a string of generator-powered lights where an officer, shouldering a bandoleer of .30-caliber long-noses, stepped forward, nodded politely toward Ram and began speaking to Chau in Vietnamese.

"This is Captain Loc Do," said Chau, quickly. "He's...he distributes propaganda pamphlets for this zone."

Loc Do removed his fatigue hat, bowed, revealing a streak of grey along his temple. "I have heard of you," said Captain Loc. He touched his bandoleer. "We are ordered on a mission--please excuse--"

"Chau told me about it..." Ram lost his train of thought. My Linh had walked from a stack of file-boxes and stood with the four other girls in the room, and even in her loose-fitting black uniform she kept a manicured smoothness about her, still gorgeous. She didn't look at him.

"And you know my companion, Dao My Linh," said Loc Do, beckoning to her. "You are special to her, so you are special to me, Sergeant Apollo. Please come a moment, My Linh?"

My Linh, keeping her head lowered, walked only a few steps forward.

"I tell my companion that I must go now," said Captain Loc. "I must go--we will all speak when we return." He turned to Ram to explain. "My Linh need to stay with me, Sergeant. I do not think she prefer this way."

"Be careful if there is fighting, Loc Do," My Linh said to him in English. "Don't be too brave in Dinh Xioa."

"I will not." Loc Do dipped his head toward Ram and left, and Chau, caught off guard by the quickness of the captain's exit, straightened up and followed after him. He gave the other women a look that brought them out behind him.

"Remember what Trung said, Ram," Chau cautioned from the doorway. "Get right out of here, okay?"

My Linh struggled to keep her gaze away from Ram as Chau left. She put her hands lightly to her face. "I cannot talk now."

"This wasn't your fault, My Linh. I mean, with Loc Do-"

"-It isn't Loc Do. I am not ashamed of being with him."

"No, I guess you wouldn't be." He reached to touch her but she shook her head.

"We cannot stay in this room together." She backed away toward the door. "I will come tonight."

"No, don't do that. That major warned against it."

"Whatever risk there is, I will gladly take." She reached the main tunnel as she said that. "I will come to you."

The other girls, after My Linh left, crowded back into the filing section and resumed thumping open the cardboard boxes. Ram made his way past them. Chau was waiting for him outside.

"I'll show you where you bunk for the night." Chau waited until Ram caught up, then walked toward another ramp entrance, stopping on the way to pick up a Mauser carbine from a stack in center-camp. "These're our best quarters." Chau yanked aside a brown canvass curtain. "Only for decadent luxury-hungry capitalist visitors like yourself." The cot inside *did* have the luxury of a mosquito net, and a table with drawers, and slot-windows near the ceiling that provided a view through the straw grass to the lavender mountains outside. "Only Russian generals and American sergeants get in here."

"Much obliged."

"I have to take off now. That village is a twelve-mile hike from here, mostly by road. But, first..." He squeaked open one of the drawers, produced a grey hardback briefcase and held it up like a banner—"*Voila.* The whole damned works on Bryan is in here, Ram. You can hang him by the balls with the documents we matched up in here."

Ram took the briefcase, bounced its weight in his hands. The Liberation Front had done its homework, the papers had gained a couple of pounds since their arrival. "It's a little late for this now, isn't it?"

"Late my ass--"

"Your father's dead, Kim Chau. And Claire's beyond our help, probably. What the hell good are these now?"

Chau tightened the strap of his carbine over his shoulder and jammed on a cloth hat. "Sooner or later you've got to risk your ass voluntarily, Ram, for *some* damned cause."

"I've risked my ass, Kim Chau. They told me it was for a cause."

"*Voluntarily*, Ram. Oh, well, hell..." He held his hand out and Ram took it. "Anyway, remember Vo Trung's warning. With that letter from the Presidium you might not be at risk, but that letter won't do My Linh any good."

"How far can he take that punishment threat?"

"All the way, believe me. He could send her north to a re-education camp, and they shoot people up there just for drill."

"Then why join these guys? What's the difference between them and the Diem people?"

"Maybe someday we'll find out," said Kim Chau. "Anyway, adios amigo. Be real careful about seeing My Linh till we get back, would you?"

After Chau left, Ram lay on his cot and wondered what he'd do if My Linh did come. Lord, he hoped she wouldn't...but if she did, what would *he* do, chase her away?

In the afternoon humidity the high slit windows allowed only hints of air to pass through, which barely reached his bed. The mosquito net intensified the stickiness inside its tent. He sweated in his half-sleep, and waited.

And she did come to him, after nightfall. She lifted the curtain and watched him, and the thin muslin curtain fell across her back like a beige mantilla, and when he opened his eyes he thought, for a moment, that he was imagining her, until she put her hand on his cheek. He looked past her, through the netting toward the doorway.

"I do not think anyone saw me, Ramirez. If they did it would not matter, I need to be with you."

"You can't stay here, My Linh."

"I need you beside me, Ramirez." She leaned over and kissed him and he started to take her but had to stop himself. He shuddered as he sat up, away from her. He couldn't keep from shuddering, for a moment. He inhaled and tried to clear his mind. "My Linh, if you don't go, *I'll* have to go. This is too dangerous for you."

She took his hand, held it against her breast. "You're with me now, Ramirez. I need no other protection."

"Like I protected your father? Christ, My Linh, I can't let you take this kind of risk. I'm having a tough enough time just...keeping my hands off you."

"I know." She stood and smoothed the hair along the back of his head. "I shouldn't have come, but I needed to sit with you, at least, even for a minute. I needed to touch you, Ramirez."

He folded his arms together, to keep from returning that touch, and he didn't look at her as she left. He wanted My Linh too badly to watch her leave, and when she'd gone he laid back with his arms still folded, and stared at the cross-bars above his bed.

That hurt worse than Con Son, he thought, and it might have been for nothing. The damage might already be done.

*

The light force company from Camp Twelve arrived at the outskirts of Dinh Xioa late that night and found a mélange of contrasting structures: triple-dannert barbed wire--a pyramid of three coils--circled a village that was smaller than Binh-An. Brick guard towers rose above muddy hog pens, trenches were carved through council meeting areas. A moat, half-dug around the north end, burrowed past a field of sugar cane, and the land was cleared for fifty meters beyond the balustrade and wire. A line of triangular-shaped mud forts with mounted machine guns circled the village, which looked like a fortified shanty-town.

Major Trung sat on a terraced hillside near the village and continued staring through his field glasses at the barricades and armaments into the night before calling his platoon leaders together. "In the morning we will destroy this village."

216

"*Destroy* it! With one company and two mortars?" Chau couldn't believe this. "They have machine gun emplacements, Major. The planes from Bien Hoa could be here in ten minutes--and in that open area-"

"-We must show this village that we will punish anyone, immediately, who cooperates this way with the Army of the Republic." Trung smacked his hands together. "Remember, in the recent Tua-Lai battle the Caodai and the Binh Xuyen destroyed a two *thousand*-man outpost."

Chau exchanged looks with Captain Loc, who stood away from the other officers. Loc Do's face had sagged into disbelief--what kind of insanity was this man *preaching* here?

"Anyone not obeying my orders will be doing so during a state of war," said Major Trung. "You fully understand what that means, Commissar Dao? Captain Loc?"

Neither man answered.

"Then there will be no more argument here."

Trung began by spreading most of the men easterly of the village, keeping the early sun at their backs. Two squads would go to the north and west with the mortars to provide diversionary fire. Five log-teams would gather heavy bamboo and logs to drop across the wire pyramids.

Chau and Loc Do took charge of the diversionary squads, an arrangement that fit into Major Trung's strategy, Chau supposed. It put Trung's two problem officers in the line of heaviest probable fire.

After their squads were positioned, Chau and Loc Do crawled out through the grass to look for trip flares and jumping grenades. There were none. They crawled almost to the nearest tower where a pair of soldiers slouched. "Like an army installation," whispered Loc Do.

"These people might fight back," Chau answered. "Trung doesn't like people who fight back."

"These people build defenses against their will--now we must kill them for it? I asked the major if this means the old people, and the women and helpless ones, and he answered exactly so, an example must be made."

"If we fight terror with terror, Loc Do, does it matter who the victor is? These people haven't done anything to us."

"Well, it was *Diem* who dishonored the 1954 treaty," whispered Loc Do. "You sound like your sister. You also think we should resist all evil, even if it means fighting *both* sides?"

"My sister is not practical," answered Chau, and left it at that.

Dawn was approaching by the time they got back to the ditch, the sky became lighter grey. Some of the men began lighting a last cigarette, against orders, hiding the glow by hunching over their smokes. At 0530 Chau checked his watch and waited, per their instructions, for Loc Do's riflemen to kill the guards, and Loc Do's rifle fire started at almost the same moment. The two guards flopped and fell against the railing of the tower. The thump! thump! of mortars from Chau's squad followed instantly, booming into the open area, stepping across the new buildings and ripping into the nearest structures.

A siren screamed from a transmission pole. Men in underwear streamed from their billets--*masses* of men. They were scrambling from all directions--these weren't village dwellings, Chau could see that. These were *bunkhouses*. The yelling defenders ran to their positions in the pits next to the barracks and into the sandbagged bunkers near the wire, mounting .30-caliber machine guns along their parapets. The inner, circular pits, frantic with gesturing men, began thudding mortar salvos back toward Chau's position.

Trung's three platoons held their positions quiet. They let the defenders concentrate on the two north squads. Then, intermittently, their log teams ran forward to flatten sections of the wire. They didn't use back-up fire until the defenders saw the flanking assault and turned their barrage toward it.

"Be ready! Be ready!" Chau called out. Seeing the Guard switch fire to the new attackers he rolled over the edge of the moat. A mortar landed on the village emplacement nearest him, blowing it apart, but someone in there was still alive, popping what sounded like a .38 pistol at the attackers.

Fire started pouring from other bunkers. Chau saw Loc Do's men surge out less than forty yards away, some of them already dropping while most of Chau's men, running like trained assault troops, stayed on their feet, using the guerrilla's soft-tread run. The men carrying heavy bamboo threw their logs across the barbed wire and Chau tried to jump over but the other guns found him first. He felt the punches in his arm, in his chest, and he fell more from surprise than pain and tried to crawl forward but the other men knocked him over as they scrambled past him. The first soldier over him stumbled toward the disabled bunker and the survivor in there killed him with the pistol. Only a pistol, but Chau's man flipped and tumbled like a shot deer.

Others clambered, clawed, sprinted through the wire but none came near the main bunkers. They began to fall around Kim Chau. This was *crazy!* he thought. How could Trung order such an attack? Then he saw Loc Do begin to fall back with the rest of the men--too late! Too late! Too late! *"Fall back!"* Chau yelled. They had to get the hell back.

With the assault collapsing, the men in the bunkers started cheering, waving *coupe-coupes*--Vietnamese machetes--at the attackers, and Chau saw the gesture and prayed they wouldn't make a sortie out for the survivors, not with *machetes*. But the whine of jets interrupted the battle, and both sides took cover.

The wing.50-calibers from a scrambled VNAF F-86 opened up and sudden fountains of dirt sprayed up from the cane, the moat, the camp. Indiscriminately. The pilot, unsure of the enemy's location, apparently, had apparently decided to kill everyone. Not even that pilot knows who the hell the enemy is, Chau thought. The bullets were rattling across his men, splashing red across the open area, across the wire, across the sandbags of the Civil Guard bunkers. The plane's guns scattered and killed both guerrillas and defenders, churning everything in the area to rubble--*who the hell was flying that thing?*

The bullets on the first pass didn't find Kim Chau. He was able to tear his shirt from the wire and crawl from the compound as more men carrying submachine guns and machetes appeared around the buildings. Small arms fire raked the defenders again with the *blat-dit-dit* from Loc Do's sector as Chau back-crawled into the sugar cane and struggled to his feet, and the cane grew enormous around him, bringing, for a moment, a sense of asylum. He could hear the exchange still going on at the other end of the village but the attack was losing any immediacy for him, for he could taste his salted blood now, and he had to keep moving from that sound. His cotton uniform clung to him, his carbine hung like a cannon from his hand--he let the thing drop. He heard, for a moment, only the cane rustling above him, around him, in the monsoon wind.

He had limped onto a farm trail when the second pass of the Sabre chattered over the fields. Chau sprawled off the path and the F-86 roared past, and he tried to get up again.

He couldn't. His leg had gone numb. His leg, what he could see of it, was torn open, his knee looked like a broken melon. Chau moved to a sitting position and felt the leg, felt the sharp jab of the splintered bone.

He worked his rope belt loose, to tie around his upper thigh.

Chapter 32

"Commissar Dao not come back." Major Trung made no pretense of grief about Kim Chau *or* the attack. He was back in his camp command bunker now, saying this in English to Ram, Loc do and My Linh. "Many Dao men die."

The major had come back from Dinh Xoai without a scratch.

"No soldiers saw Kim Chau die." Captain Loc Do had fragment wounds speckling around his neck and one of his eyes was almost closed, watering from a thickly ointmented flash-burn. "I see Republic soldiers shoot Kim Chau and he goes to cane field. Too much blood." He stopped when he remembered My Linh was in the room. He turned toward her but she had already leaned weakly against Ram's arm.

Ram saw Major Trung watching this. He helped her sit down and moved away from her. "Did anyone go look for him?"

"I come back with my soldiers into trees," said Captain Loc. "Kim Chau with his men, I think. Maybe not."

"Then he's probably still alive."

"*No.* He's not come back, so Commissar Dao die at Dinh Xoai," said Major Trung.

"Chau goes into cane field," Loc Do insisted, this time to Ram. "Republic soldiers don't follow, afraid of fight in cane field. Afraid of..." Loc Do tapped his head.

"Ambush. So they probably wouldn't follow him in there?" Ram was speaking more to Major Trung now. "That motor pool, what can I use from there? I need that jeep."

"You can't go near the village, Ram," said My Linh.

"ARVN soldiers won't bother an American-"

"-*No* jeep. Need jeep here," said Major Trung, hesitating a moment. "Use motocycle." Trung apparently wasn't unwilling to get the American out of camp.

"I can't get a wounded man out on any motorcycle."

"Use motocycle. Need jeep here, need truck." Vo Trung, saying that, stepped back. "Now we talk what happen to you, comrade Dao My Linh." Loc Do answered Trung in Vietnamese and the major responded with a rebuke toward My Linh, then spat and switched back to English, to Ram. "Something *happen*, people see. No good."

"Major, more important to find Kim Chau-"

"-You know rule, Captain Loc. Something happen here. You wait for what I decide." Vo Trung pivoted and marched from the room, and began yelling orders to the men outside.

There was no choice. Without the battalion commissar in camp, no one could stand up to Vo Trung. "We need to find him, Ram," said My Linh. "We need Kim Chau."

"But *this* bastard-"

"-You cannot do more here, Sergeant," said Captain Loc. "My Linh must be with me only now, better you are not here." He gave them a tired look. "I will protect My Linh, this is my promise." He started to say something to My Linh, but then, instead, bowed and left the room.

"Jesus."

"Loc Co is a good person, Ramirez," said My Linh. "I am not a proper companion for him." She put away that thought. There wasn't time to think about Loc Do. "You have to go to Kim Chau."

"Last night, damn it, we should have--"

"You will bring back Kim Chau." She put fingertips to his chest. "Everything will be all right."

*

Ram put on the green fatigues G-2 supplied him in Saigon, and checked the stripes on the sleeves--could be important if he met up with ARVN. Before he picked up the motorcycle he went to the sick ward for a med-kit and a canteen and strapped these next to a flashlight attached to the back seat. The bike, after the first convulsive *BAM!* kicked into a flat rattle. He steered it around toward the CQ where My Linh had come out to see him, and they watched each other from a distance.

He turned the throttle and guided the bike back around, away from her.

The road to Dinh Xoai was a small battered ribbon of pavement, a little smoother than the one he and Chau had come in on but just as empty. He tried to see the road as far ahead as possible although he doubted that the Civil Guard would do any counter-attacking along here. If they didn't have the stomach to go after an enemy this nearby, before the attack, they sure as hell wouldn't have it now.

Within minutes the towers and wire of the Civil Guard village bristled above the cane. He saw the mud-yellow moat next to the field; Chau would be in that cane, where, probably, the ARVN were afraid to go, according to Loc Do. But he needed to get past the camp first, maybe do an end run here.

Too late. The main gate was already opening, two armored field cars were already nosing through it, triggered by the noise of the motorcycle. Each carried a mounted.30-caliber machine gun.

"*Nuroi-My.*" Ram called, sliding to a stop. "American!"

They didn't seem to understand, or care. The drivers and gunners shouted at each other using a lot of hand motions and then, getting back to the American, signaled for him to go away from here. Both vehicles put it in reverse and skidded backward through the gate, back into the compound.

Ram took a deep breath and tilted the cycle up and around and continued farther along the road until the canefield blocked off the camp's line of sight, then he slowed and began looking for Kim Chau. He saw the harvesting trail, which was about a third as wide as the main road. He turned onto it and found, within a hundred yards, the empty stilted storage shed, the jagged row of.50-caliber holes, the splotch of deep red stain along the ground--it looked like a damned *lake* of blood here. Ram dumped the bike and followed the black-red blotches to the shed, where Chau lay scissor-legged against a foundation pole under the shed's platform. His face was graying from loss of blood. He didn't move as Ram kneeled over him. "Kim Chau?"

The lieutenant gave a sickly smile, didn't open his eyes. "Wha' kept you?"

"Don't talk." Ram crawled under the shed, checked underneath the soaked red patches on Chau's shoulder and side. The blood was caking around the wound, although the upper area was clean, but the.50-calibers had shredded his lower left leg.

"Couldn' make it up th' stairs."

"Don't talk, dammit."

"Fuggin' l-leg, Ram," Chau garbled the words. "No l-leg. Think i's gone."

"It's still there. You tied it off okay." Ram felt around the mangled bone. "I better hide the bike and get us inside the shed." He went back to push the motorcycle into the cane, then tore open the medical kit: one hypodermic in there, taped to a bottle of milky liquid. And gauze wrappings, and scissors, and iodine--at least what appeared to be iodine. The bottles were all labeled in Russian.

"What's this say, Kim Chau? Is this morphine?" Ram held the bottle of milky liquid near Chau's face.

"Can't...see. Shoot my leg with it anyway. God damn really hurts."

"Right." Ram cut away the pant leg, tried to locate a clear section of skin, but dirt and blood were smudged over most of the leg, overlapped with twisting flesh. Bone showed on both sides of the knee. Ram poured water on it, wiped off the leg and found the upper thigh less torn up. "Where the hell's this go?"

"Don' know."

"Right." Ram pushed the needle into Chau's leg--only half a shot, then, just in case. Ram emptied the bottle of red ointment over the larger holes in the skin, then wrapped the leg between two cane and lifted Chau to the platform, on which the farmers had placed plates to burn incense to protect the harvests. He could taste the still-sweet odor in his throat and it reminded him of things past, of the Okinawan pleasure rooms.

"Got t'get back, Ram."

"Not yet. Not yet."

"Someth'n I got t'do."

"Can't get you past that camp till after dark." Ram knew the soldiers would spot a wounded Vietnamese as one of the guerrillas. They'd chase the bike while it was still light, and there was no chance for two men on one bike to get away from a mounted jeep. But he knew the soldiers wouldn't come out after dark. That would be like going into the cane field–too much chance of their dreaded ambush once it got dark.

Ram wrapped Chau's chest with the remaining gauze strips. "You'd be too easy to spot in daylight."

Chau slumped back. "I've got th's great fear, Ram."

"So do I, Kim Chau."

"N-not them." Chau's jaw sagged as he motioned toward Dinh Xoai. "Trung. Got to get My Linh away from Trung. You get back to My Linh, Ram."

"Going to get you back first. Wait till dark."

Chau laid on his side and closed his eyes. His eyelids quivered, his breath came in long gasps, and his words grew in Ram's mind: My Linh was probably in danger, *big* danger, but he wouldn't have a chance of getting to her past Dinh Xoai, not with Kim Chau. Not while it was still light.

They waited, Ram squatting like a cockroach within the stink of incense while Gecko lizards clung to the wall above them, motionless in the afternoon heat, watching through fishbowl eyes. "Kim Chau, you awake?"

"Don' let me go now, Ram. Can't die yet."

"You better not, after the trouble I've gone through." Ram wondered if this one wall-eyed Gecko was thinking of trying to eat them, he kept eyeing Ram like he would a beetle meal. Ram tried to make the time pass, tried to think about My Linh. Was even this situation part of her great *Unreality?* He squatted like a cockroach and waited for an answer and the

223

answer came only in the hum of small noises, the rustle of crickets and sugar cane, the soundless blink of a motionless lizard. And they waited, and the day passed.

"Sun's almos' down." Chau attempted to scooch himself to a sitting position, grimaced, and settled instead on his elbow. "The bas'ards won't come out t'chase us now."

"Pretty timid, these ARVN people."

"ARVN scared shi'less of ambush... You look almos' as worried as me, Ram. Y'll get wr'nkles."

Ram smiled. "I worry about the stuff your sister puts in my head, Kim Chau."

"I sure unnerstan' that." Chau leaned on Ram, tried to stand on one leg and immediately bent over. He inhaled and pushed himself up from the platform railing. "Awful painful. Sorry."

"Don't talk so much."

"Jus' get me to th' camp, Ram. Got somethin' have to do."

Amber shade spread over the fields as the two scuffled down the short ladder, across the road to the motorcycle, which looked small and thin in the dusk. The handle-bars pressed into Ram's knees as Chau squeezed himself onto the back seat, propping his splint on the footrest. Ram kick-started the motor into its spasmodic banging, turned the handle and chugged the cycle into a careful acceleration.

No problem, now, with the military camp. The front gate blinked on yellow floodlights as they went by but no vehicles came out. Ram saw no guards on the battered outguard towers.

He shifted gears as the moon came out. The outline of trees and terrain ghosted around them.

They entered the abandoned soccer field of Camp Twelve to a looming emptiness, and Ram braked harder than he intended, and Kim Chau sucked in his breath. "Jesus Christ, Ram--" Chau had slid forward, he pushed on Ram's back to take the weight off his leg.

"Sorry."

A few lean-to poles remained tilted in the air like long thin grave markers. Except for a disabled French half-track all the equipment had vanished, only the rubble of sandbags and fire pits and shoveled-over entrances remained of the tunnel-bivouac existence of Camp Twelve.

"Too goddamned late." Ram started the motorcycle forward again, lurching into the main section of the camp.

"*Oh Jesus Christ!*" Chau's scream sent the bike into a side-slip and Ram jammed his foot along the ground to keep the thing upright. He swung around to find out what in hell Chau was...Chau was staring at one of the poles. Ram twisted around to follow the stare.

At the top of the nearest pole was a knob, a knobby ball--

"Holy shit." Ram fumbled the flashlight out and tried to center its beam on the bamboo staff. The light wavered for a moment, then crawled up the spotted rail onto the sucked and hollow bulb, still draining red beneath a hanging trail of skin.

The severed head of Loc Do, in soundless shrieking, glared down on them. Loc Do's neck had been sliced through below the jaw, and Ram dropped the flashlight with a *thunk* and the noise went through his head like an electric shock. He grabbed it up again and moved the light across the remaining poles. The thought that My Linh could *also* be up there...

The nearby poles were bare.

"*Drive*, Ram. Gi'me the flashlight."

Ram kicked the starter over as Chau shot the light around the camp. After they made a circle of the field Ram had to shut the motor down again because he was shaking too much and the engine vibration intensified it. He needed to stop for a minute to get his control back. He and Chau sat mutely in the center of the field.

Loc Do had died trying to protect My Linh, Ram knew. But if Trung had killed My Linh too, he'd left no trace.

"Got to catch up wi' them, Ram."

Ram steadied his hands on the grips. "Show me the way there, Kim Chau."

When they got back to the road Chau pointed to the right, to the west. The battalion would be headed that way toward the town of An Loc. "Jeep and trucks go this way," said Chau. "The men walking with the buff'lo would take the forest trails. Trung makes the Caodai platoon walk, so they won' be there to help...if we find him."

Chapter 33

The land leveled out after they crossed the Song Be River. The rubber plantations were all around them now, the bamboo forests disappeared. As they entered the upper Piedmont region, near the Cambodian border, a weak cluster of lights rose in front of them.

"Tha's An Loc." said Kim Chau, through his teeth. The pain in Chau's voice reminded Ram of the tourniquet; the leg would putrefy if the tourniquet weren't loosened again, soon.

Stray chickens, gray splotches in the path, squawked and scattered as the cycle entered An Loc. Yellow lamps silhouetted people against open stalls. Less than a block into town Chau pointed to a opening between two squatty buildings. "There, Ram, to the lef'."

They turned and bumped along a rock walkway to a courtyard centered around a two-story, open-air restaurant. And at its front sat the hunching mastodon, the boxy Molatova, the troop carrier of the Viet Minh 42nd Light Force Battalion.

"S'where they usu'ly go," mumbled Chau.

Rough wood tables cluttered an outside patio extending below a ragged orange canopy, where some of the villagers were eating, sitting cautiously away from a knot of black uniforms that were on the road side of the restaurant. One of the uniformed men raised his hand... Major Trung.

When Trung recognized Kim Chau his gesture froze, hanging in air like a signpost. "*Quan hai Dao!*"

"You killed Cap'n Loc, you fugging *murderer!*" Chau said this in English and Trung responded with a stream of dialect and Chau tried to raise his voice above it--"What've you done wi' *My Linh*?"

Trung answered with a yell to his men and most of the blackshirts in the restaurant came to their feet, and Major Trung, reinforced, then shouted back at his commissar. Chau sagged, snarled a response before he translated Trung's words: "Says My Linh's been sen' away for execution."

"Exe...? We'll see who the hell gets *executed!*" Ram had swung at Trung's face before he'd finished the sentence, bashing the major's cheek, whipping Trung's head back, arcing a spatter of red under the canopy as the major tumbled across the tables. Bottles of rice wine shattered along the floor and plates of rice splashed over Major Trung as the other men, jumping through the debris, circled and yelled and pointed weapons at Ram until a spectacled captain got in their way. The spectacled captain waved his hands, sending some of them to untangle Major Trung from the legs of a chair.

226

"Don' move, Ram," said Kim Chau, feebly, from behind. "Show them you don' wanna fight them, jus' Trung."

Ram lifted his hands as the officer wearing glasses continued talking to his men. Lights went on above the restaurant. People leaned from their windows, straining to see the foreigner who had dared strike a *Viet Minh* officer.

"These're mountain cadre, Ram. Be careful," said Chau. "The man talking, Cap'n Pham, he's telling them not to kill you in fron' of the village."

Captain Pham was speaking rapidly, mainly to Chau, sometimes pointing at Ram as he spoke. He stopped long enough to check Kim Chau's leg but now, wearily, Chau could only grunt his replies.

"Tell him to get you to a doctor." Ram watched the soldiers lay out--carefully lay out--the unconscious Trung, who lolled from side to side like a beached shark, his mouth leaking red and white spit, his eyes half open.

Ram could feel the sharp bite of Trung's teeth on his knuckles, a satisfying kind of pain, while the captain, instructing the nearest men to carry Chau to the truck, paid little attention to Major Trung. "I tol' Pham that you're the one tha' saved me, Ram." Chau grimaced as they picked him up. "He plans to hol' you...till Trung gets conscious. Caodai men'll be here by mornin' to help you, maybe."

"Get the hell to a doctor, Kim Chau."

"Told Cap'n Pham I'm calling meeting of battal'n leaders, as undersec'tary..."

"Get the hell to a *doctor* first."

As the truck carrying Chau pulled out, Captain Pham, bracketed by his men, motioned Ram inside and up the stairs, along an outside boardwalk to a tiny room: one cot, two hemp stools, bamboo-strip blinds. Filled with the smell of boiling fish seeping from the restaurant downstairs. Pham gave orders to two of the guards who, after the captain left, moved themselves as far from Ram as they could, eyeing the American like the feces end of a punjii stick, because this American had struck their battalion commander. That meant he must be insane. They wanted no part of this person.

After what seemed like a few hours, a commotion began at the front of the cafe, working its way up the stairs, ending at the doorway with an eruption of people--two more soldiers and Major Trung--jostling to keep their weapons in Ram's face as Trung pointed a finger at the furious purple bloat under his eye: "You look! See! Die for this!"

"What'd you do with Dao My Linh?"

"Shut up Dao My Linh! Dao My Linh die." Trung stepped back when he saw Ram's clenched fist. "We send My Linh to north for execution.

227

She go to American against order, people see. She, Loc Do, traitor--*die for this.*"

"You're a goddamn liar, Trung."

"Send to north for execution." He made a face that might have been an attempted smile when he saw the effect that had on Ram. "In morning now you execute also. You go My Linh." Vo Trung was apparently trying a sneer but the puffy mound around his eye drew his face, instead, into an ugly warp. "Why Kim Chau call meeting?"

Ram squinted at Vo Trung--at what was left of Vo Trung's face--and the major glared back through his good eye.

"Captain say commissar secretary Dao to call meeting all battalion commander," Vo Trung snarled. *"Why call meeting?"*

"The secretary plans to hang your ass, Major Trung, if you harm My Linh or me-"

"-Dao My Linh to be executed, commissar not help. Tomorrow *you* executed, first thing." Trung, satisfied with that agenda, nodded at Ram's two guards, who took their places on the stools again as the major pulled the door shut behind him.

Ram studied the two remaining guards, who, in turn, studied him. He wondered if the threat of Kim Chau's meeting, whatever the hell that meant, could help them. Not damned likely. Trung had probably given himself the night to think over Ram's "safe-passage" letter, that's why Ram wasn't already dead, probably. Whatever, he'd have to wait. He laid back again, and watched the fanless ceiling where light from the patio dappled kaleidoscopes through the bamboo window strips. He heard other steps now, people resuming commerce on the streets.

He adjusted back to the choppy straw mattress, and the scuffle and tinkle of street noise eventually faded, and the ceiling patterns turned charcoal pre-dawn gray before the first tapping came, so faint the guards didn't hear it. The second was more insistent and both guards did hear that, and they stood and positioned themselves on either side of the door as the man nearest the latch unlocked it.

In the hall two more soldiers, carrying M-2 carbines, nodded their greeting. The new men wore black-uniforms like the guards but instead of sandals and soft hats they wore white boots, belts and holsters, and white bush hats pinned up on the side... Kim Chau's Caodai had caught up with them.

Ram carefully moved himself to a sitting position as one of the Caodai, a young lieutenant, stepped past the guards toward Ram while his corporal talked with the two cadre. "We have been asked to take you with us," said the lieutenant, quietly. "We are comrades of the military commissar Dao Kim Chau."

"How is he?"

"He is still alive." The lieutenant looked behind him as the discussion at the doorway seemed to be heating up. "Your guards do not believe Major Trung would send Caodai soldiers to relieve them--be on your alert a minute." He gave this warning as one of the guards pushed the Caodai corporal away from him. The lieutenant straightened up and barked at the guards in Vietnamese. The guards responded by shaking their pistols at him.

Both Caodai dipped their carbines toward the guards as the lieutenant gave another command. Trung's two cadre hesitated, then started to return the threat but the *R-R-R-RUP* of fire from the Caodai cut them short, both carbines erupting together, emptying the clips in seconds, ripping .30-caliber holes through the guards and pitting the walls behind them.

The guards stood disbelieving, for an instant, before they fell into each other.

"*Hurry*, Sergeant."

Ram had leapt off the cot before the firing stopped, reaching the hall in three steps, jumping down the stairway. The corporal apparently had hot-wired the hammering Molatova and had already jumped in, pulling away as Ram and Tom flopped into the back. The lieutenant pulled down the canvass and fell across the troop bench inside, and tried to get his breath.

"Damn!" Ram stayed on hands and knees and sucked in air as the truck swerved around the first corner. "Won't they know the Caodai did this?"

"Perhaps not." The lieutenant had to take another deep breath. "Our friends will take care of this truck."

"Anyway, thanks for doing this, Lieutenant...didn't catch your name."

"Call me Tom, Sergeant. It is better you don't know real names."

He was breathing a little easier now. "Lieutenant Dao say to save you so you will report this to your President." After a few moments he reached beneath the bench and pulled out Kim Chau's gray briefcase. "Commissar Dao say to give you this. You go back to U.S.A., tell your President that our people will fight both Diem and the north cadre by ourselves. No need to fight the Americans too."

The message, even in that scrambled context, wasn't lost on Ram. Chau had probably hand-picked this man to deliver it. "The sister of Lieutenant Dao, what've they done with her?"

"Cannot help the girl-priestess of Gia Dinh. She is in convoy through Cambodia to camps in north. Too many guards."

"Where does it leave from? Couldn't we get more Caodai-"

"-*No*, not for that. Dao My Linh is in Loc Ninh, twenty kilometers from here, but you cannot go there."

"Is Major Trung in Loc Ninh?"

"No. Many cadre take her there."

"Then you can act like you're guarding me in Loc Ninh." Ram saw an opening here. "The squad left before you got here, didn't they? There's no way they would know...Trung wouldn't expect us to go *there*."

"We are told to hide you until Kim Chau's meeting."

"Hell with Kim Chau's meeting. We go to My Linh first, or hell with any message to my *President*." Ram waited to see if that would have any effect. The lieutenant lit a cigarette, then slid open the window to the driver's cabin and talked with the corporal.

"If we go there, we cannot stay," he said, turning back to Ram. "We need to take off Caodai belts and hats, to look-"

"Okay, good."

"-to look like other soldiers, and will need to tie your hands, hold rifles on you as prisoner, in case Trung's men see you," said the lieutenant. "But we will not fight convoy guards, and we cannot stay there."

"Do you know if My Linh is hurt?"

"I am not sure. Many prisoners in Loc Ninh going north this morning." The inside of the truck became morning-bright as Tom lifted the canvass flap to let air in. The acid smell of his cigarette dissipated in the wind.

"What do you mean, you need to hide me until Kim Chau's meeting? He wants me *at* the meeting?"

"Yes."

"What in hell for?" Ram couldn't understand that. "*Trung* would be there, wouldn't he?"

"After the meeting we will not worry about Major Trung," said Tom, who concentrated now on taking off his white belt and holster.

Screw it, thought Ram. He wasn't interested in Trung's fate. Through the flaps he saw farms chopping through crusted earth, buffalo pulling lorries... In half an hour the truck began to slow as they drove onto the main street of Loc Ninh. People squatting along the road stretched themselves sideways, curious to see what soldiers sat in back, jabbing each other and pointing when they saw the American.

The truck veered, slid to a stop inside a graveled assembly area, and Lieutenant Tom searched out a cord and tied Ram's wrists together, loosely, before calling to someone outside. Someone, in turn, called back. Two or three people called back. Lieutenant Tom, in sandals now, climbed off the tailgate and waited for Ram. "If anyone speaks to you, do not answer. We will do the talking. If Kim Chau's sister is alive she will be here."

Ram moved to the side where the voices came from, where a line of trucks, most of them already unloaded, were being guarded over and tightened down and tinkered on by about two platoons of men. But in place of the black pajamas and open sandals these soldiers wore boots and green uniforms, pith helmets with palm branches and chin straps. Ram knew enough about the Hanoi army to recognize the uniform. These were North Vietnam Regulars.

And in the middle of the line, in confused accordion rows, the soldiers prodded prisoners onto the side benches of open-bedded trucks. The prisoners mostly wore black uniforms or short-sleeved white shirts, or gray farmer's tunics, but among them, one girl, her hair braided back dark and long-formed and knotted to sworls of stretched black silk... "My Linh!"

She stood to find him among the vehicles and soldiers.

"Ramirez!"

Tom grabbed Ram by the back of his shirt. "You will get us killed, Sergeant. Let *me* do the talking."

Among the regulars three men separated from the unloading and came toward the Caodai and their prisoner, signaling by crossing and uncrossing their hands--*come no farther*. And Tom tried to speak to them, pointing to the girl and to Ram as the Regulars continued crossing and uncrossing their hands.

Tom turned to Ram. "I told them this girl was to come with us but they do not believe me. They have orders to take these people to a camp near Hanoi."

"Bullshit." Ram could see My Linh clinging to the steel bracing as she looked toward him. "I'll be damned if I let them take *her*."

The soldiers nearest Ram put their weapons to their shoulders as Ram started toward the trucks. "Ram!" My Linh screamed. "Don't try to stop them!"

"Do not do this," Tom repeated behind him. "It does no good to get us killed."

"I'm not going to just *stand* here."

The three men in front of him pushed in the bolts of their rifles.

"Ram!"

He saw the flash of Tom's rifle swing in from the side.

He could still hear the arguing between the Caodai and the Regulars when he fell, but he couldn't get up. He couldn't move. He could only hear the voices and the call of My Linh: *"Don't fight them, Ram!"*

The pain from the side of his head funneled to his neck and shoulders as the motors of the convoy revved up--on command of the harsh, tinny voice of its commander.

Chapter 34

Harry Crosse poured a beaker of vodka from the bar and settled into the overstuffed gold-brocade chair, spreading his feet on its matching pouffe. He lit a three-dollar cigar from the humidor of Bryan's waiting room, within the inner chamber of their San Francisco offices.

Capsulized luxury here, he decided. The senators and generals and diplomats who maintain links to Bryan's world enterprises--citizens of singular rank and substance--sought out this private room to preserve their anonymity. Most especially they preferred this when dealing with the likes of John Bryan.

Per Bryan's orders, Harry flicked on the intercom and adjusted the volume to pick up the voice of Major General Arnold Novinger, but the other room was quiet, for a while. Harry thought Bryan might have forgotten to turn on his microphone. Then: "How did you obtain this, Mr. Bryan?" came the general's grumble. Novinger, apparently, had been reading the memo to himself.

"Not important!" Bryan snapped. "We didn't tie your investigation to these two until I was *given* this, sir, and I demand to know why you would send such people after me!"

Harry smiled, imagining the scene in the next office: old "Banker" Novinger, slim, stern, over-serious--an eight-by-ten glossy of what generals should look like--being confronted with his own Top Secret memo re: the investigation of John Bryan. Presidential timber in there, according to the newspapers, shrinking from the rheumic outrage of this one old man. Harry took a contented puff on his three-dollar cigar. The rich smoke massaged the back of his throat.

"There was no choice, Mr. Bryan. I explained that to you when we..." Novinger's voice became gravelly. "The Bao Dai government insisted that the investigation take place, apparently."

"Apparently? Apparently? Didn't you know this memo existed? You *signed* it, sir."

"We ordered that sergeant to drop it since then, sir."

"Your avenger has *not* dropped it, General. We know for a fact that he has documents-"

"-Our avenger?"

Uh, oh, thought Harry.

"-documents in his possession showing these shipments, and if he can match them with receipts held by these Viet Cong people, he could embarrass both me *and* your National Security Council--and therefore your Administration, I might point out."

"The Administration's deniability has been completely preserved... How did you know about the Viet Cong?

"You mean the Administration does not even *know* of this?" Bryan ignored Novinger's question.

"We understood the thrust of the President's policy against resuming pre-war European colonialism, Mr. Bryan, and I implemented it, at my level. I will take the blame if necessary."

"So you signed a memo to investigate *yourself?*"

The sound of a finger tapping came through the intercom. Harry heard someone walking--Novinger, it would have to be, for Bryan now claimed his "wounds" were too intense for him to walk. The walking man dropped into a chair, creating a delayed whiz of air from the cushion.

Harry found himself chewing harder on the cigar. The caustic taste required a spit into the wastebasket.

"We called the investigation off some time ago, Mr. Bryan."

"Then why is your avenger in Vietnam today, this *minute,* sir? Why does he continue the investigation of my arms shipments there?"

Silence. The picture of the bewildered General Novinger danced in Harry's brain. It was actually quite easy to obtain this information through their connections at the Machinato depot. The whole process, thought Harry, was not much more than routine for a wheeler-dealer like myself. Claire was right, getting things done is what I do.

"How do you know such a thing?" General Novinger asked.

"It is my business to know such things. I would like an answer to my question, sir."

Over the speaker came a noise that sounded like stomach gas. Harry leaned closer to the intercom, which was not easy, requiring him to flounder a moment in the giant overstuffed chair.

"Sergeant Apollo is in Vietnam because we wanted him out of the way, Mr. Bryan. Also he has a direct contact with this new Viet Cong organization--one of our few direct sources, in fact. He's there to obtain information, and that's *all* he's there for."

"No, that is not all, General. You don't understand who and what we're dealing with here. He could also secure proof from them that we--that *we*, not just me, General--did ship arms to the Viet Minh to help fight the French."

"That's not true. That wasn't our purpose at all."

"Create whatever reason you wish. That's how it will read if this *Satan* should contact the newspapers with those documents."

"We could not allow that to happen. It would...raise too many questions."

Harry began to feel real uncomfortable about the purpose of this meeting. What the hell was going on here? Can't the general see he's dealing with a lunatic?

"A lot of Americans would wonder why you now plan a war on people you've been *supplying*," said Bryan. "There is every possibility, sir, that a congressional enquiry might be started regarding those shipments."

"No one would pay attention to such a report. We are talking here about only one sergeant."

"But the documents would give him authenticity, aren't you listening? And he is not just a sergeant. He is not even human."

But he sure isn't indestructible either, thought Harry. This conversation was getting a whole lot less amusing. It was pointing toward resolutions that Harry didn't really want to think about.

"He's a career soldier, Mr. Bryan," said General Novinger, undoubtedly confused by Bryan's last remarks. "He doesn't give a damn about any of this, we're sure of that. We frankly thought we'd gotten him out of the way, sir, by sending him into the mountains of Indo-China."

"Out of the way? He grows *stronger* with adversity, general, for a very obvious reason, since he was sent by my father to punish me."

"By who?..." Silence again. General Novinger continued his tapping for a full minute. "I could almost agree with you in one respect. He comes back from these missions like a trip to the PX. Our latest report says he got caught and was supposed to be shot by a Viet Cong unit, and he even got out of *that*."

"Of course! He always prevails, is that not proof enough?" Bryan could be heard wheeling his chair across the room. "The contest is not between your people and this man, General. It is *I* who must destroy my father's envoy."

"Mr. Bryan-"

"-Where are you sending him next? Can you keep him over there?"

"Not in Indo-China. He's going from there to Okinawa if he makes it back to Saigon. And If he makes it we'll make sure he keeps that schedule. His commanding officer will be going there to debrief him."

"Then *leave* him there on Okinawa, only for a week. Only for a few days, that would be enough."

"Mr. Bryan, we can do nothing more than discipline him."

"That is all *you* can do, General. Fine. You leave him there--what was it? Fort Buckner?--then we'll see what *I* can do."

"I don't think I want to hear any more of this, Mr. Bryan."

"Fine, but you *will* cooperate. You're no schoolboy, you know what will happen to your plans for that country--not to mention what would happen to your *career*, General--if those documents get out. So I suggest, sir, that you hold this sergeant on Okinawa and let us take steps to resolve this."

Bryan waited. Harry waited too, at the intercom. Harry understood Bryan's purpose here: If the general did not disapprove of what he just heard, *if he did not disapprove...* The general was now steeping in his own juices, military codes of honor and discipline were down the toilet. The underside of the world politick took place in these dark alleyways of the world--*my* world, thought Harry--and the general was looking directly into the bowl, *right* now.

"We will take it from here, General," concluded John Bryan. "We will deal with Sergeant Apollo from this point."

"I would prefer not to discuss this further," said General Novinger.

"No, I do not suppose you would," said John Bryan. "Only remember that you created this monster. You helped this emissary of my father to carry out his malediction against me--through this person *you* sent, sir."

"Mr. Bryan, what are you talking about?"

Jesus, here it comes, thought Harry.

"I know who he is, this Sergeant Apollo, this man who takes his name from the God of Light. The instrument of my father, of his dying...and it is *wrong.* I fought in the battle of Belleau Wood, I proved that to your--to this Apollo. I completely reconstructed that battle for him, from my own memory."

Do I really want to stay with this craziness? thought Harry. *Apollo the Angel of Death?* My ass.

"Mr. Bryan..." Novinger's voice was plainly disturbed now. "I think we might study our alternatives a little further before-"

"-Neither you nor my father nor God himself had the right to send him after my...to murder my son."

"He did not murder your son," said General Novinger. "Those two men were not even in the same regiment as your son. They had no reason to kill him."

Harry softened down the speaker. The words from it were banging around inside his head--that imaginary leg wound, all that Belleau Wood crap. "Now it's up to me," he could still hear Bryan say, over the intercom, followed by the sound of Novinger's briefcase snapping shut.

"I understand your implications," said Novinger. "I hope it will not come to that."

"But it *has* come to that, sir."

Harry never pictured Bryan taking it this far, although he didn't know why. He thought this Apollo thing represented some game that Bryan didn't want to end--was Bryan so screwed up now that he could *kill* someone? He didn't really have it in him, did he?

Where in hell did I get that idea? thought Harry. But maybe Bryan will just try to scare the sergeant again. And if Apollo doesn't scare maybe Bryan will swallow hard and take his lumps and not end the game.

Maybe a dog won't piss in Iowa today.

"Now if you'll excuse me, I will get on with this," said Bryan, adding, "Will Sergeant Apollo be allowed a firearm on that island?"

"Off the base? No, but your people certainly won't be allowed firearms there either."

"My people will not need firearms, General."

God, thought Harry, there it was. A major-damned-general nodding at an implied assassination. What in hell goes on in Novinger's mind? Harry needed to get himself back into perspective here: What the hell is this to me anyway? Let the honkies kill each other off if they want to... But he no longer felt comfortable with that cop-out. This thing was going *way* beyond his covenant with Bryan Enterprises.

As the door closed, Harry heard Bryan click the two-way button on his intercom. "Did you hear all that, Harry?"

"Yes sir."

"What do you think? I think they will all disavow any connection with our shipments, if Sergeant Apollo brings this out. What do you think?"

"They will disavow any connection, sir."

"Our fate cannot lie with that one horrible sergeant, Harry. Our country's future military assistance in that country might lie with one God-forsaken sergeant, if I hear the general right. Is that the way you heard it?"

"That's the way I heard it, Mr. Bryan."

"What if he sends the information on those shipments to the newspapers?"

"That would be the action of some kind of crusader, Mr. Bryan. Apollo doesn't strike me as any crusader."

"No, he certainly does not, but can we afford to take that chance?"

"-"

"Exactly so," said Bryan. "And Harry, I need drafts for fifty thousand dollars by tomorrow. Have Trevors and Ochoa here tomorrow morning, and Carson--tell Kenneth to be here too. He should be back from Paris this afternoon."

"Yes sir." Harry waited but Bryan didn't say anything more.

Well, hell with it, thought Harry. I'm not my brother's keeper. Let them kill each other.

Chapter 35

Loc Ninh, positioned at the northwest rim of the Mekong Delta, was the last bump of population before the vein of V.N. Highway 13 cut into Cambodia. Which made it the terminal point for the Cambodian leg, the "back-country" leg, of the Viet Minh supply route. Its location was the reason that the Inter-Zone Committee agreed to a meeting in Loc Ninh, according to Lieutenant Tom. As he explained to Ram, "From Loc Ninh, if the ARVN comes, we will more easily run to Cambodia."

Lieutenant Tom insisted on reporting to Ram on each step of Kim Chau's planned meeting. He thought this would help occupy the sergeant's mind, for Tom knew that Ram still heard the screams of My Linh, and the grind of the trucks pulling away. The sergeant still felt the thud of Lieutenant Tom's rifle against the side of his face.

The town of Loc Ninh contained a large population of Caodai, so Tom had no trouble finding a place to hide the American. They put him behind a shop that sold bicycle parts, run by an old loose-skinned Caodai papa-san, on a street saturated with the vinegar-stench of burning trash. To pass the time, Tom pointed out, Ram could watch through a ventilation hole in a flimsily boarded wall facing a stall selling chickens, which were killed and plucked as the townspeople bought them. Killed in some way that brought a terrible death scream from them.

Lieutenant Tom wore a farmer's tunic for awhile, but that proved unnecessary. As he explained to Ram, "The only people who saw me were Hanoi Regulars, who are in North Vietnam by now."

My Linh, Ram thought, was also in North Vietnam by now.

"The meeting is at an empty Catholic mission," said Tom, returning from the bedside of Kim Chau. He bowed his way into the back room past the hanging burlap door. "All have come, as far as I can see. All commanders that were given Dao Chau's message."

"How is he?"

"No good. No good. His leg has infected worse, I think."

"Worse? They didn't take it *off?*"

"He did not allow this. He said it would make him too weak for this meeting."

"That leg was infected bad, it'll kill him--the meeting can't be that important."

"Dao Kim Chau believes that it is that important."

237

"He's called this for *all* commanders? He has that authority?"

"Dao Chau is the inter-zone secretary. But for this meeting we invited only the ones that we consider...worthwhile," replied Tom. He didn't seem willing to talk about the meeting any further. "You will see them today, Sergeant. I will come for you at two o'clock."

After Tom left, Ram tried to figure just what Chau planned to do. Would the Caodai agree to *shoot* the commanders? Not likely. That would create an open break between the Viet Minh and the local Caodai.

He'd know in a few hours, apparently. Until then Ram decided to stay away from the ventilation hole. He had no desire to watch the chicken butcher, or hear the death screams of his work.

*

"Come, Sergeant, providence waits." Tom came back as promised, exactly at two o'clock. He was wearing his black Caodai officer's uniform again, accompanied by the little corporal, similarly dressed, waving from the street.

"We steal a jeep this time. First we tie your hands again. We need to tell them we catch you again."

"Tell who? Trung won't believe that."

"It is not Major Trung that we are to worry about." The lieutenant brought out some brown hemp cord as Ram stuffed his civilian clothes into his backpack, alongside the Bryan documents.

When the three arrived at the mission they attracted an instant cordon of Viet Minh, retinues of those commanders who were assembled inside, and Tom gave his prisoner a push, for effect, as they stepped from the jeep: "They think you are brought before their leaders for tribunal," said Tom. "Try to look submissive."

"Submissive?" Ram settled instead for a straight-ahead stare, avoiding the blackshirts as he entered the church, which had deteriorated to little more than an organized stack of rocks. Its broken-winged cross hung above it like a pennant, its ruptured ceiling yawed rays of light through the unsettled tomb-gray dust inside. A few guards, loosely posted along the battered pews, watched the three men scrunch across the sandy floor into the sacristy. Inside, at the end of a long, makeshift table, sat Kim Chau. He was heavily bandaged, leaning sideways, presiding over the other men at the table like a wounded Buddha.

"Ram... C'm on in." Chau tried to straighten himself up. "There're some people I wan'ed you to meet."

"What's going on, Kim Chau?" Ram saw most of the officers staring at the place where Kim Chau's hand rested on something that looked like a metal stapler, wires from it stringing down under the table.

"Only need to lean on this a half inch an' the whole fuggin' place blows up," Chau grinned. "Just got through explaining this to my fellow off'cers here."

"Lieutenant Dao go crazy." Trung, who'd fixed a glare on Ram the moment he came in, was seated near the head of the table. "You talk Lieutenant Dao, tell him stop craziness."

"You already know Major Trung," said Kim Chau.

Ram didn't acknowledge Major Trung. The feeling of this room...the pallor of death was in this room. Chau showed the yellowness of death in his face and the men at the table were pale under the hulking prospect of death. They looked at Ram as newly-arrived death, and death sat across from Kim Chau in crates, their covering torn off to show their English markings: "Caution--Granular PETN."

Putrefying death mixed with the medicine smell from Kim Chau's leg, in this room. "Dao Chau crazy. You talk Lieutenant Dao," said Vo Trung.

"The officer over there's Colonel Kam Phat, who's an Inter-Zone commander," said Chau, speaking with a fierce effort. "But Colonel Phat doesn' speak English." Chau indicated with his head a thick-jawed officer who also attempted a glare back at Ram.

"And the fat one," continued Chau, "tha's Katung-Mao, a butcher sent by Hanoi to teach us how to torture villagers. Made up his own name from *Katung Di*--Ancient Hero--and the Chinese leader Mao Tse Tsung. Dreams of being the nex' Genghis Khan, I think... The skinny one there's Lat Nu Lat, a lieutenant-command'r of Middle Rivers Division--reprimanded by Ho Chi Minh hi'self for his...excesses." Chau slipped farther sideways as he talked, and struggled to get himself up again, and the sweat streamed along his face. "I won' bother wi' the rest. Not strong enough right now."

"Kim Chau, we can get you out of here."

"*You* will get out, Ram. But I wan'ed to prop'ly introduce these men to you first. They're going to accompany me to my celestial home."

"Comrade Dao sick man, Sergeant. You must help him," said a balding officer at the far end of the table. "You talk him from plan, take him from country. We will not stop you."

"Well, Colonel Tu Lon. Didn' know you spoke English," said Chau. "Tu Lon's commander of the Northern Brigade, Ram. The cap'n next to him...Minh Duoc of the Red Climbers Brigade."

"Sergeant kill two my men," said Vo Trung. "He stay here. He to be *executed.*"

"We let go of sergeant," said Colonel Tu Lon. "Get Dao Chau to stop plan, let both you free." His frown stopped Major Trung from objecting further: First they must get *out* of here.

"You'll let S'geant Apollo go anyway, Colonel Tu," said Chau. "Otherwise *none* of us will leave here, will we?"

"The place is surrounded by cadre, Kim Chau."

"Once you're safely out of here, Ram, then these people c'n talk me out of this, maybe--tha's our agreement here." Chau started to laugh but coughed instead. "If they try t' leave, or don' let you leave, you'd be better off blown to shit right here, which I will do. They know I will."

"American can go-o," warbled Colonel Tu Lon, losing his voice. "Then we, Comrade Dao talk. Okay?"

"Okay, Colonel, then we talk," agreed Kim Chau. "Lieutenant Tom, take the s'geant from here, please."

"Kim Chau, is it worth sacrificing yourself for this garbage?"

"Is it worth...? Hell, Ram, this's what My Linh's preached at me since she's old enough to talk, for Chrissake--each person's respons'bility, you know." He coughed again and closed his eyes. "I lay these bast'rds at her feet...'cause these're the worst of the worst."

"Does this accomplish one damned thing, Kim Chau?"

The English-speakers in the room watched the American sergeant more intently now; the gray-eyed executioner had become their spokesman. Maybe their last hope.

"Jesus, Ram, you still don' see?" Chau flinched and squinted sweat from his eyes. "You and I've been called on, Ram. We're going to reach tha' Touchstone."

"I still don't buy that, Kim Chau. What good can just two of us do?"

"I's a start, Ram." Chau motioned feebly toward Tom. "Would y'take him 'way from here, please--now, Lieutenant?"

"Why the hell *us*, Kim Chau?"

Chau poked his fingers inside his bandages. "Almos' forgot. Remember this?" He tugged from the gauze the red and black lacquered knife Ram had given back to Chau in San Francisco.

"I don't understand you at all, Kim Chau."

"You will, Ram'rez Apollo." Chau reached up to shake Ram's hand, weakly, and put the knife in Ram's hand. "Don' think I ever told you, few years back my uncle Chien did zackly the same thing in Da Nang. Blew up his own damn cargo ship." He made another grin. "Himself too. Mus' be in the fam'ly blood."

Ram didn't return the smile. "What the hell am I supposed to do? Dammit..." He clenched the knife in his palm, put his other hand on Chau's arm. "If you think you've got to do this, at least go to your Cao Dai in peace, Kim Chau. Not this way. Not by taking out this pile of crap." He saw that wouldn't work. He put the knife in his pocket and turned away, because he couldn't look at Chau any longer. "Okay... Find some peace for me too, would you?"

"Tha's what this's all about, Ram."

"I still don't buy that, Kim Chau. I don't buy that at all."

The guards in the main congregation room fidgeted with their AK-47's as Tom led Ram out, then bluffed a peremptory command at them. They stiffened and jabbered back at him, then at each other, and then, in unison, started through the door behind the Caodai lieutenant.

"I told them Secretary Dao has gone mad, and that he will explode this building," said Tom. In the yard he went through the same performance, giving orders to the nearest soldiers as the three got in the jeep. The corporal drove around the church while the lieutenant, standing up, keeping his pistol visibly on Ram, continued yelling to the surrounding cadre.

The soldiers seemed reluctant at first. They argued among themselves, they motioned toward the building and then at the lieutenant and then, like a shifting herd, began to move away from the mission. A few broke and ran.

The corporal was wheeling toward the road, through the retreating soldiers, when the first blast jarred the ground, and Ram swung around in his seat to look back. The stones of the church pulsed and held an instant, then the windows spewed their remaining sprays of glass and wood outward. The last part of its roof rippled and rose from the structure and the building sagged in on itself. The stone walls sighed and joined while pieces of wood expanded skyward, arcing into sprinkles of board.

Nearby soldiers, knocked down by the blast, continued scrambling on hands and knees while pillows of dust whooshed beneath the collapsing building, wrapping over them. The jeep was fifty yards away when the explosion came, the shock jolted it to the side and the corporal had to fight the wheel to trim it back to the road.

Ram grabbed the corporal's shoulder. "We have to go back there."

The corporal shot a look at Ram, then at his lieutenant.

"Turn the hell *around.*"

"For what?" Tom yelled at him. "Lieutenant Dao is dead!"

"I need to see for myself--*turn around.*"

Tom motioned to the corporal and the jeep squealed to a stop as Ram jumped from it. The lighter shards of roof were still coming down as he walked toward the impact area. Viet Minh soldiers were shaking themselves erect and townspeople had stopped along the road, staring at the place where the church used to be. Ram walked past them and saw parts of one black-uniformed body, blown free of the building, but it wasn't Kim Chau. Of his friend he saw only a blistered arm extending from under a door. The door and the stones of the church covered the rest of him but the arm carried on its wrist a band of tarnished steel--the whore's-ware, the Okinawan i.d. bracelet Ram had bought for Chau on the Street of a Thousand Pleasures.

Ram sagged to his knees and let his hands drop to his sides "Damn, Kim Chau."

"Our people will take care of Lieutenant Dao," said Tom, behind him. "We have to go now. We have to hurry."

Chapter 36

Tom and the Caodai corporal took turns wrestling themselves into ARVN uniforms now, as they drove along V.N. Highway 13 from the dissident eastern territory to the Republic-controlled Delta to the pink-stucco buildings of the Military Air Transport at Bien Hoa. As he left the jeep Ram picked through his backpack for his passport and Army i.d., which were all still in there, along with the Bryan documents. He couldn't focus on whatever else he should check for. There were too many ghosts now in his head.

He entered the terminal, then realized he'd said nothing to Lieutenant Tom or the corporal and went back to find them. The jeep was already gone. He stared at the place where they left him off. They'd risked their lives to get me out of there, he thought, and I don't say shit to them. Don't even know their real names. Thankless ass hole. Got to get my mind back together.

According to the schedule on the blackboard there was a next-morning flight to Kadena Air Base. The cargo trips between Bien Hoa and Okinawa departed on the half-hour during daylight but it was past 1900 hours, the flights were shut for the day. He showed his papers and signed in at the scheduling desk and found a bench to lay on in the waiting room.

Next morning, a light-cargoed Boeing 377 flew him to Kadena where he caught the bus to Fort Buckner, where he left a message for Colonel Purdy at the Headquarters desk. Then he got out of camp, he had no desire to meet with Colonel Purdy just yet. He walked instead, past the push-push streets of Naha, smelled again the saccharine incense, the faint excremental aroma and exhaust fume, but noticed none of it. He wasn't interested in the things of this world, good or bad, not after watching Dao Kim Chau kill himself to "preserve" these things. And not while My Linh was a prisoner in North Vietnam--maybe worse than just a prisoner.

Maybe a lot worse.

He walked until he reached the colorless docks of Naha Bay... "I need to go to the north end, to the place where the albatross are."

"Albatross?"

"Big sea birds."

"Ah! Never big sea birds on Okinawa." The taxi driver seemed pleased with that answer. "No cabby drive to north anyway. Too damn much drive. Take bus. No big birds anyway."

But that wasn't true. Ram could remember the birds around the aging piers in the north. He'd visited with some old man there, once, who talked with Ram through wrinkled folds of skin, while they watched the sea birds there.

"Never albatross on Ryukyus," said the cab driver, worried about the silence of his potential fare. Receiving still no answer, he left, squealing his tires on his way by.

*

When Ram reported to Purdy's office there seemed to be a noticeable softening in the colonel's usual gruffness. Now, instead, there seemed to be a pale tiredness about the man, a feel of resignation. "What're we going to do, Sergeant? What do we do with you now?"

Ram didn't understand the question, didn't care what it meant and didn't answer.

"How'd you get out of those mountains? We heard you slugged a Viet Minh officer or something. You're supposed to be dead."

"Two soldiers of the Caodai helped me out."

"Of the who?" The colonel jiggled a hand across that question. "Skip it. Doesn't matter right now." He reached in his pencil drawer, withdrew and unwrapped a dark, pimpled cigar. "Whatever became of your contact there, that Lieutenant Dao?"

"Lieutenant Dao's dead. So is the officer I hit...with about seven other Viet Minh field officers."

"We've come to expect results like that, unfortunately," said Colonel Purdy, gazing around. "So goes our chance of future contact with those people, probably."

Ram thought for a moment about explaining those deaths, decided instead to just let it go.

"With regard to your recon, did you learn anything there?" asked Colonel Purdy. He placed the cigar in the side of his face so he could speak around the butt of it. "About this Viet Cong thing, I mean." His voice remained weirdly congenial.

Ram contemplated Colonel Purdy while the officer lit his cigar, and Ram waited his answer on the first exhalation. Again the stink, like burning dung.

"I learned they don't like to be called 'Cong' because a whole lot of them aren't communists. I learned that most of them went to the side of that Liberation Front because we're propping up that little dictator, Diem."

"General Staff didn't send you to come back with your assessment of President Diem, Sergeant."

244

"And I was able to get all the documents to prove Bryan was supplying that Liberation Front."

"Christ, what the hell is wrong with you?" Colonel Purdy couldn't find the right words, and gave it up. "Are you really nuts? This bull-headedness between you and Lieutenant Dao has shaken up people all the way to the damned National Security Council. Now General Novinger has okayed Bryan *himself* to come talk with you about this."

"Bryan's coming here?"

"Bryan is coming, Sergeant, ostensibly to inspect his ordnance at the Machinato warehouse, but I know damn well--and so do you--that he's coming to see you." Colonel Purdy stabbed a sausage-like finger at Ram. "My advice is to stay on base, meet him here if he wants to meet, but for God's sake don't provoke him."

"Why should I stay on base?"

The question was deliberate, and Colonel Purdy couldn't understand the deliberateness of it. What went on between Sergeant Apollo and Bryan? Some kind of goddamned *showdown*? It seemed to Purdy that General Novinger actually wanted to prepare the ground for this; Novinger had given him specific orders that Sergeant Apollo was *not* to be confined to the base.

"Am I required to stay here, Colonel?"

"Okay, no, you aren't, I'll be damned if I know why. All because of this general's--" He caught himself--he'd also be damned if he needed to explain his actions to a grunt sergeant. "Some peculiar things are happening, I just can't get a fix on what the hell they've got planned here." He had to stop there, for the conclusion he might draw was inconceivable. "I don't suppose you've heard about Bryan's daughter-in-law yet."

"Claire? What's Bryan done to her?"

"Bryan? Why would *he* do anything to her?... Whatever, it's not pretty. She got cut up in Paris right after you left, apparently." Purdy tossed an envelope on his desk that was slit along the top. "It's in there, came for you yesterday."

"You opened it?" Ram looked into the smudged gap of the envelope.

"Where you're concerned, Sergeant, we open everything. I'm taking no chances with you any more."

Ram checked to see if the envelope was from Emile St. Amand. It was. He folded it into his jacket. "Will that be all?"

"No." Colonel Purdy took another puff. "We need to talk about this Bryan visit." He stopped to watch the gray fan of smoke blow along his hand. "I don't know what the hell's going on, but something really stinks about Bryan's coming here." He apparently wanted to state this as clearly as he could, without being *too* clear. "You've squeezed a lot of balls, Sergeant. Some real perilous balls."

"I understand the warning, Colonel."

"And?"

"I'll think about what I've got to do."

Colonel Purdy raised his hands in the air. "Got the hell to do? Haven't you been listening? You've got to watch your ass, that's what you've got to *do*." He stopped, inhaled, and spread his palms on the desk to calm himself. It reminded Ram of the first time he'd stood before this man, more than four years ago now, and so many people had died since then. It seemed like everyone he knew had died since then, one way or another.

"Sergeant Apollo," said Colonel Purdy, mellowed a little by the deep-breathing. "Your friend, Lieutenant Dao, killed those field commanders, didn't he?"

"Yes sir." Purdy's knowledge of the killings wasn't surprising. Some G-2 stringers had probably reported in.

"So now you feel you've got to make some kind of stand too, right?"

"I don't feel I've got to do anything, Colonel."

"I wouldn't have guessed so, ordinarily." But Colonel Purdy obviously wasn't comfortable with Ram's answer, for the sergeant no longer spoke with his usual, marbled indifference. "You never really gave a good goddamn about the Bryan investigation."

The statement sounded more like an inquiry, but Ram's response gave him nothing: "I don't know yet, Colonel. Will that be all?"

"I suppose so," said Purdy. and Ram saluted and walked to the door before the colonel added, "What was the strength of that guerrilla unit?"

"A light battalion. Three hundred men and maybe fifty women," said Ram, half-turning at the door. "I doubt if it was typical,"

"What kind of weapons?"

"Russian, mostly. AK-47's, some American BAR's and carbines and a few M-1's. They had mortar and anti-tank missile squads. Six-man squads."

"Leave the American-made weapons out of your report, Sergeant." Colonel Purdy leaned forward, trying to bring home what he was saying. "Do it this afternoon, without mentioning the American stuff."

"That wouldn't be the truth, Colonel."

"But you'll do it because I tell you to do it, Sergeant," said Colonel Purdy. "You'll do it because your ass depends on your doing it, probably in more ways than you know." He decided not to take that any further, and said his last sentence more to himself. "We should never have started this thing."

"You did the next best thing, Colonel. You sent me and Lieutenant Dao." Ram waited for the colonel to react, but it didn't happen. "We weren't supposed to come back, were we?"

Colonel Purdy puffed his cigar and looked sadly past Ram toward a picture of the President on the wall. "You're wrong, Sergeant," he said, and that was all he said, and after Ram left, the colonel crumpled the memo from General Novinger, the memo instructing Colonel Purdy not to confine Apollo to base, and put a match to the memo, and watched the ashes curl into black carbon.

Outside the camp, along the road, the gravel baked like white charcoal. The waves of heat distorted the forest and undergrowth, and as he watched the forest Ram understood that his entire life had been played out in a place like this, against the backdrop of some kind of jungle.

The jungle is where I belong, he thought.

He took out the letter.

Wrote Emile St. Amand, someone had stabbed Claire with a turquoise-handled knife, it was found in the trash a block away. But she still lives--at least the doctors *think* she'll live--although she wasn't coherent yet. The police hadn't been able to get a name from her yet but Ram didn't need to see a name. The name wrote itself in the letter of Emile St. Amand: Kenneth Willy Carson.

Another creature of the jungle, he thought. Life begins and ends in the wetness of the jungle and maybe that's why I seek it out, and why the Montagnards call the jungle their sanctuary, which now waits in Indo-China for the next war to be played inside its belly, so the country can be blown into dog shit... Maybe it *was* time to do something, but why me? Why the hell *us*? I'm trying to understand this, Kim Chau.

The northern coast, where the albatross were, would be a fitting place. At the dock where he and the old man had talked, where the jungle could not reach him.

He wondered who Bryan would bring with him. Those two bodyguards, certainly. Willy Carson, probably. And Harry? Harry was still a riddle. Harry wasn't sure where the hell he stood in all this, Ram figured.

He was curious to see if Harry would come.

Chapter 37

Charles Trevors and Sorry Ochoa were a pair of men not easily classified. Bryan never understood them, he secretly feared them, but he did *so* relish the power that came from employing such men.

Trevors, not quite a giant, not much less than one, had been court-martialed out of World War II for killing a prisoner with his hands. Ochoa, the old one, the cherubic-faced wrestling bear, had ridden with the bandit Huerta in Mexico in the state of Guerrero, before the Obregon people chased them out. The new regime had justifiably hung all those who didn't escape, for "general atrocities."

Bryan did not originally intend using them as henchmen, not exactly. That would fly too much in the face of the Baptist upbringing that once wrestled for control of his mind, but in the last few years he'd begun to rationalize that *every* man carried this inclination--the desire to do violence, to destroy. Or so reasoned John Bryan after he'd lost the thread of reasoning, after the visit by his father's messenger. After he began to believe he'd met his father's Angel of Death.

Planted so many years ago--by his father, he at least knew that to be true--that seed would blossom within this week on Okinawa: "I will arrange a special bonus for you, a *Swiss* account. I need you with me in this my Armageddon. Trevors, Ochoa, we now must confront Sergeant Apollo." He nervously cleared his throat. "I will release twenty-five thousand to each of you for this, you understand?"

"We understand fine, Mr. Bryan," said Charles Trevors, and Bryan caught his breath at the simplicity of that answer, for he now had this Godlike ability to order men to severely punish or kill other men, as easily as a general might punish traitors.

"On the north end of the island, that is where he... One of our people there keeps track of him." Bryan was saying this to his men on the plane. "Now you know that Kenneth is with me only as my assistant. Neither he nor I can help you here."

"Won't need any help, Mr. Bryan," said Trevors. "Fact is, there's no reason for you and him to come along."

"No, I must be there. And Kenneth, certainly, to show I've not been defeated by him. Show him even my own son, the son *he* killed, can be replaced by me." Bryan mumbled something to himself that came out like a muffled protest: "He didn't win this, not at all."

248

Trevors and Ochoa watched John Bryan and said nothing. Lately they had to be real cautious about what they said around the man. He seemed to be getting screwier by the day now. At least, they had to be real cautious until they got their twenty-five thousand.

"You understand they won't allow us firearms of any kind, *any* kind, while we're on that island?"

"Won't need firearms, Mr. Bryan." Trevors gazed at his employer beneath his extended brows. "Will your black guy be coming?"

"Harry? No. No sir, I've begun to worry about Harry lately. He won't be coming. Anything else?"

"Don't need to know anything else, Mr. Bryan." Trevors grinned then, his mule teeth, in themselves, sufficient armament. "All you need do is point us to him."

*

Harry Crosse pinched the skin of his forearm and watched the welt turn pale, released it, examined the dissipating lightness until it blended to his color. His blackness re-verified, he wondered then why he would feel any empathy with someone like Ramirez Apollo. In their separate ghettos they'd be automatic enemies, wouldn't they? And they sure weren't exactly buddies now.

Look again, not *really* black, he thought. More of a rich brown, sort of, although Harry had developed a personal drive that he felt transcended color. It wasn't a racial thing, he simply wanted, demanded, insulation, so a lot of money had to be reckoned into his plans, or a lot of inner strength. Whatever "inner strength" meant. The phrase didn't translate well into street lingo.

As long as it doesn't require a conscience, he thought, for that's a quick ticket back to where you came from, child. Can't let any half-breed Mexican screw that up. I'll follow them to Okinawa, maybe, but I sure as hell am not committing myself. Still don't think way down deep that Bryan's got the *huevos* to kill anyone. Too much Christianity still down inside that garbaged brain.

Only the substitution of Willy Carson for Bryan's son Daniel, Harry figured, was saving Bryan's brain from self-destructing. Although if Carson wasn't around, Bryan would still have his grandson, he supposed. One last human to hang on to... Bryan's grandson? Harry had a terrible thought, and shook it off. Too late to help Apollo anyway. Quit coming up with these God-awful... Bryan and the goons are probably there by now, and if the U.S. Army can't protect Sergeant Apollo, what does Supernigger here think *he* can do?

249

He picked up the nouveau-antique cradle phone, flipping his Dial-Dex to the Pan American number. He would need to go through stopovers in Seattle and Tokyo to get to Naha, the flight clerk told him. It would be over one way or the other by the time Harry got there.

But maybe not, he thought. Maybe not. Harry just couldn't get this terrible thought from his head, the one event that could destroy Bryan, if Harry had the guts to use it.

*

Ram stretched and felt the muscles of his back dig and knit into a feedback of strength, and that helped his confidence a little. From the decaying pier he watched Bryan approach, pushed in his chair by Sorry Ochoa, followed by Trevors and Carson, all still wearing business suits. Ram had seen them stop on the overlook next to the road, where they stood quiet awhile. Ram turned to watch the incoming current lap the sides of a grungy rowboat secured to the floating slip below. He could still cut and run, maybe, but that would only postpone this meeting. This meeting was inevitable, whichever way it worked out.

He watched for the birds that didn't seem to be around here any more. He felt his pocket for the knife, which could probably take the old man out before...but if he killed Bryan, would that stop those other two? That's probably academic, he thought. Those two would know how to defend against a knife thrower.

He might try pushing Bryan's mind over the edge, but Ram didn't want to bet his life on pulling *that* off, not without a whole bunch of help, which wasn't in the game plan here. No, he would need to stick with plan number one, take the old man out if he could, then do some real fast talking to those bodyguards.

He cupped his hands to his face: "*Ese, cabrones*, you looking for me?" Throwback dialogue, he realized. Trash-talk from the barrio, but what could be more appropriate here?

"The God of Light awaits you, *viejo*. I'm going to *blind* you with my goddamned light." Bravado, for effect, but they didn't react. They didn't hear him, maybe, or maybe, probably, this was a real dumbass idea. He was about to find out just how nutty the old man really was.

They came: John Bryan and Sorry Ochoa and Charles Trevors. Kenneth Willy Carson. Turning onto the path like the Four Horsemen, Ram thought. Plague and locust, this malignance walking through the shoreline weeds. "You know that *proof* you constructed for me, Mr. Bryan? That's all your sick illusion. It's *make believe!*" Ram wanted to push these thoughts deep into the old man's head. "You haven't proven your courage to me with that little toy-shit battlefield. Your father's words were *right--*" As his voice rose Ram could damn near feel the spirit of Bryan's father, the long-dead evangelist. "You're the ultimate coward, old man, a feeder on war who never had the courage to *fight* in war. Your father was *right!*"

"No!" shouted John Bryan, finally. He tried to raise himself from his wheelchair, without success. "I've spent *four years* to prove him wrong, and I can still send you back to tell him that, but there is no *urgency*, don't you see? You no longer have a *reason* to torment me!"

Okay, thought Ram, follow the program now, viejo. Get that sick-ass core to surface through your withering shell.

Sorry Ochoa edged up alongside his boss. "It's okay, Mr. Bryan. We'll take it from here."

"You could still prevent this, Ramirez Apollo," said Bryan. "Your mission is at an end. There's no longer a *need* to demand your own destruction." He stopped himself. He didn't really want to give this hint of reprieve here.

"We can take and dump him from the rowboat," said Trevors toward Ochoa. He nodded over the railing at the boat.

Bryan raised his hand and held it there a moment, then dropped it onto Ochoa's sleeve. "Wait." Bryan's head dipped, his chin quivered just above his chest. "We must be *certain* here. This is still not in accordance--this still might be judged as an act...against the will of God, you must know..."

The bodyguards looked down at the old man, and Ram could see it might be over, just like that. Victory by the will of God Himself, except--now what the hell's that mean, *except?* he thought. It looks like it's over. What's this *except* crap?

"The knifing of your son's wife, Mr. Bryan, what do you plan to do about that?" Ram couldn't seem to stop this crazy obsession now--who the hell was the *nut* around here?

"What did you say?"

"Your son's wife, Mr. Bryan. Claire, the lady your boy Carson cut up, remember? What're you planning to do about that?"

"That has nothing to do with you. The fate of that woman has nothing to do with you. *I'll* handle whatever compen-sation-"

"-Not good enough, Mr. Bryan."

"There is no longer a *need* to torment me!" Bryan was getting shrill. "What do you gain, you stupid Mexican? All you need do is let me alone, let me *alone*. I am trying to follow God's commandments here!"

"Too late to let you alone, Mr. Bryan. I sent your documents to the newspapers."

Bryan was trying to wheel himself farther along, shaking off the help of his men for these last few yards until Ram's words stopped him. "To *what* newspapers? You would not know where..." His body trembled and he slumped back into the chair. Damn, Ram thought, was all of Chau's document-gathering actually *scoring* here? "You won't understand this, Mr. Bryan-"

"-The guy's a dumb-ass cholo, Mr. Bryan. Don't pay attention to him." Carson bent toward his boss but shied back as Bryan began slapping his hands loudly against the wheels of his chair.

"Daniel's wife is not your responsibility!" Bryan yelled. "She has *nothing* to do with your mission here!" The mention of the documents was working magic here; Bryan's fingers were now clamped rigidly on the wheels as Ram brought out the knife, its blade still within its thick, red-black jacket.

"You won't understand this, Mr. Bryan, but I've decided to help a friend of mine clean up this world, just a little."

"That a knife you got there, Chuko?" Trevors grinned. He and Ochoa were already shaking off their coats and wrapping them over their arms into shields, moving in front of Bryan. Bryan was almost hidden from Ram now. Shit, Ram thought, they *are* professionals.

"You trying to scare us with that crappy little knife?" said Trevors. "You making a joke with us, Chuko?"

"What the hell's wrong with you?" said Ochoa. "Bryan's giving you a way out, man."

"Not forever, amigo. I don't think so." Ram could see that Ochoa, as Ram suspected, wasn't all that enthusiastic about going through with this.

"You wouldn't use that *now*." Bryan shook his finger at the weapon. "You would not condemn yourself just to revenge that...that...*harlot!* Not even to carry out my father's-"

"Shut the hell up, old man." Ram pushed the release and the blade snapped from its handle. "Dao Kim Chau gave me this, Mr. Bryan. *Lieutenant* Dao, remember him?"

"What're you saying there?"

"Claire didn't deserve what your boy did, Mr. Bryan." He let the knife hang flat alongside his open palm.

"What're you saying there? What do you mean, *deserve*?"

"Something I recently learned from Dao Kim Chau, Mr. Bryan." Ram raised the knife. Its glossy redness reflected the afternoon sun toward the four men. "And from his sister. She's a girl-priestess of the Cao Dai, you know."

"This is madness!" Bryan bristled. "You think that weapon will help you against *these* men?"

"Be careful, Mr. Bryan," said Willy Carson. "I heard he throws that thing like a slingshot." Carson inched away from Ram's line of fire. "He could take at least one of them out."

"Hell, not them, Willy." The situation had been clarifying for Ram, maybe it had been for a while now, the sweet beauty of what he was meant to do. "I want you, little ass hole."

"Me? Why *me?*"

"You're guilty of some real bad things against Claire Bryan, *hombrecillo.* Putting her back on dope, raping her, now maybe killing her."

Carson looked toward Bryan's bodyguards but he'd moved too far away now. "You've gone *nuts!* That was just-"

"-You leave Kenneth out of this, you hear!" Bryan shuddered behind the two bodyguards. This sergeant was making an *unthinkable* threat. "He did not intend.. Kenneth may have made a mistake-"

"-You also caused the death of Dao Phuong, Willy, and went after his son Kim Chau, and his daughter My Linh. Hell, we've got a whole pile of things to settle up here."

"What's he saying?" said Bryan. *"What in heaven is he saying?"*

"I'm saying you're right, Mr. Bryan. You've been right all along. I am the Angel of Death, and I've come for your *other* boy now."

"You're thinking o'going for the little jerk instead of me?" Trevors snorted. "You are one dumb bastard."

"You've taken my son," cried John Bryan as Carson took his first step toward the protective back of Trevors. "You will not take Kenneth from me too! Kenneth is..."

The air between them sparkled. Death came in a flick of space, a silver bridge. The knife of Dao Kim Chau buried itself to the handle in the middle of the chest of Willy Carson, and Carson's eyes widened as he fell on John Bryan's shoulder and coughed, gagging on a mouthful of red spit, rolling across a wheel of the chair.

He tried to grab at John Bryan as he died.

Bryan doubled up in his chair and gaped at Carson and then at Ram, and then around at his bodyguards.

"Jeez that was a dumb move, amigo," said Sorry Ochoa.

"I thought you'd try for me first. I'm kinda insulted," said Trevors, nudging Ochoa. "Let's get this over with, compadre."

Probably not too bright, taking out the littlest one, thought Ram, beginning to back up. Maybe it's time to do some real thinking now, okay?

"Father, your devil haunts me so..." whispered Bryan.

Ochoa glanced at the old man as Trevors unwrapped his coat. "Looks to me like you're fresh outta knives, Chuko," said Trevors. "Time for us to dance?"

"Now he's killed Bryan's other boy," said Ochoa, "maybe we should double our fee here."

"Take a look at him first, amigo." Ram kept his eyes on Sorry Ochoa. His fate here rested with Ochoa now. "What you see there, that thing's going to pay you for doing this?"

Bryan had huddled himself into a ball. "He was really my last child, you know...." His voice came out flat and lifeless. He didn't notice their attention.

"Whatta you think you just done, cabron?" said Ochoa.

"It's over, man." Ram indicated Bryan. "You planning on doing this for free?"

"Nothing's wrong with Mr. Bryan." Trevors turned and leaned over the twisted form of his boss as Ochoa shuffled to the other side of the chair and pulled Carson's hand off the wheel.

"Mr. Bryan, you just tell us-"

"-The Angel of Death takes *all* of us, sooner or later, you know," said Bryan into Ochoa's face. He raised a fist toward him. "He will come for you too."

"He might really be gone, Trevors," said Ochoa. "We might have a stiff *and* a crazy man on our hands."

Ram took another step back. "You'll have enough trouble explaining *one* missing man, even if they don't find Willy's body."

"It wasn't us that killed him, ass hole," said Trevors.

"With our records, you wanna try explaining it, Trevors?" said Ochoa, who seemed kind of relieved. "A crazy guy and two missing dead men and maybe not a dime for the effort? That's a bad deal, Trevors. Let's take Carson out and dump him and just get the hell off this island, okay?"

"What kind of shit thinking's that? Jesus, Ochoa, you're just looking for any goddamned excuse--"

Ochoa put a hand against Trevors' chest. "I'll rough Apollo up if that'll make you feel better. You weight Carson's body and dump him, then we try and find if Bryan's still able to pay us *first*, okay? I'll just rough Apollo up. He's not gonna tell anyone about us. We saw him kill the little bastard, didn't we?"

The idea didn't sit that well with Trevors, but, "Make it good, damn it. Cream his ass, then see if Bryan wants us to finish it."

"Poor Kenneth," moaned Bryan. He was reaching over the chair, trying to run his hand through the hair of Willy Carson as Trevors gingerly picked up Willy's body and began to cart it to the rowboat. Bryan only stared past them, he didn't watch Carson. He no longer watched any of them.

"Sorry," said Sorry Ochoa as he stepped over to Ram. "Since you're Chicano I'll just mess you up a little, okay? Don't want to kill you, man, unless Mr. Bryan--"

Ram swung as hard as he could, trying to drive his fist deep into the stomach of Sorry Ochoa, but the mass of muscle and gristle gave solid resistance. The force of the punch wheezed a great belch of air from the bodyguard but he fell back only a step.

"Aw, *shit*." Trevors tossed Carson aside and came back, stepping around Ochoa as Ram swung at him too but Trevors swatted Ram's arm away and threw him to the boardwalk and Ram rolled, crouched and came up again, catching Trevors on the jaw with the heel of his hand, popping Trevors' head sideways as Ochoa shuffled back toward him. "What the hell're you doing, you *dumbass*." Ochoa grabbed Ram by the shoulders and growled his breath into Ram's face. Ram brought his hand back down into Ochoa's groin.

"Son of a *bitch!*" Ochoa yelled, but didn't let go. The two of them dropped together and Ram pulled himself loose from Ochoa and got up just as Trevors hit him again, and Ram tried to reach Trevors with his knee but his reflexes weren't there. The knee missed. Ram dug his fingers into Ochoa's neck but both of Bryan's men held onto him now and Ram swung his other fist uselessly through the air.

The hammering became muffled. The sky, sea and angry men whirled and blurred around him. The light of the day turned to brilliant hues--oranges and reds, coloring spinwheels--and he knew he was still standing and he wondered at this but he could no longer feel himself being hit.

And Ram did not remember falling. He did not know how long they hit him when he fell.

"*Now* we kill the son of a bitch, *okay?* Is that the hell okay *now?*" he heard them say.

"What good would *that* do?" he heard them say. "The old man's gone nutty on us. We going to dust this guy for *fun?*"

"The old man'll be okay, I tell you."

Look now, My Linh, Ram thought. We're whipping these bastards. There's a damned *transformation* coming to this world.

We're destroying the destroyers.

No response, not yet, because the singing in his mind allowed for none, and for a while he could see only the splintery black-brown deck beneath him, he could feel and smell only the dampness of its planks. For a while he heard only the tapping in his mind, which began to blend with the banging of the heels of shoes, walking so very fast... Harry was walking toward them, Ram was at least able to make that out. And then there was this high, thin scream, this long and hollow sound. This long, ugly and hollow sound--a wailing.

Within the sunset, in the corona of light, he did really see her then, for her face had become the lowering sun.

Chapter 38

Diminuendo

Harry Crosse still didn't believe what he'd done. A terrible, terrible thing, he knew, but it had worked. If it hadn't Harry would have been long gone by now, on his way somewhere south of Venezuela, preferably. Fast. But Bryan was a basket case thanks to Harry Crosse, and of course, mainly, to Ramirez Apollo.

Harry told the old man that his grandson Sean had caught pneumonia. And *died*, for Christ's sake, a lie Harry would have to live with for a very long time, but considering the alternative... After Bryan saw the killing of Willy Carson, Harry's lie had blown the remnants of Bryan's mind into hamburger, as Harry thought it would. Hell, as Harry *knew* it would.

Harry still wore his gray business suit, even here, dressed like a standing corpse along the humid coastline. The morning sun, shouldering up through the Okinawan sky, was starting to underscore the heat of the new day, but last week's events had left Harry too confused to think about the heat. And he was still a little confused--still a whole *lot* confused-- about what direction he would take now.

Harry had stuck around to see if Apollo would pull through. Ram was only half conscious now, in the Kadena base hospital, but apparently he *would* pull through. And the Ochoa-Trevors combo was no longer a threat to him; they'd made Carson's body disappear and then were gone, just like that, at Harry's suggestion. Harry would see to them later, he'd promised.

And Claire was doing okay--what a twist that situation had taken. Although the outcome should have been obvious, he thought, if he'd stopped to think about what would happen if Bryan ever got taken out. Claire was doing okay in a hospital in Paris, five thousand miles away, but *calling all the damned shots*. Hell, of course she'd be calling the shots, he realized now, finally. She was the parent and guardian of Bryan's only remaining heir.

Harry had no idea whether Claire could now kick the habit, maybe it didn't matter. She had appointed Harry as the interim president until... but time wasn't a factor. The local Army shrinks all agreed Bryan would never get his head together again. *C'est fini*. And the newspapers had lost John Bryan, their prime target, so their interest in an inquiry, consequently, would quietly fade away, with the help of Harry and a few of Bryan's friendly congressmen.

And me? Well, hell, look at me, thought Harry. Set for life, it seems. Seems old Harry's in permanent charge now, with Claire's blessings.

So where's the exhilaration I should be feeling?

Harry deferred his question to watch the flight of an immense sea bird, making its circle along the island's tip. How fine that bird becomes up there, he thought. So alone, self-contained, kind of like this Ramirez Apollo. But now from his hospital bed Apollo asks me to help find his girl-priestess-- what kind of absurd shit was he coming on with *now*? Deal with the enemy again, right? Why would I take that kind of risk, jeopardize everything I've finally achieved?

Harry folded his arms and kept his eyes on the white morning clouds, and wondered how in hell anyone, even old Harry here, could pull off something like that anyway. Get that girl out of North Vietnam? Even *he* couldn't manage something like that, he thought.

Could he?

He searched the sky for an answer, but the only response he found was the circling, the constant upward spiraling of this one, this ethereal, great-winged bird.

*

Ram didn't know if he had gone back into unconsciousness, he couldn't be sure. He seemed to hear her voice, questioning him, and he wondered if Harry had succeeded in bringing her to him.

Has he killed you, Ramirez Apollo? he heard her ask--he might only have imagined her asking.

Couldn't let him kill me, he answered. I can't die yet.

Bryan had to try, though, this vision said to him. Don't you see why?

Couldn't die yet, My Linh. I haven't found your Touch-stone yet.

Ramirez, don't you see? You have become *part* of the Touchstone. You are at a place where honor is everything, where the power of Bryan has no meaning.

Bryan must have wanted to join us here, then, Ram thought. The man tried so damned hard to prove he also had sacrificed.

When he could not be a part of your world, Ramirez, he had to destroy that world, for in that world he has no meaning.

And Ramirez Apollo knew that was true. And he slept more easily, knowing he might have begun to understand her now.

Epilogue

The Laysan albatross of the western Pacific islands, while aground, is the most ungraceful of birds. It waddles spraddle-legged, like the sway of a sumo wrestler, at the mercy of the elements on the black volcanic extrusions, the quieted eruptions, sometimes wobbling in its own excremental goo through the shallow rain catches, stones and sea grass.

The elephant bird, this, seven pounds of gooney, tall as the Canadian goose. And the largest sea bird in existence, and the most out of place while on land. Bickering with the rapid clacking of bills, like off-rhythm castanets, clumsily mating in elaborate courtship with its dancing, kazoo-like honking, beak-pecking. It arrives at its mating place individually, not in the communal formations of other waterfowl, and its landing requires room: rump up, head down, coming to rest in a rolling sprawl. Stomach-crunching, bone-rattling, tail-skidding.

And the gooney bird's leaving is not graced with the slithering takeoff of the drake or gull, or the skyward arch of flamingo's wings. Becoming airborne is serious business, requiring concentration, accelerating the waddle to a lopsided gallop, the overworked rear bobbing sideways in pre-flight, flapping over stone, sod, marsh, sand, mud, hibiscus, scavvy bush, iron wood tree.

Then, usually, backing its hind to the water's edge to take another run. The terrain that flops underfoot graduates from hard ash to macadam road to mossy wetness before the bird finally finds the wind, floats, touches down, floats again.

It tucks his legs underwing.

It becomes airborne.

Maestoso...

The Laysan albatross is a great-winged bird. From tip to tip it spans twelve, fifteen, seventeen feet. Its wings embrace the horizon.

The albatross, like the humans below, achieves grace when it does what it was created to do, and the albatross was designed to fly. The earth drifts from this bird, mythical talisman, riding the currents above the ocean without the need to touch land for the first seven years of flight.

Skimming the curve of earth in its circle, it becomes a different being from the floundering thing below, for it was not intended to be below. It was designed to soar.

ABOUT THE AUTHOR

Edward Barr Robinson, son of Scots immigrants, began writing during his high school years in Glendale, California, eventually receiving his master's degree in journalism from UCLA. At the university he was editor-in-chief of both the campus newspaper and magazine, then took a 30-year break to obtain another master's degree in business and become a successful shopping center developer.

However, the background materials for *The Godhead* were accumulating during that 30-year period. Early on he was drafted into the Army and trained for 18 months in the Ryukyu Islands with the 75th, formerly the 1075th, Regimental Combat Team--the "Merrill's Marauders." This RCT was apparently being jungle-trained as a possible backup to the French in their Indo-China war in 1954, and the Marauders were in fact flown out of Kadena Airport on Okinawa for Vietnam during the Dien Bien Phu battle, M-1's between their knees. They were turned around and returned in mid-flight, which initiated the author's curiosity about the strange twists that America's national policies were taking during the early days of Vietnam. Which in turn resulted in the writing of *The Godhead*.

Much more than just a historical glimpse of the pre-Vietnam War era, *The Godhead* to a great extent reflects Mr. Robinson's life-long fascination with physics and philosophy, specifically with the disciplines of quantum mechanics and eastern mysticism. He had begun, early on, to notice the eerily neat parallels between the two subjects, which have been buttressed in publications like *The Tao of Physics* by Fritjof Capra and *The Dancing Wu Li Masters* by Gary Zukav. But in *The Godhead* the author has attempted to extend these parallels into a basic foundation for all human action, as reflected in the thoughts, actions and developments of the novel's protagonist.

Mr. Robinson is qualified to make such an attempt. Aside from his professional credentials he is also a lifetime member of Mensa and, on more rarified level, recently served as the world-wide Regent of the Triple Nine Society, which limits its membership to those in the 99.9[th] IQ percentile. And the challenge of incorporating his observations in a novel like *The Godhead* has always been one of his life goals.

The author now lives on Lido Isle in Newport Beach, California, with his wife Jean.

Internet References:

The Godhead Web Page: *www.thegodhead.net*
Triple Nine Society Web Page: *www.triplenine.org*

Printed in the United States
60295LVS00003B/52-57

9 780759 610170